Praise for

THE SPIRAL PATH

"Bravo! Putney proves she's every bit as good writing contemporary romance as she is with historicals . . . Putney's superb storytelling skills and complex and evocative characters make for an unforgettable story."   —*Booklist*

"Putney handles her . . . material with emotional honesty and insight while maintaining the taut romantic tension between her richly developed, complicated protagonists."
—*Publishers Weekly*

"One of the most gripping and darkly emotional books to come along in a long while. As an author Mary Jo Putney never shies away from tackling the bleak and ugly elements of human behavior. Nevertheless, her books hold out such promise of hope, redemption, and triumph that you will be unable to put them down."
—*Romantic Times* (Top Pick)

"A book that will take your breath away from the first page to the last . . . Gripping . . . The climax makes the book literally impossible to put down . . . There is only one word for it: *unforgettable*. Ultimately, it's a keeper of a story that only an author like Putney can tell—and tell very, very well."   —*All About Romance*

"A book I will want to read again; hence its 'keeper' status . . . The happy ending is hard-won, which ⬚⬚⬚⬚ it all the more satisfying. And ⬚⬚⬚⬚⬚⬚⬚⬚⬚⬚⬚⬚ ⬚⬚⬚⬚ y satisfying contempora⬚⬚⬚⬚⬚⬚⬚⬚⬚⬚⬚⬚⬚⬚⬚⬚⬚⬚⬚ r

Praise for
THE BURNING POINT

"*The Burning Point* is sure to light a fire."

—Debbie Macomber

"A winner." —*Midwest Book Review*

"Passionate . . . The author has created a realistic, well-crafted story, laced with elements of suspense and mystery and featuring sympathetic protagonists."

—*Publishers Weekly*

"Powerhouse novelist Mary Jo Putney explodes on the contemporary scene with an emotionally wrenching and dramatically intense story. She tackles a very difficult subject with insight and compassion. Exceptionally powerful reading." —*Romantic Times* (4 1/2 stars, a Top Pick)

"Ms. Putney is one of the very best authors, who excels at historical romances. Now she's crafted her first contemporary and fans of both genres will be delighted to learn that her incredible talent for compelling characterization and original premises comes through on every page. She takes a taboo issue not normally found in a romance and, with touching sensitivity, creates a poignant tale about forgiveness and the awesome power of love to heal all wounds. I could not put it down." —*Rendezvous*

"A fascinating, controversial story that's sure to generate plenty of discussion." —*The Romance Reader* (4 hearts)

"A master . . . dynamite." —*Crescent Blues Book Views*

"Remarkable." —*Interludes*

TWIST OF FATE

MARY JO PUTNEY

JOVE BOOKS, NEW YORK

This is a work of fiction. Names, characters, places, and incidents either are the product of the author's imagination or are used fictitiously, and any resemblance to actual persons, living or dead, business establishments, events, or locales is entirely coincidental.

TWIST OF FATE

A Jove Book / published by arrangement with
the author

PRINTING HISTORY
Jove edition / August 2003

ISBN: 0-515-13545-3

A JOVE BOOK®
Jove Books are published by The Berkley Publishing Group,
a division of Penguin Group (USA) Inc.,
375 Hudson Street, New York, New York 10014.
JOVE and the "J" design
are trademarks belonging to Penguin Group (USA) Inc.

PRINTED IN THE UNITED STATES OF AMERICA

10 9 8 7 6 5 4 3 2 1

To Susan King,
for support and friendship
that's practical, creative, and metaphysical.
How about lunch?

ACKNOWLEDGMENTS

It's amazing the number of topics I know nothing about, but luckily there are many generous people willing to share their knowledge.

To Louis B. Curran, Julie Kistler, David Blum, Harriet Pilger, Jane Langdell, Susan Tanenbaum, and Judge Alvin Cohen, my legal advisory board, many thanks for your help, and I hope I didn't make too many mistakes in translating your knowledge to my book.

Special thanks also to Cynthia Parker and Cass Roberson, for their insights into my attempts to do justice by my African-American characters; to Denise Little for information on the Big Sister/Little Sister program; Catherine Abbot Anderson and Alice Cherbonnier on what it means to be a Quaker; and Tracy Farrell on the care and management of ultra-curly red hair.

Thanks also to the usual suspects: my fishy friend, John Rekus; my fearless editor, Gail Fortune; my ever-supportive agent, Ruth Cohen; Mary Kilchenstein, for her keen eye; and Pat Rice on general principles.

PROLOGUE

He pushed away the remains of his last meal: shrimp Creole, corn bread, chocolate mousse cake, and single malt Scotch whiskey to wash it all down. He'd been liberal with the whiskey, wanting to dull the edge of his fear. He would die as he'd lived, with cold superiority.

The guards arrived to take him to the execution chamber. He had come to know all the regulars on death row. None of them loved him—he'd made sure of that—but none of them looked happy about his last walk either. He hoped they'd have nightmares.

It was only a few steps down the corridor to the place where legal murder was done. Face composed, he refused the offered comfort of a minister and scarcely glanced at the witnesses who had come to watch him die. He made a particular point of avoiding the gaze of the one family member present. No question about the nightmares there.

The guards strapped him onto the gurney. It took effort, now, to act as if he didn't care.

Three shots—the first for unconsciousness, the

second to paralyze his breathing, the third to stop his heart. He flinched involuntarily as the first needle went in. Then the second stabbed . . .

ROB SMITH JERKED AWAKE WITH HAMMERING heart, sweat on his face. He always woke at this point, just before the end. Would the nightmare leave him if it ever progressed to the end? Or would his heart quietly stop as if the lethal drug really had been injected?

He stared through the darkness at the ceiling as he forced his breath into a steady rhythm. Gradually his tension eased. After all, he had never been on death row. He was plain Rob Smith, a man whose only crimes were the sort that didn't get prosecuted.

That wasn't the same as being innocent.

CHAPTER 1

VAL COVINGTON BARRELED INTO THE OFFICE, BRIEF-
case swinging. "Sorry I'm behind schedule, Kendra—the
judge was in a chatty mood. Has the FedEx package from
Houston arrived?"

Kendra Brooks glanced up from her computer monitor.
A paralegal and Val's assistant when one was needed, she
was tall and athletic, with a sense of style that made her
look like an international supermodel. "Yes, the documents
are on your credenza, since your desk would disappear under the pile. But you can slow down a little, Val. Howard
Reid called to say that this afternoon's deposition has to be
postponed."

"The honorable opposing counsel loves his golf and
probably decided it was too nice a day to waste inside," Val
said dryly. "Still, I can use the time to get caught up."

"You will never be caught up. Being constantly behind
is a fact of life at Crouse, Resnick, and Murphy." Kendra
Brooks returned to her computer, dark fingers moving
faster than seemed quite humanly possible.

"You are *so* comforting." With a more moderate pace,
Val opened the door that connected their two offices. After

taking off her tailored suit jacket and hanging it in the closet, she dropped into her chair and checked her voice mail. Eleven messages, three of them urgent. After dealing with those, she did a fast triage on her e-mail, shooting off quick responses to some, forwarding others, printing out a couple more.

Kendra buzzed through on the intercom. "Boss? Bill Costain wants to see you tomorrow at 9:00 A.M. Is that okay?"

Val checked her calendar. She had planned to use the time to work on a brief, but Bill's manufacturing company was her biggest client, and he was nice as well. She could draft the brief this evening. "Fine. Ask him if he prefers his place or mine?"

Kendra chuckled. "That will make his day. Will do."

Val was returning to her e-mail when the direct line telephone rang. Since only a few friends and top clients had the number, she picked up immediately. "Hello?"

"Don't tell me—you're multitasking again. You have that sound in your voice." The comment was followed by a famously husky chuckle.

"Rainey, how are you doing?" Glad to hear from of one of her oldest friends, Val tilted back the chair and rested her high-heeled pumps on top of her desk. "I promise to give you my full attention. I don't suppose you're in Baltimore?"

"No, I'm in Los Angeles for the day, doing business meetings. Tedious."

Val grinned. Raine Marlowe was a successful actress, producer, and director, but she didn't get there by enjoying meetings. Even when they were in grade school, Rainey had preferred action to talk. "Did you get a green light on the next project?"

"Close but no champagne. Soon, I hope." Raine's voice changed. "I had a different reason to call. Remember when you and I were working on the script for *Centurion,* and I told you that without your help I would have quit?"

"You were only feeling down that day. You would have

been back the next, sinking your terrier teeth in it." Rainey was not the sort to give up easily. Against all the odds, she wrote, produced, and directed a movie based on a Victorian novel called *The Centurion*, and saw it take off into a major hit that won several Oscars for her and her crew. Now she was in a good position to create other movies that excited her.

"I probably wouldn't have given up," Raine admitted, "but you were crucial both in preproduction and during the actual shooting, when I was on the verge of nervous hysterics. That's why I gave you a production credit on the movie."

Val grinned. "I got such a kick out of that. It added to my wild woman image among the staider elements of the Baltimore bar."

"Anytime you want to move to L.A. and go into production, there's a job waiting for you. Several jobs."

"No way, Rainey. I had great fun working with you on that one project, but show business is not for me. I haven't got enough gypsy in my soul."

"Do you remember me saying I'd give you a profit point?"

Val thought back. "Vaguely, but I figured you were just suffering sugar shock from an overdose of hot fudge sundaes. Everyone knows that profit points don't mean anything—Hollywood accountants are famous for making sure that movies never make any profit, even when they're a wild success."

"Accountants do not play games on *my* movies. Even with no special effects, *Centurion* was a solid success all over the world and in the secondary markets. Your percentage point is worth well over a million dollars and climbing."

Val almost dropped her phone. "You're kidding!"

"Not about this," Rainey said with satisfaction. "So what are you going to do with your windfall?"

Val sank back in her chair, a little dazed. "It will make one heck of a nice addition to the retirement fund."

"Good grief, Val, a fat portfolio is not the cure for what ails you!" Raine exclaimed. "You're thirty-three years old. Why act as if you have one foot in the grave and the other in a soup kitchen? Life is for living now—not. . . ." She chopped off her sentence. "Sorry, it's your money to spend as you like. But you're always complaining about your job. Why not take this as an opportunity to do something you love?"

Val found that she was rubbing the back of her neck and forced herself to stop. "Good question. I'll have to think about it. Starting with figuring out what I want to do when I grow up."

"Please do." Rainey's voice softened. "You've proved to your father that you're an ace lawyer. Now it's time to find work that brings you joy."

Old friends knew too much. "You make that sound easy."

"It's not, of course, but it's doable. Why not turn that razor brain of yours to the question of what you want to do with the rest of your life? It's time to fish or cut bait, Val. You have the opportunity to change your life. If you don't, you lose the right to complain about your job."

"Heavens, what would I do for a hobby if I couldn't complain about work?" Discomfited, Val changed the conversation by asking about Rainey's husband and baby girl. Her friend obliged, and the rest of the call stayed with safe topics.

Rainey signed off, but Val did not return to her e-mail. Instead, she gazed out her office window. Her spectacular view of Baltimore's Inner Harbor was one of the visible rewards for years of hard work. Having just made partner at Crouse, Resnick, she was about to go from a good salary to major bucks. She was one of the city's top litigators, and had the trappings to prove it.

But to say that she was ambivalent about her work was an understatement. She was lucky her friends still allowed her to complain. Her job was so demanding that sometimes she felt like a gerbil running on a luxurious wheel. Apart from the leave of absence she had taken to assist Rainey on the movie shoot, she hadn't had a real vacation in years. There had been no time or mental energy to think about change.

What did she want to do when she grew up? If she didn't get moving, she would still be trying to find herself when she was in a nursing home.

She pulled a yellow legal tablet from her desk, drew a line down the middle, and started listing pros and cons of her current job. On the plus side, she enjoyed the mental challenges, the money was good, and soon would be *very* good. After a childhood spent squeezing pennies until they screamed, she found it comforting to have money in the bank. After paying off her college and law school loans, she had helped her mother buy a house, then bought her own dream house. Now she was busily socking away retirement and rainy day money. She really liked having that security.

On the negative side, litigators needed to have hides like rhinos. Not being that tough could be painful, and Val wasn't sure which was worse: suffering or turning into an insensitive battle-ax. Though she had been accused of the latter, she didn't think she was there yet. But it was a real risk.

Back to the plus side. As Rainey had said, Val liked showing her corporate lawyer father how smart and successful she was. Her two half sisters were airheads, albeit charming ones. But they had grown up in the same house with their father and Val hadn't. Nothing could change that now, no matter how good a corporate lawyer she was.

Another major negative: being too busy to have a life. Like a husband and children. Much as she loved her cats, it wasn't the same.

She had almost filled the page with pro and con points when the door swung open, and a bright voice announced, "Lunch has arrived."

Val glanced up to see the elegant blond form of Kate Corsi, another old friend who had moved back to Baltimore and remarried her ex-husband a couple of years earlier. This had the huge advantage of allowing Val to see her regularly rather than having to make do with phone calls and rare cross-country visits.

"Hi, Kate." Val set her tablet aside with relief. "It's old home week—Rainey just called. What brings you downtown? Looking to implode a building?"

"Not today." Dressed in I-am-a-serious-businesswoman gray, Kate plopped a brown paper bag on the polished desk, then pulled a chair up on the other side. "Since I had a meeting nearby, I checked with Kendra to see if you were available. She said yes, so I stopped at that Mideastern sandwich shop down the block."

"Falafel in pita bread?" Val asked hopefully.

"*And* cucumber salad, a couple of pieces of baklava, and mango lassis to drink. You're responsible for coffee."

"It's a deal." Val went to her small sink and made up a fresh pot of coffee. "Rainey's flourishing. She also had some unexpected good news for me."

"What a coincidence. I have good news, too." Kate grinned.

Val halted, caught by the note in her friend's voice. On the worst day of her life, Kate was lovely, but today she positively glowed. "Are you pregnant?"

"Yes!" Kate said exuberantly.

"Wonderful!" Burying a pang, Val rounded the desk to hug her friend. "Congratulations. How does Donovan feel?"

"He's all dazed and mooshy and romantic. The only drawback is that he shows signs of treating me as if I'm made of blown glass."

"If he wants to take away your hard hat so you can't leap around demolition sites, I'm with him."

"You're both wusses." Kate pulled the stuffed pitas from the bag and set them on napkins. "I figure I'm good for a couple more months at least. Don't worry, when I start feeling clumsy, it's back to the office for the duration."

Val bit into her pita sandwich, knowing that her friend would show consummate good sense and make a terrific mother. Any baby produced by Kate and Donovan would be gorgeous, too. A child born of love . . .

"Does the news bother you?" Kate asked quietly. "After all, you and Donovan . . ."

Val gave a quick shake of her head. "When he and I dated, it was never serious. Look how quickly he ended things when you decided to come back to Baltimore. But . . . I'll admit that my biological clock just bonged rather loudly."

Kate studied her face, but said only, "You mentioned that you just got some good news from Rainey?"

"It's one of those good news/bad news things, actually. The good news is that Rainey gave me a profit point for my work on *The Centurion*, and now it's worth a surprising amount of money." Val swallowed the last of her sandwich. "The bad news is that Rainey informs me that if I don't use the money to change my life, I can't complain about my job anymore."

Kate whistled softly. "So—what are you going to do?"

"Darned if I know." Val couldn't quite manage a light tone.

"Okay, let's start with basics." Kate wiped her hands clean as she thought. "I think you must love the law, or you wouldn't be so good at it. But this silk stocking corporate law firm isn't really your style. Just because your father . . ."

"Spare me comments about my father. Rainey already went there." Val gestured at her tablet. "I've been listing the pros and cons of this job and I'm not getting anywhere."

Kate snagged the tablet and skimmed the entries, then pulled off the top page and ripped it to pieces. "This is not a question that will be solved by rational analysis. If you want to figure out what kind of work you'll love, get your head out of the loop and go with your heart. For example, you always seem to enjoy your pro bono work, which is usually more involved with people than corporations. Why not open your own office and let the windfall subsidize cases that interest you?"

Val paused in the middle of her mango lassi. "Now there's a thought. The law does fascinate me, but too often justice is measured by the size of a client's wallet. It would be hard to run a practice doing only pro bono work, though."

"If you leave, some of your paying clients would go with you. Enough to keep money coming in." Eyes sparkling, Kate leaned on the desk with crossed arms. "Imagine a life where you could decide how many hours you want to work. Where you can take cases that really interest you. Where you can say no to clients you don't like. That's the luxury that money gives, Val—choices."

Kate's vision was enticing—and darned scary. "It's an intriguing possibility, but where would I start? We're talking major, major changes. As a sole practitioner I wouldn't be able to take on the big, complicated cases I handle now."

"I'm going to pretend that question wasn't rhetorical. You need a sharp assistant like Kendra to run the office; if you give her the right bait, maybe she'll go with you. As to not being able to handle large cases, didn't you tell me once that it's possible to hire contract lawyers when more help is needed? You could create work for some of your lawyer friends who quit the corporate world to raise their kids."

"You've got this all thought through while I'm still blinking at the possibilities!"

Kate grinned. "It's easy for me, it's not my life. You'll need physical office space, of course, unless you want to work out of your house."

"I don't want an office invading my home," Val said. "If I'm going for do-gooder law, I should avoid the high-priced offices downtown and pick a neighborhood location. Some place with parking."

"What about the Hamilton area? That's pleasant and affordable and an easy drive from your house."

Val thought about Hamilton. A working-class neighborhood in Baltimore's northeastern quadrant, it was unpretentious and safe. "Does the area have any office space apart from the storefronts on Harford Road? I don't want to handle walk-in divorce clients. That's painful work."

"As a matter of fact . . ." Kate dug an electronic organizer from her handbag and hit several keys. "Donovan has a friend called Rob Smith who he met on one of those charitable weekend fix-up projects. They bonded over the Sheetrock. Rob's a nice guy who does carpentry and remodeling. He bought a vacant church on Old Harford Road and fixed it up as commercial space, but he's been having trouble renting it." Kate jotted a phone number and address on a tablet. "Take a look and see if it speaks to you."

Val gazed down at the address. "You're making this seem . . . possible."

"That's the whole point. You've proved that you can do the uptown lawyer thing, but you don't want to spend the rest of your life here. That I'm sure of." Kate glanced at her watch. "Have to run—it's later than I thought."

She swallowed the last of her coffee and stood. "You're in a position where you have lots of choices, Val. Maybe you want to throw the law over and get certified to teach kindergarten. Or become a veterinarian and set up an all-cat practice. Explore the possibilities. Find what makes you laugh. You haven't done a lot of laughing in the last few years. Change is scary, but it beats dying inside."

Kate scooped up her briefcase and departed as quickly as she'd arrived. In the suddenly silent office, Val drew a shaky breath, feeling as if she had been beaten by pillows. Nothing like having friends who gave good advice whether it was wanted or not.

A fat portfolio is not the cure for what ails you. Rainey's quick, perceptive words had made her recognize how much she had come to seek her security in money. Blindly she gazed from the window and wondered where she had gone wrong. Not by choosing law school, though her reasons had been a spaghetti tangle of good and bad. Yes, she'd wanted to impress her father, but she had also loved the challenges and discipline required by the law, and her talents suited the work well. She enjoyed analyzing cases, researching precedents, devising ingenious strategies, and performing in the courtroom. Her law firm was a decent employer, and every day was different.

Yet somewhere along the line, she'd lost her course. *A fat portfolio is not the cure for what ails you.* Her instinctive desire to save the movie money was odd considering that financially she was in fine shape, with a good job, a nice home, and a healthy amount of savings. But she had clutched at that million dollars—less massive taxes—as if saving the money was vital to keep her from destitution.

Her mind skipped to an emotionally needy boyfriend who had lived on the edge of financial disaster because he tried to fill the holes in his spirit with extravagant spending. It never worked; the satisfaction that came with buying was gone in hours while the bills stayed around forever.

Val had broken up with him regretfully, unable to deal with his chronic money problems, yet she hadn't recognized the similarities between them. They both put too much faith in material things—he by spending, she by saving. Somewhere along the line she had turned into Ebenezer Scrooge without noticing it.

Had Val ever known inner peace? Yes, as a girl there had been times when she had felt centered and content. But now she was restless and unhappy, running so hard there was never time to stop and think about her life. She needed to slow down and find a way to heal her tattered spirit before it became frayed beyond repair.

The question was—how?

CHAPTER 2

❧❧❧

VAL TURNED SOUTH ON OLD HARFORD ROAD from Northern Parkway. Unlike nearby Harford Road, a busy through street, this older route was a quiet residential road. The address Kate had given her was a couple of blocks down. Turning on to a cross street, she parked her car and studied the stone structure on the corner.

Petite and well-proportioned, the church was dangerously charming. Leave it to Kate, an architect by training, to know about such an interesting possibility.

That didn't mean the building would work for Val even if she did decide to set up her own office—a very big if. Though small for a church, the structure would be large for a sole practitioner law firm. Probably built in the early twentieth century, it had Gothic arched windows containing roundels of stained glass at the top. The clear lower panels allowed lots of light in. From here, the interior looked white and empty.

She climbed from her car and went to explore. A For Rent sign in the front window looked weathered, and she wondered how long Rob Smith had been trying to find a tenant. This was a big project for a carpenter. If he had all his money tied up in the church, he might be hurting.

Reminding herself that she shouldn't rent an office simply to make a stranger's life easier, she circled around behind the building. Neat shrubs lined the foundations, and well-grown trees shaded the corner lot. This close, she could see that the back of the structure had a second floor. Still more space that she wouldn't need.

Behind the church was a parking lot that might hold eight or ten cars. A wheelchair ramp, which was good—the carpenter knew the law. There was street parking, too, which was much nicer than the claustrophobic parking garage Val used downtown.

She was touching a glossy magnolia leaf when a voice asked, "Can I help you?"

Almost jumping from her skin, she spun around to see a powerfully built man in jeans and a worn blue work shirt standing an arm's length away. His shaggy light brown hair and beard were sun-bleached, and his eyes were startlingly light against tanned skin. The faintest tint of blue kept them from being the color of ice. Her mind made a swift association with the frontier mountain men: strong, craggy, utterly competent.

And gorgeous. Mustn't overlook the fact that he was gorgeous.

"Sorry." His voice was deep and pleasant. "I didn't mean to sneak up on you. I was doing some pruning on the other side of the building."

He seemed vaguely familiar, but she couldn't place him. His accent wasn't Baltimore, though. Western, maybe. "Are you Rob Smith?"

"Yes." His brows arched inquiringly. Again she felt a flicker of recognition, but no sense that they had met before. Maybe she had seen him in passing somewhere. For a big city, Baltimore could be a pretty small town. But no, surely she would remember seeing a man who made her nerve endings tingle just looking at him.

Reminding herself that she was here on business, she held out her hand. "Hi, I'm Val Covington. My friend Kate Corsi, Patrick Donovan's wife, said you had remodeled an old church for commercial use, so I thought I'd take a look. I . . . I'm considering setting up my own office."

His warm, strong hand was callused and marked by minor scars. A working man's hand. Maybe he seemed familiar not as an individual, but because of his general resemblance to numerous workmen she had hired over the years—strong, at ease in his body. Whether carpenters, roofers, electricians, or landscapers, they tended to have the kind of confidence that came with physical mastery of the world around them.

The workmen she knew tended to be beer-drinking, sports-watching, guy-type guys, but they were also fun, reliable, and had an innate courtesy she enjoyed. The man who had done the tile work in her new kitchen was so attractive that she might have jumped him if he weren't happily married with two children. So instead she made brownies and sent them home to his kids.

"Do you want to see the inside?"

"That would be nice, Mr. Smith." There, she sounded collected and professional.

"Call me Rob." The faintest of smiles showed in his eyes. "*Mr. Smith* sounds so generic."

And he had a sophisticated sense of humor. She was doomed. "Okay, Rob. I'm Val. What kind of church was this?"

"Originally Methodist." He unsnapped a key ring from his belt and climbed three steps to the back entrance. Arched and made of heavy oak, the door had the huge, vinelike hammered iron hinges often seen on English churches.

Rob unlocked the door and held it open for her. "They outgrew the space and built a larger church out in Parkville. A gospel church was here for a while, but they outgrew it and moved on, too."

She stepped across the threshold into a small reception hall. The interior was completely unfurnished, with warm white walls, handsome moldings, and floors of beautifully polished oak. "I suppose this area was offices for the minister and church secretary and that sort of thing?"

"Yes, with a kitchen and church hall below. There are four rooms here in the back for offices, supplies, storage, whatever."

She opened a door on the right and found herself in a sizable room with oak wainscoting. "The builders really liked oak."

"American church Gothic, circa 1910." Rob stroked the wainscoting with his fingertips. "This place needed a lot of work. The shell was solid, but the roof was crumbling and most of the larger stained-glass panels had been stolen. Luckily I was able to salvage some smaller pieces and incorporate them into the new windows."

She wondered about his educational background—the exterminator she called every spring to rid her house of wasps was a Phi Beta Kappa in Russian history. Smith spoke like an English major. Which made carpentry a good choice, since a degree in English was not exactly a career path.

She opened the door that led to the front of the church, then halted in delight. The high-ceilinged original sanctuary soared above her with light pouring through the windows. For an instant she felt that every prayer, every song, the church had ever known was echoing through her. And underneath was a sense of deep connection intertwined with sharp alarm.

Clamping down on her reaction until she could examine it more closely, she said, "How lovely. This place . . . sings."

"You can feel it?"

She glanced at Rob. Hard to read expressions under that beard, but his eyes were intent. "If you mean can I feel that this was a much-loved house of worship, yes. I'm glad you saved it. No new building would ever have such richness."

She advanced, feeling as if she were swimming in light. "Not right for me, though."

"What business are you in?"

"I'm a lawyer."

"A lawyer?"

She smiled wryly at the surprise in his voice. "People always have trouble believing that. My first week in law school, one professor called on me by saying, 'You, the barmaid in the third row.'"

"Isn't that considered harassment?"

"Probably, but at Harvard Law, the philosophy is to torment students into toughness. If you can't take it, too bad. I was warned that HLS is not a user-friendly school, but I didn't really appreciate what that meant until it was too late."

"In the case of that professor, it meant that he noticed you. Any man would."

To her surprise, she blushed. "Is that a compliment?"

"Definitely, in a nonharassing sort of way." He smiled and changed the subject. "Why Harvard? Because it looks so good on a résumé?"

"That, and to prove I could do it." Her reply was absent because her attention was on Rob, who was standing in a swath of light. With the sun gilding his hair and emphasizing the breadth of his shoulders, he was a sight well worth admiring.

Suppressing thoughts of how long she had been celibate, she continued, "My mother says that even when I was a toddler, the surest way to get me to do something was to say it was a bad idea."

"Tenacity is a useful trait for a lawyer. What's your specialty?"

"I'm a litigator, currently working for a firm that does mostly corporate work. I'm thinking of opening my own office so I have more variety and fewer hours." She gestured around the former sanctuary. "Practicing law here might ruin the beautiful energy. And the building is too large, especially with the upstairs office space."

"Actually, the upper level is an apartment with an out-side entrance. I'm staying there now, but if you wanted to live over the shop, I could find another place."

She drifted to a window, admiring the care with which the surviving stained glass had been combined with the clear glass panels. Rob was a man who liked doing things right. "That's okay, I don't want to be that close to my work."

"Will you stay with corporate litigation?"

She scanned the room, unable to stop herself from imagining it as a reception area. "Some, but what I really want to practice isn't law, but justice," she said slowly. "I want to give little guys the kind of representation that usu-ally only big guys can afford. I want to rip some fat-cat throats out."

The unnerving light eyes regarded her thoughtfully. "That's a mission this old church would approve of, I think. A modern version of driving the moneylenders from the temple."

Why had she said so much to a stranger? "Perhaps. Or maybe I'm just temporarily insane with spring fever. Thanks for the tour, Rob. Even though this wouldn't be right for me, you've done a beautiful job."

"Thank you." He ushered her toward the back door. "If you change your mind, give me a call. Do you have the number?"

"Kate gave it to me." With a last wave, she climbed into her car and headed for downtown, her mind churning. To think that if Howard Reid hadn't canceled this after-noon's deposition to play golf, she would be terrorizing his expert witness rather than having all these unsettling new experiences.

ROB WATCHED THE BURGUNDY-COLORED LEXUS turn south on Old Harford Road, wondering if she had bought the car to match her hair. Even with a schoolmarm hairstyle and her sexy little body disguised in a severely cut navy suit, Val Covington crackled with physical and mental energy. She must be hell on heels in a courtroom.

How long was it since he had been so aware of a woman? Years. Four years, three months, and seven days, to be exact. He was glad that she appreciated the church's uniqueness, but it was just as well she wasn't interested in renting. If she were that near, she would be a temptation.

Yet he couldn't resist going up to his apartment and plugging "Val Covington" into a search engine. He got plenty of hits, mostly in the *Daily Record*, Baltimore's business and legal newspaper. She had won some high-profile cases and was a newly made partner at a top city law firm. Having met the lady, he wasn't surprised.

Nor was he surprised that she was considering her own office. Not only were corporate law firm jobs murderously demanding, but no amount of dressing the part could quite hide the maverick gleam in her eyes. He hoped she did decide to go out on her own and rip some fat-cat throats.

Preferably in a neighborhood far from this one.

LUCKILY KENDRA WASN'T AT HER DESK WHEN VAL returned, since she would notice her boss's distracted mood. Safely in her office, Val closed the door and tried to concentrate on the most urgent of the briefs she had to write.

Usually work focused her mind, but not today. She gave up in exasperation and closed the file after fifteen futile minutes. Digging out her calculator, she began playing with figures, estimating expenses and cash flow if she opened her own office.

Making her best guess on the costs, it appeared that even after paying humongous taxes, the *Centurion* windfall would give her enough money to pay for start-up costs, then subsidize the business until it was established and could pay for itself.

And amazingly, that was based on a forty-hour work week. What a luxury that would be! She should be able to divide her time between paying clients and pro bono work and make enough for mortgage money, cat food, and her retirement fund. Having her own office meant she wouldn't be able to do the intellectually challenging work that required a team of lawyers, but working more closely with clients and their needs would compensate for that.

Her pulse quickened at the knowledge that she could really do this if she wanted to. Her hesitation came not from economics, but fear. The insecurities of her childhood had left her with a craving for logic and order, which was one reason the law appealed to her. Despite her frustrations with Crouse, Resnick, it was a known quantity, and lucrative. Abandoning that to become her own boss would be exciting but unpredictable, and she did not love for her life to be unpredictable.

Of course, there was a whole range of possibilities between staying at Crouse, Resnick and starting her own office. She could go to work for a corporation, or enter the government sector, which would be less demanding and still provide a steady, comfortable income. That kind of change would be safe and relatively easy.

And yet, when she had entered the old church sanctuary, she'd experienced such a sense of rightness. Exhilaration, even.

She stepped into her small washroom and stared into the mirror, knowing she was at a crossroads. One direction was familiar, safe, and exhausting. The other was unknown, enticing, and damned scary.

The mirror reflected back her lawyer costume: dark tailored suit; a discreet, tasteful gold chain around her neck and matching gold earrings; hair secured in a sleek knot at her nape. This was how she had gone to work every day for years. The image was very different from how she looked on her own time.

She jerked out her hairpins, then wet her fingers and ran them through her hair to restore the natural bounce of the energetic red mass. Little Orphan Annie on a bad hair day was how she described herself. These red curls had been the bane of her childhood. The bright, carroty color had made her stand out in a crowd no matter how much she wanted to blend in with the other girls. With age the color had darkened to a less violent shade, but even so, she was doomed to go through life looking like a short barmaid who needed to lose a few pounds.

But she didn't have to go through life wearing tailored suits. The choice was up to her. If she wanted a new life, it was time to take a few cautious steps in that direction.

If only it were possible to fast forward through change and go directly to the next secure niche. . . .

CHAPTER 3

❦

IT LOOKED LIKE VAL WAS STILL OUT, BUT JUST IN case, Kendra called, "Are you in there, Val? I've got the Mercantile files for you."

As Kendra set down the stack of folders, Val emerged from the washroom, her hair rioting around her head and looking much redder than it did when pulled back. Startled out of her usual composure, Kendra blurted out, "Girl, what have you done to your hair?"

"Nothing. After five years of working together, it's time you saw the unvarnished me." Val folded onto the sofa with one leg tucked under her, looking very unlike her usual professional self. "I'm thinking of going off on my own. If I do, would you consider coming with me as paralegal, office manager, and secretary? I could match your salary and the medical coverage, though the other benefits might not be as good."

Kendra closed the door to her office and sat down, even more startled than she had been by the hair. "You really want to leave here after making partner? You've just climbed on the gravy train. A few more years and you'll be set for life."

"This job is eating me alive," Val said bluntly. "I'm

good at corporate work, but a lot of it is just an elaborate game. I get tired of playing games, especially when I sometimes wish I was on the other side." She hesitated, perhaps finding it difficult to reveal so much of herself. "I want to do justice, Kendra. I'll need to take enough paying jobs to cover the rent, but what I really crave is pro bono work I can feel good about. I want to take on the powers that be and give some little guys a chance. As corny as it sounds, I want to fight the good fight."

Her words jolted Kendra. Justice for the little guy. "You really mean that?"

Val smiled wryly. "Yes. The big question is whether I have the courage to actually do it."

Kendra was silent for a long time as she thought about the pain and injustice that had been bleeding her soul for years. It was almost too late to make a difference—but maybe not. Val was the smartest lawyer Kendra had ever met, and she had a real heart under that red hair and fast-talking tongue. Maybe . . . just maybe . . . "If you leave, I'll come along if you'll take on a lost cause for me."

Val looked cautious. "I can try. What kind of case?"

"I want you to get a man off death row."

"Death row?" she said, surprise in her voice. "Someone you have a personal interest in?"

"Do you recognize the name Daniel Monroe?"

Val's gaze went vague as she consulted her incredible memory. "He killed a policeman some years ago. If I recall correctly, he assaulted a woman, the policeman intervened, and got pumped full of bullets for his pains. A nasty business."

"Yes, but Daniel didn't do it," Kendra said vehemently, trying to suppress her bitterness. "Seventeen years Daniel has been in jail. Every possible appeal has been filed and denied, and the State of Maryland is ready to kill an innocent man. You want to do justice? Save the life of Daniel Monroe."

Val's expression softened. "I gather he was a friend of yours?"

"More than a friend." Kendra's mouth twisted. "He's Jason's father." Jason, her tall, handsome, air force academy cadet son, who believed his biological father was long dead. Philip Brooks, the man Kendra had later married, had been a good father to Jason from the day he entered her life until a heart attack carried him off too soon, but it was Daniel's blood that flowed in Jason's veins. Daniel's life that had been destroyed for no damned reason at all.

"Good God." Shocked and sympathetic, Val chose her words carefully before continuing. "If you loved Daniel Monroe, it's natural to believe in his innocence, but if I recall correctly, the case against him was solid. His conviction was upheld on appeal a couple of times."

"Eyewitnesses!" Kendra exclaimed, then muttered some other words that she never used in the office. "Three people identified him, and they were *wrong*."

"You're sure about that?"

"Of course I'm sure! When that poor cop died, Daniel was in bed with me and we was screwin' our brains out." Kendra deliberately used the raw accents of her youth as a way of making the past real to Val. It worked, because Val's expression changed.

"Surely if you testified to that . . ."

Kendra cut off the words with an angry gesture. "No one believed me. They all thought I was just an ignorant black girl, lyin' to protect her no-good boyfriend."

Val's eyes narrowed. "Tell me more."

"There isn't much to say. Daniel had had a few run-ins with the law, but never anything serious. Never, ever anything violent. He spent some time in jail for car theft and had only been out for a few months. But he had found a job and was going straight. We were living together and planning on getting married. Look, I have his picture." Kendra went to her handbag and dug out her wallet, flipping to the fading photo of her, Daniel, and their son on Jason's first birthday. She had carried this photo since it was taken. Philip, bless him, had never minded. "Does this look like a murderer?"

Val studied the photo. "It looks like a happy family. Jason takes after his father, I see. What a darling he was at that age. They have the same smile."

Daniel had been a darling, too. Big and sweet-natured, he'd had a romantic streak that made Kendra feel like a queen. They had been so close to having it all. . . .

She snapped the wallet shut. "Then the cops came blasting in with guns one night threatening to shoot anything that moved. Jason was screaming—he was eighteen months old." She shook her head. "How Daniel did dote on that boy. He wanted to be there for him, like his father had never been there for him. Instead . . ." Her eyes squeezed shut as she furiously fought tears. She had tried so hard to put this in a mental box where she wouldn't be crippled by the pain. Usually she succeeded.

Val leaned forward and touched Kendra's hand with silent sympathy. "They arrested him and charged him with murder?"

Kendra nodded. "One of the detectives thought the description sounded like Daniel, and we lived only a couple blocks from the murder. Since Daniel had a record, they hauled him in. The witnesses picked him out of the lineup, and that was that. The police never looked for anyone else. He was tried, convicted, and sentenced to death."

"Even though you said he was with you?"

Kendra gave her a level look. "You're wondering if I'm lying. Val, I swear on my mother's grave that Daniel was with me when the murder took place. I tried talking to people. The public defender who handled the case kind of believed me and did some investigation, but he was never able to get around the eyewitness testimony."

She fell silent as she remembered the horrible time after Daniel's conviction when she struggled as a single mother to keep herself and Jason above water. "I managed to get into a state job training program so I could get a job that paid enough to support me and my son. One reason I chose to become a legal secretary, then a paralegal, was in the hopes of finding a way to help Daniel. But I never have." Instead she had learned that while the legal system usually worked, there were plenty of times when it didn't.

Val closed her eyes, tension visible in the taut skin over her cheekbones as she absorbed Kendra's story. "If you're right, a terrible injustice has been done." Her eyes opened, glinting steel. "You've got a deal, Kendra. You'll work for me, and I'll do my best for your friend. But you know the odds are slim that I'll be able to do anything after all these years."

"I know." Kendra's mouth twisted. The eleventh hour had struck, and midnight was approaching fast. "You'll have to start by persuading him to let you take on the case—last winter, he fired his lawyers, saying he was tired of fighting a losing battle. But you can charm a snake out of a hole, you're smart, and you know people all over town. You're Daniel's last chance, Val. You and God. I've been having a lot of conversations with Him lately. Maybe you can stir up enough doubts to get his sentence commuted to life."

"Why didn't you tell me about Daniel earlier?"

Kendra tried to imagine dropping that into a conversation. "This is such a white-bread, white-collar place that talking about murders and death row seemed out of place." She hesitated, realizing that in the last few minutes their relationship had changed. They had always been friendly, but they had never spoken so freely. "And to be honest, I didn't think you had the time or the interest to care about a condemned man."

Val's nose wrinkled. "I've gotten too good at showing a detached lawyer face. Believe me, I have always cared about injustice. I only hope I can help."

"You're offering a chance, and that's more than Daniel had before." And in return, Kendra would be the best damned legal assistant and office manager in Baltimore.

Val got to her feet. "It's time to resign my partnership. I found a great potential office today—a remodeled former church out Old Harford Road, not far from where you live. A good omen if I get it, don't you think?"

Kendra smiled a little as the other woman left the office. A remodeled church? Maybe God was listening after all, and this was a sign. With God, Val, and Kendra working to-gether, they might beat death row after all.

STEP FIRM, VAL WALKED DOWN TO THE CORNER suite occupied by Donald Crouse, senior partner of Crouse, Resnick. Strange how the decision she had wres-tled with was now blindingly obvious. It was time to take her career in a new direction. To do good, not just well.

She murmured a greeting to Carl Brown, the firm's biggest rainmaker, as he brushed past her with a brusque nod. Dear Carl, charming as always. The only one of the senior partners she disliked, he was hyper-competitive and had made no secret of the fact that he didn't think the firm should have female partners. Val wouldn't miss him.

As Carl turned into his office, his assistant looked up, phone to her ear. "Mr. Brown, your daughter Jenny is on the line. Can you take the call?"

"I haven't got time," he said curtly. "If she needs money, tell her to e-mail me."

Val winced, seeing herself in the absent Jenny, who was a child of Carl's first or second marriage, not the current one. Law firms were full of people too busy to talk to their own children. Her father was like that, though at least he wasn't as bad-tempered as Carl. Yes, leaving was the right decision.

Breezing into Donald Crouse's reception area, she asked, "Is The Man free?"

"Go on in," his assistant said. "And what did you do to your hair?"

Ignoring the question, Val entered the inner sanctum. Donald glanced up from the document he was reading. Tall and saturnine with a dry sense of humor, he was Val's per-sonal favorite of the senior members of the firm. He'd been her mentor and her champion even before he became her friend.

"Donald, I'm leaving Crouse, Resnick," Val said bluntly. "I've finally lost the battle to be respectable, and it's time to go off on my own."

He leaned back in his chair with a sigh. "I can't say that I'm surprised. You've always been a triangle in a round hole."

Her mouth quirked up. "Not even a square peg?"

"They're a dime a dozen. Triangles are rare." He peered over the top of his glasses. "I always wondered what you'd look like if you let your hair down. Remarkable."

She smiled and settled into a chair. "I'm rather sorry to prove to the other partners that they were right, and I'm just not their kind, but there it is. I'll start organizing my work for others to take over."

He steepled his fingers thoughtfully. "If you're opening an office here in Baltimore, would you be interested in a continuing relationship with us? We often contract some of the smaller cases out, plus there will be occasions when we'll have larger cases that would benefit from your unique touch."

The prospect of self-employment gave Val a sudden, keen interest in cash flow. "Call away. It's generous of you to be willing to maintain a relationship."

"Generous, hell," he said dryly. "You're the best litigator in the city, Val. I'd rather have you on my side than in opposition."

"I'll miss you, Donald," she said honestly. "But not the daily grind here."

"It takes courage to walk away. There were times when I was tempted, but . . ." He gestured toward the family portraits on his shining mahogany desk. "Too many responsibilities, and too used to living well."

His admission surprised her—she had thought him perfectly suited to the career he had chosen. But how much did one ever know about someone else's inner life?

After she and Donald discussed timing, finances, and other exit details, she returned to her office, making mental lists of all that must be done. The phone was ringing as she passed Kendra's door. "If that's my father, I'll take it in my office."

Kendra picked up the phone and greeted the caller, raising her brows in a how-did-you-know-that expression.

Wryly Val closed the door and sat at her desk to take the call. This prediction had been easy—if her father was available, he would call as soon as his old friend Donald let him know that Val was quitting.

Not bothering with a greeting, Bradford Westerfield III barked, "For God's sake, Val, what's this nonsense I hear about you leaving Crouse, Resnick?"

"Not nonsense, Brad," she said calmly. "I've had enough of life in a big law firm, and I'm ready to go."

"You're insane to throw away all you've achieved so far. And just after you made partner! That's more than insane, that's . . . that's *perverse*."

As he proceeded in that vein, Val half tuned him out. Ironic that he was talking about her professional successes only when she was leaving. She supposed that he loved her in his fashion, but nonetheless, she was an embarrassment—the illegitimate daughter he'd sired during his one youthful dabble in rebellion. She would never be tall, slim, blond, or legitimate.

He sighed with exasperation. "You're not listening to a word I'm saying."

"I could quote your last few sentences, but if what you mean is that nothing you say will change my mind, you're right. The decision is made." She smiled wickedly. "What if I say that I can make more money on my own? Would that make a difference?"

His voice changed. "Are you going to handle class-action suits like the ones over asbestos and tobacco? There's huge amounts of money to be made there, and you would be good at it."

"No class-action suits, at least not yet. I've just taken on my first new case—to try to get a convicted cop killer off death row. I won't make a penny off this even if I'm successful—which I probably won't be."

He snorted, recognizing that he was being baited. "You're your mother's daughter, Val."

The statement was not meant as a compliment. Val's mother, Callie Covington, was an aging hippie who lived her principles and disdained practicality. Occasionally she made Val nuts, but she was real and admirable, and she, at least, would approve that her only daughter was kicking over the traces of the establishment. "Callie will probably buy me a bottle of cheap California champagne to celebrate."

Her father unexpectedly laughed. "She would. Very well, if you're bound and determined to practice do-gooder law, I'm sure you'll do it well. But when you decide you want to return to a real firm, come to New York and work for me."

"Brad, that's probably the nicest thing you've ever said to me." She sent greetings to her stepmother and half sisters, then hung up.

When she was younger, she had wondered what it would be like to have parents she could call Mom and Dad. The commune where she had spent her early years considered anything but first names to be hierarchal and bourgeois.

The Mount Hope Peace Commune. Among her long-time friends, it was generally agreed that Val had the weirdest upbringing, though Rainey was a close second.

Callie had been a gorgeous auburn-haired earth mother, while Brad was a tall blond WASP entranced by the world outside his privileged childhood. The couple was a classic example of opposites attracting—then being unable to get along. They had lived together in the North Carolina commune until Brad tired of rebellion and returned to his real life, which meant Harvard Law School and a career in a top New York law firm.

Callie had stayed at Mount Hope practicing art, gardening, and free love until Val reached school age, then she moved to Baltimore and set up a studio. Though she was a gifted fabric artist, she had no business sense and didn't earn regular money until she began teaching art in a small progressive school. The salary wasn't much, but at least it was regular and she enjoyed the work.

Since Brad was the responsible sort who paid child support regularly even though he hadn't known Callie was pregnant when he left, they got by. Val attended the local Quaker private school on her father's dime, then made it through college and law school on scholarships and student loans. Though Val was proud of having managed on her own, unlike her mother she had never wanted to rebel against the middle class. She had wanted to join it, and she had.

Speaking of Callie . . . Val reached for the phone. Time to invite her mother to dinner and tell her the news.

After Callie accepted the invitation, Val had one last call to make before settling down to her brief. The phone rang three times before it was answered. "Rob here."

Hearing traffic in the background, Val guessed it was a cell phone. "Hi, Rob? This is Val Covington. I've changed my mind about the suitability of putting a law office in a church. Do you have time now to discuss the details?"

"For sure." There was a smile in his voice. "I'm glad you changed your mind."

"So am I." She could hardly wait to begin her new life. And apparently it would include Rob Smith, which would be . . . interesting.

CALLIE WAS ALREADY WAITING IN A BOOTH when Val entered the Kandahar restaurant's cool, dim interior. Taller than Val and dressed in flowing artsy garments of her own design, Callie would fit right into a Wagnerian opera. She rose to administer a hug. "What's the occasion? You never leave that dreary office early enough for dinner."

"Often I don't, but you're right, this is an occasion. I'm buying dinner, and I expect you to spring for some cheap California champagne."

Callie raised her voice dramatically. "I'm becoming a grandmother! You may even get married, neo-conservative that you are, though I'll settle for the grandchild. No champagne for you if you're pregnant, though."

Val grinned. "Sorry to disappoint your dynastic ambitions, but I'm sure you'll be happy to hear that I'm leaving Crouse, Resnick to open my own office, and I intend to do a lot of do-gooder law."

"Now *that's* my girl!" Callie beamed. "Tell me more."

Val repeated her new spiel about wanting to offer quality representation to those who needed it but didn't have the money. In another couple of days, she would have the concept reduced to a sound bite. After mentioning the death row case she was taking on, she added, "You'll like the office I intend to rent—a remodeled church in Hamilton. I'm going to commission you to do a huge fabric wall hanging for the entry area. The high ceilings need something big and splashy."

The wall hanging was pure impulse, but a good one. Not only would the office get a striking piece of art, but some money would be transferred to Callie. Apart from allowing Val to put a down payment on a house, Callie always refused her daughter's financial help.

A twinkle in her eyes showing that she'd deduced Val's intent, Callie said blandly, "I'd love to do a wall hanging, but it will be my gift for your office warming."

"I'll be the envy of the Baltimore legal community." Val accepted graciously since it was obvious her mother wouldn't accept payment. Callie had never cared much about money. As compensation, she had the artist's ability to make her home comfortable and attractive while spending less than most people put into a sofa. Though Val's childhood had been chaotic in some ways, it hadn't lacked color and imagination.

Callie frowned. "If you're looking for worthy clients, I have one for you. The music teacher at my school, Mia Kolski, is being harassed legally by her ex-husband, a slimeball who keeps dragging her back to court. She's a single mother and can't afford the legal fees, so she's terrified of losing custody of her kids. Her husband doesn't really want them, he just wants to punish her for being smart enough to leave him."

It was a common story, but it still made Val's blood boil. "Have her call me at home to set up an appointment. Maybe I can help her."

"That's my girl," her mother said again. "You've spent

so many years with those corporate bandits that I was beginning to think you had gone over to the dark side."

Val grinned. "You're such an unrepentant old lefty."

"Watch that word *old!*" Callie's expression turned serious. "I'm really, truly glad you're doing this, Val. Though I wasn't a very good Quaker, the principles still speak to me, which is why I took you to meetings and sent you to Friends school. I wanted you to grow up better and wiser than me. It seemed to be working, until you hit adolescence."

The waiter arrived to take their orders, giving Val time to think about her mother's words. For years the two of them had attended the Stony Run Meeting which was directly adjacent to Friends School. At the school she discovered friendship and the joys of learning; at the meeting, her idealistic young heart responded to the spiritual purity of Quaker silence and belief. Later she had fallen away from faith, while her mother moved to the Unitarians when she acquired a Jewish significant other who wasn't comfortable in a Christian church.

As the waiter left, Val said lightly, "It's hard to be a good Quaker and an adolescent, and becoming a corporate litigator is even worse. Harvard won't grant a law degree unless you swear a blood oath to deliver your soul over to the dark gods of materialism."

Callie grinned. "I almost believe that. I don't blame you for wanting to live a comfortable life. Even when you were an adorable infant with carrot-colored curls, it was clear that you weren't cut out to be an artist and live in a garret. You used to line all your toys up in neat little rows, and you always qualified your opinions, just like your father. I guess you were born to a be a lawyer, but it really makes me happy that you're going to be using your abilities to help people who need help. Now tell me more."

Val was happy to oblige. It was interesting that having given up trying to win her father's approval, she had her mother's instead.

And it felt darned good.

CHAPTER 4

ONE LONG SWEEP OF THE ROLLER COVERED MOST
of the sprawling graffiti tag, which screamed BURN! across
the side of the abandoned rowhouse. Rob eyed the paint
critically. The tan color wasn't a bad match. It would do
until they were ready to completely repaint the wall.

After obliterating the rest of the graffiti, Rob closed the
bucket and wrapped the roller. "Can you finish up here,
Sha'wan? I have to get over to the church. I may finally
have a tenant—a lady lawyer."

His partner asked, "Is she hot?"

"That's no way to talk about a lady."

Sha'wan grinned, unrepentant. "Yeah, but is she hot?"

Rob remembered Val Covington's well-curved figure
and excellent legs and found himself smiling. "She is definitely hot, and has the red hair to prove it."

Sha'wan chuckled. "Can't wait to meet her. But for
now, I'll climb up on the roof and take care of the tags on
the upper part of the next house."

"Watch your step." Rob's warning was automatic and a
sign of his age rather than Sha'wan's climbing ability. Easily finding handholds, the younger man was on the roof in

seconds. He'd been headed for a career in breaking and entering when he first crossed Rob's path. Now he used his talents in more productive ways.

Sha'wan called down, "The wall of the next building is marked up pretty bad. Send up some paint, and I'll take care of it."

"More of the tan?"

"Gray this time."

Rob moved to the graffiti removal van and pulled out an industrial size bucket of gray paint. The five basic colors stocked in the van were close enough for most situations. The idea was to obliterate graffiti, not provide a commercial painting job. After tying a rope to the handle of the paint bucket, he lugged it to the wall. "Ready?"

The younger man straddled the ridgepole near the edge of the roof. "Bring it on."

Rob threw the rope into the air. Sha'wan deftly caught it, then pulled the bucket up. "When I get through here, I'm headin' over to the Crabtown shopping center. Got a call this morning that taggers hit it last night."

"If you need help, give me a call. This meeting shouldn't take long." Rob climbed into his pickup truck to drive to the church to meet Val. Though they had reached a tentative agreement on rental terms, she wanted to see the rest of the church before making a final commitment.

He found himself whistling softly as he drove north. Strange to anticipate seeing someone so much. Even though his head knew it would have been better if she hadn't turned up on his doorstep, he couldn't help but like the idea of having her literally underfoot. With him living upstairs, he was bound to run into her regularly. If proximity proved too distracting, he could always move.

From the corner of his eye, he saw an altercation on the shabby street. A tall, skinny kid was trying to steal an old woman's purse. She clung to it fiercely and risked being knocked over or worse.

He slammed the truck to a stop against the curb, cut the engine, and vaulted out just as the old lady thwacked her cane across her assailant's ankles. As the kid squawked, Rob grabbed him and immobilized both arms behind his back. When his prisoner struggled, Rob twisted a wrist hard. "Hold still, or I'll break your arm," he ordered. "Are you all right, ma'am?"

The old woman nodded. She must be over seventy and weighed maybe a hundred pounds soaking wet. "It's not the first time I've been mugged. Probably won't be the last." Her eyes narrowed as she studied her assailant. "I know you. You're Lucy Watts's grandson Darnell."

Darnell made a choked sound. Guessing the kid was a nervous amateur, Rob released his hold, though he kept a wary eye. Even innocent-looking ten-year-olds could pull a knife or a gun. "What kind of fool attacks his grandmother's friends?"

"I . . . I didn't know it was Miss Marian," Darnell stammered. "Didn't mean to hurt nobody." He was maybe fourteen if not younger. "I never did nothin' like this before."

"Did you let your so-called friends bully you into a purse snatching?" Rob asked sternly.

Darnell's gaze dropped.

Rob continued, "The city courts are cracking down hard on violent criminals." He unhooked the cell phone from his belt. "If you try to run while I call nine-one-one, I promise that you will regret it."

"He's been hangin' out with bad company, Lucy says." Miss Marian frowned. "You want to end up in jail or dead, Darnell?"

The boy shook his head miserably. He looked very young and very frightened. Rob and Miss Marian exchanged a glance. This was, as the psychologists said, a teachable moment. If they did the right thing, maybe they could keep a basically decent kid from going off the rails.

"Do your friends tell you that mugging people makes you a man? That just makes you a coward, Darnell." Rob's voice was flinty. "If you want to be a real man, go to school, graduate, get yourself into good condition, and if you're lucky, maybe the Marines will take you. They're the real thing, not cheap street criminals."

There was a flicker in Darnell's dark eyes. "The Marines wouldn't want me."

Seeing reluctant interest, Rob said sternly, "They sure won't take a mugger, but the Corps is full of strong, brave, black men. Real heroes. If you want to do something useful with your life, go down to the Fresh Air youth center. Play some basketball, sit down at a computer, use your brain and your body both. You might surprise yourself. In a few years, you might even turn into Marine Corps material. But only if Miss Marian doesn't want to press charges."

Taking her cue, the old woman jabbed Darnell in the ribs with the head of her cane. "I won't press charges, but I will tell your grandmamma. Now go down to that youth center and make some new friends. You've got a good brain. Use it."

"Yes, Miss Marian." After a long pause, Darnell said with difficulty, "I'm real sorry. I won't never try 'n rob anyone ever again."

"See that you don't. Because if Miss Marian doesn't hear, I will." Rob gave a sharklike smile. "And I'm nowhere near as nice as she is."

"Yessir." Darnell started edging away nervously.

Miss Marian halted him with a gesture. "If you come by my house and clean the trash from the backyard tomorrow, I won't tell Lucy about this. Will you do that?"

"Yes, ma'am," Darnell said eagerly. "I'll do a good job, I promise."

"Come by after church then. And if you do really well, there will be some peach pie for you."

Darnell nodded, then took to his heels, disappearing down an alley. "Do you think he'll follow through?" Rob asked.

"There's a good chance. He was always a nice boy, but his mama's on drugs and his daddy's dead, and he's too much for Lucy to handle." Miss Marian shook her head. "Giving him something better to do is a start. Thank you for your help."

"You would make a pretty good Marine yourself, ma'am."

The old lady snorted. "I used to teach junior high school, and I learned that you can't let yourself be afraid of kids, no matter how big they are. You do your best, and hope they listen."

"Can I drive you somewhere?"

"My daughter's house is only a block away. Thank you for your help, young man." She cocked her head to one side. "Aren't you the Graffiti Guy?"

He nodded and held his hand out. "Rob Smith."

"Marian Berry." She shook his hand with a surprisingly strong grip. "It's good to get rid of graffiti, but don't the kids just come right back and paint new ones?"

"Usually not. They want recognition. Being wiped out as if they don't matter generally sends them to find a spot where their tags won't be covered immediately. If a different tagger comes around then, we paint him out and pretty soon, he's gone, too."

"Sure does make the neighborhood look better. You keep up the good work, Mr. Smith." She marched off, back erect.

Adrenaline still pumping, he climbed back into the truck and resumed his trip to the church, hoping he wouldn't be late. He had just pulled into the lot when a burgundy-colored Lexus whizzed up next to him. The car made his truck look old and tired.

He climbed from the truck, then stared at the woman who bounded from the Lexus. She wore jeans, a dark orange T-shirt that read 99 PERCENT OF LAWYERS GIVE THE REST A BAD NAME, and she had a wild mane of red curls swirling around her head. Dangling earrings and an embroidered ethnic vest completed her outfit. He said, "Who are you and what are you doing with Val Covington's car?"

She laughed. "This is the real me, Saturday style. Can you stand it?"

He climbed the steps and unlocked the back door. "Stand it? I'm fascinated. I always loved the story of Jekyll and Hyde."

"I presume Dr. Jekyll was me in lawyer drag." She

slanted him a glance as she passed by him into the building. "Which means that now I'm dangerous Ms. Hyde."

Dangerous wasn't the half of it. Her buoyancy and sheer high spirits struck chords that had been silent so long he had forgotten how they sounded, and that wasn't counting her physical attractions. Even in her tailored suit she had been sexy, but in casual attire, she was stunning. And she was flirting with him.

He didn't take it personally—today she radiated the kind of sparkling femininity that flirts with the world and probably caused males from nine to ninety to follow her around. Keeping his voice light, he said, "A killer lawyer who looks like you? Dangerous indeed." He ushered her into the back room he had been using as an office.

Val reached into her oversized tapestry handbag and pulled out a sheaf of papers. "I drafted a lease based on the terms we discussed on the phone. Look it through, consult another lawyer if you like, or let me know if you want changes."

He skimmed through his copy, noting that the rental amount and terms were as they agreed. "No need. I'm willing to sign now."

She shook her head. "You're too trusting."

"A contract isn't worth much more than the honesty of the people who sign it."

"True, but contracts come in handy if a situation implodes and the pieces need to be sorted out. I want to talk to you about a bit of remodeling before I move in, but that should be a separate deal." She grinned. "I haven't even seen the whole building. I should be ashamed of myself for not doing my homework."

"I'll give you the full tour before we sign anything, so you can back out if you change your mind."

"I won't change my mind for anything short of a cholera-breeding swamp in the basement. And probably not then."

If she found a swamp, she'd call a plumber. An efficient woman, Val Covington. He opened the door to the lower level for her. Though she seemed tall because of her energetic presence, now that she wore sandals instead of high heels she really was just a little bit of a thing. "See for yourself."

Since the sanctuary and church offices were half a story aboveground, the basement level had enough windows to admit good light, but the area was otherwise unexciting. The majority of the old church hall was open space, the white walls and neutral vinyl floor covering accented by dark woodwork.

Kitchen and bathrooms were at the back of the building, under the offices. The aged kitchen was a period piece, designed to allow a dozen or more church ladies to work in it. Since Rob wasn't sure of the eventual use of the room, he hadn't done anything but clean, paint, and check that the elderly appliances worked.

Val didn't mind. "What a great old kitchen. With a table in the middle and a new microwave, it will make a nice lunch room." She surveyed the open hall, which had been designed for suppers and meetings. "Not a cholera swamp in sight, so I'd like this subdivided into rooms for records and offices for interns and volunteers."

"Interns?"

"With two law schools in Baltimore, it shouldn't be hard to find students hot to get some real world experience. I also intend to haul in some of my lawyer friends. Since they have to do some pro bono work, they might as well do it here. I'm not the only one who yearns to do justice." She headed to the stairs. "Next stop, offices."

Rob guided her to the former minister's study, which was directly behind the sanctuary. "This is the nicest office, I think."

Val sighed happily at the sight of the bay window, which had narrow stained-glass panels at the top. "This one's mine. I've always yearned for a window seat." She crossed the room and perched on the uncushioned bench. "Diamond-shaped windowpanes and a view of the neighbor's rhododendrons. Not a bad exchange for my vulture's eye view of the Inner Harbor."

He thought about what her current job must be like. "I

imagine it will feel strange to shift from a busy uptown law firm to a quiet private practice."

She shrugged. "I'm ready. For years, every day has had six deadlines and endless streams of tense people. The adrenaline rush is addictive, but busyness is no substitute for a life."

She might find it harder to recover from adrenaline addiction than she thought; he'd had a terrible time kicking the habit himself. Simplicity wasn't easy. Of course, Val was looking to slow her life down, not turn it off completely, as he had done. "Are you really going to concentrate on pro bono work?"

"I figure on doing it about half time. We'll see." She drew her feet up onto the window seat and wrapped her arms around her knees. "I want to make a difference in people's lives, not just their pocketbooks. Not that there's anything wrong with prosperity, but I don't want my life to be about money. For years it has been, and I didn't even realize it until these last few days. I was always pushing, pushing . . ." She cut off her words, as if she had already said too much.

She was wise to see the light before her life was in crisis. He had been less wise. "How will you find worthy causes to fight?"

"They're finding me. I already agreed to take on one case, and I'll probably take another on after I've talked to the potential client—a single mother whose rich ex-husband keeps taking her to court for no good reason."

"I hope you squash him like a bug. What's the other case?"

"It's a tough one. Kendra, my assistant, asked me to see if I could do anything for an old friend of hers who's on death row. Daniel Monroe was convicted of killing a policeman. She swears he's innocent, but he's run out of appeals and the execution date will be set soon." Val grimaced. "I'll see what I can do, but it would take a miracle to save his life."

The words *death row* hit Rob like ice water, shattering his relaxed mood. "Are you sure your friend isn't indulging in wishful thinking about his innocence? Most convicts will swear on a stack of Bibles that they were railroaded."

"Kendra says she was with him the night of the murder."

"The police didn't believe her?"

"They thought she was lying to protect her boyfriend. I'm sure that happens, but Kendra doesn't lie. If Kendra says he was with her, he was."

So maybe this really was an innocent man wrongly convicted. "What was the case against Monroe?"

"I haven't seen the files yet—this only just came up—but Kendra said that he was convicted on the testimony of the three eyewitnesses."

His mouth twisted. "Eyewitness error is the most common cause of unjust conviction."

"Yes, but it's awfully hard to disprove." Her arms tightened around her knees. "If a victim gets up on the witness stand and says, 'That man there did it,' juries believe. A mistaken witness can send an innocent man to his death."

"When a crime raises public outrage, everyone is desperate to see the killer punished," Rob said cynically. "It's too easy for police and prosecutors to settle for the first plausible suspect and not look any further."

She studied his face. "You know something about crime and punishment."

His gaze shifted away from her. "I've done some reading." Which was true, though most of what he knew had been learned the hard way. "How will you go about this? As a capital case, I imagine it's been pretty thoroughly hashed over."

"I'll start with getting the case files from the public defender's office. Then I'll try to interview everyone significant in the case—the defense lawyer, the prosecutor, the police, the eyewitnesses, and hope they're all still alive. I'll have to tear apart every shred of evidence and look for weaknesses." She halted. "No, that's not where to start. First I have to visit Monroe at the penitentiary. All I know about him is through Kendra. I want to meet him for myself, then find out if he wants me to act for him. I really can't do anything without his agreement."

Rob's desire for detachment fought a brief but fierce battle with a compulsion to get involved in this case. "Take me with you. Maybe I can help with the investigation."

"Why would you want to do that?" she asked, startled.

"I don't like capital punishment," he said flatly. "How do you feel about it?"

"Ambivalent." She frowned. "I don't clamor for blood, but some people have done such ghastly things that it's hard to be upset if they meet their maker prematurely."

"By killing, society reduces itself to the level of a murderer. Not to mention the fact that innocent men die. Did you know that for every seven men executed, one is released from death row as completely innocent? A lot of prisoners have been freed when DNA evidence proved they didn't commit the crime. What does that imply about cases where there's no DNA to give absolute proof of guilt or innocence?"

She stared at him. "One in eight? Really?"

"So I've read. The figures aren't exact. Plenty of agencies keep track of crime and punishment, but not many track wrongful convictions."

"Twelve percent. That's *appalling*." She swung from the window seat and began pacing the room. "If the percentage of wrong convictions holds across the board, that means tens of thousands of innocent people are in prison."

He smiled without humor. "You wanted to do justice. The field is wide open."

"I promised to look into this case for Kendra's sake, but if the problem of wrongful conviction is so widespread, there's even more reason to take it on." She gave a quick, impatient shake of her head. "Any thinking person recognizes that the system must occasionally fail and send an innocent man to jail, or worse, to the death chamber. But if mistakes are made on such a scale, it's . . . it's horrific."

"You'll probably go home this afternoon and research to find if my figures are accurate," he predicted.

She looked startled. "I'm that transparent?"

"Lawyers believe in facts. Before you start a crusade,

you're going to make sure that you're carrying the right banner."

"Damn straight." She stopped pacing and studied his face with alarming intensity. "Rob, your desire to help an innocent man is obviously for real, but I have to ask if you have any experience as an investigator. Do you think you can handle an investigation with so much riding on it? There won't be time for second chances. If this kind of work is outside your experience, I can hire a professional investigator."

Though he preferred not to discuss his past, it couldn't be avoided this time. "I was a military policeman in the Marines. It's been a few years, but the basic cop skills of investigation, interviewing, and deduction were drummed into me pretty thoroughly."

"You're hired. Not that there's any money in this." She smiled a little. "Between now and the time I leave my job, I'm going to be swamped, so it will be a godsend if you have skill and interest in this."

"Thanks for letting me help." The words were inadequate for what he felt. Even to himself, he couldn't fully explain this urgent need to try to save a stranger. Changing the subject, he said, "You were interested in some remodeling before you move in?"

"Bookcases, closet shelving, that sort of thing. One of the back rooms needs to be set up for equipment like copiers and printers." Her eyes narrowed thoughtfully as she shifted mental gears from justice to office space. "It might be good to install double doors between this office and the one behind. I can use the extra space as a library and conference room."

"No problem. Do you want to think about what changes you'd like over the weekend, then give me a list so I can do an estimate?"

"Will do. I want to move in as soon as I wind things up at Crouse, Resnick." Her gaze flicked upward. "Your apartment can't be very large. If you want to keep your office here or in the basement for the time being, feel free. There's plenty of space."

He shook his head, both amused and bemused. "And you say I'm too trusting. What if I'm an ax murderer?"

"If you are, I hope I remember the moves from my self-defense class." She crossed to the door. "But you don't look particularly crazed, and if you're around some of the time, it might discourage other ax murderers."

A pragmatic lady. He followed her down the hall and into the former sanctuary. "What goes in here?"

"Kendra's office, so she can keep an eye on the door, plus a sitting and gathering area. Maybe knee walls or portable cubicle dividers to give her some privacy. Her choice." Val moved into the center of the sanctuary, her gaze going to the stained-glass roundels. "I love this building so much. How can justice not be done here?"

"Justice is good," he said softly. "Mercy is better."

"So we're back to capital punishment." Her gaze was uncomfortably acute. "You're an interesting man, Rob Smith."

"And the Chinese made *interesting* into a curse." He pulled a set of keys from his pocket. "Time to sign the contracts and make you the official tenant. Then you can come and go as you please."

She grinned. "Don't forget that I'm supposed to give you a check."

He snapped his fingers in mock surprise. "Oh, yeah. Money. I need to work on the business end of being a landlord. I'm better with studs and Sheetrock."

She whipped out a business card and handed it to him. "If you need a lawyer, let me know. For landlords, special rates."

They both chuckled, and to his relief, the mood lightened again. Signing the contracts took only a few minutes, after which he left Val to survey her new empire. Yet as he drove in toward the center of the city, he couldn't shake her from his thoughts.

For years, he had passed through the world like a ghost, interacting mostly with things instead of people. Val Covington made him real.

It was a damned uncomfortable feeling.

CHAPTER 5

❧❧❧

AFTER ROB LEFT, VAL MEASURED ROOMS AND MADE notes, but her mind was churning. If he was right about how many innocent people were being sent to jail—and she suspected that he didn't make many mistakes—she had discovered a subject she could feel passionate about.

Though grateful for Rob's investigative skills and desire to help, she wondered if more help would be needed. Maybe journalism students? At Northwestern University, a journalism professor and his students had done investigations that cleared so many men on death row that the Illinois governor put a moratorium on executions. But students would require some supervision, and she simply didn't have the time. She would give Rob a chance to show his stuff before she sought more volunteers.

In the meantime, she had Crouse, Resnick work to finish. More briefs. Clients paying top dollar for her full attention. But today was Saturday, and she was entitled to have her own life for a few hours. That meant pricing equipment for her new office, then kicking back over dinner with a friend.

After visiting an office furniture warehouse and a com-

puter superstore, she headed for home, thinking again
about her landlord. Definitely one of a kind. She would
love to know Rob's background, but wasn't quite rude
enough to ask. She grinned. When she knew him better,
then she would be rude.

Their relationship was developing fast, albeit in uncon-
ventional ways. She was still surprised at her impulsive
suggestion that he maintain his office in the church, but it
was true that she had space to spare, and it would be nice to
have him around.

Okay, Val, admit that you're attracted. She liked his
mind, liked his solid, practical skills, liked that he cared
about the fate of a condemned man he had never met.

Not to mention that either he radiated sex appeal, or she
had been celibate way too long. Maybe both.

She realized that she was humming a song her mother
sang as a lullaby, "If I Were a Carpenter," and smiled. How
appropriate, for under the lilting words and melody it was
a song about class. She was a Harvard-educated lawyer
and Rob was a carpenter, remodeler, and ex-Marine. Was
attraction doomed?

Hell, no. Education was all very well, but in her experience, having a bright and active mind mattered more than
having a diploma on the wall. And unless her judgment
was way off, he was not unaware of her.

Such a lovely combination of strength and practical
skills and sharp mind and appealing textures. She would
love to run her fingers through that thick, tawny beard. . . .

She cut off her thoughts before they could descend into
X-rated territory. The fact that he was interesting and attractive didn't make him date material even though he was
age appropriate, had no obvious vices, and she had always
had a weakness for beards.

But she had a longstanding rule not to date men she
worked with, and since he was both landlord and potential
investigator, a more intimate relationship had plenty of
room to cause trouble if it didn't work out. Best to keep
things on a professional level.

On the other hand—as a lawyer, Val had a lot more than
two hands—maybe she was trying to deny the possibility
of romance because she had lost her nerve. It had been a
long time since she had been in a real relationship.

The last had been with Donovan, her friend Kate's once
and present husband. He was a great guy who had treated
her well, but in retrospect she realized that he hadn't really
been emotionally available because he had never stopped
loving Kate. Luckily, they had all managed to stay friends
after Kate moved back to Baltimore and fell straight into
her ex-husband's arms.

The most intriguing man she had met since Donovan
was Greg Marino, the cinematographer on Rainey's movie.
Working as Rainey's assistant, Val had hung out with Greg
during the shoot. He also had a delicious beard and was a
real sweetie as well as very talented. He had asked her to
be his date at the Academy Awards ceremony where he
won an Oscar, which made for an unforgettable night. Yet
though she had liked him immensely, there was no future
for a show business gypsy and a conventional East Coaster
like her.

She sighed. Men. Now that she might actually have
time for a real romance, she needed to figure out better
ways to pick 'em.

Pulling into the alley garage of her house started a welcome flow of relaxation through her. The Homeland neighborhood was one of Baltimore's best, with handsome,
spacious houses and shady trees. Traditional center hall
colonials predominated, but Val had fallen in love with this
Tudor-style house the moment she saw it. Asymmetrical
and finished with cream-colored stucco between herring-
bone beams, her home sat placidly under slanting slate
roofs. Comfort with a dash of eccentricity—just her style.

As a child she had loved her father's grand Connecticut
house on the rare occasions when she visited. Not only
were the grounds larger than some Baltimore parks and a
lot better landscaped, but there were more bathrooms than
residents. Her yearning to live in such a house had made

her feel disloyal to the small row house she shared with her mother. The house was pleasant and wonderfully decorated by Callie, and Val had helped her mother buy it when the landlord decided to sell. But it would never be a Connecticut mansion.

Her Homeland Tudor house wasn't a mansion either, but it was just right for her, and a reward for years of hard work. Since she was walking away from her law partnership income, maybe it would have been smarter to stay in her first home, a row house near Johns Hopkins University. The mortgage and running costs there were one heck of a lot lower, but she couldn't regret buying her dream house. If she ended up having to cut costs in other areas, so be it.

A stop at a gourmet grocer on the way home provided the ingredients for dinner. The meal would be simple since her guest, Rachel Hamilton, had been a friend since first grade and formality was neither necessary nor desired. Val was looking forward to the evening. They hadn't managed to get together for months, and it would be fun to catch up. Rachel's good sense was always useful for keeping things in perspective. A pity she had wasted herself on medical school; she would have made a great judge. In fact, Rachel's father *was* a judge.

The cats were waiting in the mudroom when she came in the rear door. The sleek black male, Damocles, waited aloofly while the calico lady, Lilith, twined suggestively around Val's ankles, gaze locked on the plastic shopping bags. "Don't pretend you're starving, Lilith. I saw you inhaling your breakfast." Val bent to stroke Lilith's head, skritched Damocles's neck so he wouldn't feel neglected, and headed for the kitchen.

Some fast work resulted in marinara sauce with sliced Italian sausage gently simmering on the back burner, a table set with crystal and candles—why restrict elegance to dinners with men?—and a green salad chilling in the refrigerator next to a bottle of wine. Val was wrapping garlic bread in foil for heating when the doorbell rang.

She skipped to the front door to admit her friend. Tall

and serene, with short dark hair that fell naturally into soft waves, Rachel inspired confidence even when she looked exhausted, like this evening. She stepped into the vestibule and inhaled deeply. "Smells wonderful. How do you do it, Val? You're at least as busy as I am, but you still manage to be a domestic goddess."

Val laughed. "I know where to buy good food made by other people to fill in whatever gaps I don't have time to fill myself. Come on in and have some wine and tell me what you've been up to."

Over wine, pasta, and dessert, they talked with the ease of friends who can reconnect immediately no matter how long it has been since their last meeting. Afterward, they settled on the sun porch, which was cozier than the formal living room. Val curled up in her wing chair, Lilith on her lap, while Damocles sprawled across Rachel, who was conveniently wearing black so the fur wouldn't show.

Having heard Val's story about how and why she was changing her career, Rachel said, "This must be a good decision. I haven't seen you so happy and excited for years."

"I'm excited but scared, too." Val paused to clarify her qualms. "Up until now, sheer competitiveness kept me pointed in the right direction. Not only am I tackling professional areas where I don't know much, I have no idea how to manage leisure time. I'm too used to running like a gerbil on a wheel."

Rachel took the disclosure calmly; she had always been the Mother Confessor of their group of friends. "Of course you're scared—any life change worth doing is scary. But I think you'll be glad once you make the adjustment. You just have to trade some of the orderliness you like for more disorder."

Val groaned. "It sounds awful when you put it that way."

"Then impose order by making lists. You always enjoy that. What's on your list for using your new leisure time?"

"I'd like to garden again," Val said thoughtfully. "Travel more, cook more, go antiquing. Heck, it would be heavenly to be able to loaf around the house with the cats guilt-free. But the biggie is relationships, of course. Friendships are plants that need watering with time and effort. I want to be able to have lunch with a friend without scheduling it a month in advance."

"I wonder if that's why most of my friends are people I've known for years. I haven't had time to develop new friendships." Rachel scratched Damocles under the chin. "Speaking of relationships, tell me about this landlord of yours. You get a feline gleam in your eyes when you mention him."

Val made a face. "Is it that obvious?"

"Crystal clear."

"He's an interesting guy—the still-waters-run-deep sort. Very down-to-earth and practical, which should help in this death row investigation. He genuinely cares about saving Daniel Monroe's life, I think, so he'll do his best."

"That's all very well, but is he attractive?"

Val looked for a movie analogy from the years when the old gang watched films together every Sunday night. "Think of Charlton Heston as Ben-Hur after the Roman galley sinks and Chuck is rowing that raft. Lots of muscles and a blond beard."

Rachel laughed. "If he looks like that and has a brain as well, ask him if he has a brother. I await developments eagerly."

"Don't hold your breath. Rob is strictly fantasy fodder."

Rachel arched her brows in patent disbelief, but didn't argue the point. "Even if he's a nonstarter, a new job means meeting new people. Maybe one of them will be the love of your life."

"Even if I do find Prince Charming, that would lead to the biggest ambivalence of all—motherhood," Val said wryly. "My biological clock is ticking madly, but the prospect of children also terrifies me. What if I find a guy who's a keeper, have a baby, then discover I'm a total loser as a mother? It's a job that you can't quit after you start."

"Personally I suspect that you have plenty of ambivalence about the love-of-your-life part as well," Rachel observed, "but you won't be a failure if you decide to have kids. You'll read every book on parenting ever written, analyze them all, then put the best ideas into practice. The real question is not whether you'd be a decent mother, but whether it's a responsibility you want to take on."

"You're right—it's the responsibility that's so scary. Sure would be nice if we could do a test run on parenting before jumping into the abyss."

"You're over-thinking this parenting business—an amazing number of people manage it with no advance planning at all. But if it would make you feel better, there are different kinds of test runs available."

Val ran a mental list of friends with small children. "Borrow someone's child for a weekend?"

"That's a start. Or you could join a Big Sister/Little Sister program." Rachel grinned. "It would fit right in with your new do-gooder status."

"I never thought of that," Val said slowly, "but it's a good idea. Maybe I'll learn something about how well I can handle a long-term relationship with a kid."

"Maybe, or maybe not. I know plenty of people who say the only children they can stand are their own. But even if you don't get a definitive answer on becoming a parent, mentoring a young girl should be rewarding in its own right."

"I'll put 'little sister' at the top of the list." Val smiled, soothed by wine, good company, and feline purring. She had the prospect of exciting new work, an intriguing man, and finding a little girl she could play with, then hand back.

What more could a woman want?

CHAPTER 6

ROB WAS ABOUT TO START FRAMING THE NEW OF-
fices in the church basement when Val rang up on his cell
phone. "Hi, Rob, it's Val. I know this is short notice, but
can you meet me at the SuperMax prison on Madison and
Fallsway in an hour so we can talk with Daniel Monroe?"

So soon. The knowledge of what he was starting was
like a cold north wind on bare skin. "Sure, but let me pick
you up at your office."

"I can manage—it's not far from where I work."

"Do you really want to park your Lexus in that area?"

"Probably not," she agreed. "Do you know where my
office is?"

"Yes." He had learned that when he web searched her.
"See you at eleven." He hung up, thinking he had better go
upstairs to his apartment and change clothes. Worn denim
was his fabric of choice, but he needed to look like an investigator, not an inmate.

It had been years since he had made much effort to look
respectable, and he found that his navy blazer was now
tight across the shoulders and his khakis loose at the waist.

Hammering a nail was much better exercise than hammering a keyboard.

He climbed into his truck and headed downtown, thinking it felt odd to wear business casual clothing in his old pickup. The monastic simplicity of the life he had lived these last years would surely break down if he involved himself with people and causes. His feelings about that were ambivalent. The oppressive heaviness that had flattened him was slowly beginning to lift, but what kind of changes could he bear?

And what did a man who bore the mark of Cain deserve?

The offices of Crouse, Resnick were polished, hushed, and expensive. Even in his blazer, he felt like a janitor. The receptionist was impeccably polite despite his appearance, and two minutes after she called to report his arrival, a tall, stunning black woman came to collect him. Hair pulled into a sleek chignon showed off her beautifully shaped head while a fuchsia-colored suit set off an admirable womanly figure. "Mr. Smith? I'm Kendra Brooks, Ms. Covington's assistant."

He offered his hand. "I'm Rob. It's a pleasure to meet you. We'll be seeing more of each other, I'm sure."

She glanced around as she led him back into the offices. No one was in sight, but she still kept her voice low. "I appreciate that you volunteered to help Daniel."

This close, he saw the strain around her eyes, and he revised his estimate of her age from thirtyish to fortyish. Kendra Brooks was a woman who had weathered her share of troubles. "I hope I can help. This case . . . pushes some personal buttons."

Kendra gave him a shrewd glance as she opened the door to an office. Val was on the phone, and she beckoned to Rob to enter. She was in full professional mode today, with hair up and a sober gray suit. Interesting how that flaming red hair looked several shades darker when firmly restrained.

As she bent her head to take notes, he admired the delicate line of her nape, where a tendril of bright hair curled over her fair skin. A perfect place to kiss . . .

He turned away as soon as the thought formed. He was here on serious business, not to fantasize like an adolescent. He walked to the window behind her, which offered a spectacular view of the Inner Harbor. Far below, a tall ship flying the German flag was docked and an untidy line of visitors waited for a tour. A juggler entertained them, while on the other side of the Harborplace pavilion a water taxi discharged tourists. He wondered if Val would miss being in the center of the city with a nonstop carnival outside her window. He turned when the phone clicked down.

"Sorry to make you wait." Val stood and stepped from behind the desk. Today she wore a pantsuit. Probably didn't want to foment trouble in a prison by showing off those excellent legs. She also wore high heels that created the illusion of average height. He wondered how she would react if he told her she looked cute. She'd probably deck him. "No problem. Ready to go?"

She handed him an accordion file heavy with documents, then grabbed a briefcase and set a brisk pace toward the elevators. "I've done a quick review of the case documents. That file contains copies of the most important ones. After you've gone through them, we need to sit down and discuss the evidence and decide how to attack. Assuming you and I and Monroe all want to proceed, that is."

"You've had time to get the files and read them already? It's only been four days since you decided to open your own office."

"This is one case where time really is of the essence." The elevator doors opened and she pressed the button for the garage after they entered. "Anyone sentenced to death in Maryland automatically has appeals filed, so the evidence has already been studied six ways from zero. Four months isn't much time to come up with a strategy that will convince the governor to commute the sentence. Especially not in an election year when politicians are terrified of looking soft on crime."

"If he's innocent, there should be a way."

She smiled as they emerged into the parking garage and walked to his pickup. "I like your optimism."

"Optimism is easy when you're ignorant." He helped her up the high step into the pickup. Her hand was small and cool, and her composure made her seem perfectly at home on the patched bench seat of a working truck. He liked that in a woman.

Less than ten minutes of driving brought them to the area by the Jones Falls Expressway where several major Department of Corrections facilities were jammed together like rock fans in a mosh pit. Rob's skin crawled when they came in sight of the Maryland Penitentiary.

The oldest continually operated prison in America, the Pen looked like a dank medieval castle. The looming stone building sat right on one of the city's major west-bound streets without even a sidewalk to separate it from heavy traffic. High above, wicked spirals of concertina wire glinted in the pale sun. He wondered what those slashing razor spikes would do to an escaping prisoner who fell into a coil, then decided he didn't want to think about it.

As they circled the Pen on one-way streets to reach the parking lot, Rob saw women standing on the sidewalk and shouting up to inmates visible in the prison's narrow windows. Wives and girlfriends, presumably. He wondered if drugs and other contraband were ever thrown to the prisoners.

He was glad their destination was the SuperMax prison across the street. Relatively new, the brick structure hadn't had time to accumulate as many ghosts as the Pen. As they parked, Val explained, "Even though death row is here, the main purpose of SuperMax is to secure the most violent criminals. Prisoners spend twenty-three hours a day in solitary confinement, with an hour of recreation time."

"So if they aren't crazy when they're first sent there, they soon will be."

"Probably, but at least they can't murder each other."

They fell silent when they reached the entrance to the SuperMax. Though Rob had never been in this prison, the routine was painfully familiar. Guards and metal detectors, Val's briefcase thoroughly searched, and an atmosphere as toxic as poison gas.

As the guards patted him down for concealed weapons, he felt as if a steel band were tightening around his chest. Recognizing his panicky desire to bolt, Val said quietly, "If you want to wait in the truck, that's okay."

"Thanks, but no. This needs to be done." Grimly he reminded himself that he was here by choice. If he visited the SuperMax again, maybe it would be easier. "But it's a good thing you're doing the talking."

"Talking I can always manage." Her mouth tightened as she surveyed their surroundings. "Making sense is something else again."

"You'll make sense." They shared a glance of mutual support, then followed a guard to a visiting room. It was little more than a glorified closet with a transparent plastic barrier separating the prisoner from visitors. Conversation was through a pair of telephones. Val took one of the two chairs on their side, but Rob fidgeted about the small space, unable to relax. He didn't take the seat next to Val until the opposite door opened and two guards escorted a shackled Daniel Monroe into the other half of the room.

Rob's first impression was of intimidating size. Monroe was well over six feet tall with massive shoulders that stretched the fabric of his bright orange jumpsuit. A long, wicked scar marred the ebony perfection of his gleaming bald head. Another scar had been carved in his jaw. Knife cuts? Broken glass? If Rob saw this man at night on the street, he'd get the hell away as fast as he could. Even shackled and separated from the visitors' area, Daniel Monroe was scary.

Not turning a hair, Val waited until he'd taken his chair and lifted the handset, then introduced herself. "Mr. Monroe, I'm Val Covington. Kendra Brooks said she'd let you know I would be coming."

"She told me." Monroe's basso profundo voice rumbled the telephone, sounding more resigned than dangerous. "That girl just don't give up."

"Neither do I, Mr. Monroe." Val gestured toward Rob. "This is my investigator, Rob Smith. You fired your previous lawyers. Will you allow us to act on your behalf?"

Monroe turned his attention to Rob. His gaze wasn't that of a mad dog killer, nor did he have the flat stare of a psychopath. Instead, he had the wise, sad eyes of a man who had seen unspeakable things and given up all belief in justice. "Why bother? I ain't hopin' no more. When the chief justice of the Supreme Court says that actual innocence isn't necessarily a constitutional claim, it's time to quit."

Val said incredulously, "A chief justice said that? Which one?"

"Rehnquist. Look it up." Monroe's voice was matter-of-fact.

"I will." Val frowned as she considered how to reply. "Very well, since hope is a luxury you can't afford, don't hope that we can do anything. We both know that the odds of success are slim. But isn't even a long shot worth trying?"

Monroe stared at his manacled wrists. "You don't know what you're askin'."

"I think I do," Val said quietly. "And now I'm going to take a cheap shot. Will you let us do what we can for Kendra's sake, so she won't torment herself wondering if more might have been done?"

After a long silence, Monroe released his breath in a ragged sigh. "Okay, Miss Covington. For Kendra's sake. I don't want her carryin' no regrets when I'm gone."

"Good. And please, call me Val. We are going to get to know each other very well." Val pulled a legal tablet from her briefcase. "I know you've told your story a thousand times before, but would you mind doing it again?"

"Not much to say. I was never no saint. As a kid, I got into trouble with the law a couple of times. I never did nothin' violent, but I did have a record and the cops knew me. After I served six months for swipin' a car to go joyridin', I decided it was time I grew up. Kendra gave me another chance, and I got a job working in a warehouse. They treated me right and were going to make me a supervisor. I got me a GED and was set to take some night school courses at the community college.

"Then one night the cops came bangin' on the door. When I opened it, they charged in and slammed me against a wall. I moved real, real slow so they wouldn't get itchy trigger fingers. They said I had to come down to the station for some questions. When I left, I told Kendra I'd be back soon 'cause I knew I hadn't done nothin' wrong." There was a bitter edge to his voice. "I said good-bye to Kendra and the baby, and I been locked up ever since."

"What happened at the station?" Val asked softly.

"They kept askin' questions about what I'd done that night. Didn't know what was going on until one of the detectives got in my face and screamed why did I kill Officer Malloy? That's when I knew I was in deep shit—a policeman killed.

"I told 'em the truth, over and over. Then they put me in a lineup, a couple of witnesses said I was the shooter, and it was all over. I was charged, tried, and convicted. People cheered when I was sentenced to death."

His flat voice was chilling. Rob asked, "No one believed Kendra's testimony that you were with her?"

"The shooting took place only a couple of blocks from where we lived, so the prosecutor claimed there was time for me to sneak out and back without her knowing." Monroe snorted. "As if I'd leave Kendra to attack another woman, blow a cop's brains out, then calmly come home to play with my baby. But common sense didn't matter. They wanted to convict someone real bad, and I was handy."

"There was an attempt several years ago to commute your sentence to life imprisonment," Val said.

"The victim's family wouldn't hear of it, and what they think matters." Monroe's expression tightened. "Some smart folks tried to help me, Miss Val, and didn't get anywhere. It's time to let go and let God."

"We've already had this discussion, and you agreed to let us see what we can do. Personally, I prefer to think God helps those who help themselves. I'm not a criminal lawyer, but I'm a damned good attorney and maybe I can bring a fresh eye to the case." Val flipped to the next page of her tablet, revealing questions she'd written in advance. "Are you ready for a preliminary discussion of the evidence?"

Monroe gave a faint, rueful smile. "You sayin' that resistance is futile, and it will be a whole lot easier if I cooperate?"

Val smiled back. "That's about it, Daniel. Let's give it a try and see what happens. What have you got to lose?"

He rubbed a hand over his bald head, revealing the edge of a tattoo below his sleeve. "Nothin', long as I'm not fool enough to hope, and talkin' to you is a break in the boredom. Ask away."

Val obeyed, asking probing questions about the crime, the evidence, and the people involved. Rob watched in silence, simultaneously learning about the case and observing Monroe's reactions. Val's grasp of the material was remarkable, especially since she'd only just taken the case on and was working on multiple projects.

When their time was up, they left the SuperMax in silence. He inhaled deeply as they reached the street, thinking that even exhaust-tinged air tasted wonderful after the suffocating atmosphere of the prison.

He took his companion's cool demeanor at face value until they reached the privacy of the pickup truck. As he closed his door, she buried her head in her hands. "What a ghastly place! It's . . . it's like walking into a cloud of poison gas."

"Worse," he said grimly. "Prisons are soul-destroying for everyone in them."

"Seeing Daniel made capital punishment *real*. Kendra showed me a picture from before his imprisonment. He was a real teddy bear of a guy, very different from the way he looks now. As he talked, I couldn't stop thinking that his days are literally numbered. One day in September, the state intends to strap him to a gurney, stick a needle in his arm, and murder him." A wrenching sob escaped her. "It's barbaric. *Barbaric.*"

Throat tight, he put an arm around her shoulders. "That's the worst of executing people. It makes us all barbarians."

She turned into him, shuddering from her sobs. Her intense reaction was a startling contrast to the composure she had shown in the prison.

His own reaction was equally intense. As he circled her with his other arm, he realized with a fierceness beyond anything he had felt in years that he wanted her. He wanted to have and hold her, protect her and seek comfort from her. He wanted to connect with another human being as he never had before. He had been attracted to her physically from the start, and soon came to admire her intelligence and charm. But her vulnerability touched some deep, long-frozen part of his soul.

Unable to bear the cascade of his emotions, he sought for a way to restore normalcy. "Maybe you're the one who can keep the barbarians at bay this time, Val."

"Maybe." She raised her head wearily. "Sorry to cry all over you. I never do things like that, but meeting a condemned man pushed buttons I didn't know I had."

"I won't tell anyone that the SuperMax got under your skin. It got to me just as badly." He pulled out his handkerchief for her, at the same time easing away, putting as much space between them as was possible in the cab of a small truck. "I'm amazed at how much you've learned about the case so quickly."

"There are three keys to being a good lawyer—preparation, preparation, preparation. Boring, but true. The more homework I do, the better the results, and I learned early how to do my homework well."

"Do you think Monroe is innocent?"

"Quite possibly." Her expression hardened. "But even if he's guilty as sin, I'm going to do my damnedest to get him off death row. I've just become a convert to the cause of ending capital punishment."

"There's nothing like personal experience to make the horror of it sink in." Before Val could wonder about his remark, he continued, "If I understand this right, remove the eyewitness testimony and the case against Monroe collapses. No physical evidence ties him to the murder—no blood, and the weapon was never found. His only crime might be that he was roughly the same size and shape of the real shooter."

"Like he said, with a policeman dead, they had to convict someone and he was handy." She wiped her eyes with his handkerchief. "Are you still up for investigating this case? It's not going to be fun, and the potential for pain and depression are huge. If you're unsure, now is the time to bail out."

"I'm sure." He turned the key in the ignition and the truck's engine lurched to life. "Tonight I'll start work on the files you gave me. When I'm up to speed, we can talk strategy."

"It's a deal." She smiled wearily. "We're off to a good start, I think."

Rob hoped so, or Daniel Monroe was doomed. But as Rob turned into the afternoon traffic and headed downtown, it was Val who dominated his mind. Now that he knew just how much he wanted her, what, if anything, was he going to do about it?

CHAPTER 7

✦✦✦

SUNDAY AFTERNOON IN THE PARK. ENJOYING THE lazy sunshine, Val pulled into the grassy lot and parked at the end of an irregular line of vehicles. In the last eight days she had decided to open her own office, committed herself to what was going to be a gut-wrenching case with little chance of success, spent far too much time fantasizing about her new landlord, and learned that a local Big Sister/Little Sister organization was having a potluck picnic. She wasn't sure whether so much change was exciting or terrifying.

No, she *was* sure: It was both.

She climbed from her car, telling herself that attending a picnic was not a commitment. Anita Perez, the social worker who coordinated the group, had explained the program over the phone and invited her to the outing. The other people were mostly existing Big/Little pairings along with other family members, but there would also be kids in need of partners and a few other women interested in becoming Big Sisters.

Val removed the bakery fudge cake she'd brought as a contribution and headed toward the sizable crowd picnicking under the oak trees. A card table held blank nametags, so she stopped to print her first name on a tag.

She was following the scent of broiling hamburgers when she was approached by a relaxed middle-aged woman with shrewd eyes and an easy smile. Glancing at the tag, the woman said, "Hi, Val. I've been hoping you would make it. I'm Anita Perez."

"It's nice to meet you in person. I feel ridiculously nervous about today."

Anita laughed. "No need. Have some food, meet people, talk to some Bigs and Littles to see what they think of the program. The girls who need a Big Sister are wearing red T-shirts that say I'M SOOOOO COOL on them. If you want to strike up a conversation with one, that's fine, but no pressure. We take a lot of pains to make a match that will work for both parties." Anita took Val to the nearest grill and made some introductions, then moved on to greet others.

Val's nerves began to unwind. Her friends used to say that she could strike up a conversation with a flagpole, so the fact that she didn't know anyone was not a problem. These were nice people. It took a generous spirit to reach out to a child who needed some extra attention, and if Val was any judge, the relationship benefited both sides. Certainly they all enjoyed telling her what a great program this was.

After hot dogs, hamburgers, salads, and sodas had been demolished, picnickers fell upon the dessert table, where her fudge cake was rapidly reduced to crumbs. In the lazy lull after eating, the more energetic in the group decided to play softball. Teams were formed with much teasing and giggling.

Val was considering whether to volunteer for shortstop when she noticed a spot of red at the far end of the grove of trees. A girl was perched on the most distant picnic table, feet on the bench and nose in a book. She looked frail and very alone.

For an addicted reader, hiding with a good book was the most fun possible. Still, Val decided to go investigate.

The little girl was maybe ten or eleven, with a wild tangle of dark hair and one of the I'M SOOOOO COOL T-shirts. Her nametag read LYSSIE, and the wiry hair and caramel-colored skin suggested that she was of mixed race.

Val hitched herself up onto the picnic table, sitting as far from the girl as possible so as not to invade her space. "Hi. Good book?"

The girl looked up. She was not pretty. Thick glasses distorted her dark eyes, and her face was thin and wary. "My father murdered my mother and then killed himself," she said in a flat voice. "You can go away now." Her gaze returned to her book.

Val's jaw dropped, which of course was exactly the reaction Lyssie wanted. Mastering her shock, she said, "That's a real conversation-stopper, but I don't see why what happened to your parents means I should go away. I admit that a good book is usually more fun than anything, but this is a picnic. Meeting new people can also be fun."

The girl looked up again. "My parents weren't married, so I'm a bastard."

Val guessed that Lyssie had been taunted, rejected, and singled out so often that she had decided to do the rejecting herself. The combination of belligerence and vulnerability touched Val's heart. "That gives us something in common—my parents weren't married, either."

"You're a bastard, too?"

"Yes, though my mother preferred to call me a love child, which means the same but sounds nicer." Wanting to retain the girl's interest, Val added, "We have something else in common—crazy curly hair. Being illegitimate never caused me any trouble, but this hair was the bane of my existence when I was your age." She tugged on a lock. "As curly as yours, and red-orange like a carrot. I stood out in a crowd like an orange sheep."

"Now that you're grown-up, why don't you do something with it? Straighten it. Color it."

"I could, but I don't want to. I've learned to like it this way. When I want to look respectable at work, I pull it back and look very mean." She demonstrated, pulling her hair behind her head and donning a mock scowl. Then she released her hair to bounce around her shoulders. "When I let it go, I can look like a free spirit or a rebel. So be grateful—you have hair that's an instant signal system."

Lyssie's brief smile vanished. "I'm not a rebel."

"No? You're here reading a book when the herd is over there, having seconds on dessert and playing group games. That makes you at least a bit of a rebel."

The thin shoulders shrugged. Taking another tack, Val peered at the book to read the title. "Ah, the fourth Harry Potter. Good choice. Isn't the series great?"

For the first time, the dark eyes gave Val full attention. "You've read the Harry Potter books?"

"I sure have. They work on so many levels. Good stories, good characters, powerful themes, good writing, and humor. That's why readers of all ages like them."

Lyssie was definitely engaged. "Do you read other fantasy books?"

"They're my favorite leisure reading." Val hesitated, then decided to make it more personal. "Fantasy is about the struggle of good and evil, and good usually wins. I'm a lawyer so sometimes my job is also about good and evil, but real life gets pretty complicated and I don't always know if I'm on the right side. Reading fantasy novels is kind of like taking a shower to wash away the dust of the day."

She thought that might be a little over Lyssie's head, but the little girl was nodding thoughtfully. This was one smart kid.

"I want to be a writer," Lyssie said. "In books, the endings come out right."

Unlike real life. No one should have to endure what this little girl had suffered. "I know a writer, and she says that loving to read is the first step toward writing. The more you read, the better a foundation you have. In other words, as you read, don't just relax and enjoy the story, but think about what works and what doesn't."

Lyssie's face lit up, making her almost pretty. "I do that already." She launched into an analysis of several books she had recently read. Though Val had read only the Potter books, it sounded as if the girl had a good eye for story-telling.

When Lyssie's flow of words slowed, Val said, "Are you interested in getting a Big Sister, or are you here only because someone made you come?"

Lyssie shrugged again. "Gramma asked me to give it a try."

So the girl was here reluctantly. Did she fear that no one would want her, as if her traumatic background was conta-gious? Val felt a powerful wave of tenderness.

Though she knew better than to hug the girl, the strength of her reaction surprised her. She had come to the picnic because she was interested in the program, but now she didn't want a Little Sister in the abstract—she wanted *this* one. She wanted to learn more about this bright, tragic little girl. She wanted to spend time with her, make her laugh.

A little nervously, she said, "I've never been a Big Sis-ter and I need training, but if you're willing and Anita and your grandmother agree, I would very much like to have you as a Little Sister. Would you like that, too? We can get matching T-shirts that say 'Every day is a bad hair day.' " She hesitated, hoping this wasn't too soon. "Of course, if you'd rather not, that's okay. The match has to be some-thing we both want."

Lyssie's rejection wouldn't be okay, but the last thing Val wanted to do was make the girl unhappy. Hardly breathing, she waited as Lyssie pulled out a bookmark and carefully placed it between the pages. "What would we do?"

"I'm not sure—things we would both enjoy. I'd like to read and discuss books, or maybe go to movies, or work on craft projects, or cook. Do you think you'd like any of those things? We get to choose together."

For a long moment, Lyssie fidgeted with the bookmark.

Then she closed the volume and looked up with a shy smile. "I . . . I'd like that."

"Wonderful!" Val beamed like an idiot. "Shall we go find Anita?"

And later she would call Rachel and thank her for a truly great suggestion.

OVER THE YEARS, KENDRA HAD BECOME ACCUS-tomed to the SuperMax. She knew the routines and some of the guards. Most of them were good guys doing a job to support their families. But she never stopped loathing the place. Sometimes when she couldn't sleep at night, she would be haunted by thoughts of being incarcerated here. Rough concrete walls, even a concrete bed, in a room the size of a walk-in closet. Narrow slits of windows that only a snake child could escape from. Twenty-three hours a day of solitude. She would go crazy.

Daniel's calm acceptance was little short of a miracle. Though he was on death row, he never caused any problems, so he was allowed a few privileges. With books, he had given himself an eclectic education. He had stayed fit with exercises that could be done in his cell, and playing basketball with two or three other men during the brief recreation hours. After his initial rage and bitterness had died down, he had returned to the religion of his childhood with a faith that awed her. Though he didn't want to die, he wasn't eating himself alive with anger.

Only on rare occasions did she glimpse the frustration he felt with his imprisonment. What would it be like to be locked up like a rat in a cage? Be unable to eat what he wanted, go where he wanted? Lord, never to have sex except with his right hand? No matter how hard she tried to imagine imprisonment, she couldn't really understand the dark place at the center of his soul. For that, she was shamefully grateful. She wouldn't have the strength to endure vicious injustice with such grace.

She settled in the visiting room chair, waiting. Not

something she was naturally good at, but she had learned. When Daniel arrived, he was escorted by two guards. Both gave her friendly nods. Everyone politely ignored the shackles that bound the prisoner.

"Hi, baby." Daniel smiled at her, warmth in his eyes. Though he'd never used emotional blackmail to get her to come, she knew how much these visits meant to him as a break in the slow stretch of featureless days. "How you doin'?"

"Pretty good, big guy. What did you think of my boss?"

He chuckled. "She's quite a little firecracker. Wouldn't want to cross her."

"She's smart, Daniel, probably the smartest lawyer I've ever worked with. Maybe she can create some reasonable doubt."

His smile vanished. "It's too late for that, Kendra. The people who love executions keep makin' it harder and harder to raise post-conviction issues. Even if that little redhead came up with a signed affidavit from God that I'm innocent, it wouldn't be enough to save my black ass. Don't kid yourself about this. It'll just make the hurtin' worse when I'm dead."

His words chilled her. "Don't give up, honey. Val needs you to cooperate if we're going to have a shot at getting the sentence commuted."

"I'm cooperating, but not because I think it'll do any good. Even if my sentence is commuted, what would it mean? They would just move me back across the street to the Pen. Not much of a life. Maybe I'd be better off dead."

"Don't you say such a wicked thing!" she snapped. "No one is better off dead."

"We all die, sugar," he said gently. "In a way, I'm lucky to know when. Gives me a chance to make my peace."

She disliked his words, but he had given her an opening to raise the question that haunted her. "Let me tell Jason about you before it's too late."

"No!" Daniel's expression darkened. "We've talked about this over and over. What good will it do for him to know his real father will be executed as a murderer? No damn good at all. Phil Brooks adopted him and did right by both of you. Jason has already lost the father he knew. Don't make the boy ashamed of a father he didn't know."

"Jason isn't a boy, he's a man. Nineteen years old, an air force cadet. A son who's going to soar. He deserves to know the truth."

For an instant, Daniel's pain was vivid in his face. Then he shuttered his expression. "All he needs to know is that his real daddy loved him and died young."

"He has a right to meet you at least once, and to know that you're innocent." She was begging now and didn't care. "You shouldn't make this choice for him."

Daniel sighed. "I can't stop you from tellin' him. But Kendra—can't you at least let me have this?"

His words silenced her. She never had been able to say no to him, from the first time they met. He'd been playing basketball with some buddies at a local schoolyard. The ball flew over the chain-link fence as she walked by on the way home from her job flipping burgers. She was Kendra Jackson then, nineteen and feeling three times her age.

When the ball bounced in front of her, she automatically scooped it up. Daniel jogged up to the fence. "Hey, girl, will you throw the ball back?"

She turned to him and saw the most beautiful man imaginable. A couple of years older than she, he was tall and limber and fit, with a smile that lit up East Baltimore. A light-hearted Ashanti warrior. Feeling mischievous, she took aim and threw the ball over the fence. It arced through the air and snapped through the net in a perfect shot.

"Whoa, baby!" Daniel exclaimed admiringly. "You are *good*."

One of the other players scoffed. "She just got lucky."

"Maybe. Maybe not." Daniel retrieved the ball and dribbled it, his gaze on Kendra. "Want to shoot a few hoops?"

She debated a moment before saying, "Sure." Her life didn't have a lot of fun just then, what with her mama dying of cancer, so she wouldn't pass this up. She found the fence door and entered. The guys accepted her with good humor, which switched to alarm as she showed 'em her moves.

After she sank her fifth basket, Daniel recovered the ball, saying with a chuckle, "We got ourselves a ringer here. Where did you play, sugar?"

"Dunbar. I was All-State for two years." She smiled wickedly. "It isn't just black *guys* that know how to play basketball." Her smile faded as she thought of the athletic scholarships that had been offered. But then her mama fell sick, so no way could Kendra go to college. She glanced at her watch. "Time for me to go home."

"I'll walk you there." Daniel tossed the ball back over his head and the two of them left in a chorus of cheers and rowdy speculation.

On the way home they exchanged names and discovered that his family went to the same church her cousins did. She liked that she could look up to him. Too many guys were too short for her.

When they reached the small house Mama had rented because it was close to Hopkins Hospital, Daniel asked, "Like to get together for a little one-on-one this weekend?" Gently he brushed her cheek with his knuckles, his expression making it clear what kind of game he was hoping for.

Her instant, sizzling attraction was immediately drowned in a wave of weariness. "I can't. I got too much to do."

"There should always be time enough for love."

It was a slick line. Too slick. Deciding to show him why she couldn't play games with carefree young studs, she said, "Come on in and meet my mama."

That would have sent most boys flying, but not Daniel. And he didn't run or flinch when he met her mother, who was bald, bone-thin, and exhausted by the disease that was killing her. Instead, after Kendra made the introductions, Daniel solemnly took Mama's hand. "Miz Jackson, you have one mighty fine daughter here. Maybe I'll marry her someday."

Never at a loss for words, Mama said, "See that you do. I don't hold with boys who make babies but are too cowardly to become husbands."

"Yes, *ma'am.*" From then on, Daniel and Mama were friends. He was the one who sat with Kendra in the hospital at the end and held her when she was crying her eyes out at the funeral. He had moved in by then, and his loving was the only sweet spot in a sad, sad time.

Before Mama died, he asked Kendra to marry him. She had said yes for her mother's sake, but later she kept putting him off when he wanted to name a date. Though she was crazy in love with him, he wasn't ready for marriage. He didn't have a regular job or any ambitions, and he spent too much time hangin' with his idle friends. She didn't think he did drugs, but some of the friends did, and she wondered what kind of life they could build together. She wanted to marry a reliable man like her daddy, who had taken good care of his women until he died in an accident on the job at Bethlehem Steel.

Getting pregnant with Jason had been an accident, one that decided her on setting a date because she didn't want her baby born illegitimate. Then Daniel got high at a bachelor's party, and he and his homeys stole a car and crashed into some parked vehicles. Because he had a couple of priors, her man went to jail instead of the altar.

She was furious and broke everything off, swearing she would never trust him again. Not once did she visit him in jail, though she thought of him plenty, especially when her baby was born.

When Daniel was released, one of the first things he did was come to visit his son. He had the right, so she allowed it. He seemed steadier, and truly sorry for not being there when she needed him. He purely adored his baby boy. When Daniel got a job and made promises, she began to think that maybe this time they had a future. The church was reserved and she had even bought her wedding dress.

Instead, her world shattered in smashing doors and police accusations. Knowing he was innocent, she fought as hard as she knew how to see him free, but it was no use. The law wanted revenge, and Daniel was the sacrifice.

The first time she visited him after the sentencing, he told her flatly to think of him as dead and get on with her life. She must tell Jason when he was older that his daddy had died young in an accident . . . and how much Daniel had loved him.

She left the Pen with tears pouring down her face, her heart breaking even as she accepted that he was right. Getting on with her life hadn't been easy, of course. No money and a baby and a bad case of the blues. She found a state program that gave her support and child care along with job training to keep her from starving. She wrote Daniel now and then, and sent him pictures and drawings the boy made as he grew older.

Then she met Philip Brooks, fifteen years older, as steady as he was kind. He adored her and Jason, and she realized it was possible to love again. She told him about Daniel early on. A lesser man would have been jealous, but not Philip. He sympathized, and never objected to his wife keeping in touch with a man on death row.

With Daniel's permission, Philip adopted Jason so they all had the same name. She was proud of that—a real family, just like when she was small and her parents were alive. Philip never let her down, except when he went and died three years earlier.

After his death, Kendra began visiting Daniel in person. The first time, she was shocked to see a bald, scarred thug with massive shoulders and a scowl that could melt stone. She knew a man had to be tough to survive in prison, but this was a stranger. Then he had smiled, and she knew he was her Daniel still.

One of the guards said quietly, "Time's almost up, ma'am."

Kendra pulled herself out of her reverie. "Okay, Danny boy. I don't talk to Jason, and you cooperate with Val. Deal?"

"Deal." With a rattle of his shackles, he raised one large

hand and pressed it on the plastic wall that separated them. She kissed the center of her palm, then laid her smaller hand against his. She could feel his warmth through the plastic, but not touching, never touching.

"Will you sing me a song?" he asked. " 'Amazing Grace'?"

"If you like." This was their custom, and even the guards seemed to enjoy it. She closed her eyes and reached inside to the place where songs lived, then began to sing. The words were soft at first, but as the spirit moved her voice strengthened until it filled the small room with faith, hope, and solace. In song she could touch Daniel as she couldn't physically.

". . . *was lost, but now I'm found* . . ." After the last note faded, she opened her eyes. The guards were nodding solemnly and a glint of tears showed in Daniel's eyes.

Pretending not to see, she managed a last smile as she rose. Then she pivoted and walked from the room, head high, because she had promised herself she would never let him see her cry.

It was a promise she had kept. So far.

CHAPTER 8

✖

AFTER THE PICNIC BROKE UP, VAL RETURNED TO HER car, delighted at the way the afternoon had turned out. Anita had been enthusiastic about the matchup since Val and Lyssie both wanted it. Val winced a bit when she thought about where she would find the time to build a relationship with the girl, but she would manage. That's why she was changing her career direction, after all. To have a life.

Before driving away, she checked her cell phone, which had been off, and saw that she'd had a call. Rob's number. She punched it in, thinking she was on a roll today. When he answered, she said, "Hi, Rob, it's Val. What's up?"

"I've finished going through Monroe's files and wanted to set up a time to get together with you for that strategy session."

Her good mood dimmed as she thought about her schedule for the coming week. No way could she fit in a long meeting with Rob. But it couldn't wait. "It will have to be this evening. Can you make it on such short notice? If so, come for supper so we can make use of every minute."

"That would be nice, but you don't have to cook. I can pick up some carryout."

"No need. Are you vegetarian, vegan, low-fat, low salt, low carb, lactose intolerant, have food allergies, or any other special dietary requirements?"

"I eat anything." He chuckled. "It sounds like you feed a lot of people."

"As many as possible. I have plenty of recipes that can be done quickly, and a sizable freezer. How about six o'clock?"

After he agreed and signed off, she thought about dinner. Nothing too elaborate—this wasn't a date, after all. But she had her share of domestic pride. She would pick up some fish and serve it with a packaged rice pilaf and a salad. As she drove home, she admitted to herself that it was pretty primitive to want to impress the man with her cooking ability. Their relationship was business.

But she hoped he liked a nice piece of grilled tuna.

DINNER TURNED OUT WELL, IF SHE DID SAY SO HER-self. Rob arrived bearing a bottle of excellent chardonnay, then ate like a man who didn't get much home cooking. He finished the meal with a happy sigh. "I've decided that you must not sleep, which is why you get so much done."

She laughed as she cleared the table. "That's kinder than saying I'm hyperactive, which I've been accused of. Do you want coffee while we go over the case?"

"Please."

By the time she returned with the coffeepot, he was spreading folders and notes across the dining room table. "Here's the list of people I plan to interview," he said. "Obviously, the three eyewitnesses whose identification convicted Monroe are the most important. It would be great if they're having second thoughts about their identification."

She scanned the list, nodding. "Darrell Long isn't going to be possible. Though it's not in the file, I understand that he died in a shooting almost ten years ago. Armed robbery, I think."

Rob came alert. "Armed robbery? In the transcript, he

and Cady were both described as clean-living community college students and church members. I suppose Long might have taken a turn for the worse in the years after his testimony convicted Monroe, but it could be useful if he was less reliable than the jury was told."

"If we could prove that Long and Cady were lying about being so wholesome, it might persuade the governor that there's sufficient doubt to commute Daniel's sentence to life imprisonment," she agreed. "I don't think we'll get far with Brenda Harris—she's the woman whose assault led to the murder. You probably noticed that at first she was uncertain that Daniel was her attacker, but once she made up her mind, her opinion was cast in concrete. She wouldn't budge on the witness stand."

"I want to find out what the lighting conditions were like where the assault took place. By her own account, the attack and shooting were so quick that she might not have had a clear look at her attacker." Rob frowned, his thick brows drawing together. "You've probably thought of this, but it seems to me that a major angle hasn't been explored. If Monroe is innocent, who *did* kill Officer Malloy?"

Val felt the tingle across the back of her neck that came with an important idea. "I hadn't thought much about that, but you're right. A man who would attack a woman and have a gun ready to shoot was no innocent. He might be sitting in a cell now himself. But how would you locate such a suspect after all these years?"

"If the real shooter is as large as Monroe, that would narrow it down, but it will still require a lot of looking. I'll start by talking to some of the city detectives from that period to see if they remember any street dudes who fit that description. I also want to go through the full file, not just the highlights version." He gestured to the stack of papers Val had given him. "Maybe something buried in the complete file will be of use. Maybe there are people who lived in the neighborhood who might have something to say."

"All good ideas, but will you have time when you have a business to run?"

Rob gave a faint, humorless smile. "I'll find the time."

Once again, she felt the power of his personal interest in saving Daniel Monroe. She almost asked why, but decided not to pry. Better to wait and hope that he would tell her voluntarily. "Shall we go down the list of witnesses and outline the questions we want answered?"

"Okay." He pulled out a lined tablet for note-taking. "When I know what to ask, I need to talk to Monroe again. He might have some ideas how to proceed. I need to talk to Kendra Brooks, too. Maybe she had neighbors who could verify that Monroe never left the apartment."

"It's pitiful how little investigation was done at the time. Since the police thought they had their man, they sure didn't put any time into looking further." She smiled wryly. "On the plus side, we've got lots of things to look at because so little was done."

"You're really reaching for a silver lining there. But maybe you're right and we'll find the rabbit in the haystack."

"A metaphor mixer. But in this case, that's better than talking about smoking guns." Getting serious, Val pulled out her yellow-lined tablet. Despite all the high-tech devices available, at this point in a case she wanted a tablet and a blue felt-tipped pen so she could develop her thoughts on paper.

For over four hours, they discussed the case intensively, analyzing the information they had and brainstorming possible areas of investigation. She also explained the legal options. Maryland was a fairly liberal state that performed few executions, but the governor wouldn't intervene in a case unless there were really solid reasons to believe that they risked killing an innocent man. Especially not in an election year. They would have to find extremely compelling evidence.

Rob was a natural problem solver with a pragmatic approach to running down possible leads. Val found it stimulating to bounce ideas back and forth with him. Damned sexy, in fact. She had always had a weakness for smart men.

She realized she was losing concentration when she found herself admiring the way light glinted from his dark blond hair. And such beautiful strong hands . . . Smothering a yawn, she said, "Time to call it a night. I think we've done as much as we can for now. The next step is old-fashioned digging for information."

"Sifting tons of sand in the hopes of finding a nugget." He squared his files, then packed them in a battered canvas tote bag. "I may be a little rusty, but the Marines taught me well. I already have leads on some of the people I want to interview. It's a start."

As she stood to escort him to the door, she said, "You've done more than military police and carpentry, haven't you?"

She expected him to avoid the question, but after a hesitation, he said, "I used the Marine educational benefits to learn something about computers and worked in the field for a while." He got to his feet and slung the tote bag over one shoulder.

"Would you care to add computer troubleshooting to your other work?" Val asked hopefully. "A lot of our work is done on computers, and when the system goes down, we get hysterical."

"When you have computer problems I'll take a crack at solving them, but no guarantees. These days the hardware and software combinations are so complex that no one fully understands them."

"That's what I'm afraid of," she muttered.

They drifted to the door, the cats coming awake and ambling after them. Damocles liked Rob, which wasn't unusual since Damocles liked everyone, but Lilith did also, and she was usually shy with strangers.

Rob took hold of the doorknob, then paused, his strikingly light eyes focused on Val's face. She came to full alert as the atmosphere changed.

"This isn't the right time or place," he said haltingly. "There might never be a right time or place. Yet I keep thinking about a . . . non-business relationship with you."

So she hadn't imagined that tug of awareness and attraction between them. But it was clear that Rob wasn't about to jump her bones. In a complicated situation, he was simply letting her know he was interested. Any negative reaction on her part and he would drop the subject, perhaps forever.

What did she want? The reasons for keeping her distance were legion. He was her landlord, they were working together on a critical case, and she knew very little about him. Plus, her track record in choosing men was not great.

Weighing against that was her attraction, and her loneliness. It had been too long since she had met a man who intrigued her so much. She would be a fool to throw this possibility away.

She raised her hand and stroked his beard, enjoying the texture and tickle of it. Sexily male. His mouth was strongly shaped, a soft contrast to the beard when she brushed her fingertips across his lips.

He touched her hair, twining a springy red lock around his finger. "I love your hair. It's so completely alive, just like you are."

"Countercultural hair. It makes a political statement just by existing." The brush of his fingers on her hair sent tingles through her. What did she want? A partner. A man who could be a trusted friend and lover—the kind she had dreamed of but never found. Rob was in many ways a mystery, yet he had depth, kindness, and intelligence. To hell with the potential complications.

Rising on her toes, she kissed him. His stillness ended and he kissed her back, his hands going to her waist to draw her close. Warm lips, textured beard, a faint, pleasing bittersweet tang of coffee on his tongue.

At first the kiss was tentative, two strangers exploring, but attraction crackled when Val slid her arms around his neck. Her breasts tingled as they pressed into his chest and her blood began to dance with the animal chemistry that addled adolescents. She leaned into him, murmuring, "This is probably a really bad idea."

"No question about it." He began kneading her back, his strong hands caressing and energizing her tired muscles as his kiss deepened.

She tugged him over to the sofa and they went down in a sprawl of arms and legs. Her legs bracketed his as she lay across his hard-muscled working man's body. She felt like a teenager necking on the front porch after a date. She had forgotten how delightful such sessions could be.

No, "delightful" was too frivolous a word. They were communicating on a deep non-verbal level. Under the distracting tides of passion, she sensed a vast, almost frightening need at the center of his being, a hunger he was rigorously controlling. She yearned to dive into those depths, explore his mysteries.

Common sense reasserted itself barely in time. She was reading way too much into a kiss. Reminding herself that she was trying to change her life and relationships, she broke away from Rob, sliding from his lap to the other end of the sofa. "This really *is* a bad idea," she said shakily.

He checked his instinctive reach toward her and took a deep breath. "I know you're right, but remind me why."

She looked away, struggling to order her tangled thoughts. "I don't know anything about you, Rob, except that you're interesting and attractive. I don't know where you were born, what you've done with your life, why you feel such a powerful desire to help Daniel. You're the mysterious dark stranger, except that you're not dark."

Without moving a whisker he became distant, his expression turning to stone. After the length of a dozen heartbeats, he got to his feet. She thought he was going to walk out. Instead, he began pacing the room, tense with stress and indecision. She sat very still, wondering what internal demons he was battling.

"I don't want your soul," she said quietly. "But I need to know more about what makes you tick. Though I've made my share of mistakes about men, I try not to make the same one twice. This works both ways—you might want to know more about me."

"Harvard Law Review," he said promptly. "Youngest partner ever at Crouse, Resnick. Your father is Bradford Westerfield III, a senior partner at a top New York law firm, and you have two blond half sisters with perfectly straightened teeth. Your mother, Callie Covington, is a textile artist and board member of the American Visionary Art Museum. You are utterly loyal to your friends, a soft touch for stray animals, and your not-so-secret vice is hot fudge sundaes."

She stared, thinking he had just proved his credentials as an investigator. "How did you learn all that?"

"Mostly from the Internet. Some from Kate Corsi when I called her about your interest in renting the church. Of course, the things she said about you were pretty innocent. She would never talk about the really interesting stuff."

"Thank heaven for that—old friends know way too much about each other to dare dishing dirt." Val wondered if he was trying to change the subject away from himself—he looked as if he would rather be anywhere in the world except here. But he hadn't run away yet. "Not that there is anything terribly interesting about me. I've always been too busy with school or my job to get into much trouble."

His pacing stopped at the fireplace and he stared into the gilt-framed mirror as if not recognizing the reflection. "I've been hiding for four years," he said brusquely. "But if we want to have any relationship beyond the superficial, you need to know the truth."

Val felt as if ice water had been poured over her. "Are you a . . . a fugitive from justice?" The name Robert Smith sure sounded like a pseudonym.

"Nothing criminal on my part, though for a couple of years I saw way too much of the justice system. I walked away from my old life because . . . because . . ." He stopped again. She hardly breathed, not wanting to spook him.

When he spoke again, he took a different tack. "Do you recall hearing about an environmental terrorist who called himself the Avenging Angel?"

"Jeffrey Gabriel, self-righteous destroyer of projects built on coastal wetlands," she said promptly. "Started with simple arson and moved into fire bombs. Four people died in his fires and a dozen more were injured, along with millions in property damages. He was torching developments for something like eight years before they caught up with him in Texas. I saw him on television. He had the coldest eyes I've ever seen."

Rob pivoted sharply away from the fireplace. "It's time to quit before things get ugly. I'm sorry, Val. I should have kept my interest to myself."

She was off the sofa in a shot. "You can't walk out in the middle of this! Were . . . were you involved in setting those fires? A co-conspirator who wasn't caught?"

"It would have been easier if I had been." He looked down at her, his pale eyes like ice. "I'm the Avenging Angel's brother."

She gasped, riveted by Rob's eyes, which were so like those of the man she'd seen on television and in newspapers. Dear God, no wonder he was haunted. "You're Robert Smith Gabriel," she breathed. "The man who turned him in."

CHAPTER 9

ROB TENSED AT THE SIGHT OF VAL'S SHOCKED EX-
pression. He should have known she would be familiar
with the whole sordid story. "Right—the cold-hearted
computer tycoon who blew the whistle on his own brother.
Cain slays Abel. There was quite a media feeding frenzy at
the time." He turned the doorknob. "Good night, Val. Let's
pretend I left right after packing my files and forget anything else happened."

She caught his wrist in a light but tenacious grip. "You
must carry a world of guilt about this, but you did the right
thing. When the story broke, I was awed by the incredible
courage it took to do what you did. I've wondered sometimes how much it cost you." She studied his face, then
shook her head. "I saw pictures of you then, but I would
never have recognized you under that beard."

"Which was the point—to eradicate Robert Smith
Gabriel. Easy enough to drop the Gabriel and become
generic Robert Smith. It worked, until tonight."

"Now that you've started, why not tell me the whole
story?" Her voice was very gentle. "A nightmare shared is
a nightmare tamed."

He hesitated, torn between a desire to bolt back into the rabbit hole where he had been living since Jeff's arrest, and an equally powerful desire to talk with Val, who had no judgment in her eyes, only acceptance.

"Come sit down," she said. "You can tell me as much or as little as you want."

Her words tilted the balance toward talking. Val was the first person he'd met who made it possible to imagine a life beyond paralyzing guilt and betrayal, so it was time to bare his soul. She already knew the essentials; he wondered how she would handle the grim details that had festered inside him for so long.

When he gave a jerky nod, she tucked a hand in his elbow and guided him back to the sofa, taking the chair opposite herself. "You weren't kidding about the media feeding frenzy," she said. "They loved that you were a Silicon Valley honcho while your younger brother was burning down marinas and expensive condominium projects."

He lifted a figurine of a Chinese dragon from the end table, rolling the silky, polished wood between his hands. "Jeff was always kind of an oddball—very bright, with a mind that worked differently from most people. He had lousy social skills, but he never hurt anyone. Mostly he just wanted to be left alone. He used to talk about how he should have been born in the time of mountain men like Jim Bridger, so he could live in the wilderness and never have to see anyone. Looking back, I can see the signs of what he became, but at the time, he was just my smart, eccentric little brother." His little brother, now dead. "He . . . he looked up to me."

"You and your family lived in Baltimore when you were young, didn't you? The local angle was always mentioned in the newspaper."

He nodded. "That's why I came back after Jeff died. It was the one place where we had been happy. After our father left and my mother married a guy called Joe Harley, we moved to Florida and life went to hell. Harley was a vicious drunk and couldn't hold a job, so we moved around a lot. I had terrible fights with him—it's a wonder we didn't kill each other. As soon as I finished high school, I enlisted in the Marines. I told myself everything would be better if I wasn't home to piss Harley off, but the real reason I enlisted was to escape. The first and worst betrayal of my brother."

"It's not a crime for a young man to grow up and move away."

He set the figurine down. "I was older. I should have stuck around and stood up for Jeff. It never came out at the trial because Texas doesn't much care about mitigating circumstances, but Jeff's lawyer learned that after I left, Harley started beating on Jeff. He was a skinny kid and couldn't defend himself except by running away. That went on until Harley died in a fire."

She caught her breath, understanding instantly. "Did your brother do that?"

"In hindsight, it seems likely. The fire was caused by a smoldering cigarette in Harley's favorite armchair. He smoked and drank himself into a coma every night, so his death was ruled an accident. But . . . I don't think so."

"If Jeffrey could arrange that kind of fatal accident in cold blood, he was probably well beyond any help you could have offered." Her face was pale, but she didn't look away. As he'd seen in the SuperMax, she was tough. "He may have been mentally ill from the time he was very young."

"I think he was, but his behavior was normal enough that he was never diagnosed. Moving through different school systems meant he wasn't in one place long enough to attract much attention." Rob had spent endless hours digging through his memories, thinking of times when he'd covered up for his brother. If he hadn't, maybe Jeff could have been helped.

"I used to take him on camping trips along the coast or in the Everglades. He loved that. He'd talk about the two of us living in the woods when we grew up, but I never took that seriously. I went from the Marines to college to being a hotshot computer wizard and didn't see my family more than once every year or two.

"In the process, I failed Jeff. While I was having a fine time working twenty-hour days and having people say how smart I was, he was getting sicker and sicker until he began torching coastal developments. If I had stayed in closer touch, had seen how things were going, I could have prevented the worst of his excesses. I'm sure of it."

"Maybe you could have, but maybe not," she said quietly. "If he was incapable of empathy, it might have been impossible to fix."

"He wasn't completely callous. He cared about wildlife and nature, and about me. That's why I'm the only one who might have made a difference." And Rob cared for Jeff. Despite his younger brother's cool, warped intelligence, he hadn't been a monster, at least not when they were kids. That had come later.

"He might have looked up to you, but he still stole that security device you were developing. You might have been arrested for your brother's crimes."

The damned security detection device had led to Jeff's downfall. "I hardly ever heard from Jeff, just an occasional e-mail, so I was tickled when he showed up out of the blue at my office in Menlo Park. It was great to see him, but I was about to leave for Japan so there wasn't time for much more than a tour of the company and a lunch. He asked about the different products I was working on, but didn't show any special interest in the security device. I didn't notice that he stole one of the prototypes.

"Eventually, that's what tipped me off. I read an article about how the Avenging Angel had destroyed that upscale resort near Galveston just before it was due to open. It mentioned that the arsonist had used a sophisticated device to detect and neutralize security. I thought, 'That sounds like what I've been working on.' Alarm bells went off when I remembered Jeff's visit and things he'd said over the years. I knew he hated the development that's destroying our coasts, and calling himself an angel from the family name fit, but I couldn't really believe that Jeff had turned terrorist.

"Still, I was spooked enough to do a web search and construct a timeline of the attacks. Jeff lived in Florida, and most of the arson attacks were on the Gulf Coast between Florida and Texas. The only two in California were right after he visited me—and they were the first attacks where the security device was used."

"Did you call your brother and confront him?"

"I tried, but all I had was an e-mail address and P.O. box number in a tiny place on the Florida panhandle, and he wasn't answering messages on either. I was getting more and more worried, because the fires were getting more frequent."

"And more dangerous," she observed. "All of the fatalities came at the end, when he started using those military-type explosives."

He nodded wearily. "I dropped everything and flew to Florida to try and find him, but again, no luck. He hadn't been in town to pick up his mail in weeks. When three fire-fighters were injured in another Texas fire, I realized I couldn't wait any longer. I had my lawyer call the FBI and say that a client of his might have a line on the identity of the Avenging Angel, but wouldn't talk to them unless they swore not to go for the death penalty if he was prosecuted. After some arguing, they said they wouldn't." He smiled bitterly. "You know how well that worked."

"The feds might have kept their word, but Texas got him first and tried him for crimes committed there." She sighed. "It was over so quickly. Since he refused all attempts to appeal his sentence, the State of Texas was able to oblige his death wish pretty quickly."

"People gathered outside the prison in Huntsville to cheer when he died." No longer able to sit still, Rob rose and began pacing again. "I understood why he didn't want the sentence appealed. For someone who loved the outdoors, being caged in a concrete box for the next half century was a hell beyond imagination."

"Did Jeff understand why you blew the whistle on him?"

Rob smiled bitterly. "I don't know. He certainly didn't forgive. He refused to speak to me after he was arrested, just like he refused to cooperate with the expensive lawyers I hired to defend him. If he had given them anything to work with, maybe he would have received a life sentence instead of the death penalty."

"Even if your lawyers could have gotten him acquitted on the grounds of insanity, which is highly unlikely, it would only have meant imprisonment of another sort."

"But as long as he was alive, there was hope. Maybe someday they would have developed medications to control his kind of mental kinks." It had been a slim hope, but Rob had clung to it as long as possible.

"You never saw him again after he visited you in Menlo Park?"

His mouth was so dry he could barely speak. "I saw him. I sat in court every day of his trial and sentencing. He would never look at me. When he requested that I be present at the execution, I hoped that meant he wanted to see me—maybe say good-bye. Instead . . . he just wanted me to see him die."

"Dear God," she whispered. "How unspeakably cruel."

Even frantic pacing couldn't relieve his crawling skin as he remembered the execution. "The worst of it was that at the end, I think he was afraid. I don't know if anyone else saw it, but I could. Having rejected everyone who approached him, even the prison chaplain, he was completely alone. No one should die so alone."

He stalked the length of the room, feeling like a bird beating his wings against a cage. "Sometimes I have nightmares that I'm Jeff, screaming inside as they strap me to the gurney and stab in the needles."

She shuddered. "After he died, you felt you had to get away from your old life?"

"What really sent me packing was receiving the million-dollar reward that had been established for information leading to the arrest and conviction of the Avenging Angel."

He had been horrified when he received that news, and Val now looked equally horrified. She asked, "What did you do with the money?"

"Gave it to the victims and survivors of Jeff's crimes." Even now, thinking of that blood money turned his stomach. "Before he died, Jeff publicly accused me of turning him in for the reward."

"Horrible. *Horrible*." Val drew her legs up and wrapped her arms around her knees, shivering. "What about your mother—did she understand why you had to act?"

"When Jeff was arrested, she called me screaming, asking how I could do such a thing. Where was my loyalty?"

"Duty and loyalty often clash, but you couldn't stand by when your brother's actions were threatening other people's lives. No reasonable person could. I hope your mother realized that eventually. Where was she during the years Jeff was growing up?"

"Tending bar. She loved a smoky, down-home bar better than anything, and since her job supported us, she had a perfect excuse not to be around." He rolled his shoulders, trying to unknot the muscles. "When Jeff was arrested, she was already suffering from lung cancer after smoking three packs a day for decades. She died between his trial and execution. If she ever understood why I acted, she never mentioned it."

Val was so white that the ghosts of childhood freckles were a golden haze over her cheekbones. "Do you have any other family?"

"No one close enough to count. My real father might be alive somewhere, but he sure as hell didn't come forward to claim his sons during all the publicity. He's probably dead, too—he was another one who smoked like a fiend. I barely remember him."

"Where did you learn to be such a good carpenter?"

He guessed she wanted to change the subject to something less grim. Hard to do when it came to his past. "From Harley. He was a carpenter and not a bad guy when he was sober. In other words, before noon." He paused by the bookcase, where a much larger dragon tossed its head, the gilded hide embedded with mirror fragments. He wondered what dragons meant to Val. Symbols of invincibility, maybe.

"During the computer years, I lived in my head all the time. After Jeff died, I needed to get away and do work that was real and physical in a place where no one knew who I was. I'd always liked working with wood and doing household repairs, so I came back to Baltimore and bought a beat-up row house and fixed it up to sell."

"You also learned how to restore things of beauty like the church, and help fix up the homes of some of Baltimore's poor, elderly citizens. Small acts of redemption."

"Too small. A lifetime of Sheetrock and plumbing repairs will not make up for the lives of Jeff and his victims."

"Saving an innocent man from execution would help balance the scales."

"Yes—if it can be done." He was startled at how quickly and easily she made the connection. In retrospect, it was obvious: a life for a life. He wanted to save Daniel Monroe as he had been unable to save his brother. Guilt or innocence were secondary—what he yearned for was the preservation of life.

She uncurled from the sofa and crossed the room to where he had finally halted his pacing. "Together, we have a chance to save Daniel," she said, her amber eyes steady. "If we fail, it won't be for lack of trying."

She slid her hands into his hair and drew his head down for another kiss. Their previous kisses had been heated. This one seared to the bone. He responded fervently, desperate to bury himself in her. Though the emotional bond between them was new and tentative, the physical connection flooded his senses.

"Shall we go upstairs?" she said huskily.

He tried to think, not easy when desire was dissolving all reason. "I can't believe this is any better an idea now than it was half an hour ago."

"On the contrary—the whole playing field has changed.

I said then that I didn't know enough about you. Now I do." She exhaled warmly in his ear.

He gasped, resolve crumbling. "A starving man doesn't refuse a banquet, but . . . I really, really don't want you to be sorry later for giving in to a charitable impulse tonight. I don't need someone new despising me. Especially not you."

"This isn't pity, Rob." She rubbed her cheek against his chest like a cat. "I've been interested in you since we first met, and unless my radar is broken, you reciprocate. We're both adults, unencumbered by spouses. At least, I am, and I assume you are, too."

He nodded when she gave him a slanting glance. "I was always too busy for that kind of serious relationship."

"See how much we have in common," she said wryly. "Now, about going upstairs . . ."

With sudden exhilaration, he caught her around the waist and swept her off the floor. She laughed and wrapped her arms around his neck and her legs around his hips. It was sexy as hell. Of course, everything she did was sexy as hell. Securing his grip on her, he said, "Just tell me where to go."

She wriggled against him so provocatively that he was tempted to drop her onto the couch and start tearing her clothes off right there. "Much as I admire intelligence," she said, "there's also much to be said for being swept off my feet by an alpha male. Up the stairs and to the right."

He laughed with her. "An alpha male. I've just achieved a goal I didn't know I had."

She leaned forward and licked his throat as they ascended the stairs, cats trailing behind. The past was disaster and the future unknown, but for this precious moment, he remembered what it was to be happy.

CHAPTER 10

※◆※

THE LIGHT SWITCH IN VAL'S BEDROOM TURNED ON a single Tiffany lamp in the corner, illuminating the room with a gentle glow. Enough light to see and admire, not so much as to be unromantic. The room was like her, warm and unusual and welcoming, with a bed of elegant curving cherry and a comforter in sumptuous tones of gold, russet, and amber. Chosen to go with her hair and eyes, no doubt—she looked equally sumptuous when he yanked back the covers and laid her on the tawny sheets, her hair a flame and her eyes a golden lure.

Val pulled him down on top of her, laughing exuberantly as she molded her body against his. "How fast can we get each other's clothes off?"

"Not fast enough." He peeled off her cotton sweater, revealing a satiny apricot-colored bra. "It would have been more efficient to stay on our feet and undress."

"Where's the fun in that?" She made short work of his shirt buttons while he removed his jacket.

He shivered when she flattened her palm on his bare chest, one finger teasing his nipple. Laughter vanished into cascading lust. He'd been celibate so long that this felt like

the first time. In a way it was—his life divided into before
and after Jeff's prosecution and death, and he was not the
same man he had been.

He wanted to take his time and savor the sight and taste
of her. Even more, he wanted to incinerate himself in raw
sensation and leave savoring for later.

Val had ideas of her own. As she pulled his zipper
down, he remembered to say, "I didn't come prepared for
anything like this."

"I was a Girl Scout, so I'm *always* prepared. Check the
drawer in the nightstand."

A small packet of condoms waited demurely. As he
pulled one out, she said a little defensively, "I hope they
haven't passed their expiration date."

Guessing that she was afraid of looking too experienced, he said, "It's damned unfair that a man who is prepared is considered responsible while a woman who does
the same risks being considered a . . ." He halted, groping
for a term that wasn't insulting.

"I think the word you're looking for is *slut*," she said
helpfully.

"An ugly word that has nothing to do with you." He
smiled wryly. "I hope *I* haven't passed my expiration date.
It's been so long I may not remember how to do this."

"It's been a long time for me as well. Too long." She slid
her hand down his body. "But I'm sure we'll work it out."

And they did, despite his being aroused to the point of
mindlessness. Every garment removed was a new opportunity to kiss smooth female flesh, to inhale her intoxicating
scent. She was vibrantly alive, a full-color woman who had
come blazing into his monochromatic existence. He rolled
onto his back, pulling her on top of him.

With a purring sound, she feasted on his mouth while
adjusting her body over his. The touch of bare skin on
bare skin was electrifying. He was almost unbearably excited, and when she sank onto him, exquisite pleasure almost pushed him over the edge. His long celibacy had

deepened his awareness, made every nerve ending painfully sensitive.

She held very still, her breasts brushing his chest, while he struggled for the control to prolong their lovemaking. Then she began pulsing into him with small movements that drove him mad.

Intoxicated, he knew nothing beyond the moment, the woman, the joy and freedom of passion. Their mating was swift and sweaty, with Val's climax triggering his own. He came with a shuddering groan, saying her name over and over as he buried his face in the springy tangle of her hair.

As he struggled for breath, he realized that this was more than great sex—this was emotional transformation that had dragged him from paralysis into a new and dangerous world. One where he could be hurt again. He had an absurd desire to say that he loved her—but how could that be when they still had so much to learn about each other? And what did he know about love?

"Oh, my . . ." Val said on a soft exhalation. "I've forgotten all the reasons why this might not be a good idea." She slid off him to her side, where he could study her beautiful little body. What a symphony of curves she was, every part of her an invitation to touch.

Under his scrutiny, Val shifted uncomfortably and reached for the sheet. He covered her hand with his. "Don't hide. I want to admire you."

"Rubens would have admired me, but this body isn't fashionable right now." Though her tone was light, she was clearly self-conscious.

He felt a wave of tenderness that even a woman as smart as Val couldn't quite escape the feeling that she ought to be skin and bones. What a crazy society they lived in, where a beautiful woman considered herself flawed. "You aren't even close to Rubens proportions." He cupped her breast, his thumb slowly teasing the nipple. "You're what used to be called a pocket Venus—petite but perfectly, sexily proportioned. A feast for the eyes, and all other senses as well."

"That does sound much nicer." She arched apprecia-
tively into his hand. "I'm going to be tired tomorrow, but
this is worth it."

"I didn't think angels of mercy got tired."

"I'm no angel of mercy. Actually, I don't think that
lawyers get to be angels at all—it would be professional
misconduct."

He smiled, but realized that this was the moment where
second thoughts might appear. Luckily, Val didn't appear
to have any. She skimmed her palm across his chest. "If I
had known it would be like this, I would have jumped you
the first time we met."

"It wouldn't have been like this then." He tried to keep
regret from his voice as he recognized that emotionally
they were in very different places. Though she was happy,
open, and glad to be in this bed, the earth hadn't moved for
her as it had for him.

Catching his mood, if not the reason for it, she said,
"You were concerned that I might have morning-after regrets. I won't, but will you?"

He caught her hand, lacing his fingers between hers.
"None at all, but . . . I guess I'm wondering what comes
next."

"We take it one day at a time, of course. We seem to
get along well both in and out of bed. Isn't that enough for
tonight?"

"I don't think I'll ever get enough of you."

He could feel her withdraw fractionally. She was definitely not in a mood for emotional declarations. Lightly he
continued, "I hope I don't get added to the list of mistakes
you've made with men. Where would I fit in?"

She smiled, relaxed again. "So far, you show no signs of
being a mistake. I've done all the stupid things. Believed a
married man once when I was so young my stupidity was
almost forgivable. Dated a few separated men over the
years, until I realized that every time I got even a little bit
involved with one, bad things happened because separated
people are always screwed up. I tried to fix a few wounded

guys that I thought needed me." She wrinkled her nose. "That one is *really* dumb. And let's not even start on the workaholics. What about you? I seem to recall seeing a picture during the scandal days when you were with a woman described as your fiancée."

"That was Janice Hale, a terrific game designer who was as involved with her career as I was with mine. It suited us to hang out together when we both had time." They had been safe, pleasant sleeping partners who knew better than to ask too much of each other. "I mostly made only one mistake, but it went on and on and on—I was always too busy to get seriously involved. During the media feeding frenzy Jan was a loyal friend, but never my fiancée. When my concern with Jeff's case took over my life, there wasn't any room left for her."

He had been relieved when Jan phoned him and said calmly that it was time to go their separate ways. He had nothing left for her, and she deserved better. "She married another game designer a couple of years ago, had a baby, and the last I heard, she was working on games for toddlers. Dancing elephants and playful bears and the like."

"Thereby proving that workaholics can change their stripes, at least partially." Val grimaced. "I should ask her for tips on how to do it."

"Surely the first step is to want to change, and you're there already."

"My mind is, but my body is still racing like a gerbil on a wheel. I'll be glad when I wind things up at Crouse, Resnick and move out to the church. Being in that atmosphere is bound to slow me down."

Her voice was a little wistful. Maybe the earth hadn't moved for her, but she was trying to change her life. If he was patient, perhaps she would find the time to fall in love. "Only a couple of weeks until you move into your new office. Since my apartment is upstairs from that, I can volunteer my services in helping you to relax if you find yourself getting too wound up." He leaned forward to kiss one lovely full breast, moving his tongue in a slow circle.

She sucked in her breath, eyes glowing. "Oddly enough, I'm beginning to feel wound up again right now."

He blew gently into her navel. "We'll both be tired tomorrow, but at the moment, it's impossible to give a damn."

She laughed as she reached for him again. "Luckily, I don't need much sleep."

"Good. I have a number of years to make up for. This time, let's not rush."

He had wanted raw passion to be succeeded by slow savoring, and that's what he got. Though the first time might have been mostly sex, now they made love with emotion rooted in a desire to please. She was exquisitely responsive, like a musical instrument created by a master craftsman. He hadn't known how intensely arousing it was to make love to a woman who was so open and joyous in her pleasure.

Long rapturous orgasms left them both drained to the point of incoherence. Val managed to pull the covers over them before falling asleep. He was grateful for her tacit permission to spend the night—it would have been hell to haul himself from her bed and make his way home. Infinitely better to fall asleep with her tucked against his chest, flyaway red curls tickling his chin.

Yet despite the exhaustion of their lovemaking, he slept lightly and woke early. There was just enough dawn light to show the planes of Val's face. He supposed she wasn't technically beautiful, but he found her face enchanting. A wickedly intelligent elf.

He was tempted to kiss that full lower lip, but when he tried to move he found that he was sandbagged between Val and the cats. Not wanting to wake everyone, he relaxed again, his only movement to cup his hand around Val's breast.

Sleep hadn't eliminated his feeling that he had found something rare and special with her. He needed to develop a better understanding of love—for starters, he'd like to believe he was capable of it. Then he needed to figure out how to be lovable enough that a woman like Val might fall in love with him. Like that was going to happen.

Living a life in full color wasn't going to be easy after so many years in monochrome.

VAL AWOKE WITH A SHIVER OF PURE DELIGHT AS she registered the feel of Rob's body against hers. She stretched, every cell in her body tingling with satisfaction. She had almost forgotten how great sex could be. No, it wasn't just the sex that made her feel so good—it was Rob, who brought mesmerizing concentration to making love. She had never been with a man who was so wholly in the moment. And he really was a beautiful physical specimen—firm and fit and splendidly proportioned.

His eyes opened. The light color was still startling, but not icy at all. She leaned forward to brush a kiss on his lips. "I feel like Cinderella after the ball, returning to her work of scrubbing bricks or whatever it was Cinders did on a normal workday."

He returned the kiss with interest. "I don't suppose there's any hope of persuading you to have one last dance."

She was calculating whether there might be time for a quickie when her alarm clock went off. She bopped its button, resenting the way it had blasted her into reality. "Alas, no. I have time for a fast shower and if you're interested I can rustle up some eggs and bacon, but I have to be out the door in an hour. I have a ton of work to do if I'm ever to break free of my uptown job."

She liked that he released her rather than trying to change her mind. There was a time for play and a time for work, and a man who tried to seduce her when her mind was on the job was irritating, not romantic.

"I'll console the cats while you shower." He raised her hand and kissed it with a tenderness that melted her. "Breakfast would be great. Is it okay if I use your shower?"

"Of course." Reminding herself of her day's calendar, she slid from the bed, grabbed her bathrobe from the closet, and headed for the bathroom. Days like this, she was glad for her bizarre but low maintenance hair. Within ten minutes she emerged from the bathroom finger-combing the curly red mass. "The shower is all yours."

"You're fast." He removed Damocles from his chest and climbed from the bed. "Don't you have to dry your hair?"

Frankly staring at his splendidly naked body, she tossed him a set of navy blue towels. "A dryer would turn my hair into a frizzy red tumbleweed. If I had to go to court or see clients today, I'd pull it back, but since I'll be working in the office, I can take the easy way, which means shaping my hair with my hands and letting it dry on its own."

"What about when the weather is cold? Won't a wet head give you pneumonia or something?"

She laughed. "I've actually had my hair freeze when I've dashed out in icy weather, but no pneumonia yet."

He shook his head. "Amazing. The things I don't know about women."

She liked the twinkle in his eyes as he headed into the shower. In fact, she liked everything about him. Despite the short night, she glowed with energy as she donned a tailored pantsuit, made a swift pass with her makeup, and skipped downstairs to the kitchen.

First, feed the cats. That was inviolable law. By the time her furry friends had completed their first graze at the bowls, she had coffee dripping and bacon in the microwave. Mixing eggs with parsley and a dash of cheese was done while a burner heated up on the stove. As a woman who liked to eat proper food but never had enough time, she had kitchen efficiency down to a science.

When she heard the shower turn off, she pushed down the toaster lever and started scrambling her eggs, setting the table in the bay-windowed breakfast nook while they cooked. She was pouring orange juice when Rob entered the kitchen.

His appearance triggered sharp dissonance as his quiet,

professorial image clashed with the memory of last night's passionate lover. The result was unexpected shyness.

The silence lasted only a moment before he crossed the kitchen and drew her into a reassuring hug that dissolved all morning-after awkwardness. "You're incredible," he murmured. "A beautiful woman, a kitchen perfumed with bacon and coffee, and enough memories of last night to keep me smiling like the Cheshire cat all day. May I call you Wonder Woman?"

She laughed, at ease again. "As long as you smile when you say it."

Breakfast was relaxed, if not lingering. Rob was easy to have around. Just when she was thinking she needed to get moving, he glanced at his watch. "Time for me to go if you're to keep on schedule." He got to his feet and cleared his plate and silverware to the sink. "I'm not quite sure what one day at a time means in this situation. On the work end, I'll let you know if my investigations turn up anything interesting. On the personal side, I'd like to take you out to dinner when you can fit me into the schedule."

She thought a moment, glad he understood how busy she was at the moment. "Next Saturday?"

"It's a deal." He bent to give her a light, sweet kiss. "Thank you, Val. I feel more alive than I have in years."

Then he left, tote bag of files in hand. Instead of bolting from the house herself, she stood motionless, touching her fingertips to her lips. Rob was the nicest thing that had happened to her in a long, long time.

But she didn't have time to think about that now. With a quick shake of her head, she darted up the steps to renew her lipstick and put on earrings, which she had forgotten earlier. The morning would be spent preparing for a hearing the next day. In the afternoon, she had to brief another partner on a case he was taking over since she was leaving. Plus, at least three important phone calls that must be made first thing . . .

Delicately perched on the Corian vanity in her bathroom was an origami bird. She lifted it wonderingly, balancing the feather weight on her palm. Rob had taken a piece of yellow lined legal paper and transformed it into this magical creature. A crane, she thought.

She unexpectedly found herself blinking hard as she remembered Jimmy, a young musician she had dated in college. Charming, talented, and self-destructive, he was the only other man she'd ever known who might have done something so whimsical and romantic. One of the boyfriends she had tried to save, Jimmy had died of a drug overdose a year or so after they broke up.

Who could have guessed that a carpenter/Marine/computer wizard could be as romantic as a doomed musician? Not that Rob didn't have plenty of baggage of his own, but at least he didn't seem self-destructive. Maybe she was making progress on the relationship front.

Or maybe not. Time would tell. Lightly she kissed the origami beak before setting the crane down and heading into her day.

CHAPTER 11

✦✦✦

ROB FOUND HIMSELF WHISTLING AS HE SWUNG into his truck. Life might have become more complicated overnight, but for the first time in years, he was looking forward to challenges rather than trying to hide from them.

Since he and Val had laid out plans for the investigation, today he'd discover how rusty his skills were. Luckily, his most recent renovation was finished with the new residents ready to move in, so he could devote all of his attention to Daniel Monroe's case. Despite the years that had passed since the original crime, there would still be some information out there if he dug hard enough. Given how cursory the original police investigation had been, there might be a lot of information if he looked in the right places. The question was where to start.

As he headed toward Northern Parkway, his cell phone rang. He sighed and pulled over to the curb. If there was one thing he should have learned by now, it's that life seldom went according to plan.

"Hi, boss, it's Sha'wan," his caller said cheerfully. "The Crabtown shopping center got hit by taggers again last night. Can you come help clean it up?"

Rob hesitated, thinking of his investigation. But it was important to obliterate graffiti quickly, and Sha'wan was teaching a class at the Fresh Air community center that afternoon. The two of them should be able to take care of this job in a couple of hours if they worked together. "I'll be there in half an hour."

As he headed for his apartment to change his clothes, he realized that the Crabtown shopping center was near where Officer Jim Malloy was killed, and Kendra and Daniel had lived only a few blocks away. It looked like he was being given some direction on where to start his investigation.

LIKE KENSINGTON, THE NEIGHBORHOOD IT SERVED, Crabtown had seen better days but still functioned. The small strip center included a locally owned supermarket, a dollar store, a hair salon, a fried chicken and crab house, a shoemaker, and a couple of other small shops. Today, the center also had graffiti blaring on the sides and the upper level, which was home to several offices.

Sha'wan was already on a ladder painting out the sprawling obscenities on the upper level. Rob opened the graffiti van and set himself up with paint and a roller.

As he headed for the end wall, Sha'wan lifted his roller in salute. "Hey, boss. There's less tags this time than last, so we're making progress. The supermarket manager and three other business owners have already been out to thank me. They say the company that manages this place wouldn't have done anything for months." He grinned. "The dollar store guy says he'll give us some paint, and the supermarket guy said lunch is on him if we want sandwiches and soda."

"Sounds good." Rob turned the corner and set to work. There were people who thought that graffiti was art, and maybe some of it was. But mostly it was vandalism—an angry shout that intimidated and signaled a community at risk. Having lived in neighborhoods like this one, Rob felt a deep sense of satisfaction in helping to maintain a civil, stable environment.

With the two of them working, by noon the graffiti had been vanquished. Rob went to the van where the younger man was starting to clean up. "Sha'wan, do you know this neighborhood well?"

"Sure, I mostly grew up here in Kensington. Lived with my grandmother over on Hurley. She's been in that house for forty years."

"Really?" Rob removed the paint-saturated roller and dropped it into a trash bag. Time to start prospecting for new information. "Did you ever hear of a police officer who was murdered in this neighborhood seventeen years ago?"

"Oh, yeah, I know about that. He was shot just around the corner from Grandma's house. It was a big deal around here." Sha'wan stripped off his painting coveralls to reveal jeans and a garish T-shirt. "It's taken 'em long enough to get around to fryin' the murderer."

"My new tenant for the church—"

"The fox?"

Rob tried not to grin fatuously. "The *lawyer*, Val Covington, is now Daniel Monroe's attorney. He says he's innocent. I've met him and think he may be telling the truth, so I'm helping with the investigation. Think your grandmother would be willing to talk to me? Maybe she knows something or someone that might help clear Monroe."

"Gran will talk to anyone and feed you pie along with gossip." Sha'wan pulled an Orioles baseball cap onto his head backwards. "You really think the guy didn't do it?"

"It's a distinct possibility. He certainly deserves a better investigation than the murder got seventeen years ago."

"Then Gran's the one to talk to. She's been active in the community association forever, so she knows everyone. She's in Atlanta visitin' her sister until next week, but when she comes home, give her a call and say I sent you." Sha'wan jotted a phone number on a piece of paper and handed it over. "You might want to talk to the old guy who runs the shoe repair shop, too. Mr. Sam is older'n God and has been there forever. He might know somethin'."

"Thanks. I'll talk to both of them," Rob said, thinking that he was off to a good start. A brief thought of Val flashed through his mind. No, he certainly had no excuse to call her. "Shall we go collect that free lunch?"   .

AFTER LUNCH WITH SHA'WAN, ROB BOUGHT A steno pad at the dollar store and headed to the shoe shop, but he hesitated outside the display window. He hadn't considered all the implications when he volunteered to help investigate the case. Though he had learned in the Marines that interviewing people got the best results if rapport was established, "rapport" meant at least an illusion of closeness, and that was something he'd avoided for years. The fact that he hadn't even known that Sha'wan grew up in this neighborhood was a sign of how much distance he had been keeping between himself and others.

If he could bare body and soul to Val, he could let some barriers down with a shoe repairman. Steeling himself, he entered the shop. "Good afternoon."

The shop was empty except for a wiry older man behind the counter. He glanced up from polishing a lady's shoe. While not older than God, he was at least sixty, with grizzled hair and a shrewd gaze. "Afternoon. What can I do for you?"

"You're Mr. Sam?" When the man nodded, Rob continued as he had planned. "I wouldn't be able to leave my boots today since I'm wearing them, but would you repair these? I took them into one repair shop, and the man said he threw away boots that looked better than these."

Mr. Sam chuckled. "Take one off and let me have a look."

Rob obliged, handing the lopsided, paint-spattered, and scuffed boot over the counter. The story about the cobbler who refused to repair his boots was no lie.

Mr. Sam examined the boot closely before handing it

back. "Yep, these can be fixed if you like 'em well enough to pay the price."

"I do. It takes years to get boots this comfortable." As he accepted the battered boot, Rob spotted something that might create a sense of connection: on the shoemaker's forearm was a faded tattoo of the Marine Corps insignia. "You were a Marine?"

"Once a Marine, always a Marine." The old man's teeth flashed white in his dark face as he glanced down at the tattoo. "Da Nang. First Battalion, twenty-seventh Marines."

"I was a Marine, too, but more recently, when we were between wars."

"Be grateful. Vietnam taught me a lot more about life and death than I wanted to know." Mr. Sam glanced at the steno pad. "Now what's your real reason for coming in?"

So much for subtlety. At least the older man sounded curious rather than hostile. "I'm investigating the murder of Officer James Malloy, which took place in this neighborhood seventeen years ago. Sha'wan Baker suggested that you would be a good person to talk to since you were in business here then."

Mr. Sam squinted at him. "You're one of the graffiti guys. Sure, pull up that stool and ask away, but I don't know much. Want a cup of coffee?"

"Thanks. I take it black. As to whether you know anything useful—well, I'm just starting out, so I have a lot to learn." Rob sat on the stool as he'd been told. "Just so you know, I'm working for the attorney of the convicted murderer, and we're looking to find evidence that the man might be innocent."

"You're trying to clear Daniel Monroe?" Mr. Sam set down a mug of steaming coffee that looked strong enough to etch glass. "I've always wondered if he was the shooter. The boy was in here a time or two. He was real hard on sports shoes. Might've been a little wild, but he didn't strike me as no murderer."

Rob took a cautious sip of the coffee. He'd been right about the strength. "Monroe was convicted by eyewitness testimony, which isn't always reliable. He's a very tall, strong, broad-shouldered man. Distinctive. I'm wondering if someone of similar height and build might have killed Malloy. Do you recall any young men around this neighborhood who could have been mistaken for Monroe, and who might have been more likely to pull a trigger?"

"Oh, yeah, there were others who fit that description. There was a fellow called Shooter—he was killed a few years after Malloy died. A couple of cousins named Omar and Isaac Benson. Alike as peas in a pod. Both of 'em went to the Pen." He shook his head sadly. "No shortage of punks who fit that description close enough so that in bad light someone might mistake 'em for Monroe. Could be any of a dozen guys."

"I checked the sunset time for the day of the shooting and it was dusk. The light can be misleading then."

"There had been rain and overcast all day, so it was darker than usual." The shoe repairman grimaced. "It's easy to remember a bad day."

"That's interesting." Rob noted the weather comment so he could check it out later. If the evening was unusually dark, it undercut the eyewitness identification even more. "Did you know Officer Malloy?"

Mr. Sam nodded. "He was a good cop. Young and idealistic. He'd drop in on these shops regularly so we could get to know and trust him. I'm the only owner who's still here—the other businesses have closed or changed hands. The day before he was murdered, he showed me a picture of his wife and kid. His daughter was just the same age as mine."

Time didn't diminish the sense of tragedy. A pleasant, idealistic young man who worked hard at his job had died for no good reason. "What was the neighborhood like at the time?"

"There were problems then with open air drug markets and outsiders coming to buy drugs. Wasn't as bad as some of the neighborhoods farther in the city, but bad enough.

Luckily a honcho in the police department lived nearby so we got extra attention, which kept the worst of the drug dealers out of Kensington. We still have problems, but mostly this is a pretty good place to live and work."

"Were there any police detectives who worked the neighborhood regularly then and might remember who was hanging out here?"

"There were a couple. Saw 'em here regularly. Now what were their names?" Mr. Sam thought for a long time before shaking his head. "One was named Washington. Can't remember the first name. The other was Xenon Barkley. A smart, tough guy. He knew all the players by their street names and rap sheets. Not much got by Barkley. He was part of the Malloy investigation."

"Any idea if he's still with the police department?"

Rob didn't expect an answer, but the older man said, "He quit a few years back when a fancy new police chief decided the detectives were thinkin' too highly of themselves so everyone should rotate into different jobs." Mr. Sam snorted with disgust. "So the experienced detectives were forced out and a lot less murders were solved. The newspaper had a big article about it. Barkley was mentioned as one of the detectives who retired rather than be rotated into traffic or somethin' like that."

"Sounds like an easy name to find in the phone book if he's still around." Rob held out his hand. "Thanks for your help. I'm not sure where I'm going with this, so is it okay if later I come by with more questions?"

"Sure. Too many black men sittin' in jail who don't deserve it. If Daniel Monroe is one of 'em, more power to you." Mr. Sam's handshake was Marine tough.

Rob gave him a business card in case he had any other thoughts, then left. So maybe the murder had taken place under conditions more like night than dusk. It was a start. Now he had more names to trace, and maybe, after enough slogging, he would come up with something that might save Daniel Monroe.

* * *

LIKE MOST LAWYERS, VAL WAS CAPABLE OF LASER-
like concentration when she worked, so she managed to
keep thoughts of Rob at bay all morning. That ended
when she completed her brief. Kendra had picked up a
salad for her, and by the time Val had poured on the dressing, her hormones were rioting. If Rob was in the room,
she would plaster herself to him like suntan lotion. She
hadn't felt so crazed since adolescence. Pent-up demand
after long celibacy, but knowing that didn't reduce her
yearning.

She glanced at her watch. Twenty minutes until her afternoon meeting, and she couldn't think of a single good
reason to call Rob. If she were sixteen, she might have
done it and been content to giggle into the phone, but she
was a grown woman, for heaven's sake.

The best way to keep from calling Rob was to call
someone else, and she owed one to Rachel. Doctors were
harder to track down than lawyers, but it was worth a try.

She got lucky, and Rachel called back within two minutes of being paged. After they traded hellos, Val said,
"Thanks for suggesting I look into the Big Sister/Little Sister program. I met a real sweetheart—well, not a sweetheart maybe, but Lyssie is a totally cool little girl—and the
paperwork is now in process. Did you know how many
forms have to be filled out? Practically every address I've
ever lived at, interviews, references—even a police check!
Not that I blame them for being careful."

"You sound as excited as Kate did when she announced
that she was pregnant. Are you still having doubts about
your parenting instincts?"

"One thing at a time—the match isn't official yet." Val
took a quick bite of salad. "The caseworker said that since
I've lived in Baltimore most of my life, the paperwork
should be processed fairly quickly. I hope so—I'm really
eager to get started, though heaven knows where I'll find

the time. By the way, I need references from four people who have known me for at least ten years. Will you give me one? I figure *Dr. Hamilton* will look good on the list, but I warn you, there's a long form to fill out."

"I'm a doctor—long forms are my life," Rachel said dryly. "I'd be happy to do it, but maybe you would be better off with my father. *Judge* Hamilton is even more impressive than *Doctor*."

Val shuddered. "Having watched me grow up, I'm afraid what your dad might say. Do you think he's forgotten the time I built a fort out of his law books, including the ones he had carefully laid out for research?"

"He hasn't, but nowadays, he likes to think that was an early sign of legal talent on your part." Rachel's voice changed. "So how are you doing with the handsome landlord? Do his waters still run deep?"

Val almost choked on her salad. A good thing Rachel wasn't here to see her blush. "Very deep. We're having dinner together on Saturday."

"Splendid! Will it be your first date??"

Val sighed. "Not exactly. Further details classified under the Privacy Act."

"That was fast," Rachel said with a chuckle. "He must be something pretty special to get you interested in dating again."

Val wished she could discuss Rob's tortured history with Rachel—her friend was wonderfully insightful about what made people tick. But Rob's confidences were not to be shared. "He is. One of a kind and really, really nice." She thought of something she could mention. "This morning, I found an origami crane that he'd made and left for me to find. I almost swooned on the spot."

"A romantic! Val, if you decide you don't want him, I want an introduction."

"Not your type—you don't like beards." Val glanced at the clock. "Have to run. I'll mail the reference form tonight. Thanks for agreeing to vouch for me, and even more, thanks for suggesting I get a little sister. Kids in the program have to lack access to at least one parent, and poor Lyssie has lost both. She deserves special attention."

"Thank me after you know her better, and she's thrown a teenage hissy fit," Rachel said. "And when you and Lyssie are better acquainted and in the mood, let's all do something together. A trip out on the boat, maybe."

"It's a deal, Doc." Val hung up the phone and reached for the handle of the wheeled luggage carrier that held three file boxes she must transfer to her replacement on this case. Someday soon, she promised herself, she would have a life where she wasn't always eating and running.

But for now . . . she sighed and grabbed the last cherry tomato before heading out the door.

CHAPTER 12

DESPITE THINKING OF ROB WHENEVER SHE SLOWED down enough to take a deep breath, Val managed to keep her hormones at bay until Thursday. There was no point in wanting to see him when she didn't have the time to do so.

Yet despite her impeccable logic, she still wanted to see him, dammit, which is why she decided to stop by the church after leaving Crouse, Resnick on Thursday afternoon. It wasn't far out of her way, and if Rob's pickup truck was there, she could stop and ask a question about her rapidly approaching move. Just a couple of minutes of friendly conversation to appease her hunger to see him. Then she would go home and eat before meeting with Mia Kolski, the legally harassed single mother.

She had half-convinced herself that he would be away, but his truck was in the lot. When she pulled in beside it, she felt unexpectedly shy about going inside. Two years on the wagon had made her rusty on the rituals of the mating dance. Or had she always felt this craven neediness? If so, no wonder she had sworn off men.

Reminding herself that she was changing her life and this time was supposed to be different, she took a slow breath and climbed out of the car. A quick look around the church showed that the final finishing work was complete, but there was no Rob. She would have to be obvious. No, think of it as direct. Direct was good. Yet she still felt like an anxious teenager when she climbed the stairs to the apartment.

She rang the bell. Nothing. The truck in the lot didn't mean he was home.

The door opened as she was turning to leave. Rob loomed over her, casual in his jeans and a T-shirt that showed off his splendidly developed muscles. He lit up like a candle when he saw who was on his doorstep.

Val swallowed, feeling even more like a skittish teenager. Ridiculously so, given that they'd already been to bed together. "Uh, hi. Sorry to interrupt you, but I stopped by to see how the office is coming and thought I'd say hi."

"I'm glad you did. Come on in. Would you like a soda or something?"

He stepped back so she could enter the apartment. Clean, spare, and white-walled, it made her think of a monk's cell. Not that she had ever seen a real one. "I have to be home to see a client at seven o'clock, but a glass of ice water would be nice."

"Iced tea?"

"That would be even nicer."

He moved into the small kitchen and pulled a jug from the refrigerator. "Drinking iced tea is one of the few signs of my years in the South."

"You've moved around a fair amount. Does Baltimore feel like home, or was it just a place for you to go to ground?"

"Some of both." He poured tea into two ice-filled tumblers and handed her one. "Plus, it was about as far as I could get from California and still be in the U.S."

She leaned against the edge of the table, which was as casual as she could get when wearing one of her power suits. The kitchen matched the living room's austerity. The only color was a set of whimsical ceramic canisters in radioactive shades of fuchsia, magenta, and orange. "Lively canisters."

"You mean they stand out like a sore thumb. They were a gift from the family that moved into the first house I renovated. The wife made them herself. She likes bright colors more than I do, but she's a good potter. If you'd like sugar for your tea, it's in the orange one."

Val didn't want sugar, but she liked the canisters. "They're fun. You need more color in your life."

"You're right." He ran a slow gaze over her. "Your hair adds a nice bit of brightness to the apartment."

She didn't quite blush. "Any progress with your investigation?"

"Not really. I'll write a report for you, but this is a slow process of talking to people who may lead me to other people who might be able to fill in the missing pieces of a very old puzzle. Investigation takes lots of time and patience."

Even though Rob had the patience, they didn't have much time. "It must be hard to work on a case this cold when most people can't remember what they ate for dinner last week."

"True, but there are a few pluses. Relationships and alliances that were compelling at the time of the murder might have changed. Someone who knew something then but wouldn't talk out of fear or loyalty might be willing to tell the truth now . . . if I can find the right people and ask the right questions."

She paused in mid-swig, arrested. "That's an interesting thought. In fact, it could be our best hope. If the real killer was involved with drugs, he was part of a world where alliances can shift in an eyeblink. Finding the right threads could lead into a network of guys who were hanging together then. Criminals often boast of their crimes—that's why prison snitches are useful even though they're unreliable."

"All true, but folks like that have a high mortality rate. I've already had a couple of lines of inquiry literally hit dead ends." He grimaced. "I would really, really like to talk to Darrell Long and Joe Cady, the eyewitnesses, but as you know, Long is dead and so far I've had no luck finding Cady. I have leads to a couple of people who knew them. If we know more, maybe they can be discredited as witnesses."

"That would help, though when a death sentence is this close to being carried out, it takes something really, really major to get official attention." Such as incontrovertible evidence of who the real murderer was—and even that was no guarantee of saving Daniel. The legal system had its procedures and was not easily swayed from its accustomed progression.

The thought triggered the recognition of why she had been feeling jumpy about Rob all week—matters had progressed too quickly, from businesslike to spending the night together with no intervening steps. It had felt right to offer Rob the most primal form of comfort when he revealed his haunted past—it still did—but now she didn't know whether it was the beginning of a relationship or a one-time event brought on by unusual circumstances. Which is why they were chatting like two people who barely knew each other.

"You're frowning," Rob said. "Does that mean you've thought of something helpful? Or detrimental?"

"Actually, I wasn't thinking of the case," she said slowly. "I've been feeling uncertain about you all week— I'm not sure whether or not we have a relationship or a . . . a one-night stand."

Instead of blanching at her frankness, he said, "I don't do one-night stands. Do you?"

It was a fair question since she had raised the subject. "Never deliberately, but sometimes . . . things happen. A promising spark dies rather than growing into a flame." Her mouth twisted. "I told you I've had my share of problems with men. Usually because of wishful thinking on my part. You and I skipped the usual dating stages and went straight to bed, which made me wonder if . . . if there's more here than sex, or if I'm thinking wishfully again."

He regarded her thoughtfully. "Should we pretend the sex didn't happen and just date for a while so we get to know each other better?"

She blinked. How many men would suggest a moratorium on sex in favor of getting acquainted? A gold star for Rob. Still, when she thought of the mind-blowing night they had spent together. . . . "I don't want sex to be declared off limits, but the real reason I came here today was because I wanted some reassurance that Sunday night was a beginning, not an . . . an aberration."

"I certainly hope it wasn't an aberration." He set his glass aside as the energy between them turned electric. "In fact, I can think of a very good way to prove that it wasn't a one-night stand."

With a mischievous smile she hadn't seen before, he caught her around the waist and sat her on the edge of the table, then proceeded to kiss her with a thoroughness that rocked her to her toes. "Do the math."

"You're right, if we do it again, it's no longer a one-time fling." Doubts vanishing, she set her tumbler down and abandoned herself to the kiss. The worst part of her two years of celibacy had been the lack of touch. Now his vivid physicality exploded through her senses like the wild, sweet tang of raspberries. "All week I've wanted so much to wrap myself around you like a boa constrictor."

"If we're getting Freudian here, I think I'm the one entitled to the snake imagery." His laugh was a sexy rumble from his chest to hers. "I'm so glad you're here, Val. I've been wanting to call you all week, but knowing how busy you are, I didn't want to be a nuisance."

She yanked out the tails of his T-shirt and spread her hands on his taut back. "I would have loved to talk to you. I think we like each other, so it's okay to call or visit."

"Much more than like." He slid his hands under her and cradled her tailored bottom. "You have almost an hour and a half until your meeting. I could nuke some Mexican food I have in the freezer and feed you supper, or . . ." He buried his face in her hair, his breath warm against her throat. "I could show you the bedroom. It's not much to look at, but the appearance sure would improve if you were on the bed."

The heady excitement of a new romance bubbled through her like champagne. "I want to see that bedroom. After all, you've seen mine."

Since his apartment was smaller, they got there a lot quicker than they had reached hers on Sunday night.

HALF AN HOUR LATER THEY LAY TWINED TOGETHER on Rob's bed, passion satisfied but the urge to touch still strong. Lazily Val toyed with his beard. "This gives you a misleading teddy bear look."

"A teddy bear?" He made an exaggerated face. "And here I thought I looked like a Hell's Angel. So much for your thinking I'm an alpha male."

"Alpha enough for me." She snuggled closer. "Are we still on for Saturday night?"

"I certainly hope so." His hands were as active as hers, stroking, caressing, kneading. "Do you have any favorite restaurants you'd like to go to?"

"Surprise me."

"Okay. Fairly dressy, seven o'clock."

She nodded, her face against his shoulder. "I have to get up and go home."

He sighed and tightened his arm around her. " 'The world is too much with us; late and soon.' "

Since she had also studied her poetry, she continued the quote. " 'Getting and spending, we lay waste our power: Little we see in Nature that is ours.' To think that Wordsworth came up with that two hundred years before voice mail and faxes."

"I wonder how he would react to life today? Probably freak out."

"Who could blame him?" Regretfully she disentangled herself and slid from the bed. After a quick wash-up in the bathroom, she collected her randomly strewn garments and began to dress.

As Rob pulled on his jeans, he asked, "When I was looking you up, every reference was as Val. Is that your full name, or did you decide you didn't like Valerie?"

"Neither." Since her stockings were wrecked, she slipped her bare feet into her neat little lawyer pumps. "My eternal hippie mother had a thing for Prince Valiant. She considered naming me Valiant, but ended up with Valentine, since I was born on Valentine's Day. That's better than Valiant, though not by much."

"I like the name Valentine."

He came up behind her and wrapped his arms around her waist. She leaned back, enjoying the playful affection in his embrace. There had been passion before and would be again, but for now, it was enough to be held.

And she was no longer worried about whether they had a real relationship.

ROB WALKED VAL TO HER CAR AND SENT HER OFF with a last lingering kiss. Though she left his arms reluctantly, by the time she pulled out of the lot she looked like a woman who would be able to keep her mind on business during her evening meeting. No way could he do the same. He would much rather sit around with a dopey smile on his face.

Fizzing with buoyant energy, he changed into shorts and jogging shoes and went for a run along the quiet, tree-lined streets of the neighborhood. Val might not be as head over heels as he was, but she had liked him well enough to come by voluntarily. Ever since Sunday night, he had been wondering if they had ended up in bed together because that was her way of expressing sympathy. The fact that today she had found time to visit despite her hectic schedule made him want to turn cartwheels.

She had seemed surprisingly shy when she first showed

up on his doorstep. After a startled moment, he'd hustled her inside before she could change her mind and leave. His motives had been pure—a few minutes of her company would have been enough to make his day. That they had ended up in bed again was a glorious bonus.

Exuberantly he broke stride, leaping into the air and batting at a clump of leaves on the maple that overhung the street. He felt like a seventeen year old who was in love for the first time.

Except that he had never felt like this as a kid. Then he was always worrying about what new domestic explosions awaited, and counting the days until he could escape to a new life. The real reason for his good high school grades was because studying at the library kept him away from home.

As a child he hadn't known he was intelligent—his family hadn't looked at the world in those terms. But as his home life deteriorated, he discovered solace in books. He enjoyed reading and using his mind, liked the approval of his teachers, liked demonstrating that he was smarter than kids who came from normal homes.

He had ended up as the class valedictorian without even trying. It had broken his math teacher's heart when he chose the Marines over college, but higher education was something else that wasn't part of his family's worldview. Hell, Harley never graduated from high school. Despite his grades, in his heart Rob hadn't believed that a kid from his side of the tracks belonged in a university even though his teachers swore he could get the scholarships that would have made it possible.

Would Jeff have turned out differently if Rob had gone to a college close enough that he could have been there for his little brother? With Rob as an example, Jeff could have gone to college, too. His swath of destruction had been brilliantly executed—what might he have achieved if he had been encouraged to channel his intelligence in constructive ways? If he hadn't stolen and used the experimental security detection device, he would still be alive—and probably still burning developments and people.

Rob's elation crashed. While he was enjoying himself in various libraries, his little brother had disappeared into some rough, woodsy hideout he had created for himself. Jeff was a classic loner. School bullies learned to avoid him because he fought like a berserk buzz saw if attacked. So he spent his time alone, growing ever more angry and twisted. It hadn't occurred to Rob to pry into his brother's life—at the time, it seemed that they owed each other privacy. But he should have been more aware. He should have done something.

Sweaty and leaden-limbed, he slowed to a walk as heaviness settled over him. To him, Val was like the world's greatest Christmas present, glittering and beautiful and infinitely desirable. But he had learned early not to trust gifts. Once, not long after his mother had married Harley, the old goat had taken his stepsons to an ice cream stand when their mother was at work. The specialty of the place was something called a Brown Derby—soft ice cream swirled onto a sugar cone, then dipped into melted chocolate which solidified over the ice cream in a crackly, delicious coat.

The counter girl had made the Brown Derbys extra large and brought them over. Rob had stared at the cones, his mouth watering. On a steamy Florida night, the smoothness of the ice cream and the richness of the chocolate melting on his tongue was the next thing to heaven.

Harley presented a two-for-one coupon only to be told that it had expired. He exploded into curses and waved the ice cream away. The boys watched the cones disappear, paralyzed with shock and yearning. The family wasn't that poor; there was always enough for food and Harley's booze, but to save a buck, the bastard had acid-etched a memory in Rob's brain that still filled him with a disappointment so painful it ached. That stupid ice cream cone had become an emblem of everything that was wrong with his childhood.

It didn't take much to keep a kid happy. A little affection, a full belly, and an occasional treat—and no physical violence that the kid hadn't earned. Instead, he and Jeff had been taught that they didn't deserve the good things in life, and whenever it seemed that they might get lucky, the prize would be taken away.

The wonder was that they hadn't both turned into arsonists.

MIA KOLSKI PROVED TO BE SLENDER, BLOND, AND tired-looking. She was perched on the top doorstep when Val arrived home. Val climbed from her car, apologizing. "I'm so sorry I'm running late, Mia." To be precise, she was sorry she was late, but not sorry for why. Firmly she blocked out thoughts of Rob, since Mia deserved her full attention.

"Not a problem. Sitting here for ten minutes on this peaceful street is practically a vacation." She stood and offered Val her hand. "I really appreciate your willingness to look at this. My dear ex-husband is putting me in the poorhouse by constantly dragging me back into court, and while music teachers are underpaid, it's still too much to qualify for Legal Aid. Sometimes I'm tempted to grab the kids and run so we can start over somewhere else under an assumed name." Though she managed a brittle smile, it was clear that Mia was at her wits' end.

"Running is not a good idea. Come on in and we'll see what can be done," Val said. "And trust me, something can be done. Want a cappuccino?"

"That would be absolutely heavenly. Go heavy on the caffeine."

Val escorted her visitor into the den. By the time she returned with two cappuccinos, Damocles had settled on Mia's lap and was purring comfortably. "Do you have a cat? If not, you should get one. They're wonderful stress relievers." Val set the foaming drink by Mia, then sat down with a tablet to take notes. "Now, where do you want to start?"

Mia brushed her hair back nervously. "Steve and I were married for seventeen years. For the first twelve, he was in the army, and we moved around a lot. He was always a negative, controlling sort of guy, and he got worse over time. I could stand it when his criticism made me cry, but when I found my daughter sobbing as if her heart would break because he'd destroyed all her pleasure in something she had worked hard to achieve, I hit the snapping point and told him to leave."

"Was he violent? Did he hit you or the children?"

"Never that, but I've come to realize that his behavior was emotional abuse," Mia said wearily. "After the divorce he moved to Atlanta for a couple of years, and life was great. Then he moved back here and started taking me to court, trying to reduce the amount of child support, trying to force me out of the house, which we had agreed I would keep until the kids are both twenty-one, quarreling about visitation. Now he's threatening to ask for full custody on the grounds that I'm unfit."

"On what grounds does he claim you're unfit?"

Mia relaxed into a smile. "I've acquired a boyfriend, a great guy who has kids of his own and treats mine well. They think he's terrific. We never spend the night at my place, or do anything that might upset the children, but the mere fact of having a boyfriend makes me a slut in Steve's book."

"He won't get far in court with that." Val leaned back in the sofa. "Does Steve love his children?"

Mia thought about that. "Yes, but he doesn't *like* them much. Teenagers are just too noisy and headstrong and un-controlled. He's also such a narcissist that he doesn't really see how his constant feuding with me hurts the kids even though I try to keep as much of this petty nastiness from them as possible."

"Does he spend a lot of time with the children?"

"Not really. He has them two weekends a month. He's never gone out of his way to see them more often even though I wouldn't interfere if they all wanted it. I think it's important that their father be part of their lives, even if he is a pain." She smiled ruefully. "For the record, I never criticize him in front of the children. They're smart enough to make up their own minds."

"It doesn't sound as if he has any grounds for taking custody away from you, and likely it would crimp his bachelor lifestyle," Val said cynically. "Probably he's just threatening that to upset you."

"With great success. Or maybe his mother put him up to it. She'd love to get the kids away from me and under her control."

"Don't worry, it won't happen." Usually a lawyer didn't make sweeping guarantees, but Val figured that Mia needed some reassurance. Since Callie had worked with Mia for years and vouched for her all the way, it wasn't likely that any skeletons would tumble out of the music teacher's closet. "When we talked on the phone, I asked for copies of your legal history?"

Mia opened a capacious handbag and pulled out a plump accordion file. "This covers the basics. If you want the nuts and bolts, I can copy everything but it's enough to fill a couple of file drawers."

"This will do for a start." Val took a quick look through the records of Steve Kolski taking his ex-wife to court. "As you know, I'm a business litigator, not a family law practitioner, but I have friends who can guide me." She tapped her pen on the accordion file. "As a litigator, one lesson I've learned is that the best defense is a good offense. We need to find a point where he's vulnerable, then attack."

Mia looked shocked. "I couldn't accuse him of something he hasn't done. I don't care about things like getting all his pension money—I just want him to stop bothering me and keep paying child support until the kids are grown."

"Pension money? Did you waive your right to half of his military pension?"

"Not that I recall, but when I looked into it, I found I won't get any. If I have to teach until I drop in my tracks, that's okay. I love teaching music, and I'll always manage to support myself." Mia smiled a little. "My daughter wants to be a doctor. She says she'll support me when I'm old and gray. She would, too. But for now, I just want to be left alone to raise my children and teach my music and . . . and have a life without worrying about when Steve will strike next, and how I'll pay for the latest round of expenses. Not to mention the Prozac!"

"Are you taking antidepressants? That could potentially be used as evidence that you're unfit. I doubt he'd get very far, but it's well to be prepared."

"No Prozac—that was just a figure of speech. When I'm upset or depressed, I play my piano." Mia made a face. "One thing I'll say—with all the harassment from Steve, my playing is the best it's ever been."

"A silver lining if I ever heard one." Val looked at her tablet and made a mental note to look into the matter of the pension. Maybe Steve had slipped a waiver in with other paperwork and Mia had signed unknowingly. If so, it might provide some leverage, though it would be Mia's word against Steve's as to whether she had signed voluntarily. "Tell me—why do you think Steve is so persistent? Is he still in love with you?"

For the first time, Mia laughed. "No way. He has a gorgeous girlfriend fifteen years younger than he is. His lawsuits really aren't about me or the kids. He just doesn't like losing."

Val showed her teeth. "Neither do I. And trust me, a Harvard-trained litigator can rip the throat out of a retired army officer any day."

Can, and would. Mia Kolski needed some justice, and Val was going to see that she got it.

CHAPTER 13

THE HIGH GENERATED BY HER VISIT TO ROB CAR-
ried Val through the rest of the week. Link by link, she was
severing her ties with her old job, except for a couple of
cases that Donald Crouse wanted her to stay with until
completion. In two more weeks, she would move into her
own office and become officially self-employed. She could
hardly wait.

Her Saturday morning was devoted to an in-home visit
by Anita Perez, the Big Sister/Little Sister caseworker. Besides checking that Val had a respectable domicile, Anita
grilled her on how she would handle anything that might go
wrong when she and Lyssie Armstrong were together. What
would Val do in the event of accident? Illness? Temper
tantrum? Please show proof of up-to-date car insurance.

Val would also need to sign a contract that spelled out
the ground rules for being a Big Sister. These included a
commitment of at least six hours a month to Lyssie, promising to pick her up on time and return her to her grandmother promptly. Lyssie would be signing a similar
contract about her responsibilities in the relationship.

At the end of the meeting, Val said wryly, "It's amazing

to think that people go ahead and have babies without any of this. It seems downright irresponsible."

"Off the record, if I had my druthers no one would be allowed to have a baby without passing a test, sort of like getting a driver's license." Anita grimaced. "I worked in child protective services for years. Far too many kids pay the price for being born to irresponsible parents who shouldn't be trusted with a goldfish, much less a complex, demanding, lovable, fragile baby."

"People think being a lawyer is hard, but what you do is far harder. If I worked with abused kids, I'd be a basket case in no time."

"That's why I left that job—burnout after ten years of seeing man's inhumanity to child. This work is much more fun. With a good Big/Little match, everyone benefits." Anita collected her files and tucked them into her briefcase. "I'm so glad that you and Lyssie hit it off. I was worried that she would be a difficult match because she's prickly. She has a pretty horrible past."

"I know," Val said quietly. "At least, I think I know the worst of it."

"She told you? You two really did connect."

"Actually, I think Lyssie was trying to scare me off, but it didn't work."

"Good. Her grandmother does her best, but she's in poor health. Lyssie needs someone like you to be a steady, supportive presence." Anita offered her hand. "I'll expedite the paperwork, and with luck, you can meet with Lyssie and her grandmother next weekend. If there are no problems, you've got yourself a new sister."

"I've always wanted a little sister. Thanks for moving this through the system so quickly."

"Not a problem. Your friends sent in the references very promptly. They all think very highly of you."

Val grinned. "I picked them very carefully. Have a good weekend, Anita." She closed the door behind the social worker, thinking that of all the changes she was making in her life, this was the one that carried the greatest responsibility. The prospect was scary but exciting. Rather like real parenthood, she suspected.

BETWEEN ANITA'S VISIT AND HER DATE WITH ROB, Val concentrated on the business of living—laundry, grocery shopping, basic house straightening. It was a sign of how much time she spent at the office that she actually enjoyed doing ironing and vacuuming.

As she folded sheets from the dryer, she pondered what to wear to dinner. Usually on a first date she aimed for attractive but a bit reserved, so she wouldn't have to fight if the guy was the sort who thought cleavage was an invitation to jump her bones. Since she and Rob were way beyond that point, they wouldn't experience the walking-on-eggs caution usual on first dates. That meant that it would be possible to relax and enjoy a romantic dinner; and because she knew how the evening would end, she would wear something that would dazzle him until his eyes popped.

She studied her closet, looking for an outfit that was feminine, slightly demure but definitely sexy. After she showered and fluffed her hair to have lots of bounce, she donned a flowing outfit of black silk with painted borders in shades of garnet, gold, and amber. The ankle-length skirt was slit to the knee, the tank top made the best of her cleavage, and the long, drifting jacket lent an air of spurious respectability. Night-on-the-town makeup, several tiny, sparkling butterflies in her hair, and garnet-colored, dominatrix-style spike heels completed the effect.

Rather than waste time biting her nails waiting for the doorbell, she spent the last minutes making notes about strategies to pursue on behalf of Mia Kolski. The bullying Mr. Kolski was going to regret using his money to harass his ex-wife. The trick was to find a vulnerable place and file a countersuit. When he had something to lose himself, he might be more willing to back off.

The doorbell rang, and she made a quick appearance

check. Outfit looked nice, butterflies safely tethered. She opened the door, prepared to be admired—and halted in astonishment, her greeting dying on her lips.

Rob had shaved off his beard. Standing on her front porch was Robert Smith Gabriel, the well-tailored tycoon brother who had turned in the Eco-Arsonist. If she hadn't recognized him from the old news stories, she would have thought a stranger was on her doorstep. Blankly she echoed what he had said when he first saw her in jeans. "Who are you and what have you done with my dinner date?"

"I wasn't sure the teddy bear look was a plus for an investigator. And . . . it seemed like time to come out of hiding. A little, anyhow."

The beard had been a good disguise—clean-shaven, he projected a totally different image. Though she had sympathized with his terrible moral dilemma when the Eco-Arsonist story broke, she hadn't felt particularly drawn to his photos. He seemed too icy-eyed and controlled, too much like his brother.

Beardless and in person, those qualities were even more visible. His sharply planed face was more handsome than she remembered, and even more formidable. She said randomly, "You'll scare the truth out of a few people now."

"Am I alarming you?"

"No," she said, not quite truthfully. "But your new look will take some getting used to."

He sighed. "Sorry. I cut the beard off on impulse this afternoon."

"It's your face—you're entitled to change it. You look very striking this way. Just . . . different than I'm used to." Since they were still in the doorway, she stepped back. "Come on in before the cats escape. They're going to want to check you out."

"What if they reject my new look?"

She laughed. "Then you're in big trouble, Robert."

Damocles appeared and rubbed adoringly against Rob's trousered ankle. If Rob had backed away from getting cat hair on his suit she would start to worry, but he bent and scratched the cat's head as casually as if he wore jeans.

Straightening, he said, "Now that I've been cat-scanned, can I say that you look absolutely stunning? I'd love to kiss you, but if I did, I think we'd miss our dinner reservations."

"Where are we going?"

"The Milton Inn. I'm sure you've been there but I haven't. It sounded like a nice place for our first real date."

"No kissing then. I love the Milton Inn." She picked up her small tapestry evening bag. "Shall we be off? Or do you have more surprises in store?"

"Well—I didn't bring the truck. I was afraid they wouldn't let us in a fancy restaurant if we arrived in that. So I brought my old car instead."

She stepped outside and blinked at the shimmering silver convertible parked by the curb. "Good God, what is that?"

"A Rolls-Royce Corniche." He put a light hand on her back and guided her to the car. "Though I did pretty well with my business, I didn't live lavishly. Serious consumerism takes time, and I never had enough of that to waste it shopping. Then one day I drove by a Rolls-Royce dealership. I'd always thought of them as the ultimate in quality and class—way out of my league. Suddenly it occurred to me that I could afford one if I wanted it. So I marched inside and ordered a Corniche on the spot."

He circled the vehicle to climb in on the driver's side and pushed a button to bring up the powered top. "I walked away from just about everything else in my California life, but I couldn't bring myself to sell the car. I drove it cross-country with one duffle bag and a laptop computer in the trunk. Since a Rolls didn't exactly fit my new life, I rented a garage for it when I reached Baltimore. I pulled the car out of storage for you, since you're the ultimate in quality and class yourself."

"I'd always fancied myself as a latent Ferrari, but I'll settle for this." She stroked the buttery leather of the seat, understanding why the car had been an irresistible symbol for a boy who had grown up the hard way. What did cars like this cost? Surely at least a quarter of a million dollars. "Are you rich, Rob? Ignore the question if you prefer, but you wear the trappings of wealth as easily as your battered blue jeans."

There was a long silence while he put the car into gear and pulled away from the curb. Val began to regret asking the question.

They were on Northern Parkway before Rob said, "If wealth is a state of mind, I was never rich, though my business sold for one heck of a lot of money. After Jeff's execution, I set up a foundation for funding grassroots projects in poor neighborhoods. I kept a chunk for myself—I worked too hard to give it all up, and I don't ever want to be poor again. I guess I qualify as comfortable, but rich? Not now, and I never really was, not in my mind."

A foundation? Another attempt at redemption, Val guessed. "You're using the money well. Are some of your projects here in Baltimore?"

"A couple of them are. The Brothers Foundation is the chief sponsor of the Fresh Air Community Center. It's been successful, so they're looking to open a couple more in other neighborhoods. The foundation also contributes to several existing community housing organizations, plus it supports our graffiti eradication program."

"Graffiti? Like the Graffiti Guy I read about in the newspaper a while back?"

He smiled faintly. "I *am* the Graffiti Guy, or at least the original one. These days, most of the work is done by Sha'wan Baker. He's a terrific kid."

She shook her head, impressed but unnerved. "I feel like you didn't just shave off your beard, but had a personality transplant."

He frowned. "This sounds like something that needs to be talked about. Do you really feel that I'm that different? I can grow the beard back."

"Don't worry, I'll adjust." She studied his face, trying to integrate this glittering man of the world with the warm, sensitive lover. "But you're a real moving target, Rob. When we first met, I thought you were a hardworking, un-complicated carpenter. Since then you've become a cru-sader, a Marine, an investigator, a man with a past, and now a philanthropist who looks like a world-class tycoon. Even though all these things are true, it's kind of like sleep-ing with a male harem." She smiled a little. "Not that that's necessarily a bad thing. But I keep wondering if I really know you."

He pulled the car over to the curb and turned to face her. "Close your eyes."

When she obeyed, she heard the creak of his weight shifting on the seat as he leaned across the console. A large hand smoothed back her hair before cupping her cheek. The callused hand of a carpenter, not the smooth fingers of a businessman. Then he kissed her with the warmth and tenderness that were so much a part of their lovemaking. This was the man she thought she knew, not the soulless overachiever who had showed up on her doorstep this eve-ning. The vulnerability was still there under his polished surface, as was the indefinable quality that made him Rob.

"Now do I seem familiar?" he whispered before deep-ening the kiss.

Liquid heat pooled demandingly, making her ache for his touch. "Point taken," she said shakily. "You're still you, and you were right—kissing puts dinner in jeopardy."

"How hungry are you?" His lips moved to her throat, unerringly finding a pulse point that magnified the erotic effect.

She considered and pulled away. "Pretty hungry. Re-member, pleasure delayed is pleasure multiplied."

He took a deep breath and put the car in gear again. "You're right. We can continue this later in a less public place."

"Given the attention this car is attracting, that's a good idea." Val glanced in the mirror and decided her new no-smudge lipstick worked pretty well. "Where did you get your computer training? You mentioned it so offhandedly that it sounded like you went to a trade school, but now I suspect it was some high-class place like MIT."

"Why would I want to study at a second-rate dump like MIT?" He gave her an appalled glance. "I went to Stanford."

She laughed, glad his sense of humor was still recognizable. "Silicon Valley. California boy. Of course Stanford. I should have guessed. I've always thought of myself as open-minded, but you're a real challenge to my preconceptions, Rob."

"If I'm hard to classify, it's because I don't fit into any normal framework."

Though his voice was level, Val heard the underlying bleakness. "Normal is a myth," she said quietly. "It sounds to me as if you create a place for yourself wherever you go." She rested her left hand on his thigh. After a moment, his right hand came down to rest on it.

As they drove north into the Maryland countryside, Val observed Rob from the corner of her eye. He was a remarkably fine-looking man with or without the beard, but she couldn't help feeling that their relationship was built on ever-shifting sand.

ROB SHOULD HAVE KNOWN BETTER THAN TO TRY to make the evening perfect. The first crack had appeared as soon as Val opened her door, looking like an invitation to sin, and froze at the sight of his shaved self. Though she claimed she would adjust quickly, for the rest of the evening she seemed more than usually reserved.

He should have warned her that he was taking the damned beard off, but as he'd said, it was an act of impulse. The decision to come out of his shell was only one of his reasons. Equally strong was looking in the mirror and deciding the beard looked sort of silly with his CEO suit. Since he wanted to impress her, out came the scissors and razor.

Belatedly it occurred to him that since she had spent her

formative years in a commune, she might prefer a beard to the clean-shaven look. He'd discovered that the beard made him seem more approachable. His unadorned face made people wary, and it was having that effect on Val.

His attempt to impress her with the Rolls hadn't been much better. Though she liked the car, he should have realized that a woman who was perfectly okay with a battered pickup wasn't going to swoon over an expensive set of wheels.

His optimism revived when they reached the restaurant. Well north of the city, the Milton Inn was a genuine coaching inn built in the first half of the eighteenth century, and as romantic a setting as anyone could want. But a getaway it wasn't. Not only was Val greeted by name, she waved to several acquaintances as they were escorted to a table in one of the charming rooms.

She even stopped at the table of an older couple to perform introductions. "My checkered past is about to be exposed, Rob. As a kid, I was a member of a girl gang, and this tolerant couple here, Judge Charles Hamilton and Julia Corsi Hamilton, were parents of a couple of my buddies. Folks, this is my friend Rob Smith."

The judge, a distinguished man with silvered hair, rose to shake hands. "Val was the gang's attorney," he said with amusement. "Even at age ten she had an amazing ability to construct watertight defenses when the girls got out of line."

"She can certainly talk circles around me," Rob agreed, nodding to Mrs. Hamilton. The judge's sharp glance made Rob wonder if he had been recognized, but if so, he said nothing.

After taking leave of her friends, Val moved on to their table on the other side of the room. "Sorry," she said after taking her seat. "Having lived here most of my life, I just about always see people I know. Incidentally, Julia is the mother of Kate, your friend Donovan's wife. She and the judge are newlyweds. They were both widowed, so when they married, Kate and my friend Rachel became stepsisters as well as friends."

"You mean fellow gang members." Rob studied Val, admiring the way the silk draped over her lush figure. "It must be wonderful to have such long-term friendships."

"Yes, but it's hard to get away with anything when every time you turn around, you see someone who knew you when you were knee-high to a squirrel."

He tried to imagine being so much a part of a place, and failed. Maybe if he stayed in Baltimore long enough, he'd find out.

After a quick scan of the menu, she made her decision and set it aside. "Tell me about being the Graffiti Guy."

Her choice of subject broke the ice, and over food and wine they deepened their knowledge of each other. He approved of her becoming a Big Sister because he knew how valuable such programs could be, but hoped the Little Sister didn't take up too much of Val's time. He wanted as much of that time as he could get.

By and large they stayed away from the subject of Daniel Monroe, except when Rob said, "It's occurred to me that Monroe might be a good one to ask about other young men in the neighborhood who might be confused with him. Do you mind if I visit him in prison without you there?"

"Not at all." She swallowed a bite of fruit tart and closed her eyes in brief ecstasy. "Kendra might also have some ideas. She and Daniel are primary source material, after all."

"Another primary source is the police detective who handled that case, Xenon Barkley. I have a meeting with him on Monday. He might be able to tell me things that never made it into the police report."

Val nodded approvingly. "I'm scheduled to meet with the public defender who handled the original case next week. It's going to be tricky—I don't want him to feel that I'm attacking his work. If he's cooperative, he might have some good information."

Rob said, "Looking the way you do tonight, there isn't a man alive who wouldn't cooperate with you."

She smiled, tilting her head to one side. "You make me feel like the most irresistible woman since Cleopatra."

As she moved her head, one of the tiny shimmering butterflies in her hair came loose and drifted to the table. He picked it up with one fingertip and gently replaced it in her red curls. "If Cleopatra was anything like you, Marc Anthony was a lucky man."

Yet despite the romantic banter and the passionate lovemaking that came when they returned to Val's house, the evening wasn't what he had hoped for. As she slept in his arms, he stared at the dark ceiling, knowing that they were further apart than when she had visited him at his apartment.

He wanted more from her, and didn't know to get it.

CHAPTER 14

❧

"MR. BARKLEY?"

The man at the desk glanced up from his computer. "C'mon in and have a seat. I'll be through with this in a minute."

Rob took a chair, thinking that the private security industry had done well by the former police detective. This discreet, expensive agency offered a range of services from detecting white-collar crime to providing bodyguards for international businessmen. As a vice president, Barkley had a sleek, spacious office that resembled an upscale law firm.

There was nothing sleek about Barkley, though. Muscular and bullet-headed, he'd broken his nose more than once and was clearly not a man to be trifled with. He would have been a scary interrogator in his detective days. Rob's style was quieter, depending on persuasion rather than the coercive power of the law.

Barkley finished at the computer and stood to offer his hand. "I'm glad you called. Always ready to talk about when I was at the cop shop." His shrug indicated the comfortably furnished office. "Private security put my kids through college, but it hasn't got the same excitement." Taking his seat again, he said, "You're writing an article about the Malloy case now that his murderer has run out of appeals?"

"Sorry, I didn't mean to give you the wrong impression. I'm a private investigator, not a journalist."

Barkley's bushy brows arched. "Why are you investigating this case? It has human interest for a news story, but the facts were established years ago. There's nothing left to investigate."

Rob hesitated, sensing that Barkley would not approve of his purpose, but he didn't want to lie. "I represent the family of Daniel Monroe. Monroe has always maintained his innocence, so this is a last ditch effort to find evidence that might exonerate him."

"Innocent!" Barkley slammed his chair forward, his affability vanished. "The bastard is guilty as sin. The night he's executed, I'm breaking out a bottle of champagne I set aside for the occasion."

Rob kept his voice level. "He was convicted on eyewitness testimony, which is notoriously unreliable."

"Tell that to Brenda Harris, the woman Monroe attacked. The other witnesses were across the street, but Monroe physically assaulted her. He was right in her face, and she knew damned well who she was identifying."

"Yet she couldn't pick him out of a photo lineup. It wasn't until later, when he was the only familiar face in a real lineup, that she decided he was the one."

Barkley shrugged. "Harris was badly rattled by the assault and seeing a man murdered right in front of her. Not surprising that she couldn't make a positive ID a few hours later. The other two witnesses picked him out easily enough."

But they had been farther away under poor lighting conditions. Brenda Harris, who had the best look at the killer, hadn't recognized him when she first saw his picture. Only later did she become certain of his guilt. Rob said mildly, "There are cases when a victim has misidentified a rapist.

The assault was over in seconds, and she might have had a much better impression of his general build than his face."

Barkley snorted. "Of course Monroe's family wants to believe it was mistaken identity. Every criminal in the world has a mother who will claim that he's a good boy who fell in with bad company. If you believe 'em, the prisons are full of innocent men, every damned one of them."

"Most convicted criminals are guilty," Rob agreed. "But mistakes are made. DNA tests have proved that."

"Yeah, but Monroe is no mistake." Barkley's face was like granite. "You've read the case files, so you know that he started by shooting Malloy in the face. When the kid fell to the ground, screaming, Monroe stood over him and pumped five more slugs into him. As cold-blooded a murder as I ever investigated."

"It was cold-blooded all right," Rob agreed. "But not necessarily committed by Daniel Monroe. He had an alibi for the time of the shooting."

"That hot girlfriend of his?" Barkley leaned back in his chair again. "You can't have been a cop or you'd know that girlfriends lie. Families lie. Suspects lie. Everybody lies, most of all convicted criminals. Monroe and the girlfriend lived only a couple of blocks away, and she admitted that she gave her baby a bath that evening. Even if she's telling the truth, which I doubt, Monroe had plenty of time to sneak out of the house, commit murder, and sneak home again."

"There was no physical evidence connecting Monroe to the crime. No blood, no fingerprints, no weapon."

Barkley waved that off. "It's always harder to find good physical evidence at outdoor crime scenes, and there are dozens of ways he could have gotten rid of that gun. Probably passed it to a friend who tossed it into the Inner Harbor."

"There weren't any other guys in the neighborhood who had the same build as Monroe?" Rob asked. "No junkies or gangbangers who might have resembled him in low light?"

"Sure, there were other guys as tall, but it was Monroe's

face that was picked out of the lineup. That and the tattoo on his wrist. You're beating a dead horse, Smith. Don't waste any more of my time."

Rob got to his feet, knowing he'd get nothing more. "Thanks for seeing me."

Frowning, he left the security firm. From the beginning he had accepted that Daniel Monroe was innocent because the man was convincing, and Rob wanted to believe him. But maybe Barkley was right. Rob's experience in the military police was nothing compared to Barkley's years as a detective, but he did know that people lied all the time, and the most convincing criminals lied with conscienceless brilliance.

Even if Daniel had brutally killed a young policeman, Rob would try to save his life because he didn't believe in legalized murder, but he wanted to know the truth. He needed to talk to Daniel, and to Kendra. It was also time to check distances and times between the crime scene and the apartment where Kendra and Daniel lived. He needed to do a reenactment with a stopwatch. He also wanted to ask Daniel about that tattoo, which was a specific enough point to make the eyewitnesses more believable.

He also needed another car, he decided as he climbed into his pickup. The truck was great for remodeling and construction, and the Rolls was a perfect setting for Val, but both vehicles were way too distinctive for an investigator. He needed a sedan that was five years old and nondescript.

It was easier to think about cars than to wonder if Daniel really had murdered a young policeman in cold blood.

KENDRA WAS HANGING UP THE PHONE WHEN HER boss roared in. These days, Val was in perpetual motion even by her standards. Kendra picked up a file folder and held it out to be grabbed. Anticipating questions, she said, "Yes, I made all the calls you requested, and wrote a memo to you with the answers I got. Here's the Hampton file, and your sweetie was just on the phone to enlist me in reconstructing a crime. If he hasn't asked you yet, it's because you never slow down enough for him to get a hold of you."

Val paused on the way to her office at that. "Too right. Hard to believe that in a few days we'll actually be in the new office. Thank God for your organizational skills. Am I paying you enough?"

"For now." Kendra smiled wickedly. "But you will give me a salary review in six months, won't you?"

"I guess." Val opened the file she had just received. "If I survive that long. What's this about reconstructing a crime? Malloy's murder, I presume?"

"Right. He wants to do a run-through, literally, to see how long everything took, with me there as a consultant and you to hold the stopwatch or some such."

Val's brows drew together. "Late Saturday afternoon is the soonest I can do that, if the time is all right for you two."

"It works for me. As for Rob—I suspect his time, among other things, belongs to you. Just don't wear the boy out before he finishes his investigating."

Val's redhead complexion showed blushes beautifully. "I haven't got time to wear him out just now, but maybe later, when things settle down. For the moment, we haven't gotten much beyond a Saturday night date."

A date which lasted until Sunday brunch, Kendra suspected. "Are you serious about Rob, or just out to break his heart?"

Val looked up from her file in surprise. "I'm always serious about relationships, Kendra. What makes you think I'm in the heartbreaking business? Rob is very special, and maybe . . . maybe even a keeper."

Kendra hesitated, trying to define why she had asked the question. "You may be serious about relationships, but Rob, I think, is *really* serious. Vulnerable. Be careful with him, Val."

Other bosses might fire an assistant for a remark like that. Val merely looked thoughtful. "That's perceptive of you. Trust me, I have every intention of being careful. One of the nicest things about Rob is that he listens, and will talk about something besides how the Orioles are blowing another season. I'm hoping that once we get past the giddy stage and hit a few potholes, we'll be able to talk them through." She made a face. "Time to hit the computer. This ninety-second chat is my break for the afternoon. Maybe for the whole day."

After Val vanished into her office, Kendra tried to visualize her boss and Rob together. Over the years, Kendra had developed a reputation as a fortune-teller among her friends because of her ability to predict which romances would last and which wouldn't.

Kendra wasn't sure herself how she did it, though her mother and grandmother had had the same ability. Sometimes when she visualized two wildly unlikely people together, they seemed to mesh just fine despite superficial appearances. Other times, she just couldn't see two people as a couple even though they seemed well-suited.

How about Val and Rob? On the surface, very different, but their traits complemented each other. He was a serious guy, and if he decided he was in love with Val, he'd be there for her come hell, high water, or the IRS. Val, sparkly as a hummingbird, would contribute the warmth and laughter and charm Rob needed. They could be a great, forever kind of couple.

Yet when Kendra visualized them together, there was something a little out of kilter. She frowned. Based on her experience as a part-time wise woman, there would have to be some major changes if Rob and Val were going to make it.

ROB'S SECOND TRIP TO THE SUPERMAX PRISON WAS a little easier than the first, though he would have preferred to be almost anywhere else. Daniel Monroe looked even larger and more ominous than Rob remembered when he was escorted in by the guards. Seeing the man's puzzled look, Rob picked up the communicating phone. "I'm Rob

Smith, the investigator working with Val Covington. If I seem unfamiliar, it's because I had a beard the first time I was here."

"Sure makes a difference." Monroe studied his visitor's face, then gave a low whistle. "Damn. Your last name isn't really Smith, is it? No wonder you're interested in whether or not I get chopped."

Rob sighed. "You're the first one to recognize me."

"Better grow the beard back if you don't want to be spotted. Of course, most folks don't follow news of executions as closely as someone on death row."

Rob couldn't help responding to the other man's wry humor. "To most people, I was a bit player in a story that's old news. I prefer it that way."

"Were you there when your brother was executed?"

Throat tight, Rob nodded.

Monroe looked away, his deep voice a whisper. "When they do me—don't let Kendra be there. Please."

"The whole point of this investigation is to keep that from happening."

Monroe's mouth twisted. "I told you before, I think you're gonna fail. I'm willin' to be surprised if you get my sentence commuted, but I don't expect it. Will you promise to keep Kendra away?"

Rob wondered if he would be as philosophical about approaching death if he were in Monroe's place. How had Jeff felt? Had he been resigned, like Monroe? Angry? Eager to get out of prison in the only way available? God only knew. "I'll do my best to keep Kendra away if you're executed, but I can't make any promises. She's a determined woman. Maybe you can get the warden to bar her from attending."

"Good idea. I'll see if that can be done. Now what are you here for?"

"Mostly I want to ask questions that are answered in the case files plenty of times already, but I'd like to hear your point of view on what happened."

"Ask away. I have nothin' better to do."

"I talked to Xenon Barkley, the detective who investigated the Malloy murder."

Monroe snorted. "He did damn all investigatin' once he had me in custody. He never even considered that someone else might've done it."

"Do you think he did anything illegal to set you up?"

Rob was curious to see if Monroe would take the opportunity to blame someone for persecuting him, but the other man shook his head. "No, his sin was not looking hard enough for other suspects. He may or may not have set other guys up, but I don't think he messed with the case against me. He didn't have to, with the witnesses all pointin' their fingers at me."

"Was your lawyer any good?"

"Cal Murphy was kinda rushed, but he was smart and did his best. The public defenders have guys who specialize in capital cases, and they try real hard." Monroe's eyes narrowed. "Why are you askin' about all this legal stuff? I'd've thought that was more Miss Val's job."

"I'm just trying to get a feel for what happened, and how you felt about it." What the hell, might as well ask him straight out. "A lawyer probably wouldn't ask you this for fear of what you might say, but I want to know. Did you do it? I'll work just as hard if you did, but I want to know."

Instead of exploding, Monroe said dryly, "If my word wasn't good before, it won't be now. I could be the sort of twisted sister who has spent so long lyin' to myself that now I believe I'm innocent even if I'm guilty as sin. Or I could just be lyin' to everyone else while knowin' I'm a stone killer. I still say I didn't shoot that cop, but whether or not you believe me is an act of faith. You choose."

Rob felt his doubts ease. Maybe it was irrational, but he had trouble believing that a man with Monroe's detached insight was lying. "I choose to believe you're innocent, and that a real stone killer got away with murder."

"Happens regularly. With somethin' like the Malloy murder, people want to see someone pay, but they aren't real picky about who. If Kendra and I had lived in another neighborhood, I wouldn't be here today."

Now there was a depressing thought. "Since it figures in the identifications, I want to ask you about that tattoo on your wrist. Does it have a story?"

Monroe held up his right forearm, back of his hand turned to his visitor. The lines of the tattoo weren't much darker than his skin, but the image of a striking snake twining around his wrist was clear. "Yeah, but it's less interestin' than you might think. You know I went to prison for car theft? When I was inside the first time, it was kind of a fashion among the younger prisoners to get a tattoo to show you were a real man. There are plenty of ex-cons who have 'em."

That was useful information. "Was the snake a popular image?"

"That or a skull or flames were the top choices." Monroe inspected the tattoo. "I was lucky. The guy who did this was pretty good, and I didn't get AIDS from his needle. I hear he's a legit tattoo artist down in Fells Point now."

Rob surprised himself by asking, "I've wondered. Do you work at looking scary?"

Monroe smiled with an alarming flash of white teeth. "Hell, yes. The best way to get left alone in prison is to look like someone that only a fool would mess with. I'm tall to start with. Years of prison exercise, a few scars, shave my head, and I look like someone I wouldn't want to meet in an alley myself."

"The two men who identified you—did you know them?"

"Sort of. They were street corner homeboys. Not friends of mine, just to recognize. They had no reason to frame me, if that's what you're wonderin'."

As he had told Val, alliances can shift and change, especially in the drug culture. "Maybe they weren't after you in particular, but what if they were trying to protect a friend who looked something like you. Is that possible?"

Monroe looked startled, then intrigued. "Could be, but

hard to prove since one of 'em, Darrell Long, is dead. He served some prison time after fingering me. Maybe if you could find a cell mate of his, you might learn something more. Prison is so damn borin' that it's easy to spill your guts to anyone around who'll listen. Of course, it's easy to make up stories, too, which is why the word of a jailhouse snitch ain't worth much."

"Definitely worth checking. I'm still looking for the other witness, Joseph Cady. I can't find any evidence that he's dead or alive."

"His street name was Jumbo, if that helps. A skinny little guy."

Rob made a note. "It might."

As he continued asking questions and following them where they led, he wondered if any of these fragments might be the key that would unlock Daniel's prison.

CHAPTER 15

❧

ALL THE BIG SISTER/LITTLE SISTER PAPERWORK WAS complete, Val had attended the training classes, and she had passed the background checks. Finally it was time for the official match meeting. She and Lyssie were unusual in that they had met each other at the Big-for-a-Day picnic—usually matches were based on careful analysis by the case managers, and today would be the first meeting. But even though they had already met and connected, this was still a big event. Val spent as much time choosing her outfit as she had for the previous week's date with Rob.

Refusing to allow herself to be distracted by the fact that she would be seeing him in a few hours, she studied her closet. No power suits today. She wanted to look lady-like and responsible for Lyssie's grandmother, while ca-sual enough not to intimidate Lyssie. She settled on a long, flowing print skirt in cool blue cotton with a navy tank top and a loose chambray shirt with sleeves rolled halfway to the elbows—jacketlike but much less formal. Add navy sandals, and she was ready to go from the match meeting to the crime scene reenactment.

Match meetings were set in neutral places, in this case a

spiffy McDonald's restaurant with a playground attached. Val felt a shiver of nerves as she pulled the car into the restaurant lot. Representing the interests of legal clients was a big responsibility, but making a commitment to a child was much greater. Who was she to mentor a kid who had endured what Lyssie had?

Too late to back out now. This was just nerves, like waiting to make her opening statement in court. She entered the restaurant and saw that the other three had arrived and were sitting under the hanging plants in a sun porch–like room. Lyssie's grandmother was a heavy woman of indefinable ethnicity. Though very dark-skinned, her salt-and-pepper hair was straight and her features hinted at Asian or Native American blood.

With a smile, Val joined the others. "Lyssie, Anita, it's wonderful to see you." Turning to the older woman, she offered her hand. "Mrs. Armstrong?"

The older woman gave Val a swift, comprehensive examination that seemed to look through blood and bone to the soul. Apparently approving, she took Val's hand. "So I am." She had a lovely smile, full of wry wisdom. "It's a pleasure to meet you, Ms. Covington. I knew you were a good match for Lyssie as soon as she said the two of you could talk Harry Potter together."

Val laughed. "We have that and ultra-curly hair in common." She glanced at the table. "Shall we get a bite to eat, or at least something to drink? My treat."

Over sundaes and drinks according to taste, Anita outlined the responsibilities of all parties to the match, adding that she would always be available to discuss any problems that might arise. The case manager ended by saying, "Val and Lyssie, why don't you go outside and chat while Mrs. Armstrong and I have another coffee?"

"Good idea." Val got to her feet and glanced at Lyssie, who hadn't spoken except to answer questions.

Head down, Lyssie got to her feet and accompanied Val out to the colorful playground, which was empty of other children at midafternoon. Wearing blue shorts and a

T-shirt, Lyssie was all glasses and bony limbs and bushy dark hair.

As her new little sister fidgeted around the playground, Val plopped down on a large plastic hamburger. "Are you as nervous about this as I am?"

Lyssie glanced at her. "How can you be nervous? You're a rich lawyer."

"Being a lawyer mostly means that I'm good at acting because that's really handy in a courtroom, so today I'm acting as if I'm not nervous," Val explained. "Money is a really interesting, complicated topic since people are often judged on how much money they have. It's stupid, but that's how things are. I earn enough to feel sort of valuable, but I wasn't rich growing up, and I can't say that I feel rich now."

Interest caught, Lyssie asked, "What does rich feel like?"

"I think it means having enough money that you don't have to think about it. In college, I would think three times before buying a daily newspaper because even twenty-five cents was money I couldn't afford. But I never had to worry about whether I had enough money to eat, even if some weeks I lived on tuna noodle casserole. Now I can buy lots of things without having to think about it." Val grinned. "There's an old joke that says if you have to ask how much a yacht costs, you can't afford one. Maybe that's what rich means—never having to think about money. Which means anyone who doesn't worry about money can consider herself rich."

There was a hint of smile before Lyssie turned away, her thin shoulder blades sharp against her yellow T-shirt. "I've always had enough to eat."

"To some people, that would seem rich." What to say next? Val had counted, wrongly, on the way they had clicked at their first meeting. But Lyssie was a guarded, wary child, and one brief meeting did not a relationship make.

Hoping honesty would help, Val said, "Lawyer or not, I

feel nervous. We've signed contracts that say we're going to try to become part of each other's lives. This means more than taking you to movies or the aquarium or a mall. It means sharing thoughts and ideas and interests. It will be great if it works, but if not, it will be pretty darned uncomfortable. I think we can make this match work, but we're both entitled to be nervous. I probably look like a bossy do-gooder, while I can't help wondering if you'll prove too tough for a wimp like me. Drugs or gangs or something."

"No drugs. Ever. My father did drugs." Lyssie's voice was granite hard. "No gangs, either. I don't have friends."

Val felt a disabling wave of tenderness. Reminding herself that she was supposed to be a friend and mentor, not a parent, she said, "Then we can skip worrying about drugs and go to the fun stuff. After all, sisters are supposed to have fun together."

She drew her knees up and looped her arms around them, her long skirt falling over her ankles. "What would you like to do together? I like to cook. Would you like to try some cooking or baking? Or if you think you'd like gardening, we could take a shot at that, though it's a bit late in the season to start." When the girl just shrugged, Val said, "Your turn to make a suggestion."

Lyssie tugged a curly lock straight. "We can read together."

"Flopping down in my den to read our separate books will be fun, but there are other kinds of reading fun. A friend of mine founded a mother-daughter reading club. Each month, everyone reads the same book, and then they talk about it. She says they have some great discussions, and everyone learns from each other. Members take turns suggesting the books."

"Other girls?" Lyssie didn't look enthused.

Guessing why, Val said, "They're girls who like books, which is a good start to making friends. Shall I look into it and find out when they get together? They've done all kinds of books, including Harry Potter."

Lyssie nodded, looking mildly interested. Encouraged,

Val said, "Do you like making things? I used to love doing craft projects, but I've gotten too busy. I need an excuse to do them again."

Lyssie met Val's gaze fleetingly. "That might be okay."

"Shall we schedule a trip to a big craft store for our first outing? I'd like to do it next Saturday if that's okay with you."

Lyssie nodded, and this time there was a shy smile.

SINCE ANITA HAD DRIVEN LYSSIE AND HER GRAND-mother to the meeting, Val volunteered to drive them home. The small but impeccably neat Armstrong row house was in a neighborhood near Sinai Hospital, about fifteen minutes from Val's house. When Val pulled up, Lyssie climbed out of the car and skipped into the house, but Mrs. Armstrong lingered. "Be patient with her," she said softly. "Life hasn't been easy for my grandbaby."

"I understand," Val replied. "Don't worry—I know this will take time. She's a very special little girl to have endured what she has so well."

"She hides in her books."

"There are worse places to hide. Books and cats have been good friends to me."

"You have cats? Lyssie will like that. She dotes on my old tabby." Mrs. Armstrong's smile faded. "She's all I have left, Ms. Covington, and I don't know if I can be as strong as she needs. That's why I want her to have someone like you."

"I'll do my best, but I warn you, I haven't had a lot of experience with little girls since I was one myself. And please, call me Val."

"You've got a good heart, and you take her seriously, just as she is. That's what any child needs. Any person, really. I was a home health care aide for years, and the first thing anyone needs is to be taken seriously, and treated with kindness." She opened the car door. "Call me Louise, Val. I hope we'll be seeing each other regularly."

"If it's all right with you, Lyssie and I were thinking of getting together next Saturday and making a raid on a craft store."

"Oh, that's good. Let her use her imagination to make things." Louise climbed from the car, but turned back to say, "It's a good beginning. Thank you, Val."

As Val drove off, she realized that more was being asked than in a typical Big/Little match. Anita had said that Louise's health was poor. Diabetes, maybe? Perhaps she had put Lyssie into the Big Sister/Little Sister program in hopes of providing stability if something happened to her.

Hoping Louise's health improved, Val turned the car and headed toward the Kensington neighborhood. Time to think about murder.

KENDRA WAS FEELING A MITE BIT TWITCHY WHEN she met Rob and Val in the Crabtown shopping center so they could do their crime scene reenactment. Her nerves were temporarily forgotten when she saw Rob. "Man, did you run into a buzz saw? You sure look different without the beard."

"So everyone says," he said dryly. "Val still hasn't forgiven me."

"I've always loved teddy bears and beards." Val grinned at her paramour. "But I'm adjusting."

It shouldn't be hard to adjust to a guy as good-looking as Rob. Not liking beards herself, Kendra had thought him merely pleasant when he was shaggy. Clean-shaven, he was definitely hot. Not that she noticed except intellectually, of course.

She glanced around the shopping center parking lot, noting cracked asphalt and a couple of empty storefronts. She hadn't been here since Daniel was convicted—she had moved out of that cursed apartment as soon as she could. The neighborhood was in pretty good shape, but returning depressed her. "You're in charge of this party, Rob. What do you want us to do?"

"Let's start at your old apartment. I'd like to get a sense of the layout. You tell us everything you did that night. Then I want to go to the murder scene and walk through what happened. Maybe it will give us some new ideas. Maybe not. But it's worth a try."

Kendra nodded, and they walked the two blocks to her former home. The building had started as a pair of semi-detached houses. Later each had been divided into two small apartments. She and Daniel had lived in the upper apartment of the right-hand house. There was a nice-sized yard with a magnolia tree and impatiens blooming in the shade, but she shivered when she looked up at the curtained windows of her old home.

"This must be upsetting," Val said quietly.

"An understatement." Kendra wrapped her arms around herself, though the late afternoon air was warm. "Yet it was a happy place when we lived here—quiet, hardwood floors, a nice yard. My baby took his first steps in the kitchen. Daniel was getting his act together, and we sure had some good times, right up until . . ." She bit her lip, remembering the pounding on the door when the police came to take her man away. Val touched her arm sympathetically.

Rob said, "When I talked to Detective Barkley, he said you were bathing the baby so Monroe could have left and returned without you noticing. Is that possible?"

"In theory." Kendra pointed upward. "That little window on the side of the house is the bathroom where I washed Jason. The entrance to the apartment was at the back of the house—that sidewalk leads around to it. Daniel could have gone down without me seeing, but that evening we were talking on and off. He was all excited because his boss wanted to promote him, so we were both in a good mood."

She forced herself to recall events she had tried to forget. "About halfway through bathing Jason, Daniel came into the bathroom and gave me a glass of beer. He was making a suggestive comment when the baby splashed water over both of us. We laughed about it and Daniel went to change his shirt. There weren't more than a couple of minutes at a time when I didn't know right where he was." She hadn't known that it was the last time they would be together as a family.

"Barkley didn't mention any of that. He seemed to think you were busy with the baby and not noticing anything else."

Kendra's mouth twisted. "He had decided I was lying, so anything that didn't fit his theory he ignored. After Jason was washed and dried, I put him to bed. His crib was in the corner of the living room. We were thinking about getting a larger place soon, when . . . when we got married. After I put the baby down, Daniel and I—well, we went to bed, too, but not to sleep. We had just gotten up and put on some clothes, and I was going to rustle up a snack when the cops came."

"What time was that?"

"A little before nine o'clock. A TV show we liked came on then, and I was trying to think what I had in the kitchen that would fix up fast so we could watch the show while we ate."

"The murder took place just before eight, so the police moved fast," Rob observed. "Onward to the crime scene. Kendra, what do you think would be the most logical route for Daniel between here and the site of the shooting? I want to see how long it takes to cover the distance."

"Will you question along the route to see if anyone saw a running man that evening?" Kendra asked. "I'm sure that the police never questioned anyone."

Rob shook his head. "Maybe if I had the time and manpower, but it wouldn't help our case. The time for questions was then. Everyone for blocks around the murder should have been questioned because the murderer ran somewhere, though not necessarily in this direction. Not much point in doing it now."

"Now what would the best route be?" Kendra oriented herself before setting off at a brisk walk down the block. She turned left, then crossed the street and cut into the alley that ran down the middle of the next block between narrow fenced backyards and a few small garages. "We used this alley a lot," she explained to her companions. "It would have been the most natural way for Daniel."

As she led the way, she admitted to herself that this was probably an exercise in futility, but physical activity gave her the feeling that she was doing something useful.

FIVE MINUTES OF WALKING BROUGHT THEM TO THE scene of the crime. It was a quiet street of brick row houses with cars parked in a solid line on both sides, leaving a narrow driving lane in between. Each house had a small roofed porch several steps above street level, most adorned with hanging plants and kids' toys.

Rob had visited before, but his skin still crawled. This street seemed too quiet, too safe, for murder. "It took us five minutes to walk, so a fit young man could have run the distance in a couple of minutes. I suppose that supported Barkley's theory." He stopped under a sycamore in the middle of the block. "It happened right here."

"There ought to be a black mark on the sidewalk or a cross. Something else to say that a man died here." Kendra turned slowly, scanning the quiet street. "I never came here after the shooting. Couldn't stand the thought. You have the police files, Rob. Exactly what happened?"

"That's what we're going to walk through. Val, will you play the part of Brenda Harris? She was heading east on this side of the street. She had gotten off work and taken a bus home, and she was tired. Not paying a lot of attention to her surroundings because she was almost home and felt safe." Rob scanned the street. "Even now there aren't a lot of lights on the block. The assailant was lurking in this cross alley. It was pretty dark and a bit chilly—dusk on a cloudy day. A lot of people would have been eating supper, so the street was almost empty.

"Kendra, would you cross the street to the second house from the end? That's where Malloy was when Brenda Harris was attacked. He had been patrolling around the Crabtown center and decided to visit the residential streets nearby so he wouldn't be too predictable. He was conscientious. When I pull Val back into the alley, you come running as if you've heard her scream."

Kendra trotted across the street while Rob withdrew into the alley and waited for Val. Getting into her part, Val trudged along the sidewalk with her head down, a tired woman at the end of a long day.

Rob tried to put himself in the mind of the assailant. Maybe he was hopped up with some kind of drug, itchy inside his skin, looking for trouble. Here comes a woman, youngish, not bad-looking, not watching what was going on. An easy mark.

He darted from the alley. A half dozen steps to grab her. She stiffened in his grip. "Should I fight?"

He looked down at her small face, felt her petite body between his clamped hands. How could any man wish to injure an innocent woman? God, how would he feel if someone attacked Val? Brenda Harris had a husband and two children. How had they been affected by the incident? "If you like, but not too hard. No one gets hurt tonight."

She began to wriggle and flail, but he easily overpowered her and forced her back into the alley. He imagined himself as the kind of man who was aroused by resistance. He was excited by what he was doing, not thinking about consequences. "Brenda wasn't as small as you, but she wasn't huge, either. The attacker clamped his hand over her mouth, but she managed to turn her head and call for help just as he was getting her out of sight of the street."

He signaled to Kendra, who raced toward them with the grace of a natural athlete. As she joined them, she snapped, "Halt in the name of the law!"

"The bad guy swears and slams Brenda down so hard she's stunned." He set Val aside and whipped around to face Kendra, imagining rage at the sheer bad luck that put a cop on the scene.

"You try to pull me away, but you've gotten too close.

I'm bigger than you and a lot meaner, so I slug you in the jaw. You reel back and before you can go for your weapon, I pull out my fancy European handgun." Rob whipped out a purple plastic water pistol from the small of his back, where it had been concealed by his jacket. "I blast you in the head at point-blank range, and you fall to the ground."

Miming shock and horror, Kendra dropped onto the narrow edging of lawn. Rob aimed the empty water pistol into the grass, unable to point even a toy weapon at another human. "*Bang, bang, bang, bang, bang.*"

Heavy silence fell, along with aching awareness that a young man had died here, a victim of casual, meaningless violence. A hole had been left in the lives of everyone who knew him. Complete strangers had mourned the loss of a brave man who had sought to serve and protect. Kendra and her son's lives had been changed irrevocably.

The silence was broken by a husky voice saying, "Then you ran back into the alley, swearing."

CHAPTER 16

✥

STARTLED, VAL GLANCED UP FROM HER SPOT ON the grass to see a white-haired man smoking a pipe on the porch of the right-hand house. "You know what we're doing?"

The man exhaled a mouthful of aromatic apple smoke. "You're acting out the Malloy murder."

Val got to her feet, brushing off her full skirt. "If you lived here then, did you see something?" The police files hadn't mentioned that a neighbor saw the shooting.

"I heard a scream and came out just as the first bullet was fired, so I ducked back into the house and called nine-one-one. All I said was that I heard shots. I didn't want to get involved, so I told myself that I hadn't seen enough to tell the police anything useful." The man drew on the pipe again. "Now I'm kinda sorry I didn't speak up."

"But you heard him swearing and saw which way the shooter ran?" Rob asked.

"I could hear his voice through an open window, and I saw him run off, but I was looking through curtains so I couldn't see much except the direction he was moving." His gaze moved to the cracked asphalt of the alley. "In all the years since, I've never once come or gone from the house without thinking of what happened here."

"How do you stand it?" Kendra asked softly.

The old man sighed. "You can get used to anything. What are you all up to? Odd sort of thing to do for fun."

"I'm the lawyer representing the man who was convicted of the murder," Val explained. "We're investigating his possible innocence, so we're walking through the crime to get a better feel for what happened. You say the killer ran back into the cross alley. Did you have any sense of his build, or the way he moved?"

"Tall. Broad. Probably young because he sure moved fast. As I said, nothing useful." He gestured with the stem of his pipe. "Once the killer ran back there, he could continue straight across to the next block, or turn north or south behind the houses. By the time the police arrived, he could have been anywhere."

Rob asked, "Did you see the two men who were witnesses?"

"Nope." He pointed the pipe stem again, down the street to the left. "They were supposed to be down there."

Noting the wording, Val asked, "Did you have any reason to doubt their claims?"

The older man snorted. "They were a couple of useless troublemakers who were regulars at a crack house round the corner. When they testified at the trial, the prosecutor made 'em both out to be Boy Scouts, but they weren't. I wouldn't believe either of 'em if they said the sun rises in the east."

"You're saying they were unreliable witnesses?" Val asked, interest quickening.

"Yeah, but no one asked my opinion." The old man emptied the charred embers of his pipe into an ashtray on the railing. "I don't know any more now than I did then. But whoever killed Malloy deserves to die." With that, he went inside.

Rob looked at his notes with a frown. "The report implies that one of the policemen recognized Daniel from the description so they went right to the apartment, but the report is ambiguously written. Maybe it wasn't a policeman who originally fingered him."

Guessing where his thoughts were going, Val said, "Do you think one of those helpful eyewitnesses could have suggested Daniel? I'm using my imagination here, but what if they recognized the shooter as some kind of buddy of theirs? To cover for him, they might have decided to throw blame on Daniel. It would be easy to stick to the story if they agreed on the details in advance."

"Your theory would explain a lot," Rob said thoughtfully. "Assume that Brenda Harris was mistaken, which is very possible given the circumstances. If she was wrong, and the other two witnesses colluded in a lie, the whole case against Daniel collapses. But how the heck can we prove it with Darrell Long dead and Joe Cady vanished?"

"Maybe I can help with Cady." Kendra gazed along the darkening street. "If the guys were down there, they couldn't see much unless there were no cars parked along the street, and in row house neighborhoods like this, there are always cars parked."

"Val, come with me. I want to see how much was visible from there."

Silently Val took Rob's hand and they crossed to the second house from the end. The reenactment was depressing her, and she felt better touching him. When they reached the right spot, Rob turned and looked back at Kendra. "In this light and with the cars in the way, it's almost impossible to see any detail."

"I can't see anything," Val said. "I wonder how tall Long and Cady were?"

"Taller than you." Rob caught her around the knees, boosting her up so she was perched on his shoulder.

She clutched at head and arms, both alarmed and amused. He knew how to sweep a girl off her feet. "Even this high, I can't see much except that someone's standing there. Since Kendra is wearing slacks, I couldn't even swear to the gender. It's hard to believe those two crack-heads saw anything."

"I suppose they might have recognized the shooter by the way he moved or dressed." Carefully Rob set Val back on the pavement. "But no way did they see his face clearly."

Val frowned as they rejoined Kendra. "We need a lot more than the possibility they were lying to get Daniel off. Has inspiration struck about finding Joe Cady?"

"I know someone who might know where Cady is. Care to have dinner at a soul food bistro?" Kendra smiled a little. "Even if I'm wrong, you'll get the best smothered pork chops and peach cobbler in Baltimore."

"It's a deal," Rob said. "Where is the restaurant?"

"On the west side. I'll take you in my car," Kendra said. "Your pickup would be tight for three, and Val, you do not want to take your Lexus into this neighborhood."

"Okay, you drive and I'll pick up the check. Now that I'm becoming self-employed, I'm up for deducting everything I can find."

"Deducting all possible expenses is the first rule of self-employment," Rob said as he slung his arm around her shoulders. "It took me years to remember that after I started my business."

As the three of them walked back to the shopping center where the cars were parked, Val burrowed as close to his side as she could get and still manage to walk. The reenactment had given them more information and theories, but gloomily she recognized that they were no closer to saving Daniel Monroe.

ALL THREE OF THEM WERE SILENT AS KENDRA DROVE to West Baltimore. For her, the visit to her old home had stirred up memories both bittersweet and angry. She had mostly kept her fury under control since Daniel's arrest and conviction; a girl struggling to better herself and care for her child couldn't afford to waste energy on anger. But her rage at the injustice still burned, scalding hot, at the bottom of her soul.

She was glad to find a street parking spot only a block and a half from the restaurant. Though the neighborhood had improved in recent years, suburbia it wasn't. As they climbed from the car, Val surveyed their surroundings. "You're right. I don't want to bring my Lexus into this neighborhood."

"It isn't as bad as it looks." Kendra locked the car doors. "The city has put a lot of money into this area and new businesses are opening now that most of the drug dealing has been shut down. Not the sort of place where partners of Crouse, Resnick are usually found, though." She was glad to be with Rob. No smart mugger would tackle a group that included him. Once a Marine, always a Marine.

Though the sun had set, the air was still oppressively hot. Summertime in the city. When she was a kid, nights like this she and her parents would sit on the marble front steps of the house, enjoying the occasional breath of cool air and chatting lazily with neighbors. She had been too young to realize that she was living the good old days.

The restaurant, Soul Survivors, was in an old row house next to a small storefront church with a very long name. The restaurant seemed larger inside than it looked from the street, with exposed brick walls and colorful primitive paintings of Southern life. Kendra breathed in the wickedly tempting scents of a soul food kitchen. She'd kept her distance from the restaurant for a long time, and it was good to be back. "This place smells like my grandmother's house."

As always on a Saturday night, the dining room was packed. Below the chattering voices a lazy piano could be heard playing classic jazz. Kendra was amused to observe Val, who was absorbing every detail while doing her best not to look as if she was gawking. Apart from her and Rob, there was only one other white couple, and actually, they were kind of brown. For a liberal, Val hadn't seen enough of life.

A hostess dressed in colorful African cotton approached. "Welcome. The dining room is full, but if you want dinner, there's a table downstairs."

"Perfect." Kendra followed the hostess to the narrow stairway that descended to the bistro, a cozy, low-ceilinged room with more exposed brick and a performance area at the far end. On the shallow dais, a white-haired man played honey-sweet jazz piano, music soft enough to allow thought, seductive enough to reward closer listening.

When they were seated, Kendra asked the hostess, "Would you ask Luke to stop by when we get to coffee and dessert? Tell him it's Kendra Brooks."

The hostess nodded and left. As Val studied her menu, Kendra said, "Don't try to eat healthy here, Val. Nothing on this menu is intended to be healthy."

"I noticed." Val grinned at the specials of the day. "I eat rabbit food regularly so I can indulge now and then. Bring on the smothered pork chops!"

The food was as good as Kendra remembered, simple but perfectly prepared traditional Southern cooking. All three of them attacked it with gusto, right down to the peach cobbler with rich homemade ice cream. It was hard to be angry when you'd just eaten an orgasmic dessert.

They were working on second cups of coffee and Val had paid the check, but still no Luke. Kendra was beginning to wonder if he wouldn't speak to her when a tall, broad-shouldered man picked his way between the closely-spaced tables. As always she was struck by how much Luke resembled Daniel though they were only half brothers.

There was no pleasure in his face at seeing her. She got to her feet warily. "It's good to see you, Luke. Pull up a chair and sit for a spell."

His eyes narrowed. "It's been a long time."

"Too long."

"Whose fault is that?" His deep voice was also like

Daniel's. "Have you ever told that boy of yours who his real father is? Or is he still an ignorant bastard?"

Good old Luke. Kendra was tempted to slug him, but she controlled the impulse. "Watch who you call bastard, Luke. If your parents were married, this is the first I've heard of it. You know why I didn't tell Jason. Do you think he would have been better off knowing his real daddy was convicted of murder?"

"If there's one thing I learned in rehab, it's that honesty is essential."

"In principle, maybe, but it's already hard to raise a black boy in this city. I didn't want to make things worse. Jason has always been a great kid, but other great kids have been lost to the streets."

Luke grimaced. Like Daniel, he was always fair-minded. "You got a point there, but he's my nephew, Kendra. I want to get to know him."

Her voice softened. "Someday, Luke. But if he ever met you, all he'd have to do is look in the mirror to start wondering about his daddy, and start asking questions Phil and I didn't want to answer."

"When will *someday* come?"

Kendra had thought about this over the years. "When he's twenty-one. I swear I'll tell him, Luke. And . . . I appreciate that you've respected my wishes on this and not contacted Jason directly."

"It was Daniel's wishes I respected." His expression eased. "I guess your way worked since the boy's at the Air Force Academy. I didn't think much of officers when I was a grunt in Vietnam, but now the academy sounds good. You must be proud of him."

"I am, and so is Daniel." She grinned. "Since we haven't hit each other, will you sit down now? These are my friends Val Covington and Rob Smith. Val and Rob, meet Luke Wilson, Daniel's brother, who runs this fine establishment with his wife, Angel."

Rob stood to shake hands. "Pleased to meet you, Mr. Wilson. That's a strong resemblance to your brother."

"Call me Luke. Danno and I are only half brothers, but we both look like our Mama, God rest her soul." The chair squeaked under his weight as he took the fourth seat at the table and signaled the waiter for coffee. "How's it hangin', Kendra? Somehow I doubt you came just for the chicken fried steak."

"Val is my boss," Kendra explained, "and she's agreed to make a last-ditch attempt to get Daniel's sentence commuted."

Hope and doubt passed over Luke's face. "Any chance of that?"

"I honestly don't know, Luke," Val said soberly. "Daniel didn't want us to get involved, and he only agreed to cooperate for Kendra's sake. I won't lie—it will take something major to get your brother off death row. But so little investigation was done at the time that maybe we have a chance to turn up strong new evidence. Rob has been working on that almost full-time."

She glanced at Rob. Taking her cue, he said, "That's why we're here. Tonight we visited the crime scene, and we're wondering if the two male witnesses might have colluded to cast the blame on Daniel to save some friend of theirs."

"That's why I thought of you, Luke." Kendra leaned forward intently. "Darrell Long is dead and Rob hasn't been able to locate Joe Cady. You ran with that crowd. Any idea where we might look for Joe? Is he still alive?"

Luke frowned and scratched inside one elbow, where the faint scars of old needle tracks showed under his short-sleeved shirt. He was in a position to know that basically decent kids could go off the rails if they succumbed to the dangerous lure of the streets.

"Joe was an addict who never came clean, and he was in and out of jail. I haven't seen him for years, but I heard a couple of weeks ago that he's dying of AIDS. I don't know where." His gaze dropped to the needle scars. "Some of us were lucky with needles. Joe wasn't. Not a bad guy, but if Darrell told him to lie, he would."

"Assuming our theory is true, do you have any idea who they might have wanted to protect?" Rob asked quietly. "Someone who looked a little like your brother?"

"I've thought about that. I even suggested it to the cops after Danno was arrested, but they blew me off." Luke began rubbing at the scars again. "A couple of cousins ran the nearby crack house. Omar and Ike Benson. Both of 'em were tall, tough-looking guys, and they carried guns. Easy to imagine either one assaulting a woman and shooting a cop who tried to stop it. Since they controlled the neighborhood crack supply, Darrell and Joe might have figured it was worth getting on their good side."

Rob wrote down their names. "The Bensons were mentioned to me before. Time I looked them up. Any idea where they might be now?"

"Both dead. Omar was knifed in the Pen, and Ike was shot a few years later when a drug deal went bad. Another guy who worked for them, Shooter Williams, fit the same general description. Hell, if you don't insist on much resemblance to Danno, there were plenty of homeboys drifting in and out of that crack house who might have done a rape and a murder if they were high."

"We haven't time to look at them all." Rob added the new name. "I'd like to start with Joe Cady, if he's still alive." He pulled out a business card and handed it over. "If you get any more ideas, let me know."

"I'll do that. I'll ask Angel, too." Luke pocketed the card. To Val and Rob, he said, "My wife is my angel for sure. Without her, I never would have managed to stay straight, and I sure wouldn't have this business. She's the genius in the kitchen."

"Say hi to Angel and the kids for me, Luke," Kendra said. "You're a lucky man."

"Don't I know it." His gaze went to her face with some of the warmth they had once shared when they were practically in-laws. "Will you do me a favor, Kendra? Sing a couple of songs before you go."

Luke was thinking of the old days. "It's been years

since I did club singing," Kendra said uncertainly. "Your customers deserve better."

"Don't sing for them. Sing for me and Angel." His voice was soft and coaxing, just like Daniel when he wanted something.

"Okay, Luke. For you and Angel." As Luke left the table and went upstairs, Kendra buried her head in her hands for a moment as she mentally shifted back twenty years to the days when she was young and carefree and full of dreams.

When she recaptured that feeling, she tunneled her fingers through her hair to loosen it, then stood and gave her head a shake so that the dark mass danced wantonly around her shoulders. Though her slacks and shirt were casual, the slacks revealed her long athlete's legs and as she strolled to the dais she undid the top buttons of her shirt to show off what the good Lord gave her. She didn't have to see a mirror to know that she didn't look like an uptown paralegal anymore.

She waited until the pianist finished his piece, then conferred with him. His name was Ernie and she'd known him once in another lifetime. After they agreed on three songs, he handed her a microphone, and she turned to face the bistro full of diners.

Val was staring in round-eyed amazement while Rob had the expression that meant he'd just realized Kendra was hot, the way she had noticed him earlier. She grinned and waved at them, swaying to the beat as Ernie played the intro to her first song.

The shape of the mike was as familiar as if she had last sung in a club yesterday. Her first choice was "Body and Soul," a Billie Holiday standard song for lost love. What woman, or man, for that matter, hadn't felt the same way? In a voice plangent with yearning, Kendra sang the sorrows of her life—the losses of her mother, her lover, her husband—but she also sang as an indomitable survivor. Black women personified the blues, because they had suffered and endured and found new joys.

As Kendra sang, the chatter in the room quieted and

people turned to listen. Luke and Angel, his pretty, rounded wife, appeared at the bottom of the stairs and stood swaying together, arms around each other's waists.

When the song ended, Kendra bowed her head during the applause, feeling the heady rush that came with capturing her audience. After a glance at Ernie, she broke into a lively version of "Ain't Nobody's Business If I Do." The room began filling with diners from upstairs, some carrying drinks or coffee cups.

This time, the clapping threatened to loosen the bricks in the walls. She grinned and waited for the sound to die down before she signaled Ernie to begin her last selection. She had chosen to close with a raucous, high-energy rendition of "I Will Survive," a female power song written long after Billie Holiday's soulful laments.

At the end she bowed from the waist, laughing with intoxicated pleasure. Then she returned to her companions, refusing requests to sing more. "Time to go."

Val stood. "I never knew you could sing!"

"These days, I stick to gospel singing at church. Just as much fun, and it praises the Lord. Now let's scoot."

With Rob to cut a path, they made their way through the crowd. When they passed Luke, he took her hand. "Come back anytime, Kendra. Anytime at all."

"Thanks. Maybe I'll visit more often." Kendra gave Angel a long, warm hug. "I've missed you and the kids, sister friend."

"Then come back to us, girl," Angel said softly. "I know why you stayed away, but it's time to come home."

Blinking back tears, Kendra made her way up the steps and outside. The night seemed cool after the intimate warmth of the restaurant. Once they were outside, Val said, "Kendra, why aren't you singing professionally?"

"I'm good but not great." She shrugged, though a smile lingered. "I did a little club singing a long time ago, but it's no life if you have a child. That's why I only sing in the choir, or for myself."

"I've got the church, so I expect you to sing!"

Laughing, the three of them headed toward the car. Rob said, "Thanks for taking us there. Not only did we get some good leads, but that's a terrific place."

"Now that I've made my peace with Luke, I can go back again. I've missed Angel's cooking."

"I want to duplicate that cobbler," Val said. "Would Angel give me the recipe?"

"Not a chance!"

"I think there was a hint of cardamom." Brow furrowed, Val paused to get a pebble out of her sandal while the other two walked ahead. The real trick was having fresh, luscious peaches and using cornmeal for the cake part . . .

On the dimly lit street, she didn't even see the shape emerge from the alley until her shoulder bag was wrenched away. As she stumbled off balance, a hard shove between her shoulder blades knocked her to the pavement. From the corner of her eyes, she saw the flash of a blade.

She didn't even have the breath to scream.

CHAPTER 17

❧

"LUKE SEEMS LIKE A GOOD GUY," ROB SAID. "AND useful, too. Thanks for taking us to meet him."

Kendra sighed, her long strides matching his. "Hearing about all those young black men who died—it breaks my heart. Most of them weren't born bad. Instead, they were raised badly, made bad choices, and died before they had time to grow up."

"It's tragic." Rob thought of how his own brother went wrong, and how Sha'wan Baker could have gone off the rails but hadn't. "Your son has done well, though, thanks to good parenting. There are plenty of other dedicated parents who do equally well. Kids have to be saved one at a time."

Kendra was about to reply when Val gave a strangled cry behind them. Rob spun around to see her sprawled on the pavement, a lanky form bolting away with her handbag.

Instinctively he went after the mugger. After a dozen swift strides, he managed to catch the long strap of the handbag. Unwilling to let it go, the mugger jerked to a stop, then swung around and slashed at his assailant with a wickedly gleaming blade. Rob dodged and caught his attacker's wrist, twisting it with crushing force.

Rob was forcing the thief to his knees when a moan from Val distracted him for an instant. The mugger seized the moment to abandon the handbag and escape. Rob considered pursuit, but Val was more important. He went to her, damning himself for letting his attention wander in a rough neighborhood.

Kendra helped Val sit up. To Rob she said, "You're good at that macho stuff."

"If I were better, it wouldn't have happened." Rob dropped to his knees beside the two women, heart pounding. "Are you all right, Val?"

She gave a shaky laugh as he put his arm behind her. "I think so. Took some skin off my hand when I hit the pavement, and that kid scared me out of a year's growth, but he didn't try to use his knife on me."

"Did you get a look at him?" Rob pulled out his handkerchief and dabbed at Val's abraded left hand, which had taken the brunt of her fall. Thank God she hadn't been seriously injured. He thought about the mugger's knife and felt ill.

"It all happened so fast." Val's expression changed. "You know, the lighting here is similar to where Malloy was killed. I couldn't describe anything about the mugger except an impression that he was a tall, thin, young black man. I can't say anything about his face, or his age, or his clothes except that they were sort of loose and sort of dark. No wonder Brenda Harris had trouble making an identification when she saw the police lineup. Everything happened quickly, and she was badly rattled. I wouldn't be able to identify this vicious little toad, either."

Rob had to laugh. "Your brain never quits, does it?"

"Afraid not."

With Rob's help, Val got to her feet. He kept his arm around her. Despite her calm words, she was shaking violently.

"After this, I'm absolutely convinced that the eyewitnesses who fingered Daniel were lying." Val accepted her handbag from Kendra. "Rob, I want to be there for the Joe Cady interview, assuming he's still alive. We might not get another chance."

Kendra pulled out her cell phone. "I'll call nine-one-one."

"Don't bother. There's no longer an emergency," Val said dryly. "I didn't see enough to describe the mugger, I got my handbag back, and no one was hurt. It's just an unsuccessful purse snatching. I doubt the police could or would do much."

"It should be reported," Rob said. "Muggers don't strike only once."

With a sigh, Val agreed and Kendra called the police. A patrol car was there in minutes, but as Val had predicted, there wasn't much to be done. The policemen said there had been other purse snatchings in the area, and if they caught a suspect they would like Val to come and take a look. She promised to do that, but for now she wanted to go home. She stayed within the circle of Rob's arm the whole time.

It was only half a block to Kendra's car. When they reached it, Rob climbed in on the passenger side, then pulled Val into his lap. She cuddled against him gratefully.

Kendra locked the doors and pulled away from the curb. "On the surface, nothing happened tonight except that Val got shaken up. She didn't even lose her wallet. But confidence and trust and feeling safe have taken a hit for all of us."

Rob stroked Val's springy hair. "I shouldn't have let this happen," he said softly.

"Cut that out," Val said, her voice stronger. "You are not responsible for the world. I violated all the rules of safety by falling behind, not watching my surroundings, and generally looking like an easy mark. No wonder that kid came after me."

"It's a bitch that we live in a world where safety means always having to be alert, but that's the way it is," Kendra added.

Rob smiled wryly. "You are two tough chicks. Can't I wallow in my inadequacy for not defending you the way a macho man should?"

"No!" the women said in chorus.

"Fear and alertness are more natural than feeling secure," Val mused. "Ancestors who didn't dodge saber-toothed tigers became lunch. They were the quick or the dead."

All very articulate, but Val's small body still felt chilly in his embrace. "I like to think we're evolving beyond that."

"It's a slow process," she said wearily.

Too damned slow.

HOME WAS LIKE SAFE, SHELTERING ARMS. VAL SIGHED with relief when she stepped inside. As she bent to pet Lilith, who was stropping her ankles, Rob said, "I hope you don't want me to go, because I do not want to leave you alone tonight."

"I don't want that either." She turned gratefully into his arms. "One lousy little failed purse snatching, and I'm still shaking. What a wimp."

"Violence is like a stone in a pond that sends ripples in all directions." His comforting hand stroked down her back. "It cracks the world."

She guessed he had learned that too early from his stepfather. He'd dealt with violence as a child, in the Marines, with his brother, and in the work he did on Baltimore's meaner streets. Her life had been mercifully sheltered by comparison. She raised her head. "Would you like a glass of wine? I'm tempted to stress the air-conditioning by lighting a fire even though it's high summer. Fires are comforting."

"And they keep the saber-tooths away. Do you need help treating those brush burns on your hand?" When she shook her head, he continued, "Then I'll get the fire going while you take care of the wine and bandages."

Nerves unwinding, she went to the kitchen. None of her scrapes were deep, so she spread salve on the raw skin, covered it with a light dressing, and poured two glasses of wine. In the den, flames were starting to lick at the logs in the fireplace. Rob was crouched on one knee, watching, the flickering light playing across the planes of his face.

She realized that she no longer felt that he was an elusive chameleon. Whether he was a bearded cuddle bear or a chiseled executive, she was coming to understand him pretty well. A man of conscience and integrity, humor and guilt. A man who was complicated and very human. Glad he was here, she turned the lights down and settled on the sofa, shoes off and one leg tucked under her. "This is nice. Thanks."

His gaze still on the fire, Rob said, "Would you like to live together?"

She choked on her wine. "Where did that come from?"

He glanced up, his expression somber. "It seems like the next logical step. My apartment is too small, so I could buy a house here in Homeland to prove that I'm not just after you for your real estate. There's a FOR SALE sign on a terrific looking place over on Springlake. It's another Tudor house and has a nice view of the ponds. You could move back here if you decided you couldn't stand living with me."

She stared at him. "You are definitely moving too fast for me."

"I'd love an excuse to buy a house. I had a condo in California because I didn't want to be responsible for anything except my business." He adjusted a log with the tongs, then uncoiled from his spot by the fire. "You're looking at me as if I'm nuts. Do you hate the idea of living together that much?"

She hesitated, trying the idea out for size and wondering why his suggestion made her want to bolt. "I've never lived with anyone before, though a couple of times in the midst of a hot and heavy affair, there was a sort of de facto cohabitation."

"How very legalistic."

Regretting her choice of words, she asked, "Isn't this a bit sudden?"

"Perhaps." He began pacing with short, taut steps. "I've never felt like this with anyone else, Val, and I've wanted to get it right. Not too quick, not too slow, but just right, like Goldilocks. Then that mugger went after you, and now I have this enormously primitive desire to stay close and defend you, sort of like a glorified Doberman pinscher."

"The cats wouldn't like that." Though she had imbibed feminism with her mother's milk, his desire to take care of her was appealing, not to mention sexy. "But I like the idea of having a protector. I've always been responsible for my own defense."

His expression eased. "Then I'll try for attack tiger. It's not just protectiveness, of course. I love being with you. I love the idea of spending all my available time with you. And . . . I want to give this relationship every chance."

Beginning to feel uneasy with his seriousness, she said, "It's a scientific fact that people who live together before marriage are more likely to divorce than those who don't, so if you're looking at the long-term, shacking up is probably not the way to go."

He looked startled. "Maybe in that case we should . . ."

She cut him off, afraid of what he might say. "It's too soon, Rob, and there's too much going on. If we moved in together, it would take time and thought and energy, all of which are in short supply now. Ditto on buying a house. How about we revisit the subject after . . . after Sept. ninth?" The date scheduled for Daniel Monroe's execution.

Rob hesitated, then nodded. "Okay. This is too important to treat casually."

"But in the meantime, dating is good. Becoming a couple is good." Wanting to move the conversation to more comfortable territory, she set her wine aside and rose from the sofa to corner him by the bookcase. "I think my subconscious had a hidden agenda when I decided a fire would be nice." She wrapped her arms around his neck and murmured, "The rug in front of the fireplace is very comfortable."

Gently he lifted her left hand and brushed his lips across the dressing that covered the abraded skin, his touch so light it caused no pain. "Are you sure you're up for this? You had a bad experience tonight."

"Nothing would make me feel better or safer than making love with you, Rob." Before he could suffer another attack of nobility, she rose on her toes and kissed him.

The tensions of the evening flared into passion, and in moments they were ripping at each other's clothing. Her lingering distress over the mugging vanished, seared away as she pulled him down on the fireplace rug.

She gasped as his mouth found her breast. She might not be sure about living together or marriage, but this sweet, fierce passion—*this* she was sure of.

ROB PROPPED HIMSELF UP ON ONE ELBOW AND studied his sleeping bedmate. Val's curving form was silvered by moonlight and her hair rioted darkly across the pillow. The sex, as always, had been phenomenal, maybe even better than usual because of the scariness of her being attacked.

But dammit, he wanted more than sex. There *was* more than sex between them, a lot more, but suggesting that made Val skittish. Since she didn't cotton to living together, he had been ready to propose marriage when she had jumped his bones. A most effective means of changing the subject.

Maybe she wasn't in love with him and never would be, or maybe she just needed time to fall in love and get used to the idea of marriage. But he was a computer geek with a lot of experience in solving problems, and Val was definitely a problem, albeit a beautiful, sexy problem who made him feel more alive than he had ever felt in his life.

He smiled wryly, remembering why he had spent so many years buried in computer development. It was a simpler world, where something either worked or it didn't. If it didn't, you fixed it. Problems had solutions, if you worked hard enough.

Maybe the same was true with romance, but he wouldn't bet on it. He whispered, "I love you, Valentine."

Perhaps it was his imagination, but it seemed that even in sleep, she pulled away a little.

* * *

VAL CAME AWAKE SUDDENLY. IT WAS STILL DARK, and a glance at the bedside clock showed that it was a little after 3 A.M. Rob slept beside her, one arm over her waist.

Lilith glided up from the foot of the bed to stand on Val's chest and give an almost inaudible *mrowrr*. To a cat, human movement meant it was breakfast time no matter what the clock said.

Knowing she was too tense and uneasy to return to sleep, Val slipped out from under Rob's arm, found her robe by touch, and descended to the kitchen, the cats circling and threatening to trip her. After dividing a can of cat tuna between them, she crossed her arms and leaned back against the counter as she regarded her pets broodingly.

The reason for her disquiet was obvious—her behavior with Rob had been straight out of the twilight zone. Why had she come unglued when he suggested they live together? And then cut him off when he seemed on the verge of proposing marriage? She should have cartwheeled with happiness. Instead, she had panicked and used sex to change the subject. Tacky, Valentine, very tacky.

Was she in love with him? Her heart tightened painfully. At sixteen, questions like that had been easy to answer. At her age, everything was more complicated. There were many kinds of love, and she wasn't ready to try to label her feelings for Rob.

But if in doubt, make a list. She sat down at the kitchen desk, pulled out one of her ubiquitous legal tablets, and wrote "Rob: Pro and Con" at the top.

Her felt-tipped pen raced as she listed the pros. Smart, funny, sexy, responsible, compassionate, liked her cats, reliable, wanted to get serious. She could have listed his virtues for pages, but stopped after about twenty, figuring that she'd hit the highlights.

Cons were harder to find. He had major emotional baggage, but he had survived the worst and was dealing with his issues honestly. Professionally he was rather adrift, but his dedication to helping those who were less fortunate touched her soul in a way his earlier commercial success didn't. He was a truly good man, and she found that incredibly, ravishingly, appealing.

She stared at the list, long on pros, short on cons, and came to an inescapable conclusion: The problem wasn't with Rob, but with her. Granted, the relationship was still fairly new, but considering that she was crazy about him, she shouldn't be this skittish. What was going on?

An old anecdote flickered through her mind, about a man who had spent years looking for the perfect woman. Eventually he'd found her, but to no avail because she was looking for the perfect man—and he wasn't it.

She had been looking for Mr. Right, and now that she had found him, she realized that she wasn't Ms. Right. For years she'd been telling herself that she hadn't found the right guy when the truth was she had chosen Mr. Wrongs so she wouldn't have to face what were obviously some major commitment issues. Rob had slid under her defenses almost by accident. Now that he was there, she didn't know what to do with him.

She shivered, suddenly tired and cold. She didn't want to lose Rob, but . . . marriage? The prospect made her want to flee to the high timber.

Smiling wryly, she stood and headed to her bedroom. When life settled down a bit, she would have to call Rachel and find out what was wrong. Rachel could always explain the twists in her friends' psyche. Better yet, she never did so unless asked.

In the meantime, she returned to her bed and rejoined Rob, burrowing as close to his warm body as humanly possible.

CHAPTER 18

⬥⬥⬥

CAL MURPHY'S OFFICE WAS A RIOT OF PAPERS gone mad. Val wasn't surprised—public defenders were notoriously overworked. She knocked on the open door to let the office's inhabitant know she was there. "Cal? I'm Val Covington."

The man at the computer looked up, blinking behind thick glasses. Val said helpfully, "You said I could come by and talk to you about Daniel Monroe."

"Oh, right, right." He stood and offered his hand. Tall and angular, he had thinning hair and an engaging smile. "I'd apologize for the mess, but it's chronic so there's no point."

"Not a problem. You PDs average what, forty cases or so at once?"

He grimaced. "That's when things are going well. At the moment, I have almost a hundred. Pray for more city funding before the OPD goes under for the third time."

"I brought you some fuel." Val had checked with Murphy's secretary beforehand, so she opened a paper bag and produced two steaming containers of coffee. Handing over the larger one she said, "Your preference is for the largest white chocolate mocha latte in the Western Hemisphere, right?"

"My God, woman," he said reverently as he accepted the latte. "Are you married? Do you want to be?"

For a fleeting moment she thought of Rob's near proposal, and her bizarre reaction. He had not raised the subject since, and she had been embarrassingly grateful for that. "Sorry, I'm just opening my own office. No time for a husband."

"Just as well." He took a deep swallow of the latte, delicately licking whipped cream from his lips. "Not only would Val and Cal be ridiculous, but my wife would probably have something to say on the subject."

"A lot to say, if she's another lawyer. We never lack for words."

"Ginny is an ER doctor. I met her when one of my clients got himself shot in the gut by an angry drug dealer."

Val winced. "Did he survive?"

"Of course. Why do you think I married his doctor?" He grinned for a moment before turning serious. "All right, Val, what do you want to know?"

"Anything you can tell me about defending Daniel Monroe that doesn't show up on the official records."

He sighed and took another swig of coffee. "That was my first capital case where I sat first chair. Will you try to get Daniel a stay of execution based on my failings?"

"The appeals court has already looked into that without finding any problems with Daniel's trial." She sipped her own modest cappuccino. "I'm no criminal lawyer, but it looked to me as if he got a pretty darned good defense."

"Thanks for that," he said dryly. "It's easy to blame any failures on the public defender, since everyone knows we're all drunken morons who can't hold a real job."

"And corporate litigators like me are greedy beasts with long fangs and no conscience." They shared a smile of lawyerly commiseration before Val continued, "If you had Daniel's case to try over again, would you do anything differently?"

He slouched back in his chair and thought about it. "Not really. There wasn't a single damned shred of physical evidence either for or against Daniel, so it all came down to the eyewitnesses. A single one could have been explained away as mistaken identity, maybe even two, but three?" He frowned. "Knowing what I do now, I could have done a better job of undermining the two male witnesses. At the trial the state's attorney presented them as practically altar boys, but both of them eventually went to prison. That was no use to me at the time of Daniel's trial, though."

"They were not upstanding citizens," she agreed. "Darrell Long got himself shot, and I understand Joe Cady is dying of AIDS."

"No surprises there." Murphy shook his head. "Against the eyewitnesses, all I had was Daniel's girlfriend who swore he was with her. She was a good witness, but it's assumed that girlfriends and mothers will lie to protect even the rottenest criminal, so everything she said was discounted. I wonder what happened to her and the baby. I forget her name, but she was a bright, very together girl."

"Her name is Kendra Brooks now. She's my right-hand woman and the best paralegal in Baltimore. She's also the reason I'm involved in this case. The baby, Jason Brooks, will be starting his second year at the Air Force Academy."

"Well, I'll be damned. My favorite niece is a classmate of his. They might know each other. I'm glad Kendra and the boy are doing well." He sighed. "I see so many broken lives. It's good to be reminded that some people not only survive, but flourish."

She hadn't expected to get any real leads out of Murphy, but she was enjoying this discussion. "Any suggestions as to ways of saving Daniel's life?"

"Since appeals have been exhausted, you need some new evidence that casts strong doubt on Daniel's guilt. If you can find Joe Cady, lean on him. If he lied about the shooter, he might know the real killer, and he might be willing to talk now. If he's convincing, it might cast enough doubt on Daniel's conviction for the sentence to be commuted to life. Apart from that"—he grimaced—"pray for a miracle."

She tilted her head. "You've been a public defender for over twenty years. How do you keep doing what must be heartbreaking work?"

He took off his glasses and began polishing the lenses. "You mean because most of them are guilty and some of them have done truly horrible things? It helps to believe passionately that everyone is entitled to the best possible defense. Besides, sometimes clients who look guilty as sin aren't."

"Everyone deserves a zealous defense, and I've got a thing about wrongful convictions, which is one reason I'm seeing what I can do for Daniel," Val said. "I considered becoming a public defender, but decided I was too much of a wimp to deal with so many cases involving violence."

"That part isn't easy, but someone needs to do it." Frowning, Cal shoved his glasses back into place. "Clients tell some pretty incredible stories, but you sort of have to believe them since truth is so often stranger than fiction. A lot are drop-outs who started life with the deck stacked against 'em, and the streets and dealing drugs are the only road they can see that's open to them. Hope gets consumed and protecting your *honor* is worth your life, 'cause your life isn't worth much anyhow, and at least if you go down people will respect the way you fell."

He leaned forward and started talking faster. "Cops do a tough job and heaven knows we need them, but some are cowboys who figure that if a suspect didn't do this particular crime, he did something else just as bad so he deserves punishment, and beefing up the evidence is really just justice. So maybe a cowboy says he had a clear view of when something went down even though he didn't see anything, or maybe he has some drugs picked up on another bust so why not plant them on this no-good dude who deserves whatever he gets?"

Cal stood, shoving his chair backwards, and began to stalk around the office. "So, by God, the state damn well needs to *prove* every element of a crime beyond a reasonable doubt, not just seventy-five percent. Innocent until proven guilty—it's the American way, because even when the system works perfectly, which it never does, it's an imperfect process and innocent guys go to jail and sometimes they're even executed, and even one wrongful execution is too many.

"Society needs to remember that justice should be about freeing the innocent and giving just punishment to the guilty. It can't be about revenge, because most criminals will get out of prison someday, and we better hope they've turned themselves around, which they're unlikely to do if they're bitter because they were hammered by a judge or thrown by their counsel or screwed by the police. If there's to be any hope at all, there has to be *justice*, dammit. Justice. And that means people like me fighting the good fight on behalf of people who don't always deserve it, but justice is worth the fight, always."

Val stared at him, and all she could think to say was, "Wow."

He stopped, embarrassed. "God, I'm preaching. Sorry, but you did ask."

"I'm glad I did. I just remembered one of the reasons I went to law school. It's easy to forget in the daily grind of a legal practice."

"You're in it for justice?" His mouth quirked up. "Most of my female classmates claimed they wanted to be lawyers for the money."

"That was another factor for me, but not the biggest." She rose and offered her hand. "Thanks, Cal. I'll do what I can for Daniel, and prayer goes at the top of the list, because if you couldn't save him, it will take a miracle for us to do it now."

"I hope you get one, because that's a case that's haunted me. Maybe eighty percent of the time the courts get it right, but I don't think this was one of them, and death is different from other penalties. So . . . final." He shook her hand, then dropped into his chair and returned to his computer screen. By the time Val reached his office door, he'd forgotten her existence.

Thoughtfully she left the building and walked along busy St. Paul Place. She was only a few blocks from Crouse, Resnick, but very different kinds of law were practiced in the two locations. Both were needed. Neither was exactly right for her. In a matter of days she would officially open her own office, and it was up to her to develop the kind of practice that would suit her best. The prospect was still a little scary, but exhilarating. She could do this. She just wished that she could begin by freeing Daniel.

Crouse, Resnick was quiet. Kendra had officially left and was setting up the new office. Val had a lot of loose ends to tie up, but for all intents and purposes, her uptown law firm career was over. The biggest event left was her going-away luncheon.

After returning a couple of Crouse, Resnick calls, she checked her cell phone for personal messages. One number was Rob's. Glad to have an excuse to talk to him, she called his cell phone. "Hi, handsome, what's up?"

His deep voice had the remarkable ability to soothe and arouse at the same time. "I've located Joe Cady. Still alive, barely, at a nursing home in South Baltimore. Since you wanted to go with me, will tomorrow afternoon be okay?"

She felt a rush of excitement. "It would have to be first thing in the morning—tomorrow is my farewell luncheon." She jotted a note on her schedule. "I hope we get something useful from Cady. This morning I talked to the public defender who handled Daniel's case. He's a cool guy who gave a rant on justice that curled my toes. He also thought Cady might be our best chance for new evidence."

"Let's hope the poor schlub is well enough to talk."

"What's on your schedule for this afternoon?"

"I'm visiting Brenda Harris, the assault victim. If I can persuade her to admit that she wasn't absolutely sure Daniel was the attacker, it would add weight to the case."

Worth a try. "Have you had any luck investigating the other two witnesses' backgrounds?"

"I sure have. Though neither Long nor Cady had an adult arrest record at the time of the trial, they both had juvenile records, and they lied about their circumstances at the time of Daniel's trial. Long said he was a student at Coppin State College, but they never heard of him, and Cady claimed that he worked at Johns Hopkins, only he had been fired months earlier after about two weeks on the job. Will this undermine their credibility?"

"It might help support any stronger evidence we find." She sighed. "Cal Murphy suggested we pray for a miracle."

"If that's what it takes, I'll give it a try."

She wondered if he was joking. They had yet to discuss spiritual beliefs, which was odd considering how spirituality—or lack thereof—was a vital part of one's character. "Are you free for dinner tonight? Or a late night snack?" When he hesitated, she said, "I sleep better when you're with me, and it's been three whole days."

He chuckled. "That's a romantic proposal if I ever heard one. I'd love to come, but I'm not sure yet what time that will be. I'll call you."

She smiled. At least the day wouldn't be a total waste if she would see Rob later.

PETITE AND BLOND, BRENDA HARRIS WAS AN ATtractive woman in her late forties. She allowed Rob into her suburban home with a certain wariness. "I don't know what you want to talk about, Mr. Smith. Everything I have to say about Daniel Monroe and the murder trial is a matter of public record."

"An investigator needs to be thorough." It hadn't been easy to persuade Brenda Harris to see him, and Rob wasn't surprised to find a large man in the Harris living room.

"Marty," she said, "this is Rob Smith, that investigator I told you about."

As the men shook hands, Rob got the clear message that if he upset Marty's wife, he was in big trouble. "My intention isn't to disturb you, Mrs. Harris. I only want to hear in your own words what happened when you were assaulted, and Officer Malloy was killed. Maybe there's some small detail that didn't seem important or that you didn't remember till after the trial. Anything like that might be useful to my investigation."

Marty snorted. "How can this not be disturbing? She couldn't stand living in Kensington any more, which is why we sold that house and moved here to Essex."

"My mother worked nights, and she was assaulted once when I was a kid," Rob said soberly. "She fought back and ended up in the hospital." After that, she started carrying a gun. "It's a crime that women can't walk the streets in safety."

"It's a crime that murdering bastard Monroe is still alive when Officer Malloy is dead," Marty said vehemently. "Malloy never got to see his kids grow up. He never got to play ball with his son, or give his daughter away at her wedding. It's a damned crying shame that it takes so long for a murderer to get executed in this state."

"There's no question that Malloy's killer deserves punishment, but I'm conducting this investigation because there's evidence Daniel Monroe wasn't the killer. An innocent man might die, and no one wants that." He caught Brenda's gaze. "Mrs. Harris, the lighting was poor that evening, and you testified that the attack seemed to come out of nowhere. Have you ever wondered if it was Monroe who attacked you?"

"Never. It was him," she said flatly.

"Yet when you saw him in a photo lineup, you couldn't identify him," Rob said, careful not to sound confrontational.

"I was too upset then! I couldn't have identified my own mother. Later, when I saw the real lineup, I knew it was him. I could feel his filthy hands on me again. And he had that tattoo on his wrist, a nasty snake . . ." Her voice broke. "I still dream about that poor man screaming as Monroe shot him. And the blood . . . there was so much blood. It was the most horrible thing I've ever seen."

Even after all these years, pain was vividly real in her eyes. That still didn't mean her identification was correct. The police should never have put Daniel's picture in the photo lineup, then included him with a bunch of strangers in the real lineup. Seeing his face a second time had turned Daniel from a man she didn't recognize into a familiar face. But Brenda Harris was not going to concede the point.

"According to the case files, you were knocked to the ground in the cross alley beside the corner of the house on the south side. Is that correct?" When she nodded, Rob continued, "You would have seen the killer silhouetted against the only street light nearby. Were you able to see the man's features clearly?"

For an instant he thought he saw uncertainty in her expression. Then she shook her head. "It was Daniel Monroe I saw. I've never doubted it for a moment. I recognized his face and his tattoo."

"It was common then for young men in prison to get tattoos on their wrists," Rob said. "I've been looking up police files on possible suspects, and I've already found three men who had tattoos of the same general type as the one Daniel Monroe had."

"I recognized this one! Monroe is the one who attacked me and killed Malloy."

Rob would get nothing more from her. Suppressing a sigh, he got to his feet. "Thanks very much for taking the time to see me, Mrs. Harris. If you should think of anything else, here's my card."

But he would never hear from her. She might be wrong, but even if the memory had been artificially constructed after the fact, after all these years it was as firmly rooted, as convincing to her, as a genuine memory.

A pity the human mind was so suggestible, and so stubborn.

THOUGH TEMPTED BY VAL'S OFFER OF DINNER, ROB finished his work before calling her to say that he was on his way over. It was after eleven o'clock when he rang her doorbell. If they were a couple, which they seemed to be, having a key would be handy, but he hadn't asked for one because he didn't want to spook her again.

Within seconds, the door swung open and she tugged him inside so the door could be shut to prevent the cats from escaping. Then she was in his arms, hugging him hard. "It's soooooo nice to see you," she murmured into his shoulder.

"Ditto." He wrapped her close, feeling the tension ease. "Did the mugging make you uncomfortable here alone? I can come over every night until you're okay again."

"No, I wasn't afraid of being alone." She stepped back and slid her arm around his waist, guiding him toward the kitchen. "I just—missed seeing you. Hungry? I've got some nice sliced corned beef and cheese from the best deli in Pikesville."

He laughed. "When you were little, did your mother teach you that the best way to a man's heart is through his stomach?"

"Nope, I figured it out for myself." They reached the kitchen, and she headed for the refrigerator. "I also picked up a six-pack of that microbrewery beer you said you liked, and some German potato salad. Interested?"

He kissed the back of her neck. "Very. Many thanks."

As he sat at the table, he told himself that he should stop trying to analyze how Val felt about him. She might feel skittish about getting serious too quickly, but surely her consideration and pampering was proof of caring. In time, they would get this right.

He had to believe that.

CHAPTER 19

JOE CADY WAS ALIVE, THOUGH ONLY JUST. HE LAY on his hospital bed like a cadaver, eyes closed and tubes in his arms. Outside the small room could be heard the voices and rattling crockery of the nursing home, but here the quiet of near death prevailed. Only Cady's labored breathing proved that he still lived.

While Val hung back, Rob turned off the wall-mounted television and said quietly, "Mr. Cady?"

The sunken eyes opened. His dark skin had a yellowish tinge and deep lines were carved in his face. He looked a hundred years old. If he lived until October, he would turn forty. "Who are you?" His voice was as thin and lifeless as the rest of him.

"My name is Rob Smith, and I'm looking into something that happened a long time ago." He nodded toward Val. "This is Val Covington, my partner."

A flicker of life showed in Cady's eyes when he looked at Val, who couldn't help but look sexy even in her lawyer clothes. The patient wasn't dead yet. "Why'd you come here? Nobody ever comes to see me." His mouth twisted.

"Even my own family don't visit 'cause they're afraid I'll give 'em AIDS."

"We came because you're the key to understanding what happened the night Officer James Malloy was killed."

Cady's gaze shifted away. "Don't know nothin' about that."

Rob pulled a chair next to the bed and sat so he wouldn't loom over Cady. "Are you sure? It's been over seventeen years, but it was a big deal then. A police officer was shot and killed, and you and your friend Darrell Long were key witnesses at the trial."

Cady plucked fretfully at the bed covers. "Darrell weren't no friend of mine. Stole my money and shot my cousin."

Rob had done some investigation before coming and learned that one night Darrell chose to rob Cady's cousin, who owned a small liquor store in East Baltimore. Big mistake. There had been a shoot-out that left Long dead and Cady's cousin alive, and apparently destroyed any loyalty Cady had felt to his former friend. "Darrell identified Daniel Monroe as the man who killed Officer Malloy, and you confirmed that. Is the statement you gave then the whole story on what happened that night?"

"Don't want to talk about it!" Cady still refused to meet Rob's gaze.

Val motioned Rob to move away and took his place in the chair. "Mr. Cady, this is really important," she said in her soft, persuasive voice. "In a few weeks, Daniel Monroe is going to be executed for the murder. He claims he didn't do it, and his girlfriend swears he was with her at the time of the shooting. Is it possible that you and Mr. Long made a mistake that night?"

A tremor ran through Cady, and Rob realized tears were seeping from under the man's eyelids. Val took his hand. "Mr. Cady, if a mistake was made then, it's not too late to correct it."

There was a long silence while Cady drew ragged breaths, his thin chest rising and falling. "I didn't see nothin', just heard the shots. Then Omar Benson came racing along the street behind us. He saw me and Darrell and waved Darrell over to talk to him. I was too far away to hear what they said, but when Omar left, Darrell came back and told me to say that we saw a shooting, and it looked like this Daniel Monroe guy did it."

"So Darrell asked you to lie for Omar."

Cady's hand tightened convulsively on Val's. "Didn't want to, but Darrell said if we did, Omar Benson would give us all the crack we wanted, so I . . . I agreed. Didn't have enough money, and I needed that crack. I'd seen Monroe in the street a couple of times so I was able to pick him out of the lineup, but I figured he'd probably get off, if not from his girlfriend's testimony, then later, on appeal." He gave a racking cough that shook his thin frame. "They really going to execute the guy? I . . . I didn't mean for him to be fried."

"But he will be, because of the testimony of you and Darrell Long." Val's voice was gentle but uncompromising.

Cady released his breath wearily. "I didn't mean no harm. I just wanted to help out Omar so's he'd help out me."

"Omar is gone now, and so is Darrell. Daniel Monroe will be gone, too, if you don't speak up." Val waited a few beats. "Mr. Cady, would you be willing to let us videotape you while you describe what really happened that night?"

Cady's eyes flicked to Rob. "I dunno . . ."

Val leaned forward, her hand still holding Cady's thin fingers. "If we can't find new evidence, an innocent man will die. You're the *only* person who can make a difference. If you've made mistakes in your life—well, who hasn't?— this is a chance to clear the record."

Cady's eyes closed again. "All right, use the fuckin' camera. Ain't nothin' nobody can do to me now."

Rob opened his briefcase and pulled out Val's compact camcorder, trying to conceal his excitement. So Daniel had really been convicted with perjured testimony! On some level of his mind, a whisper of doubt had lingered. Finally it was gone. And if more evidence was needed, Omar Benson's police file had listed a wrist tattoo of a snake as one of his identifying features.

He set up the camcorder on a lightweight tripod and began to tape. Drawing Cady's attention back to her, Val stated the date, place, and time for the video, then asked, "Mr. Cady, will you tell us in your own words what happened the night when Officer James Malloy was shot?"

Stopping frequently for breath, Cady described how he and Darrell Long had left the crack house, heard shots, testified to the police that they thought they had recognized the killer. Joe had felt increasing reluctance, but he'd held to his story because he was afraid of what would happen if he changed it. He was a good liar, he said with some pride. Knew how to keep a story simple and not mess up.

At the end, he looked directly into the camera and repeated, "I did not see Daniel Monroe shoot Officer Malloy. Darrell Long recognized Omar Benson as the shooter because of what he was wearing. Later Omar admitted to me what he had done and promised me plenty of crack to keep quiet. As God is my witness, this is the truth."

After Rob turned off the camcorder, Val said, "Thank you, Mr. Cady. You may have saved an innocent man's life today."

He sighed, seeming to shrink now that he'd said his piece. "I feel better for tellin' the truth finally. I'm glad it ain't too late."

Val glanced around the room, which was clean but dismal, with the faint scent of failing bodies always found in nursing homes. "Is there anything we can do to make you more comfortable? Hospitals aren't happy places."

"I won't be here much longer," Cady said bluntly. "In a week I'll be gone, and I ain't sorry. This is no kind of life." He hesitated. "But there is one thing."

"Yes?"

"I got a dog, Malcolm. He ain't much, just a mutt, but . . . well, he's a nice mutt. My sister Lucy has been keepin' him, but she don't like dogs, and I'm afraid that when I'm dead, she'll get rid of him. Could you find Malcolm a good home?"

Val and Rob exchanged a glance. He could see that her

first instinct was to volunteer to take the dog, but her second thought was how her cats would react. "I'll be happy to take him in," Rob said. "I like dogs, and I haven't had one in too long. I promise Malcolm will be well cared for as long as he lives."

"And I'll spoil him with treats," Val added. "How can we find your sister?"

Voice shaking with fatigue, Cady recited his sister's phone number. Val bent to give him a kiss. "God bless you, Mr. Cady."

Cady closed his eyes, but there was a faint smile on his lips as they left the room.

Rob waited until they were outside the nursing home to express his exhilaration. "We've done it!" He scooped Val up in his arms and whirled her around exuberantly. "By God, we did it! We've found substantial new evidence to clear Daniel." He kissed a laughing Val and set her back on her feet. "Now what happens?"

"We're not home free yet. A reprieve isn't easy this late in the game," Val said warningly, but she was beaming. "The next step is to write the best damned brief of my life reinforcing all of the factors speaking to Daniel's innocence, and showing what a weak case the state had to begin with. Then we take it to court. The Maryland code of justice says that a court may revise a sentence at any time in cases of fraud or mistake."

He whistled softly. "That sure is liberal compared to Texas."

"Some states won't accept new evidence more than three weeks after a conviction. Three lousy weeks! It's absurd." She brushed hair from her face and headed toward her car. "Did you know that the execution rate is highest in the states where lynchings were common? All you have to do is cross the Potomac from Maryland to Virginia and the number of executions skyrockets."

"Now that we know who the real killer was, I can start searching for people who knew Omar Benson." He fell into step beside her. "There's a darned good chance that he boasted about the murder to others, and now that we know where to look, we can probably get more statements to that effect. Even though they would be hearsay, they would surely help support our case."

"Good idea. I'll also call Cal Murphy and see what advice he has on how to proceed from here." She popped the trunk of her Lexus so Rob could put his briefcase and camera inside. "The first thing you do is get multiple dupes of Cady's statement."

"After you drop me off, I'll take the tape to a place I know out Bel Air Road. I'll get a dozen copies made so we can spread them around."

When they were both seat belted in the car, Val said soberly, "Rob—this really isn't a sure thing. Daniel won't be safe until we get a court or the governor to agree that there is reasonable doubt about his conviction."

He grinned, refusing to worry. "We'll get it. And in the meantime, after I drop off the tape for duplicates—I've got to see a woman about a dog."

BARELY ABLE TO CONTAIN HER EXCITEMENT, KENDRA paced around the visitor room until Daniel was brought in to see her by the usual stone-faced guards. His smile lit up the dingy room. "Baby, this is an unexpected pleasure," he said into the connecting phone. "What's with the corn rows? You look good enough to eat, but you haven't worn them since I got sent up."

She laughed and swung her hair so that the brightly beaded mass of small braids danced across her shoulders. "Now that I'm out of Crouse, Resnick, I can be funkier, so from now on, I'm going to look like a stylish, black, professional woman. Val doesn't mind. In fact, she's wondering if her hair is curly enough to do the same."

He grinned. "I'd like to see that. She's a cute little thing, your boss."

Not interested in small talk, Kendra leaned toward the plastic wall separating them, wishing they could touch.

"She's also smart as a whip. Daniel, she and Rob have come up with the new evidence we need to get you off death row! This morning they interviewed Joe Cady and shot a videotape of him recanting his testimony against you. He's dying of AIDS, and it's been bothering him the way he and Darrell Long lied to cover up for Omar Benson, who was their crack connection. Val says he spelled it out in very convincing detail. Honey, this is it!"

The spark in his eyes when she began to speak vanished as quickly as it had appeared. "It won't work, Kendra. A dying con might say anything, and a lot of 'em have. The court will say too bad, this is too little and too late."

Startled, she said, "They'd ignore a death bed confession?"

"Damn right they will. Jailbirds don't have a lot of credibility. When they ask if I have any last words, I could say that I offed Jimmy Hoffa if the spirit struck me, but why should any court believe it?" He closed his eyes for a moment, then opened them and spoke with chilling detachment. "Joe Cady hasn't had a real strong track record with the truth. Val will have to come up with a lot better to make a difference."

Kendra felt the way she had when an older cousin told her there was no Santa Claus. "How can you be so . . . so cold about this? We're talking about your life, and you've already given up."

"I've accepted reality. Beating against the bars hurts too much and doesn't do a damn bit of good." His voice softened. "There's lots of arguments against capital punishment, but one that gets missed is how hard it is on the friends and family of the man who's executed. You're being made to suffer like Malloy's family did, and you don't deserve it any more than they did." He spread his large hand on the plastic barrier in an attempt to comfort. "Try to accept, Kendra. The worst thing about what's going to happen to me is knowin' how much it will hurt you and Luke and the rest of the family."

She raised her hand and rested it against his, feeling a

hint of warmth radiating through the plastic. For an instant, she could almost feel them really touching, flesh to flesh, and couldn't bear it. "I can't accept, Daniel, not when this is so unjust. Up 'til now, only you and I were sure of the truth."

And, God help her, there had been times when she had searched her mind feverishly, wondering if she had been so busy with the baby that Daniel actually could have slipped out of the apartment without her knowing. "Now we have someone testifying that it was lies that put you here. It ought to make a difference."

"It ought to, but it won't." He pulled his hand from the barrier and kissed the palm, then replaced it against hers. His warm eyes profoundly serious, he said quietly, "You've suffered enough for me, baby. I wish to God that you could walk away today and never think of me again. No more tears or regrets or anger."

"I can't," she whispered. "You've been part of me ever since we first met. You're Jason's father. How can I not think of you?"

His sad smile acknowledged the truth of that. "Will you sing for me? At night when I'm lyin' on my bunk, I hear your voice in my mind."

She nodded, wondering what would fit tonight. Ah, yes, perfect.

Closing her eyes, she lowered her voice to a husky whisper and began the spiritual "Go Down, Moses." It was a slave's cry for freedom, and as the verses continued, her voice rose to echo through the small room.

When Israel was in Egyp' Lan', Let my people go.
Oppressed so hard they could not stand, Let my people go.
Go down, Moses, Way down in Egyp' Lan',
Tell ol . . . Phar-roah, To let my people go.
Tell ol' Pharoah, To let my lover go.

CHAPTER 20

⚜

"MRS. MORRISON?" ROB STUDIED THE SLIGHTLY built woman through the screen door of her house. Though there was some resemblance to her brother Joe Cady, she had a no-nonsense expression and an air of competence. This pleasant house in Hamilton, not far from the remodeled church, suggested a comfortable, prosperous life. "I'm Rob Smith, the one who called about taking your brother's dog off your hands."

"Oh, yes." She opened the screen door and gestured for him to come in. "Could you go over that again? When you called earlier, two of my grandchildren were running around, and I didn't catch everything you said. Would you like some iced tea?"

"That would be nice." He followed her to the kitchen, where an ungainly hound sprawled in front of the refrigerator. A heavy body and drooping ears suggested that basset was prominent in the dog's ancestry, but something with longer fur and a sharper nose had contributed. The dog regarded the visitor gloomily. "Is this Malcolm?"

Lucy Morrison prodded the hound with a gentle foot to encourage him to move far enough for her to open the refrigerator. "Yes, and a beast less like Malcolm X would be hard to imagine."

Rob grinned as he knelt and ruffled the long, floppy ears. "The name and the dog do seem mismatched, but I suppose he's used to it by now. Will you come home with me, boy? Joe is afraid you'll dump the dog or turn him over to a shelter."

"I wouldn't do that, but I'll admit I wouldn't miss having him underfoot." She handed Rob a tall glass of iced tea. "My husband and I run a printing business, my youngest girl is still at home, and I've got grandchildren here three afternoons a week. I don't really need a dog to look after as well. If you like him, he's yours. Now sit down and tell me why you were visiting Joe." She took the lid off a shallow bowl of chocolate chip cookies and set the bowl on the kitchen table. "Help yourself."

The tea and cookies made a decent lunch as Rob explained the investigation, and how Joe Cady had confessed to giving perjured testimony.

As he gave his account, Lucy gazed sadly out the kitchen window. "So my little brother lied and sent an innocent man to jail. I wish I could say it was a surprise, but it's not. A lot of women talk about how their boyfriends and sons and brothers fell in with bad company. Sometimes they're kidding themselves, but not in this case.

"Joe was the sweetest-tempered little boy you ever did see. He sang in the church choir. Wanted to be a fireman so he could help people. Did you know that if you live in the inner city and need help, it's the fire department you call because they always, always come? And they bring cool equipment, too." She shook her head, her eyes dark with ancient sorrow. "Then Joe started to run the streets. I used to be glad that at least he hadn't killed anyone—even at his worst, he was never violent. And now I find out that he stole an innocent man's life as surely as if I shot him with a gun."

Knowing the grief and guilt for a brother, Rob offered, "For what it's worth, Joe wasn't the one who came up with the idea of perjury. That seems to have come from his friend, Darrell Long."

"As I said, bad company," Lucy said dryly. "They were thick as thieves for years. In fact, they were thieves. Half my attic is filled with boxes of stuff belonging to Joe and Darrell from the days when they were best buddies. They had an apartment together and had to move, so I foolishly agreed to store some boxes. Worthless stuff, or they wouldn't have left it. One of these days I need to sort through and toss, but it's easier to put it off."

Rob was having trouble reconciling Joe's words with this warm, nurturing woman. "Your brother said his family never visits because they're afraid of getting AIDS. Is that true, or was he just angling for pity?"

Lucy looked startled. "Joe said that? He may be have been trying to manipulate you—he's good at that. Or maybe he really believes we're afraid. Different people in the family do visit now and then, but it's hard for us to see what he's become."

"When we saw Joe, he looked as if a high wind would blow him away. He may not have a lot of time left."

"It's that bad? Then I'll call my sister and go visit him tonight." Her smile was wistful. "He's still my baby brother, even though he did go off the rails."

Driven by impulse, Rob said, "My brother did, too. He was executed in Texas."

She studied his face. "So you understand. I'm sorry about your brother."

"And I'm sorry about yours, but at least Joe has done a better job of redeeming himself than my brother ever did." Knowing it was time to go, Rob got to his feet. "Will you go with me willingly, Malcolm, or will I have to carry you?"

"This will be easier than you think. Walkies, Malcolm!"

The dog was instantly on his feet, plumy tail wagging hopefully. Even his expression looked less gloomy. "There's hope for you, Malcolm, my lad." Rob glanced at Lucy. "Anything I should know about him?"

"He's probably six or seven years old, he doesn't bite,

and he has an amazing baritone bark that will scare the hair off anyone who might even think of breaking into your house." She bent and scratched the dog's head. Malcolm responded with a friendly slurp of her hand.

Noticing her expression, Rob asked, "Are you sure you want to let him go? You seem to like each other pretty well."

"It's hard not to like a beast that so loves to be fed, but I really don't need the extra work." She straightened. "I'll get his leash and dog food and toys."

Rob pulled out a card. "If you or anyone else in the family want to visit Malcolm, just give me a call."

"Don't hold your breath," she advised, but she was smiling as she went for the dog's paraphernalia. Rob knelt and scratched Malcolm's head again. Sensing that this new person needed buttering up, the dog leaned against his leg affectionately.

It occurred to Rob that only a few weeks before, he had been living as solitary a life as he could manage, deliberately avoiding interaction and possessions. Now he had an amazing girlfriend, a dog, and a commitment to a cause.

Maybe he just wasn't meant to travel light.

VAL ACCEPTED STILL ANOTHER HUG AS SHE PREPARED to leave the going-away luncheon Crouse, Resnick had thrown for her at the gorgeous, late-Victorian Engineers' Club. She suspected much of the reason for the lavish event was to demonstrate to the Baltimore legal community that she was leaving with no hard feelings on either side—and to suggest that there would be a continuing relationship between Val and Crouse, Resnick. Whatever. It was a heck of a good party.

Donald Crouse appeared to give her another hug when she was almost at the door. "A good thing this is such a small town, Val—I'll probably see almost as much of you now as when you actually worked down the hall."

She laughed and hugged him back. "Very likely. Thanks for everything, Donald. I've learned a lot from you."

"I invited your father to come down," Donald said, "but he was too busy."

"The story of his life." And Val's as well for too many years. "He's promised to attend the open house I'm holding to celebrate my new firm and my new offices. The invitations just went out. Are you coming?"

"Wouldn't miss it." With a last smile, Donald waved her out the door.

Buoyantly she left the club and headed for her car. A good going-away party was fun and many maudlin comments had been exchanged, but mostly she was delighted to finally be done with her old job. Crouse, Resnick was as good a corporate law firm as she could have found, but her own practice was already more rewarding.

There was no one at her new office since Kendra was visiting Daniel, so Val had to make a fast drive to the church to let her mother inside. Today Callie was installing the soft sculpture hanging she had created, and Val couldn't wait to see it. Her mother hadn't even showed her the drawings, so it was going to be a complete surprise.

Callie and her long-term companion, Loren Goldman, were climbing out of Callie's minivan when Val arrived. Still in a hugging mood, Val embraced her mother, then Loren. "I'm officially a free woman!"

"Enjoy that while it lasts," Loren advised. "Freedom is mostly an illusion."

An oboist for the Baltimore Symphony Orchestra, Loren had a lugubrious expression belied by the wry sparkle in his gray eyes. Callie had dated widely and sometimes chaotically when Val was young, but she had settled down when she met Loren. Though he had never been a father figure for Val, he was a fine surrogate uncle. Lean and lanky, he had a neatly trimmed beard and a graying ponytail that went well with Callie's artsy earth mother style.

Though the two had been hanging out together for a

dozen years, they preferred having separate homes because it gave them more elbow room. Val had never decided whether they were gloriously liberated or merely commitment-phobic, but she had to admit that in some ways they had the perfect arrangement. It would be nice to have a relationship that was so warm and supportive, yet not extremely demanding.

Following her mother to the back of the van, Val said, "I can't wait to see what you've done, Callie."

"Maybe you won't see it. Perhaps we'll hang the tapestry with a sheet over it so there can be a grand unveiling when you have your open house."

"Mo-o-o-o-mmmm!"

Callie grinned. "Don't worry, dear, I was only teasing. I know perfectly well that even if we covered it, you'd be looking as soon as I turned my back. I never could keep Christmas presents hidden from you."

"The unveiling idea isn't a bad one, though," Val said thoughtfully. "I'll cover it up again before the open house so we can have a dramatic moment that will impress everyone so much that you'll be offered lots of new commissions to make up for the fact that you won't let me pay for this."

"How could I let my only daughter pay for a gift honoring her new business? Especially now that you're doing good work, not just grinding down the masses in service of corporate profits." While Val rolled her eyes, Callie opened the rear door of the van so she and Loren could carefully remove the long, fat roll of fabric. "Besides, I have a spy camera hidden in the hanging so I can keep a maternal eye on you."

"I do hope you're kidding." It was always hard to tell with Callie, but Val figured this was more teasing, since her mother had never been the overprotective sort. Usually she'd had sublime faith in Val's ability to cope. It was a mixed blessing.

Inside the building, Callie said, "Go check your e-mail

or something. I'll call you when we've finished the installation."

Reluctantly Val headed to her office. She was a big girl, she could stand the suspense of waiting to see what her mother had done.

There turned out to be enough messages that she was surprised when Callie stuck her head in the office. "It's up." She looked excited and a little nervous.

Val followed her into the main sanctuary, then stopped, awed. The tapestry was almost two stories high and hung against a plain wall painted the soft gold that Callie had specified. Silk and velvet and brocades were combined with feathers and leather and other materials to create a whole that was difficult to describe, but utterly stunning. Val tried to decipher the images, which suggested soaring birds, the scales of justice, and a rising sun. "My God, Callie, it's the best thing you've ever done!" She crossed the sanctuary and reached up to stroke a soft shape that stood out like a bas-relief.

"You really think so?"

Knowing what was expected of her, Val described in detail everything she loved about the tapestry, ending with, "If this doesn't get you more work, I will wash my hands of the Baltimore business community."

"It *did* come out rather well." Callie regarded her work with pride. "This is the beginning of a new direction for me, I think." With her height, exuberance, and roan-red hair, she was every inch an artist. That identity was more central to her than motherhood had ever been, Val suspected.

The door opened, and a familiar voice said, "Good God. That's amazing."

Val turned to Rob, who was followed by a long, low hound with a solid chassis and an aura of zenlike calm. Malcolm, no doubt. Since he promptly flopped under Kendra's desk, Val crossed to join Rob. How would Callie react to him? She would certainly notice that he was handsome. Though the mountain man look was gone, his sun-streaked hair was still a little on the long side, which reinforced a faintly maverick air. This was a man who could be management or consultant, but never an underling.

Figuring she might as well make the relationship clear to Callie, Val rose on her toes to kiss Rob. He returned the kiss with enthusiasm, and she almost forgot to pull away. Later. "My mother just installed the hanging. Isn't she an incredible artist?"

"She certainly is. Are you going to have the hanging photographed and prints made, Ms. Covington? I know some people who might be interested in this sort of work if they see a sample of what you can do."

Given his entrepreneurial past, he probably did know such people. As Val performed the introductions, Callie studied Rob with some skepticism. She probably would have accepted him without reservations if he still had the beard, but in a navy blazer and khakis, he looked perhaps too respectable for her tastes.

Deciding that business was business, Callie said, "Thanks for the thought. Loren is doing a Website for me. In a couple of weeks it will be online and include pictures of this and some of my other work. Val will let you know it's up."

He nodded, then shook hands with Loren. After a brief exchange of small talk, Callie and Loren left to join friends for dinner, so Val was free to meet Malcolm. "What excellent manners. This is a dog in a million." She knelt to scratch his neck. He moaned softly. "In fact, I'm willing to bet there isn't another dog like this anywhere."

Rob grinned. "That's a bet I won't take, but he's a good-natured fellow. I'll take some pictures of him and drop them off with Joe Cady. His sister, Lucy, is a nice lady. She says she wouldn't have dumped Malcolm, but she was happy for me to adopt him. Tonight she's going to round up another sister and visit Joe."

"I'm glad he'll have company. What a wonderful day this has been." Val stretched out her arms and spun in a circle, wanting to soar. "Everything is going so well it's almost scary, Rob. My new office is off to a great start, we're making progress on saving Daniel, tomorrow Lyssie and I are going to have our first get-together"—she spun breathlessly into Rob's arms—"and there's you. How lucky can I get?"

In his eyes, she could see the same exhilaration she was feeling. He gave her an exaggerated leer. "If you like, you could get really lucky right now."

One passion led to another, and the emotions of the day flared into pure lust. She cradled his face in her hands and kissed him again, murmuring, "My mother claimed to have installed a spy camera in the hanging. Shall we see if we can shock her?"

"I doubt your mother is easily shocked." Laughing, Rob dropped onto the carpet and pulled Val down beside him. "But we can try."

She slid her hands under his polo shirt, stroking his chest while she rubbed her face against his throat in an attempt to absorb his essence into her. A distant part of her wondered if such good luck couldn't last. But that was mere superstition. She had wanted to change her life and she had. Nothin' but good times ahead . . .

CHAPTER 21

❧

SPRAWLING ON THE SOFA IN HER MOST COM-
fortable sweats, Kendra glanced up in surprise when a key
grated in her front door. Four people had keys to her house,
and she wasn't expecting any of them.

The door swung open, and her son entered. "Jason!"
She dropped her magazine and flew across the living room
to engulf her son in a hug. "I didn't think you'd be home
until the weekend. It's been way too long since you've had
leave." She stepped back, her hands on his shoulders. "You
look so gorgeous I can hardly believe we're related."

That wasn't just motherly love, either. Six-foot-plus like
his daddy, broad-shouldered and with an athlete's fitness,
her boy would be a hunk anywhere. In his air force cadet's
uniform, he was to die for. Lovingly she touched his uniform insignia. "I've been waiting to see this. The star for
academic excellence, the wreath for military leadership, a
thunderbolt for being an outstanding athlete. You rock,
boy. We better get you into civilian clothes before girls
start beating the door down."

Unsmiling, he set down his duffle bag. "I asked if I
could start my vacation a couple of days early because of

family reasons and was lucky enough to hitch a ride to Andrews Air Force Base."

"Family reasons?" Kendra began to feel tense. It wasn't like her laughing son to look grim. "Is something wrong? Has some old girlfriend claimed you knocked her up?"

He took her arm and led her from the hall back to the living room. He was unnervingly adult. The words "an officer and a gentleman" flashed through her mind. "You're making me nervous, Jay."

"You might want to sit down."

Reminding herself that he was obviously hale and hearty so the worst hadn't happened, she did as he suggested and sat on the sofa again, though this time she wasn't relaxed. He stood with his hands locked behind his back, a hammering pulse in his throat proof that he was less calm than he looked. "Okay, Jay, level with me. What's wrong?"

He caught her gaze, seething anger and hurt in his eyes. "Why did I have to find out who my real father is from a classmate?"

She gasped, feeling her blood drain away. "What are you saying?"

"It's a small world. One of my classmates, Cass Murphy, is from Baltimore, so of course we know each other. She stopped by my room last night and said that her Uncle Cal had defended my father, Daniel Monroe, when he was tried for murder. Because she's a nice girl, she offered her condolences on the fact that he's going to be executed in a few weeks."

So after Val talked to the public defender, Murphy must have e-mailed his niece about the coincidence, and this was the result. As Kendra tried to decide what to say, Jason said sharply, "Don't even think about lying to me! I did a web search on the case, so I know the details, I know what Monroe looks like. At the time he was convicted of murder, he looked just like me." The skin tightened across his cheekbones. "How could you let me grow up not knowing that . . . that my real father is a murderer?"

Kendra dropped her head into her hands, temples throbbing. When in doubt, tell the truth. Looking up, she said, "I didn't tell you because Daniel didn't want you to know. He thought that even though he's innocent, it would be too hard for you to grow up with the knowledge that your father was a convicted murderer. He and I have argued about it. I could sort of see his point when you were younger, but the older you got, the more it bothered me that you didn't know the truth."

"Did Philip Brooks know he wasn't my real father, or did you lie to him, too?"

"Of course he knew! You were almost four when Phil and I married. And don't you dare say Phil wasn't your real father. He adopted you and raised you and loved you. You were his pride and joy, and you know it."

"So if Phil was my real father, what does that make Daniel Monroe? A sperm donor? What a great set of genes I've inherited." His face twisted. "Naturally he's innocent. Isn't every man on death row?"

Kendra bit back a surge of anger. He might look full-grown, but he was only nineteen. "You have every right to be upset, but don't push it. You have two fathers, both of them fine men. Daniel was a little wild as a kid but he had straightened himself out. We were planning our wedding when he was arrested. You asked, now you sit down and listen to the answer."

He wavered, looking suddenly very tired. Realizing that he'd endured a long, tormented day since Cass Murphy had unwittingly broken the news, Kendra stood and put an arm around his shoulders. "You must be hungry. How does fresh lemonade and sliced ham and potato salad sound?"

"That would be good. I didn't get much sleep last night." His voice sounded very young. "Mama, how could I not know something so basic about myself for so long? My father could have died, and I never would have known."

She guided him to the kitchen, wishing she had obeyed her instincts and overruled Daniel's wishes. "Though

Daniel is pessimistic, we may be on the verge of getting his sentence commuted. If not . . ." She swallowed hard. "For years I've asked myself how I could justify it to you if he was executed before you found out."

"No way could you justify that," he said vehemently.

"I was afraid of that." She shook her head. "Hiding the truth is hard work. Just a couple of days ago I saw Daniel's half brother Luke. He resents that you've been kept away from that side of your family."

"I've got more relatives I don't know about?" Jason's startled expression showed that he hadn't thought of that.

"Quite a few of them around Baltimore, and they're mostly pretty nice. With Phil's family all down in Mississippi, you never had enough cousins. You'll have about ten days leave, won't you? I can throw a Monroe family cook-out for you if you like. One of your Monroe cousins is at the Naval Academy. You'd have a lot in common."

He ran his hand over his militarily short hair. "I don't know about a party. Maybe. I'll think about it later when I know who the hell I am."

They reached the kitchen and Jason took his usual chair while she poured lemonade for both of them, then sliced ham and set out potato salad and pickles for her son. She waited until he'd consumed a sizable amount of food before asking, "Ready for the whole story?"

"As ready as I'll ever be." His gaze was level. "Is he really innocent?"

She met his gaze. "As God is my witness, Daniel was wrongly convicted. I know that for a fact because I was with him when the murder took place, but the prosecutors and jury didn't believe me. We've only just learned that two of the three eyewitnesses lied to protect their drug dealer."

"And the third?"

"Made a mistake. That happens a lot, especially when the light's poor and something awful is happening."

Jason exhaled, some of the tension going out of him. "So my father was convicted because they needed to nail someone, and he was black and the right size and general location."

"That's about the size of it—a lousy, rotten twist of fate that changed all our lives." She went through the familiar story crisply, answering any questions that Jason asked along the way.

When she was done, Jason said, "I want to meet him."

"It's time." She rested her hand on her son's. "Prison isn't easy, Jay. Daniel has had to be tough to survive, but he's a good man who has learned a lot of wisdom the hard way. Give him a chance, and remember that he concealed the truth for your sake. Can you say it wouldn't have made your life more difficult when you were growing up?"

Jason glanced away. "No, I can't. But easy isn't always better."

"You're right," she agreed, "but when you have kids, every instinct is to protect them even if that's not always the best choice. At the beginning, I was so wounded by the trial and his conviction that I wanted to bury the whole awful subject. Thinking about it hurt."

He studied her, his eyes softening. "You couldn't have been much older than I am now. That was a lot of grief for you to carry."

"We do what we have to do." She grimaced as she remembered the sheer weeping terror she had experienced at the time. Daniel's family had helped her out as best they could, and she'd responded by taking Jason away from them. At the time, it had seemed right. "I had you to take care of and a powerful desire not to stay on welfare any longer than necessary because my mama raised me to be independent."

"You were on welfare? You never told me that!" he said, scandalized.

She was wryly amused by his shock. "There isn't much about that time of my life I wanted to talk about, but you have a right to know. The program I was in provided support and child care while I got job training, if that sounds better than *welfare*."

"It's not much better." He grimaced. "Did you and Dad try to have kids?"

"We tried. And failed." It was her turn to look away. She had so much wanted to have a baby with Phil. Preferably a little girl with her daddy's sweet smile. "Do you want to meet Daniel tomorrow? He's at the SuperMax downtown."

"That's too soon. Maybe at the beginning of the week. For now, I just want to be home." Jason sighed and reached for the last pickle. "There were times this past year when all I wanted was to be back in Baltimore in my own bed. Normal life, like when I was in high school, before Dad—Phil—died. But life will never be like that again."

She squeezed his hand. "Afraid not. When we're little, our worlds seem immutable. Then we grow up and life becomes one rotten change after another. But usually there are compensations once we get used to the new order. Mostly you love the air force, don't you?" After he nodded, she said, "And while you won't see Phil again in this lifetime, you still have a father to get to know. It can't be the same as with Phil, but you can have a relationship that matters." She pushed back her chair and got to her feet. "Would you like some strawberry shortcake to top that off?"

His face eased into a smile. "I sure would. I dreamed of that sometimes in Colorado." She was taking the bowl of strawberries from the refrigerator when he asked softly, "Mama—did you love my dad? Phil?"

She set the bowl on the counter and turned to face him. "Daniel was the love of my youth, and I'll never stop caring for him. If he hadn't been the victim of a horrible injustice, we would have married and been happy, I think. But I loved Philip, too. There wasn't a day of our marriage when I didn't give thanks that he was my husband. You know how it was after he died—you and I were both numb for months. Your grades slipped to Bs that semester, and I sleepwalked through my job. I was lucky they didn't fire me. Phil was one of the best things that ever happened to me."

Jason stood and wrapped his arms around her. His

rangy frame made her feel small. "Loving is your gift, Mama. I'm lucky to be your son."

She hugged him back, tears in her eyes. Thank God for Cal Murphy's niece, who had precipitated this confrontation. Even Daniel would be glad eventually. She hoped.

OVERSCHEDULED AS ALWAYS, VAL CUT THINGS TOO close and showed up ten minutes late for her first afternoon with Lyssie Armstrong. Lyssie let her into the house, her expression closed but her hair neatly pulled back in a scrunchy and her T-shirt and jeans immaculate. Val said apologetically, "Sorry I'm late. I was drafting a petition and lost track of the time, then ran into some traffic problems."

Lyssie used her forefinger to push the bridge of her glasses farther up her nose. "I was beginning to wonder if you were coming."

Val started to reply that she wouldn't have gone through so much effort to become a Big Sister if she wasn't committed, but stopped herself when she realized that Lyssie was speaking from insecurity, not reason. Her careful dress showed how important this afternoon was to her, which meant she was probably nervous. "I'll always come, Lyssie, though I can't swear I'll always be as punctual as I should be. Let me give you a business card with my cell phone number on it so you can call me anytime, especially when I'm running late."

The girl cocked her head to one side. "Anytime?"

"Yes. If I'm in a meeting or can't talk for some reason you'll have to leave a message, but I promise I'll call back as soon as I can." She pulled her wallet from her bag and handed over one of the cards.

Lyssie turned the card over in her fingers. "You really won't mind?"

"Really I won't." Val made a face. "But I'd better confess that I often take on too much and have to scramble to keep up. I always manage to do everything I promise, but sometimes it takes a while, and sometimes work has to come first." She glanced around the small, neat living room. "Is your grandmother around? I'd like to say hi before we take off."

"She's in the backyard." Lyssie led the way out through the kitchen and down half a dozen steps to a concrete patio shaded by an awning and surrounded by flower containers made of old tires, all of them overflowing with brilliant geraniums and petunias and other annuals. Centered under the awning was a dinette set with table and chairs. Louise sat by the table with an iced drink and a magazine while a snoozing tabby sprawled in the chair opposite.

"Hi." Val scratched the cat and got a soft rumble in return. "I'm about to take Lyssie off. I'll have her back by six."

Louise smiled. "You two have fun. I look forward to an afternoon of doing nothing."

Val thought the older woman looked relaxed but not well. It was too early in their acquaintance to ask about her health, though. "I've been looking forward to this all week. I never seem to have much time to play, so I'm using Lyssie as an excuse."

Lyssie gave a fleeting smile before kissing her grandmother on the cheek. Once they were in Val's car, she asked, "Where is the crafts store?"

"In Towson. The place is huge, with things you never imagined. We'll have trouble deciding where to start." She pulled the car from the curb and headed toward the Jones Falls Expressway. Deciding to ask something she had been wondering about, she said, "I'm always fascinated by our national diversity, but it's hard to guess the family background of either you or your grandmother. Do you know much about where your ancestors came from?"

Lyssie perked up. "They came from all over—Scotland and Africa and Spain and Germany, but the most interesting is Gramma—she's half English and half Lumbee Indian. There are quite a few Lumbees in Baltimore, you know."

"I've read about the Lumbee community center in the city, but I don't know much about the tribe except that they aren't federally recognized. They aren't originally from Maryland, are they?"

"The tribal homeland is in North Carolina, mostly along the Lumbee River. It's the largest tribe east of the Mississippi. There's argument about the tribal roots, but our leadership is trying to get recognition. It's said that members of the lost colony of Roanoke were taken in by the Lumbee—they were called the Cheraw then—and they sheltered runaway slaves, too. That's why Lumbees don't look like other Indian tribes."

Noting Lyssie's use of *our* when referring to the leadership, Val said, "They sound like generous people. Can you be a member of the tribe with one-eighth blood?"

Lyssie nodded vigorously. "Yes—to be enrolled, you have to trace your descent from someone in the Source Documents and keep in touch with the tribe. Keeping in touch is in the tribal constitution. I do it through the community center here." After a pause, she said, "My mother ignored her Indian blood, but Gramma likes that I'm proud of mine. She tells me stories from her mother, and says that maybe someday we can go to North Carolina to visit cousins."

Val listened, impressed, as Lyssie moved into tribal history. Her little sister had clearly made a serious study of the subject. When Lyssie wound down, Val said, "I'll bet that wonderful stories could be told using Lumbee history."

"I've already written stories about them," Lyssie said shyly.

"Really? Will you tell me one?"

Lyssie only needed to be asked once. Voice bright with enthusiasm, she began a lively tale of a young English girl from the Roanoke colony and the handsome Cheraw youth who saved her from starvation and took her home. When the story reached a happy ending after many adventures, Val said, "That's terrific, Lyssie. If you want to be a writer, I think you have the talent."

Lyssie looked like she wanted to accept the compliment, but didn't quite dare. "Do lawyers know about stories?"

"Do we ever!" Val grinned. "I also worked with an actress friend when she was writing the script for a movie she wanted to make. In the process, I learned a lot about the mechanics of what makes stories work."

"Did the movie get made?"

"It did indeed." Val decided to save Rainey's tale for another day since they were pulling up in the craft store parking lot. "Are you ready to be overwhelmed?"

Lyssie bounced from the car and they entered the huge, warehouse-style store. The girl halted a dozen steps inside, her eyes rounding at the explosion of colors and scents and objects. "Awesome!"

"For sure. Where would you like to start?" Val peered into the distance. "It's been a couple of years since I've had time to come here so they've probably added whole new departments. I know for sure that there are aisles and aisles of art supplies, frames and rubber stamps, scrapbooking and jewelry making and flower arranging, and as much glitter and sparkly stuff as you could use in a lifetime."

"Let's start here." Lyssie gestured toward the center of the store directly ahead of them. A silk flower sale was in progress, and dozens of tubs overflowed with masses of richly colored blossoms.

"Aren't the silk hydrangeas fantastic?" Val compared two stems of cream-colored blooms. "I think the small blossom flowers are more convincing than the ones with large petals, but these can look great if they're used right."

As Lyssie nodded gravely and selected several stems of mauve and burgundy hydrangea, Val commandeered a shopping cart. "Arrangements are usually made in vases or baskets or sometimes on vine wreaths," she explained. "Let's start by choosing flowers we like, then find settings that will do them justice."

Working their way happily around the flower island, they had the cart over half-filled by the time they finished their circuit. "Onward to dried plants. A lot of them are really just interesting weeds, but they mix well with the silk flowers and give the arrangement a more natural look." Val headed deeper into the store, then swung the cart into the right aisle. "I love this section. It smells like a hayfield in summer."

Lyssie picked up a cellophane wrapper holding half a dozen heads of dried wheat with long, delicate spines. "I've seen pictures like this, but never the real thing."

"Put a couple of those bunches in the cart, and some of those dried lilies, too. I think they look like starbursts."

Lyssie bit her lip. "This is going to be awfully expensive."

"It won't be cheap," Val agreed, "but I can afford it, the results are lovely, and we'll have fun making arrangements. For years I've worked so hard that there hasn't been time to do projects, and darn it, I want to have fun with you!"

"Since you put it that way . . ." Lyssie gave a very adult smile as she selected an armload of different kinds of dried plants. "I love the fragrance of these." Her hand lingered over bunches of leggy red eucalyptus. "Sort of like pines, but not really."

Val picked up a bunch and inhaled deeply. "The scent of California. Two of my old school friends moved out there and whenever I visit, I make sure to spend some time driving through the eucalyptus hills. The trees came from Australia originally, and they settled down happily in California as all immigrants do. Someone told me the eucalyptus live off the coastal fog, but I don't know if that's true or not."

"I'd like to visit California someday," Lyssie said wistfully. "Maybe even Australia."

"Then someday you will, after you've seen North Carolina." Seeing the girl's skepticism, Val said, "It's really possible, Lyssie. We can't have everything we want in life, but we can usually get the things we want the most. If you want to travel, you can make it happen. Travel isn't the hardest thing in life to achieve."

"What is the hardest?"

She'd always heard that kids asked tricky questions. Val crossed her arms on the push bar of the shopping cart as she thought. "Well, it's really hard to have a nice relationship with someone who doesn't want one. It takes two people to create a friendship or a romance, but only one to end it."

Lyssie's small face shuttered. "Especially if that one has a gun."

Val winced. "I'm afraid so. Usually it's not that dramatic, though. Most relationships that never happen are things like a girl you'd really like to be friends with, but she has enough friends. It's a boy you'd like to ask you out, but he only dates tall blondes. You can earn the money to fly to Australia, but you probably can't change the mind of a guy who likes tall blondes if you're a short redhead."

"But somewhere there is a tall blonde who likes a guy who only likes short redheads."

Val laughed. "Exactly. The silver lining is that often the girl you thought was cool and wanted for a friend turns out to be a lot less interesting than the quiet girl at the next desk." She pulled out more tangy bunches of green, blue, and red eucalyptus. "Shall we move on to the baskets and containers?"

Lyssie nodded and they headed deeper into the store. So far, so good, Val decided. A Big Sister/Little Sister match was supposed to be fun, and this one was.

CHAPTER 22

❦

FRIDAY NIGHT WITH VAL, AND NOW SATURDAY AS well. As Rob rang her doorbell, he decided he could get into doing this regularly.

"Hi!" She swung the door open, casually·dressed in a long-skirted summer dress. Glancing down, she added, "No Malcolm?"

"I didn't want to upset the cats. Or Malcolm, for that matter, since he'd be outnumbered." Rob stepped inside and shut the door behind him so the cats couldn't escape before enveloping her in a hug. "You're a sight for sore eyes, Valentine. What better way to end a long, hot day than in the arms of a small, hot woman?"

She rubbed against him like one of her cats. "I hope that's a compliment."

"It is." He rested his cheek on her bouncy curls, feeling his tension unwind. "I can't think of anything nicer than coming home to you, even if it's not my home."

She laughed. "June Cleaver I'm not."

"For sure—you're much sexier. June needed to get a life. I've always suspected that when the boys were grown, she dumped Ward, went to law school, and became an environmental litigator."

"What a delicious thought!" Disengaging from their embrace, Val linked an arm through his and steered him toward the kitchen. "Dinner isn't ready yet, but soon."

He paused to study two silk flower arrangements on the floor, one in a large basket and the other in an antique-style Mediterranean urn. "These are attractive. Did you and Lyssie spend the afternoon shopping?"

"First we shopped, then we made the arrangements." Val contemplated their handiwork fondly. "Since I have that whole large church to decorate, I figured I could use some sizable floor baskets to brighten boring corners. Lyssie did the Greek urn. Isn't it nice? She gave it to me for the office, then made a beautiful autumn wreath for her grandmother. Next week we'll try some tabletop pieces."

He tried to remember if he'd ever paid attention to a dried flower arrangement before. "These will brighten your office, but I'm a little surprised that you enjoy doing this. With your mother an artist, I would have thought you would prefer to work on something more . . . more sophisticated."

Val made a face. "I would if I could, but I have no artistic talent. I realized that early since Callie is so amazing. Not just her fabric art but drawing, painting, ceramics. You name it, she can do it. My friend Laurel is a born artist like Callie, and they've always gotten on like a house afire. It was a great disappointment to both my mother and me that I was a nonstarter creatively, but even a no-talent can put together a decent silk flower arrangement. It's fun and satisfies the need to make something pretty."

He recognized the underlying wistfulness in her voice. "You may not be at Callie's level—few people are—but you create wonderful, harmonious surroundings, not to mention being a knock-out dresser."

Val beamed. "What wonderful things you say. I think I'll keep you."

He'd like to think she meant that literally, but he knew a figure of speech when he heard one. "We all have our talents. Mechanical and computer things come naturally to me. You're a word child. While you didn't get your mother's artistic sense, you inherited your father's legal brain, and the law usually pays a lot better than art."

"True, but my artist mother has a lot more fun than my lawyer father." She resumed towing him toward the kitchen. "Would you like to unwind with a glass of chardonnay while I make the salad and the pasta for the shrimp scampi?"

"Please." He loved this unexpected domestic side of Val as much as he adored her delicious body and razor-sharp mind. He and Janice had always been so blasted busy that their social life was pretty much a matter of meeting somewhere for a late dinner, then going to his place or hers to spend the night. It was rare even to share coffee and bagels the next morning.

He smiled to himself as he thought that with a husband, a baby, and a dog, Janice was probably up to her ears in domesticity. She seemed happy with it, though. The last time they had talked had been a year or so ago, when he called to congratulate her on the release of her first computer game for preschoolers. At that time domesticity had seemed a dream beyond his grasp but maybe, if he wooed Val with sufficient patience, it would be possible to have the real, welcoming home he'd always longed for.

As Val poured and passed a glass of white wine, she said, "I got a good start on drafting Daniel's petition this morning."

"What happens when it's ready to go?"

"I'll deliver copies to the state's attorney's office and to the circuit court judge who tried Daniel originally, since he's still on the bench. Needless to say, it will be flagged as urgent." She shivered. "Only about three weeks now. It seems so . . . so strange to watch this deliberate countdown to death. Barbaric."

"Very." He sipped the chilled wine. "What will the judge do?"

"Hold a hearing. It can be either in open court or in his chambers. Based on his usual habits, probably Judge Giordano will opt for his chambers. I'll be there to argue the merits of the new evidence while the state's attorney's office will send someone to explain that the original sentence was correct and Daniel deserves to burn in hell." She frowned. "Cal Murphy says Giordano is fair but a tough-on-crime sort. He wouldn't be my first choice. His court is the logical place for us to start, though."

"Can I come to the hearing?"

"Maybe. It depends on what the judge wants. I'll ask to bring you and Kendra. Having non-lawyers there would be unusual, but not unheard of."

"Should Kendra go to the hearing? It will be painful."

Val gave him a look. "Don't be overprotective. Kendra is a strong, strong woman who has been fighting for Daniel for years. It's for her to decide whether or not she wants to come to a hearing, or to the execution, if it comes to that."

"You're probably right. I was just thinking of all the court proceedings I attended during Jeff's passage through the legal system." His hand tightened around the wineglass. "Gut-wrenching."

"No doubt," she said coolly. "Yet you had the choice to attend or stay away, and you chose to attend. The easy way isn't always the best."

"I suppose not." He sighed. "The whole clumsy apparatus of capital punishment is one long exercise in torture for everyone concerned. That's why I want it ended once and for all."

"I'm beginning to agree with you." She opened the refrigerator and removed a bowl of mixed salad greens. "Was your day productive?"

"Not half bad. In the afternoon I had to teach a class in Sheetrock installation and finishing for some kids at the community center, but in the morning I managed to run down an old cell mate of Omar Benson's."

"And . . . ?" Val paused in tossing the salad.

"He says Benson several times boasted of killing a cop and getting clean away."

"Great! Will he talk on the record?"

"Since Benson is dead, yes. Omar was one mean dude. Everyone was scared of him when he was alive. The cell mate is out on parole and working as a mechanic now, and he doesn't like the idea of someone else dying for Omar's crime."

"Excellent. It's hearsay, but compelling hearsay, and the judge can consider it if he wants to." She finished tossing the salad and sprinkled a handful of cashew bits on top. "We not only have testimony that Daniel was elsewhere when Malloy was killed, but we've located the likely murderer. Do you think you can find some more people who might have heard Omar boasting? I'll be filing my petition at the end of the week, I hope, and the more supporting material we have, the better."

"I have leads on several more of Omar Benson's associates. A lot of the people who knew him well are dead, though." He shook his head again. "What a waste of human potential."

The cell phone on his belt rang as Val dropped a large handful of fettuccine into the pot of boiling water. "Sorry, I thought I'd turned this thing off," he said. "Do you mind if I answer?"

"No problem. Dinner is still a few minutes away." She moved into the dining room and began setting the table.

He clicked the cell phone button to answer the incoming call. "Hello, Rob here."

"Mr. Smith? This is Lucy Morrison."

Recognizing the soft voice of Joe Cady's sister, he said, "Hi. Are you checking up on Malcolm? He's doing fine. I took some photos today. When they're developed on Monday, I'll take some prints to the nursing home for Joe to see. I warn you, if you want that dog back, you'll have to act fast. By the end of next week, I won't be able to bear losing him. He's a great dog."

"I'm not calling about the dog." Lucy drew an audible breath. "Joe . . . Joe died this afternoon. I thought you'd want to know."

His levity vanished. "I'm so sorry. I knew he was very weak, but I didn't think . . . Not so soon." He thought of Joe Cady's dark, haunted eyes, and his willingness to set the record straight. "I hope the end was peaceful."

"It was. My brother and sister and I were all there. Everyone who remembered what he once was." Her voice broke. "It had been weeks since I visited him, so the night you came for the dog and told me he was failing, my sister and I went by. He was happy to see us. I took him some warm cornbread. He . . . he enjoyed getting it even though he couldn't swallow more than a mouthful.

"Before we left, we talked to the head nurse of his floor. This morning she called to say that the end was near. I . . . I think maybe Joe had been waiting to say good-bye to his family before he was ready to pass over."

Rob closed his eyes. "My brother did not 'go gentle into that good night.' I'm glad that Joe did."

"So am I, and I need to thank you for making it happen. I'd had my head in the sand, not wanting to deal with the pain. This way, a lot of healing was done at the end."

"If there's anything I can do . . ."

After a moment's thought, Lucy said, "Maybe you can send me some of those pictures of Malcolm, and I'll put them in the coffin. Joe surely did love that dog."

Rob promised to develop the pictures and drop them by Monday. After offering condolences again, he signed off.

Val was watching from the doorway to the dining room, her eyes enormous. "Joe Cady is gone?"

He nodded. "At least his family was with him."

"May he rest in peace, poor fellow."

A timer rang and she moved to the stove to take the fettuccine off the heat. As she poured it through a colander, she said, "I'm glad we got that videotape when we did, and sorry he won't be available if the state's attorney's office wants to interview him."

"You think it will make a difference in the petition?"

"I don't know. Probably not." Abandoning dinner for the moment, she crossed to Rob and hugged him hard.

"What a day it's been. You need more wine and a good dinner. And next time you come, bring Malcolm. It's time he met Damocles and Lilith."

That sounded distinctly domestic. He held her close, soothed by the softness of her body against his.

But he couldn't escape thoughts of dying brothers.

AFTER MUCH INDECISION, KENDRA DECIDED IT WAS best not to let Daniel know she was bringing Jason to the SuperMax because he might refuse to meet them. If that happened, there might not be another chance. She had lived with the prospect of Daniel's death for so many years that the looming execution didn't seem quite real. Yet every now and then, the reality that he might be killed in cold blood slammed into her gut like a hammer.

As she and Jason went through the prison security routine, she saw the system as if for the first time. Like all visitors, Jason was sobered by the atmosphere of the prison, but he was in firm control of himself. As he submitted to being searched, she asked, "You sure you want to go through this?"

"I'm sure," he said tersely.

She was glad of that. No matter how difficult this visit was, it would be better than Jason learning later that his father had died before they could meet.

They reached the visiting room and Kendra sat in the chair by the phone while Jason quietly stood by the door. After about five minutes, the prisoner's door opened and Daniel stepped inside with his escort of two guards. He sat down, smiling at Kendra as he picked up the handset on his side of the barrier. "Wasn't expectin' you, sugar."

"I have a surprise for you." She half turned and gestured at Jason.

Daniel looked across the room. Since Jason wore his air force uniform, Daniel had probably vaguely registered his presence as a guard, but he instantly recognized his visitor when he looked into his son's face. "No! He shouldn't be here."

He jumped to his feet, knocking the chair over in his agitation. The guards instantly snapped into full alert mode.

"Don't go!" Expecting his reaction, Kendra held his gaze as she spoke swiftly. "Jason knows, Daniel, and he wants to meet you. Don't deny him the right to know his father." The words "for as long as you have left" hung unspoken in the air.

Daniel hesitated, his expression tormented but his eyes avid as he studied his son. "You broke your promise."

"I swear I didn't. By pure, weird coincidence, your old public defender has a niece in Jason's class at the academy. Murphy mentioned you and the case in an e-mail, she talked to Jason, and here he is." Her voice dropped. "Don't throw this chance away, Daniel. I think it was meant to be."

She glanced at her son. Face set, he stepped forward and took the handset, settling into the chair when she moved away. As the two men looked at each other through the plastic, she marveled at the similarities of face and build. They had identical anxious expressions, too. *Choose your words carefully, Jay, or he'll bolt, too ashamed to look you in the eye.*

"Hello." Jason swallowed, his Adam's apple bobbing. "It's . . . strange to discover that I have a second father."

"I can guess." Daniel's grip on the phone was pale-knuckled. "I never wanted you to see me like this."

"Mama says you're innocent, so any shame belongs to the State of Maryland." Jason's voice was stronger. "She also says maybe the sentence will be commuted."

Kendra saw one of the guards snort. Luckily, Jason missed that.

"Maybe. I'm not countin' on it." Daniel's voice was soft as a whisper. He reached toward his son, dropping his hand when it encountered the plastic. "I truly didn't want this—I've caused my family enough pain. But now that you're here, you are surely a sight for sore eyes. You were just a toddler the last time I saw you, splashin' your mama with water when you took a bath. I called you Little Bit."

A muscle jerked in Jason's jaw. "I've only known about

you for a few days, yet you seem familiar," he said hesi-
tantly. "Maybe part of me remembers from when I was a
baby."

"I hope so. We had some good times together. You sure
did love ridin' on my shoulder, and when I whirled you in
the air. These days they say you shouldn't swing babies
around like that, it might scramble their little brains, but
you and I didn't know any better, and we sure did have fun."
Daniel gave a rumbling chuckle. "Doesn't seem to have
scrambled your brains, either. Maybe that's where you got
your first taste of flyin'. But don't let's waste time talkin'
about me. I want to hear about you. Tell me about the academy. I want to hear about your basketball, your classes,
your military trainin', your friends. I want to hear it all."

Slowly at first, then with increasing fluency, Jason began describing his classes, the things he was learning both
inside and outside the classroom, the beauty of the Rock-
ies. Even though Kendra had relayed much of the information from Jason's e-mails, Daniel listened hungrily,
absorbing every syllable.

Kendra watched the conversation with relief. She hadn't
been kidding when she told Daniel that she thought this
was meant to be. Sometimes when people were being stupid, God stepped in. Jason and Daniel were doing their part
by moving beyond anger to deal effectively with the situation as it was. There was a similarity in how the two
thought that was making it easy for them to converse.
Maybe the plastic barrier between them actually helped at
this stage, when they were virtual strangers even though
they shared blood and bone and DNA.

Closing her eyes, she prayed that the day would come
when her son and his father could actually touch each
other. Hug each other. And if that day never came—well, at
least they had *this* day.

CHAPTER 23

❦

VAL LET HER VOICE MAIL PICK UP THE INCOMING call, wondering how she could ever have thought that starting her own office would mean she'd be less busy. Two days into her official occupancy of the church, she was running in circles like a tail-chasing kitten.

The previous morning she hadn't even poured coffee before receiving a phone call that one of her Crouse, Resnick cases had suddenly become hot. While Kendra pulled the files on that, a call had come in from Bill Costain, her biggest Crouse, Resnick client. Not only was he transferring much of his business to her, he had a big project that had needed discussing immediately.

She had complied, driving down to Annapolis for a waterfront lunch meeting. Not only was he a good friend and client, but most of his work was on a scale that she could handle either alone or by subcontracting to another lawyer. She needed him as a client for the financial security of her fledging legal business. But she had hardly had time to draw a deep breath, and she absolutely couldn't neglect work on Daniel's petition.

Nonetheless, it was great to have her own place, and at

Crouse, Resnick having a snoring hound in her office would have been frowned on. She glanced at the patch of sunlight that Malcolm had claimed. Since Rob was going to be out most of the day, he'd brought Malcolm downstairs. Not only was the dog pleasant, undemanding company, but now she didn't have to listen to his stubby claws tapping upstairs in Rob's apartment.

Val was reaching for another document when the doorbell rang. Kendra had taken the morning off for personal business, so Val hiked from her office to the front door herself. She made a mental note to talk to Rob about putting in a video camera and solenoid system so she could check out visitors and let them in from her desk.

Standing on her doorstep was Mia Kolski, the music teacher whose ex-husband kept taking her to court. "Hi, Val. Since I was nearby, I thought I'd drop off the documents you requested in person."

"Come on in." Feeling guilty that she hadn't been more aggressive on Mia's behalf, Val stepped aside and led the other woman to the small conference room. "Did you find anything interesting?"

"That's why I need to talk to you." Mia sat and opened her tote bag to remove a fat file. "When I contacted the army pension office to find out why I wasn't entitled to any of Steve's pension, they sent me a copy of this waiver." She handed over a photocopy.

Val studied the document. It was signed and notarized. "Is it possible Steve slipped this in without you noticing when you were signing a bunch of papers?"

"That could have happened, but it didn't. To begin with, that's not my signature. It was signed and notarized in Georgia during the time he was living in Atlanta." Mia tapped the copy of the notary seal. "I've never been in Atlanta except passing through the airport, and I sure as heck wasn't there for this notary to testify to my identity."

"Good grief, Steve forged this? And convinced a notary to witness?" With rising excitement, Val studied the signature and the seal more closely. "I suppose he could have gone to the notary with some female friend who claimed to be you. This does look more or less like your signature, though, and graphologists don't always agree on authenticity. Can you prove that you were in Maryland when this was signed?"

"Darned right I can." Mia smiled triumphantly. "That happened to be the day of the school's spring music recital. I taught in the morning, rehearsed in the afternoon, and directed the production in the evening."

"You've got witnesses who can swear to this?"

Mia nodded. "The water pipes in the girls' restroom broke and made a terrible mess that morning, and we had to scramble like mad to put the show on. The day is engraved deep in all the teachers' memories. Including your mother's, I'm sure."

Val whooped with glee. "We've got him, Mia! This is fraud, and we can prove our case. Shall we start with a threat to his lawyer saying we'll take him to court if he doesn't return your pension rights, or shall we go right to the police?"

Mia hesitated. "Steve is a jerk but I don't want to send the father of my kids to jail. I'd be willing to give up my half of the pension to get him and his sleazy lawsuits off my back. Is there some way we can use this as leverage to stop him from dragging me to court every few months?"

Val sat back in her chair and thought about it. "I'll have to check with one of my family law friends to be sure. A lot depends on whether he wants the money more than he enjoys driving you crazy."

"He likes harassing me, but he *loves* money. He's making far more now than he did in the army, and it just seems to have made him want even more."

"Then maybe I can draw up an agreement which you would both sign, in which he acknowledges that the waiver is fraudulent, and you promise not to press charges nor claim any pension money as long as he doesn't take you to court again. It gives him a major incentive to find other ways of getting his jollies."

"If you can get him to agree to that, it would be great!" Mia sighed blissfully. "Being able to get on with my life. What a concept."

Val jotted a note on her tablet. "I'd also want to include a clause saying that from now on, the child support will be sent automatically from his bank account. If he doesn't have to personally write that check every month, he might be less cranky about it."

Mia rose and hugged Val. "You're a genius!"

"A lawyer is only as good as the ammunition she has to work with." Val grinned. "And you just handed me a bazooka."

After Mia left, Val called and left a message for a friend who specialized in family law to find out if her plan was feasible, then returned to work on the Crouse, Resnick case. She lost track of time and was startled to realize that it was well after noon when Kendra appeared in the door of Val's office.

"Jason is here with me," Kendra said. "Do you want to say hi?"

"I'd love to." As Val moved from behind her desk, Jason followed his mother into the room. It was the first time Val had seen him since he'd entered the academy almost a year earlier, and the intervening time had filled out his muscular frame and matured him. In his uniform, he was enough to make young women swoon, and older ones draw a deep breath. "Look at you, Jason! The air force obviously agrees with you."

"It does. Nice to see you, Miss Val." He took her proffered hand briefly. "We just came from the SuperMax prison."

Uh-oh. Val cast a quick glance at Kendra. "It's a suffocating place, isn't it?"

"No need for evasive tactics, Val. Jason found out about Daniel from Cal Murphy's niece, so we decided it was time he met his other father." Kendra smiled a little wearily. "It went pretty well, didn't it, Jay?"

As Jason nodded, Val said, "Sit down and tell me about

it if you have time. If you have any legal questions, ask away."

Kendra and Jason took chairs while Val came around the desk and perched on the edge so she wouldn't look so formal. Jason asked bluntly, "What are the odds of getting him off death row?"

Val wished she could offer whole-hearted assurance, but she couldn't. "We've got a decent shot. At the least, we should be able to get a postponement while the new evidence is evaluated. If the court finds it compelling, maybe his sentence can be permanently commuted to life imprisonment."

Jason absorbed that. "What is the chance of his getting released from prison?"

"We'd have to come up with some really stunning evidence, like the long-lost murder weapon, or hope we could persuade the governor to pardon him." She grimaced. "Since capital punishment is very political, that's not terribly likely."

"It's so unfair." Jason's low voice vibrated with emotion. "I grew up not facing any real racism. Sure, I knew it existed, and that older folks had fought a lot of tough battles, but I never realized that it affected me. And it does, doesn't it? Would my . . . my other father be on death row if he was white?"

It was a question Val had already asked herself. "Given the facts of this case, it's hard to say. He might be. Malloy was killed by a black man—that's never been in dispute, and Daniel did fit the description. A number of the police and prosecutors involved were black, and he certainly wasn't railroaded, not with three eyewitnesses swearing he was the killer. Kendra, did you feel that Cal Murphy was a smart, capable attorney who did his best?"

Kendra nodded. "Even at the time, I thought Murphy was pretty good. He wasn't drunk, didn't sleep through testimony or any of the other awful things you hear about. I appreciate him even more now that I've worked in law offices for so many years."

Val turned back to Jason. "But would your mother's testimony that she and Daniel were together have been dismissed so quickly if she were a white doctor instead of a black clerk? Maybe not. Would the police have done a more thorough investigation if they hadn't had a convenient black suspect with a criminal record? Maybe. There's racism in the system, but it's hard to prove in any given case."

Jason's lips tightened. "If he were white, maybe he wouldn't have been sentenced to death."

"Again, it's hard to say," she replied. "The best predictor of the death sentence is not the race of the killer, but the race of the victim. Death sentences are much more common if the victim is white."

"I find that particularly offensive," Kendra interjected. "As if a white life is worth more than a black one."

"Damned right it's offensive." Val looked down at the floor, trying to formulate ideas she'd never put into words. "Race is the karmic burden of America. Every other immigrant group that came here did so willingly. The brave and the ambitious made incredible sacrifices and took great risks to come to America for the chance to build better lives. African Americans are the only exception. They were brought here against their will, enslaved and brutalized, deliberately deprived of culture, education, and the opportunities others took for granted. Now, for our sins as a nation, race haunts us." She raised her gaze to Kendra. "I'm almost afraid to say such things out loud because race is such a volatile, painful subject, but how can we heal if we can't even talk?"

"I've often thought similar things," Kendra said quietly. "Even all these years after the Civil War, race matters. I grew up feeling as if there were invisible walls around me, walls a black girl couldn't climb over. I didn't want Jason to feel the same."

"You succeeded." Jason studied his mother's face with new respect. Val guessed that he had taken his sheltered, supportive upbringing for granted, as young people usually did. At nineteen, for the first time, he was beginning to understand how much conscious parenting had gone into raising him. He'd probably have to have kids of his own before he truly understood how lucky he had been.

Turning back to Val, Jason asked, "Is there anything I can do? I . . . I like my new father. I don't want to lose him before I have a chance to know him."

"If I think of anything, I'll ask pronto." Val glanced at her clock. "Shall we order in a pizza for lunch? Serious conversation always gives me a desire for saturated fats."

The atmosphere lightened and they began negotiating preferences for pizza toppings. While holding out for onions and Italian sausage, Val gave private thanks for the chance that had informed Jason of Daniel's sentence. If the worst happened . . . well, Kendra wouldn't have to mourn alone.

AS SOON AS HE ESCAPED THE ROOF WHERE THEY'D been working, Sha'wan Baker poured water over his head from a bottle stashed in the cooler of his van, then wiped himself dry with a towel. "Thanks for helping out with this job, Rob. If I'd had to spend twice as long painting out that graffiti, I'd've ended up shriveled like a raisin."

Rob used another towel to wipe down his face and neck. "Nothing like standing on a black roof on a hot day to appreciate air-conditioning."

"With the weather so hot, the taggers haven't been as busy as usual." Sha'wan peeled off his soaked T-shirt, then pulled on a dry one. "Gran wants to know how you're doing investigating that Monroe guy? She's still sorry that she couldn't come up with anything useful when you talked to her."

"Lots of leads go nowhere. At least by talking to your grandmother, I got a better sense of what the neighborhood was like at the time the murder took place." He grinned. "I also got a really sensational piece of fresh blueberry pie, so it was time well spent."

"Gran sure can cook, but I guess she didn't know enough criminals for your purposes. She's a real straight shooter, my Gran."

"You can tell her that we've actually made some progress—it looks like a drug dealer from a nearby crack house, a bad dude called Omar Benson, probably did the shooting. He was killed in prison a few years later. Though he was a suspect in some gang killings, they never nailed him for murder." Rob pulled a bottle of water from the van's cooler, this time to drink. "If you were a drug dealer who tried to rape a woman, got interrupted, and killed a cop, what would you do with the murder weapon?"

Sha'wan popped a rootbeer as he thought about it. "For sure the police would come down on the neighborhood like gangbusters since one of their guys was killed. As a drug dealer, I'd be high on the list, so I'd get rid of that gun right away. Can't just toss it in the trash or under a bush because guns turn up real fast. Can't take it back to my business establishment, because that might be searched, me being a suspicious citizen. Probably I'd give it to a homey to hold. A dude I really trusted, maybe a guy who owed me one. Someone who wouldn't be a suspect himself so he wouldn't be searched."

"Makes sense." Rob suppressed a sigh. He hadn't had a lot of luck running down Benson's associates from the crack house; Omar had led an untidy life. "Would I throw the gun out later, toss it in the bay or something? Or would I retrieve it from my buddy and keep carrying it?"

"That might depend on the gun. Was it cool?"

"Very likely. It was a 7.65 mm handgun, which is about equal to an American .32, only this one was European and probably expensive."

"You've checked out this Benson dude's guns in his later life?"

"Yep. He was never arrested carrying a gun this size. He seemed to prefer larger stuff. Fancy show-off guns."

Sha'wan considered. "Suppose Omar shot the cop with a fancy European gun. He knows he can't carry it again anytime soon but he wants to keep it, so maybe his homey stashes it somewhere. Omar goes to prison and dies before he can reclaim it."

"So the gun might be out there somewhere with one of his friends, if I can find any of them alive. That makes sense. Thanks for the thoughts."

"Anytime." Sha'wan grinned. "I'd rather talk than paint in weather like this."

Rob finished his water and dropped the bottle in the recycling bucket Sha'wan kept in the van. "See you later. I might be talking to one of Benson's old buddies today, so I'll be sure to sound him out about guns."

He climbed into his pickup, grateful for the air-conditioning that blasted on. He was about to put the truck in gear when his cell phone rang. He unclipped it from his belt and pressed the answer button. "Rob here."

A soft, cultivated female voice said, "Hello, I'm Julia Hamilton, Kate Corsi's mother. We met at the Milton Inn. My husband is the judge."

"Of course." Julia was the tall, elegant blonde who looked so much like her daughter. "What can I do for you?"

There was a stretch of silence before she said, "This is a bit awkward, but . . . you're Robert Smith Gabriel, aren't you?"

He tensed. So he had indeed been recognized. "Yes, though I haven't used the name Gabriel lately."

"Understandable. You must have felt you'd been caught in a tornado for several years." A wry note entered her voice. "You have the right to lie low, and I don't blame you if you prefer to stay in deep hiding. But if you're up for it, I want to ask if you'd consider speaking to a group of prisoners' families."

"I beg your pardon?" Rob blinked in astonishment. "Why would you want me?"

"Because you have suffered as they have, and may have something useful to say." She laughed a little. "I'm one of those useless society types who tries to justify her existence with volunteer work, and this is a good cause."

"There are plenty of good causes. This one isn't an obvious choice," Rob observed, wondering if a member of her family was in prison. "Did you get involved with it because your husband is a judge?"

Another silence. "No. Someone close to me was murdered, though that wasn't immediately obvious—it seemed like an accident at the time. When I found out the truth, I was ready to do murder myself. I might have if the killer weren't already dead. Dealing with the whole wretched business made me realize how much damage was done all around by violence. It's like throwing a stone into a pool of blood—the ripples go on forever, in all directions."

He sighed. "The perfect metaphor."

"Pain is easy. Forgiveness and healing are hard, but essential if the anger and pain aren't to warp one's life. I became involved with the Convicts Circle, the group I mentioned, because I knew a member and I realized these were people largely overlooked by the system. Victims, victims' families, and prisoners have their advocates, but they aren't the only ones damaged."

He suspected that she seldom revealed what she had just told him. "I agree, but I don't know if I have anything particularly useful to say. I'm still dealing with the effects myself, and can't say I'm handling them brilliantly."

"Maybe that's how you feel, but you've done positive things with your grief. The graffiti obliteration campaign, the community center, the way you gave the reward money to the victims and their families. In the midst of disaster, you discovered compassion. That's admirable, and perhaps by telling your story, you can help others who are still paralyzed with grief and guilt."

How far had he moved beyond paralysis himself? Not far enough. "I'll have to think about this, Mrs. Hamilton. I really don't know if I have anything to say."

"Take your time. When and if you decide you have something to say, let me know and I'll schedule you to speak to the group. With your experience, I think you'd make an articulate spokesman, and not just in the Convicts

Circle. Have you thought about speaking out against capital punishment?"

"I get the feeling that you have been poking around the Internet," he said dryly. "Too much of my past is recorded there for comfort."

"My son is a computer wizard, and I've picked up some good search techniques from him." She laughed. "It's a sure sign of age when you learn more from your children than they're learning from you. Thanks for hearing me out, Rob, and don't agree to talk unless you're really sure you want to. We committee women can be ruthless, but I'm trying to reform."

If she was ruthless, it was disguised by immense charm. "I'll bear that in mind. Thanks for thinking of me even if I stay in my hole."

After they exchanged good-byes, he hung up, bemused. Though he had plenty of opinions, the idea of him being a useful advocate was strange. But—maybe he could get to like it.

CHAPTER 24

❧❧❧

ROB QUIETLY TOOK A CHAIR IN THE BACK OF THE judge's chambers. As Val had predicted, Judge Frank Giordano had chosen to hold an informal hearing to review new evidence in the case of Daniel Monroe, and had even granted Val's request to let Rob and Kendra attend the meeting. The state's attorney's office had sent a senior prosecutor, Morris Hancock, who had worked on Daniel's original trial, plus a young female associate.

With the judge, his clerk, and a court recorder present, the judge's chambers were crowded. Rob did his best to look unobtrusive so Giordano wouldn't throw him out. Not only was he intensely involved with this case, but he wanted to see Val in action.

With her hair pulled smoothly back and wearing one of her serious lawyer suits, Val looked sensational—capable, professional, and discreetly sexy. She'd spoken little on the trip to the courthouse. He guessed that she was mentally immersed in the case and didn't want to be disturbed, rather like an actor who was deep into a character.

With her height and presence, Kendra was equally striking, but under her surface composure she was thrumming with tension since she had the deepest emotional investment in the results of this hearing. Jeff's various hearings and trials had torn Rob up every time, despite his brother's unquestionable guilt. How much worse was it for Kendra, who knew that Daniel was innocent? Rob had met her son, a youthful, confident version of his father. Jason had returned to Colorado, but he would surely be watching the clock at the academy and wondering when he might have news.

Rob shifted his gaze to Giordano. A stocky, balding man in his sixties, he wore black judicial robes and had the deeply lined face of someone who had seen it all. But he was fair, Val said, which was what they needed.

The judge glanced at the court reporter. "I had to squeeze this hearing into a tight schedule, so let's get this going. Miss Covington, state your case. I don't want to hear a lot of rhetorical flourishes. Just present this new evidence that you claim warrants a change in the sentence of Daniel Monroe."

"Very well, your honor." Val's voice was calm but commanding. Rob could almost see the wheels spinning in her head. She had probably planned some rhetorical flourishes and was now reformulating her approach so as not to irk the judge. "I'll briefly review the facts of the case. Then I will show that the state has tragically imprisoned an innocent man for seventeen years."

"Keep it very brief," the judge said dryly. "Mr. Hancock and I were trying this case when you were in grade school."

Refusing to let him rattle her, Val gave a succinct, vivid description of the shooting and went on to explain how Daniel, a hardworking young man with a decent job and plans to marry, had been dragged from the home and falsely accused of murder.

"I'm waiting for something new, Miss Covington," Giordano said impatiently.

"Not only do we have proof of Daniel Monroe's innocence," Val said coolly, "but we know who the real murderer is. Let me show the videotape."

Val had arranged with Giordano's clerk for a television/VCR combination to be available. After Cady's damning statement was played, Val presented the corroborating affidavit from Omar Benson's cell mate, then proved how Long and Cady had lied about their lives when they were witnesses, and the police had failed to check them out. She finished by weaving all the material Rob had found into a compelling indictment of Benson. Rob watched with awe. He'd been right that she was hell on heels when it came to arguing a case. Crisp, eloquent, and passionate, she demonstrated why she was one of the top litigators in the city.

The judge listened intently, his expression unrevealing. When Val finished her argument, Giordano turned to the prosecutor. "And the state's position, Mr. Hancock?"

"The state is surprised that hearsay from convicted criminals is considered significant evidence." No stranger to courtroom histrionics, the prosecutor gave Val a patronizing smile. "Of course Miss Covington is new to the practice of criminal law, so she doesn't realize how thin her material is. Daniel Monroe is a murderer, convicted on unimpeachable evidence, and the only tragedy is that the family of Officer James Malloy has had to wait so long to see justice done."

He launched into a review of Joe Cady's medical records, suggesting that at the end of his life, Cady had been out of his head. Hancock was good, dammit. Val maintained her composure, but Rob saw Kendra's increasing frustration. She looked ready to explode.

When Hancock finished, Giordano asked Val, "Do you have any rebuttal?"

Val blasted the reliability of Joe Cady and Darrell Long and pointed out how Brenda Harris had failed to identify Daniel in the photo lineup, only singling him out when she saw him in the police lineup, where his face was the only one that was familiar. After pointing out that this was an error in police procedure, she finished by declaring that the state's case was nonexistent once the eyewitness testimony was discredited. Rob was convinced, but Giordano looked unimpressed.

Val ended by saying, "Since we have clearly demonstrated Daniel Monroe's innocence, I ask that the court order his release. If the court prefers to await further investigation until the guilt of Omar Benson has been established beyond the shadow of a doubt, I ask that the scheduled execution date of Daniel Monroe be postponed. Given the gravity of the charges against Mr. Monroe and the irreversible nature of capital punishment, I believe that the State of Maryland can do no less."

Giordano pursed his lips and tented his fingers as he considered. Surely a postponement wasn't much to ask . . .

"Petition denied, Miss Covington," the judge said gruffly. "I've been following this case through sixteen years of delays. Mr. Monroe has benefited from skilled defense by some of Maryland's best public defenders. He has received every possible benefit of the doubt, including this hearing. Yet after all this time, the best evidence you can present is the deathbed account of a hallucinating junkie and a piece of hearsay from one convicted criminal to his equally criminal cell mate. Enough is enough. At some point there must be finality. It is time for justice to be done."

No! This couldn't be happening. Rob stared at Giordano, shocked speechless that a judge could allow the death sentence to stand when there was such strong reason to believe Daniel was innocent.

"This is *not* justice!" Kendra was on her feet, blazing like an Amazon. "I am the woman who was with Daniel Monroe when Officer Malloy was killed. I *know* that he is innocent. I will swear any oath, take any examination, to prove that I am telling the truth. The state will have blood on its hands if Daniel is executed."

"That's enough! Sit down!" the judge thundered, pointing a furious finger at her.

Kendra sat.

Glaring as if she had threatened him with a gun, Giordano said, "I remember you. The girlfriend. No doubt by this time you believe your claim and could pass a lie detector test easily. Your loyalty is commendable, but no less than three eyewitness refuted your testimony, and a loyal girlfriend is hardly the most credible witness."

Kendra opened her mouth to speak again, and Giordano snapped, "Not another word or I'll hold you in contempt! The petition is denied."

Val placed a restraining hand on Kendra's wrist. Her skin tight across her cheekbones, Val said, "I shall pursue this at a higher level."

"Feel free. I doubt you will get a different result." Giordano consulted his watch. "I'm due in court. Good day, ladies and gentlemen."

He ushered all the visitors from his chambers before sweeping down the hall, his black robes billowing like crow's wings. The prosecutor told Val, his voice friendly, "Not bad, but this close to execution, you'd need a smoking gun to make a difference. Next time pick a case you can win." He departed with his junior attorney in tow.

"How can he be so casual, as if this is a game?" Rob asked through gritted teeth.

"To him it is. He played his cards and is happy that he held the winning hand." Val's mouth twisted humorlessly. "It's a lawyer thing."

"What's next?" Rob asked. "Court of appeals?"

"I have a better idea," Kendra said tightly. "The court of public opinion. This is a great human interest story, and since Jason knows the truth now, I can blast it all over Baltimore. 'Local basketball star and straight arrow military cadet's father about to be executed for a crime he didn't commit.' 'Court ignores exonerating evidence.' I can see the headlines now."

"Will Jason mind being used?" Val asked. "And it's an open question whether a media frenzy will help or hinder an appeal."

"I'm not asking your permission," Kendra retorted.

"Don't worry, I won't risk getting you disbarred by putting you in the middle. This is my crusade, and I know a reporter at the Sunpapers who will be glad to get his hands on a story like this during the August dog days."

Val glanced at Rob, her face pale against her red hair. "What do you think?"

He forced his numb mind to focus. "It's worth a try. Judges and governors read the papers, and maybe publicity will flush out more information about Benson."

"It will also flush out more information about you. Your days of anonymity would probably be over." Val's expression was troubled.

He hadn't thought of that. Sooner or later, probably sooner, his identity would become part of this story, along with the details of Jeff's crimes and well-publicized death. Everything would be raked up—his former life, and the way he had run away from it. But it wasn't like he had a choice here. "My privacy is less important than Daniel's life. Do your damnedest, Kendra."

"I will." She gave a swift, dangerous smile. "Val, I'll be out of the office most of the afternoon. I need to visit Daniel and . . . and tell him the results of the hearing."

Val shook her head. "I'm his lawyer. Breaking bad news is my job."

Kendra started to protest, then accepted Val's argument. "Very well, I'll call my Sunpapers contact, and there's . . . another person I want to talk to."

"Okay, I'll see you whenever." As Kendra walked away, her strides long and swift, Val turned to Rob. She let her composure drop, revealing anguish. "I really thought we'd get at least the delay, and maybe even get the death sentence commuted."

"You did a terrific job," Rob said. "We knew going in that Giordano was a law and order type. It's obvious now that his standards for granting a petition were impossibly high. Kendra's right. Maybe this can be done through the courts, but maybe not. We need to use any weapons we can find."

Val took a deep breath. "One thing's for sure—none of us are giving up."

"Damned straight." He put his arm around her shoulders. She leaned tiredly into him, her small body soft and vulnerable. If they weren't in the middle of the courthouse, he would do more than hug her. They could both use some comfort.

Though Val had warned him that success couldn't be taken for granted, he had really believed that Cady's recantation would be enough to block the execution, at least temporarily. Now the reality of failure numbed him to his bones. How could a modern, civilized society cold-bloodedly destroy an innocent man?

Daniel Monroe was his chance for redemption. If he failed the other man, he failed himself.

IT MIGHT HAVE BEEN EASIER IF DANIEL HAD RAGED or cursed Val out. Instead, he simply looked down, the harsh fluorescent lights emphasizing the scar that ran across his skull. "I didn't really expect anything, Miss Val. Like I said the first time you came in here, it's easier not to expect much."

"It's hard to predict how any given judge or jury will act, but I was really hopeful." She still felt the defeat like a kick in the stomach. "But it's not over yet. Giordano is only a circuit court judge. I'll go higher. There's still time."

He shrugged. "Don't kill yourself tryin'. The justice system is like a string of boxcars—real hard to stop once it gets goin'."

"By God, it *can* be stopped!" she said fiercely. "And it will be even if I have to lay down on the tracks myself."

"If this is about you winnin', go to it," he said with wry humor. "But you don't have to do it for me. I've made my peace, met my son, and said good-bye to the few people still willin' to care about me. That's more than I hoped for a few weeks ago." He got to his feet. "Good-bye, Miss Val. Thanks for tryin'."

He inclined his head with grave courtesy, then turned and left with the guards. Val had never seen such dignity in her life.

As she blindly left the prison, she wondered if dignity was the best one could hope for in a world that seldom pretended to be fair.

KENDRA DROVE TO THE CHURCH TO PICK UP A videotape and a photo. After leaving a message for Al Coleman, the *Sun* reporter, she e-mailed Jason. "No luck at the hearing, but we're still fighting. Brace yourself—I'm about to go public. Love, 'The Mom.' "

She felt a sting of tears when she sent the message, but she blinked them away. There was no time for crying.

To establish that her quarry was home, she made a quick phone call, then hung up after apologizing for a wrong number. Then she drove out to the Harford County home of Anne Malloy Peterson, widow of Officer James Malloy.

It took the better part of an hour to reach the upscale subdivision set among woodsy green hills. The Peterson home was a pleasant, well-landscaped brick colonial. There wasn't another person in sight when Kendra climbed from the car, but the woman of the house answered the doorbell readily enough. A business suit did a good job of making a black person respectable even in a white-bread place like this.

"Yes?" Anne Peterson's brows drew together. "We've met, haven't we?" Petite and pretty, she was only a few years older than Kendra. Her light brown hair had streaks of silver and she looked like a typical well-kept, well-adjusted suburban matron. But she had the eyes of a woman who had paid more than her share of life's dues. Before remarrying and moving to the country, she had spent ten years as a struggling single mother.

"We didn't exactly meet, but we were connected by a tragedy." Kendra held the smaller woman's gaze. "My name was Kendra Jackson. Do you remember now?"

Anne Peterson looked puzzled for a moment, then gasped with recognition. "Good God, you're Daniel Monroe's girlfriend! We sat on opposite sides of the courtroom every day of the trial." Her fingers tightened on the edge of the door.

Guessing that it was about to be slammed in her face, Kendra raised a hand. "Please, Mrs. Peterson. I don't want to probe old wounds, but this is critically important. A man's life is at stake. Will you hear me out? Please?"

Reluctantly the other woman stepped aside so Kendra could enter. "Very well, but I can't imagine what we might have to talk about, Miss Jackson."

"It's Mrs. Brooks now." Kendra deliberately avoided the "Ms." she usually used, since she guessed that Anne Peterson leaned toward the traditional. "A couple of years after Daniel Monroe was convicted of murdering your husband, I married someone else."

Mrs. Peterson remained standing, her arms tightly folded across her chest. "Monroe is going to die in ten days. I have a bottle of champagne that's been waiting a long time for this moment."

"Mrs. Peterson, your husband was a hero who died in the line of duty," Kendra said softly. "His murder was a terrible crime that deserves a terrible punishment. But Daniel wasn't the killer, and he doesn't deserve to die. Will you watch a videotape that proves Daniel's innocence?"

The other woman's mouth thinned. "What does your husband think of your running around trying to free an old lover?"

"Like you I was widowed, though at least my husband had the blessing of dying of natural causes. Believe me, Mrs. Peterson, I know about loss, and about being a single mother." Kendra pulled the videotape from her handbag. "You have every right to want justice, but do you really want Daniel Monroe to die if he's innocent?"

"No one wants to see an innocent man executed." The other woman frowned at the videocassette. "Come on into the family room and we'll take a look at that thing, but it will have to be very, very convincing to change my mind."

Silently Kendra followed her into the comfortable family room that adjoined the country kitchen. Equally silent, the other woman picked up a remote and turned on the VCR and the big screen television, then handed her guest the control.

Kendra slid in the tape and fast forwarded to the beginning before pausing at the first frame. The large screen displayed a life-sized Joe Cady, every bone visible under his yellowish skin. "You might not recognize him, but this is Joe Cady, one of the key witnesses against Daniel. This tape was made less than two weeks ago. Cady died this past Saturday." She hit PLAY, and Joe Cady began to talk.

Anne Peterson stiffened when she realized what he was saying. Throughout the short tape, Cady looked directly at the camera as he recounted his perjury in short, choppy sentences with long pauses as he gasped for breath.

When the tape finished, Kendra asked, "Do you want to see any of it again?"

"No." Anne slumped onto the sofa, her expression agonized. "You said all along that he was with you, and I thought you were lying. But you weren't, were you?"

"I was telling the truth," she said softly. "Daniel was home the whole evening."

"May the Blessed Mother forgive me. For all these years my . . . my anger and hatred have been aimed at the wrong man."

A pity that Judge Giordano had been too jaded to believe the plain truth when he saw it. Anne Peterson was more clear-sighted. "You weren't the only one who was wrong. At least now you're capable of seeing the truth. Not everyone is."

"Seventeen years. He's been in prison for seventeen years." Anne shook her head slowly. "What about Omar Benson?"

"You'll be glad to know that he's long dead—stabbed to death in prison about five years after your husband died. It was messy and painful." Kendra pulled out the photo that Rob had obtained and duplicated. "Here's the booking shot for the last time Benson was arrested. Your husband has been long since avenged."

"He looks like a stone killer." Anne's mouth twisted into a thin, hard line. "May his soul rot in hell. Now sit down and tell me why you came out here. Not just to enlighten me, I'm sure."

Kendra sat. "I'm a paralegal now. My boss, Val Covington, agreed to see if she could help Daniel. You see the results, but this tape isn't enough for the justice system. This morning Val asked Frank Giordano, the original trial judge, to commute Daniel's sentence or at least postpone the execution until we could finish investigating Benson. Her petition was denied."

Anne's brows drew together. "Did Giordano see this tape?"

"He did, but from his point of view, Daniel has had plenty of chances and it's time he was executed."

"But he's innocent!"

"That isn't always good enough." Kendra tried to keep bitterness from her voice. "I plan to go to the Sunpapers and raise hell. It would help if the widow of the murdered man said she believes the wrong man was convicted. Would you be willing to say that to a reporter if one called?"

Anne bit her lip, distress in her eyes. "I really don't want to rake all this up. It hurts too much."

"An innocent man's life is at stake."

The other woman bent her head and ran her fingers through her short, tousled curls. "You're right. As a good Catholic, I shouldn't really believe in capital punishment in the first place, though my parish priest granted me an unofficial dispensation on that after Jim was murdered. All right, if a reporter calls, I'll tell him that I've seen your evidence, and I found it convincing."

Kendra exhaled with relief. This could have gone either way. "Thanks so much, Mrs. Peterson. I know this won't be easy."

"Jim was a great believer in the truth." Anne blinked tears back. "Good luck in saving Mr. Monroe's life, Mrs. Brooks."

"Thank you. We're going to need all the luck we can get." Kendra stood. "The tape is a duplicate. Would you like to keep it and the photograph of Benson, maybe show it to your husband?"

"Please. Bob was a school friend of Jim's. He'll want to see justice done, too." Anne set the photo on the end table and rose to her feet. "Maybe we'll drink that champagne tonight. It's strange to think Jim's killer has been dead for so long. If I'd known when he died, I would have celebrated, but now it's just ashes."

"Ashes is what Omar Benson deserved." Kendra offered her hand. "Thanks again. You're a brave woman, Mrs. Peterson."

"I'm not. But don't most women do what must be done?" She gave a shaky smile as they shook hands.

Kendra drove back to Baltimore feeling a little hope. But only a little.

CHAPTER 25

VAL AND ROB RETURNED TO THE OFFICE TOGETHER.
"After I change, I'll try to hunt down more of Omar Benson's associates," Rob said. "Is it okay if I leave Malcolm down here after I walk him?"

"Sure. I'll be glad of the company."

Rob gave her a light kiss, then headed up to his apartment. Val kept a couple of casual outfits in her office, so she swapped her tailored suit for an ankle-length skirt and loose knit top. Long hours of work were easier when she was comfortable.

First on the agenda was phoning Cal Murphy, who, amazingly, was even available. When she told him about the decision, he swore under his breath. "Damnation. Even though Giordano is a hard-liner, I thought you had a good shot at getting at least a short reprieve."

She rubbed the tight knot between her eyes. "Do you have time for me to pick your brain about strategies for the next round? Monroe can't afford the learning curve I'd need to figure out the protocol on this on my own."

"I'll make the time."

Val started taking hasty notes as Murphy rattled off suggestions. They were darned lucky that he was willing to lend his expertise.

In the middle of their conversation, Rob stopped by her office with Malcolm, both of them panting. He wore the kind of shabby garments that meant he'd be visiting some places that might be rather unsavory, especially for a white guy. She blew him a kiss, and a mental wish for his safety.

With his master gone, Malcolm ambled across the office and flopped under her desk. She paused in her note-taking to scratch his neck. He was a good dog. Maybe she should get an office cat to keep him company.

Cal ended his discussion of ways and means with, "Hope that helps. Let me know if I can do more."

"Believe me, I will," Val said. "My assistant, Kendra, intends to persuade the Sunpapers to turn this into a media scandal. Will that help or hinder?"

"Judges are very touchy about being coerced, but if enough public heat can be generated, it could help. No one likes to think of innocent people being executed. Too threatening."

"If a reporter calls, would you be able to talk to him?"

"You'd get better mileage out of the guy who prosecuted this case. He's retired now and can say anything he wants. If he agrees there is grave doubt after seeing the tape, it would be a big plus for you." Cal hesitated. "But I'm doubtful that he's changed his mind. The lead prosecutor on this case was a real pit bull."

Val took down the retired prosecutor's name, thanked Cal again, then set to work. Technically she wouldn't be doing an appeal, which was a review of how a trial had been conducted. That had already been done in this case, and the trial had been accepted as fair and correct. Now she was working on collateral challenges, which were done after all appeals had been exhausted. They had new evidence; surely the higher state court judges wouldn't all be so pigheaded.

She went online to a legal database to research; she wrote and took notes, constantly aware that the minutes were ticking away Daniel's life. By the time Malcolm raised his head and nudged her calf with his long hound snout, it was dinner time.

With a sigh, she stood and stretched, the   ped on the dog's leash for a walk. The evening was quiet, the air summer hot and heavy. After the melodrama of the day, the streets were eerily quiet. Normal.

Back in the church, she refreshed Malcolm's water and food bowls, then descended to the basement kitchen to forage. She chose a small tin of chicken salad packaged with crackers. With a glass of milk, it was supper.

While waiting for coffee to brew, she climbed the stairs and drifted through the building. She halted in the door of the sanctuary and raised her gaze to the circular stained-glass window over the front door. Though stained glass had not been a part of the Quaker tradition in which she had been raised, the spiritual energy in this old church often reminded her of meetings.

Callie had been a pagan at heart, but she believed a child should be raised in a religion. Because she deeply admired Quaker values and integrity, she had chosen to take Val to the Stony Run Meeting. The meeting house was on the same campus as Friends School, where Val had been educated.

Though she hadn't attended a meeting for almost two decades, the Quaker passion for justice had been bred into her bones. That passion was one of her reasons for choosing the law as a career. More and more, she was seeing how much it was behind her decision to open her own office.

The rule of law was at the heart of civilized values, and injustice outraged her. It was an interesting combination of traits inherited from both Callie and Brad. She turned away from the stained-glass window, on the verge of tears because the knowledge that she was failing Daniel was breaking her heart.

Sinking into a chair, she closed her eyes and for the first time in many years began to pray. *Please let justice be done for the sake of Daniel, for those who love him, and for our society, which is tragically diminished by the murder of innocents. And, if it be thy will, help me develop the strength and wisdom to do work that matters always rather than settling for prosperity and shallow approval.*

Though she tried to still her mind into Quaker silence, it was impossible. Too many strategies and anxieties ricocheted around her mind. With a sigh, she rose and returned to her office. As she entered the room, her gaze fell on the handsome silk flower bouquet that now graced her credenza. She and Lyssie had spent a second afternoon making arrangements. Next Saturday would be wreaths, and then maybe they would consider other kinds of crafts.

Val touched the attractively worn brass vase that held the bouquet. The arrangement was Lyssie's work. Not only was the girl a natural storyteller but she had a good feeling for design, color, and texture. After a mere two Saturday afternoons she was beginning to open up with Val. Occasionally she laughed now, and she was beginning to develop confidence in her creativity. Val smiled a little. In a couple more years, her little sister would be wearing all black and pining to move to Greenwich Village. At least this relationship was developing satisfactorily even if Daniel's situation was critical.

Pouring a mug of coffee, she settled in front of her computer again. She should be good for at least three or four more hours before her concentration burned out.

She worked until Rob's return a little after midnight. Malcolm noticed first. Hearing his new master's footsteps, the hound rose and galumphed across Val's office, meeting Rob in the doorway.

"Hi, old boy. How's it hangin'?" Rob knelt to give Malcolm a good double ear scratch before rising to greet Val.

She went straight into his arms, feeling every particle of the fatigue she had been keeping at bay through sheer willpower. What a wonderful, warm, comforting body and warm, comforting spirit he had. Her eyes drifted shut. "Did you find anything useful?"

"I located another man who remembered Omar Benson

boasting about killing a cop, but he'd make a lousy witness. Shifty and mostly brain-fried. Joe Cady looked like a pillar of the community by comparison."

"Still, it's another weight on our side of the scales even if he is a sleaze."

"I suppose. He didn't have any insights about the long lost murder weapon." Rob massaged her knotted shoulders with one large hand. "How are you doing?"

She shrugged without stirring from her comfortable position in his arms. "I'm drafting a new petition for the Maryland Court of Appeals. When that's done, I'll start on a petition to the Supreme Court for a writ of *certiorari*, meaning a request that they hear the case if Maryland turns us down, but that's a really long shot. This Supreme Court is a conservative one, and there simply aren't any compelling constitutional questions to give us traction with them."

He raised her face for a kiss. Even when she was mentally and physically drained, he could rouse her. She began to come alive, kissing him back with increasing interest.

He ended the kiss and rested his forehead against hers. "With so much going wrong, I feel a powerful desire to build on what's good and true. Let's get married, Val."

Her nerves jumped in a spasm of shock. "Married? It's way too soon to think about that!"

"You know me better than anyone else, and I feel as if I know you pretty well." Taking her hand, he sat on the sofa and pulled her down beside him. "Granted we've been together for less than three months, but it's been intense since we're working together as well as dating. How much better do we need to know each other? Since you don't want to live together, I think it's time to at least put the idea of marriage on the negotiating table."

She stared into his quartz-clear eyes and realized that he was dead serious. Heart hammering, she rose and began pacing. "I believe that the traditional response is 'But sir, this is so sudden!'"

"Is it?" He watched her like one of her cats eying a

chipmunk. "I've been serious about you since the beginning, but I've been trying to keep my feelings under control so I won't send you skittering off."

He did know her pretty well, because she was definitely unnerved by his declaration. Maybe if she had been more receptive to the idea of living together, he wouldn't be brandishing marriage like a whip now. "Sorry about the skittishness. I've never been proposed to before."

His brows arched. "Never? With your looks and charm and active dating history, no one ever asked to marry you?"

"Not seriously."

"Not seriously—or you wouldn't let it become serious?" He leaned forward on the sofa, elbows on knees and hands clasped between. "What's wrong, Val? Is it me, or marriage in general?"

"There's nothing wrong with you." She forced herself to stop pacing and look at him. His sun-touched hair needed cutting and his eyes were shadowed with fatigue, but he was still irresistibly attractive. "Even when I thought you were a common carpenter, I knew there was nothing common about you. Your intelligence, your consideration, your honesty." She smiled, wanting to lighten the mood. "Not to mention the fact that you turn me on like crazy. It's just . . . marriage? So soon?"

"When will be long enough to talk about it? Six months? A year? Ten years? Or do you prefer a relationship like what your mother and Loren have?"

She hesitated. Though she had rolled her eyes at Callie and Loren in the past, it looked pretty good at the moment. "Their arrangement does have some major pluses. They're together when they want to be but never under each other's feet."

"That's fine for them, but not what I want." His clasped hands tightened. "I want to do the old-fashioned love and marriage and kids thing. I want to live under the same roof with you and work our way through the ups and downs and learn how many new ways I can love you as we grow old together. I . . . I want the kind of secure roots I've never

had. What I don't want is to be a permanent boyfriend and
sex toy like Loren is for your mother."

She caught her breath. "That's not fair! Maybe you
were serious from the beginning. I think I have been, too.
But it still hasn't been very long."

"So when is long enough?"

She felt too tired for this discussion. Not to mention
suffocated by his persistence. "Can't we put our relationship on hold until Daniel's fate is decided?" She went to
him with a kiss, trying to convey the passion and caring
she didn't know how to express in words. "I don't want to
lose you, Rob. Just . . . don't rush me."

Settling on his knee, she used her weight to carry them
back against the sofa cushions before running her hand
down his body. She craved passion, the profound connection of body to body that had always served her better than
sweet-talking words.

He responded instantly, hardening under her hand and
returning her kiss hungrily. She was about to unzip him
when he broke away and transferred her to the sofa beside
him. "No." His breathing was ragged. "Sex is great but it's
not the answer this time."

Startled from her sensual haze, she said shakily, "Does
it have to be an answer? Isn't it enough to be comfort and
pleasure and laughter?"

He started to reach for her, then froze, anguish in his
eyes, before standing and putting the width of the office
between them. When he was a safe distance away, he
turned to face her, his eyes bleak. "Maybe it is for you. It's
not enough for me. I want commitment, Valentine. I love
you, and it's getting harder and harder to bear when you
slide away from anything that might be too demanding. If
we put things on hold until after Daniel's case is resolved—well, how long will it be until you're involved in
another crusade? Not that I have anything against cru-
sades, but I don't want them to be more important than our
relationship."

She felt like crying, but refused to allow it. "You say I

know you better than anyone, but I certainly didn't know what you've been thinking. I thought we have a good thing going, and it keeps getting better. I sure didn't guess that you think I slide away from anything demanding."

"We *do* have a good thing, but I'm afraid of the pattern that's being set. There's too great a risk that I'll come to accept less than I want because it will become impossible to walk away from you." He closed his eyes for a moment, his expression unutterably weary. "So I guess the solution is to . . . walk away now."

She froze with a chill that ran straight through her. "This is an ultimatum—take the ring or else?"

He smiled humorlessly. "I don't have a ring. Would you accept an engagement Rolls Royce? The keys are upstairs. I'd be happy to go down on my knees and present them to you."

"This is turning into a really bad joke." Wrapping her arms around herself, she said pleadingly, "We're both too tired to have a sane conversation. Let's go to bed and talk about this in the morning."

"Very well. You go to your bed, and I'll go to mine."

"I'd much rather sleep with you." Not only did she crave his warmth, but it would give her a chance to exercise nonverbal arguments.

"I'd prefer that, too, but it's not going to happen until, and unless, you're willing to take this relationship to a deeper level."

"This is the strangest conversation I've ever had with a man." She shook her head, still not quite believing. "Don't quit now, Rob. I can't bear the thought of losing you."

She thought she'd won when he returned and bent for a kiss, but his touch was fleeting. "We don't have to do rings or set a date. I just want you to seriously accept the possibility of a lasting commitment. But even now you're not considering that, are you?"

Anger began burning away her shock. "I don't respond well to pressure tactics."

"Who does?" He sighed. "I'm drawing a line here for

the sake of my own emotional health. I'm not optimistic that you really want to be married. If you did, it would have happened already."

"You're hardly in a position to talk!"

"Until I met you, I wasn't interested in marriage. I was running away, building a business, burying myself in work, then running away again. Exactly what you're still doing." His gaze on hers was compassionate. "Over the last four years my brain has slowly reprogrammed itself, and now I know I want more than I've had. I want commitment and emotionally intimacy."

She drew a shaky breath. "You ask a lot."

"I know. Maybe too much." With visible effort, he looked away. "Good night, Val. I think it's time that I started looking for another place to live." He snapped his fingers for Malcolm, who rose on bowed basset legs and obediently waddled to the door.

She leaped to her feet, unable to believe that the best relationship she'd ever had was splintering in her hands. "Are you dropping Daniel's case?"

"Of course not." He paused in the door. "Trying to save him is a way of trying to save my soul—a soul I risk losing if I allow myself to stay with you in the twilight zone. I'll continue to work on the case and rent you this church, but when the investigation is done, you won't be seeing me around here."

This time she couldn't halt the stinging tears. "Don't leave me."

He looked at her for an endless moment. "You know what I want, and you have my cell phone number. Think hard, and if you decide you're ready to take the next step, I'll be there. But to be honest, I think we have a better chance of saving Daniel—and the chances there are slim to none."

Then he and the dog left, leaving only the sound of Malcolm's clacking claws to echo through the church.

* * *

BLINDLY ROB STEPPED OUT INTO THE HOT, HUMID night air, not quite believing what he had just done. No way had he intended to have a confrontation with Val when he stopped by her office. He hadn't thought beyond losing himself in her arms and maybe persuading her to come upstairs for the night.

Instead, he'd become demanding and ended their relationship. Val was right to be startled—three months of dating wasn't long at all. There was plenty of time to think about marriage.

And yet, he was right, too. Though all she'd had to do was agree to think seriously about marriage, she wouldn't. She was like smoke, wafting through his hands whenever he tried to hold her.

At least she was honest. Maybe it would have been better if she had lied. . . .

He squeezed his eyes shut as he remembered her anguished face. He was insane to walk away. Yet he was falling deeper and deeper into love with her. If he stayed, how long would it be until leaving would take more will power than he had?

Even the best of relationships contained elements of power struggle. If he gave Val all his power, he knew in his bones that she would never be the wife he wanted. They might be friends and lovers and playmates, but not husband and wife. Though Callie and Loren's relationship suited the older couple, it wasn't enough for him.

After all of the years when marriage hadn't even been on his radar, how come now he would settle for nothing less?

CHAPTER 26

VAL DROVE HOME ON AUTOPILOT, GRATEFUL THE streets were empty because she was too numb to avoid emergencies.

When she entered her house the cats greeted her, Lilith bouncing while Damocles ambled up, yawning. Not quite intending it, she folded down onto the floor of the entrance hall and gathered the cats to her as she began to weep uncontrollably. With feline intuition, they cuddled against her rather than bolting at her strange behavior.

Could Rob be right that she avoided any relationship issues that threatened to become too demanding? She had certainly been quick to sweep under the carpet their earlier conflict about living together. Though her automatic response both then and tonight was to say it was too soon to talk about long-term commitment, she could no longer deny that she had deep, possibly incurable, emotional hang-ups when it came to romantic relationships. She had finally found a healthy, attractive, highly eligible man whom she cared for deeply, and his proposal tied her into frantic knots.

If you'd wanted to be married, it would have happened already. The subject of marriage had come up once or twice in earlier relationships, but she hadn't thought of them as serious proposals because the men drank or were unreliable or chronic workaholics. Come to think of it, when marriage was mentioned, she'd reacted with the same kind of panic she was feeling now, but had assumed it was because the men weren't suitable, which gave her a good excuse.

Rob was different—the sort of man she ought to grab with both hands. Kind, compassionate, funny, smart, supportive, and he lived by his principles even though they had cost him deeply. The lust level was through the roof, she adored his company whether they were working, eating, or just lazing together, and he loved her.

If she had ever truly loved any man, it was Rob, but it had been easier not to analyze her feelings because she'd been busy, because they'd only been dating for a while, because she hadn't wanted to really look at the situation.

Wearily she set the cats down and climbed to her feet. She'd feed them, then go to bed. Maybe her brain would be working better in the morning.

As she opened a can of cat food, her gaze drifted to the kitchen phone. If she wanted Rob back, all she had to do was pick up the handset, dial his number, and tell him that she was ready to consider a serious, long-term, committed relationship. He'd be here in twenty minutes, and they'd be together till death did them part.

Even in her mind, she didn't like to use the word marriage.

She drew a shuddering breath. Making a phone call was such a simple thing—yet to save her life, she couldn't do it.

KENDRA'S TELEPHONE RANG AS SHE STEPPED FROM the shower. Glad she had a phone in the bathroom, she wrapped a bath sheet around herself, shook the mass of narrow braids back over her shoulder, and picked up the handset. "Hello?"

"Hi, Kendra, it's Al Coleman. What's this great story you have for me?"

She smiled to herself. From the interest in Al's voice, he was ready to take the bait. Kendra knew his wife, Mary, who used to be a legal secretary at Crouse, Resnick. Al was smart, tough, and ambitious. Perfect for this purpose. "Hi, Al. Think you can get some front page news out of the fact that the State of Maryland is going to execute an innocent man in just over a week, despite new exculpatory evidence?"

He whistled softly. "The Monroe execution? Hot stuff, but not much time to act. Have you got proof?"

"You bet I do. I've got a big fat file, including the video-tape of a dying eyewitness as he confesses to perjury, clears Monroe, and names the real killer. Shall we meet for breakfast so I can turn everything over to you?"

"Can you be at the Bel-Loc Diner in half an hour?" he asked, not bothering to disguise his excitement.

"See you there." Kendra hung up and patted her braids with a towel to remove any droplets of stray water. Al was right, there wasn't much time, and the *Sun* wouldn't print a story that hadn't been checked out, but the newspaper must have a hatful of summer interns dying to do something useful. It was a slow news time of year, so Al should be able to pull this story together fast.

After jumping into her clothes and doing a fast job on her makeup, she paused to check her e-mail. As she'd hoped, there was a reply from Jason. What had parents and kids done to keep in touch before e-mail?

She opened the note. All it said was, "Go, Mama!"

She smiled a little tremulously. If he'd objected to her go-ing public, she'd have had to think long and hard about going through with this. Jason would be part of the story, dragged over the coals of publicity because of a father he'd barely met. No kid wanted to be different in this way, but he hadn't faltered. She and Phil had done a good job with their boy.

Would publicity help save Daniel? Maybe not, but at least she was doing something. Jaw set, she left the house and swung into her car, remembering a Latin line from Julius Caesar she'd learned in high school. *Jacta alea est.*

The die is cast.

* * *

"YOU WANT TO KNOW ABOUT OMAR'S GUNS?" Virginia Benson-Hall, Omar Benson's white-haired mother, straightened from tending the flower boxes on her front porch to give Rob a suspicious glance. Though she had agreed to talk, she was still wary.

"Your son was implicated in a murder for which another man was convicted," Rob explained. "The murder weapon was never found. I've heard that Omar liked guns, but as far as I know, he didn't own a European handgun of the right caliber. I figured there was a chance you might know since you were his heir."

"He left a pile of guns for sure. I sold 'em for enough to pay three years' tuition at the parochial school for my two girls. But a European handgun? I didn't sell one of those." She pinched off a dead geranium blossom. "He owned all those fancy weapons but he was killed with a shank, one of them homemade prisoner's knives. That's what they call an irony."

"A big one," Rob agreed. "Did Omar ever tell you that he'd murdered a policeman and gotten away with it?"

That caught her attention. "Lordy, no. Even if he had, no way would he tell his disapproving mama. Did . . . did he really do that?"

The grief in her eyes made Rob soften that as much as possible. "He might have. If he did, it was an impulse shooting when he was shocked and scared. Not premeditated, and quite possibly while he was high."

"As if that makes it less of a murder." She sighed. "In the last ten years or so of his life, I didn't see him more than maybe three times a year. Christmas, then on the birthdays of his half sisters. He really loved those little girls, brought them fancy presents and paid their school fees until he went to prison. I never dared ask where the money came from." She shook her head sorrowfully. "He was a real nice boy before he took to the streets. Wanted to join the army and carry a gun and see the world. Ruined by bad company."

Lucy Morrison had said the same of her brother Joe, though Rob had been more inclined to believe it in that case. From all he'd learned, Omar was the original bad company. But his mother had loved him, and Omar had loved his little sisters. What might he have become if he hadn't succumbed to the lure of drugs and danger?

"Do you have any idea who his friends were? Maybe one of them might know if Omar owned a gun of the right caliber."

She snorted. "Can't help you there. His friends weren't welcome in my house."

Another dead end. Rob wasn't surprised. "Thank you for your time." He handed her a business card. "If you think of anything that might be of use, don't hesitate to call."

She set the card on the porch railing. "You say someone else was convicted of this killing Omar may have done?" When Rob nodded, she said, "Then I'll pray that the truth will set that poor man free."

"Thank you, ma'am." He nodded politely and left, thinking that his Southern boy manners were beginning to reassert themselves after too many years in California.

When he drove away from the West Baltimore neighborhood, he wondered what to do next. He'd been staying as busy as possible to keep thoughts of Val at bay, but he didn't have any more interviews until this evening. Maybe he should see if Sha'wan needed some help.

Unless . . .

He pulled over to the curb and considered an idea that kept flickering across his mind. When he and Val talked, he had mentioned in passing a house near hers that looked like it might do for the two of them. Though he loved Val's house, it was very much hers. If they were planning to marry, it would be better to find a home that would belong to both of them.

Though he hadn't much hope that they would be together, there was no reason why he couldn't house hunt for himself. Maybe it wasn't smart to look at properties so close to Val, but the one that had caught his eye sure was farther from her house than his present apartment was from her office.

And dammit, he wanted a place of his own. When he was a kid, they had always lived in rent. The condo he'd bought in California had been convenient, and it had a great view of San Francisco Bay, but it was merely a slick apartment that he'd happened to own. He wanted a real house with a lawn to cut and leaves to rake and space between him and the neighbors.

Most of all, he wanted a home. Buying a house wouldn't automatically provide warmth and connection, but it was a start. And now that he had Malcolm—well, he had the beginnings of a family.

He leaned across the truck and dug a steno pad from the glove compartment. The first time he drove by the Springlake Way house and noticed the FOR SALE sign, he'd pulled over to the curb to admire the handsome Tudor-style facade, then copied down the name and number of the listing agent in case Val was interested in seeing it. No harm in calling the agent now.

Five minutes later, he was on his way to the real estate office to meet the agent. Presumably she wanted to look him over to make sure that he wasn't dangerous. He approved of such caution. As to the house—maybe he wouldn't like it that much once he got inside. But at least looking would prevent him from thinking.

IT HAD BEEN A FULL PHONE MORNING, FOR WHICH Val was grateful. Having to talk helped keep her mind off Rob, which was fortunate because thinking of him had a bad effect on her emotions and composure.

Kendra had come to work late after meeting with a reporter from the *Sun*. The wheels had been put in motion. Since her material was so well-organized, it wouldn't take Al Coleman long to check his facts and write a story about Daniel's wrongful conviction and looming execution. With sidebars.

Though publicity might help, Val concentrated on polishing her petition to the Court of Appeals. She was deep into the document when Kendra put a call through from Rainey Marlowe. Thinking how much had changed since her friend had called to announce the profit points her movie had earned, Val picked up. "Hi, Rainey. How are you and the baby and the Sexiest Man in the World?"

Her friend laughed. "Very well. One of the nice things about the entertainment business is the long quiet stretches between projects. Which is why I have time to think that we really ought to throw a baby shower for Kate. If so, could you and Rachel organize it? I'll help where I can, but there's a limit to what can be done long distance."

"I should have thought of that myself, but I've been too darned busy. So much for opening my own office and taking time to smell the flowers." Val leaned back in her chair, thinking how wonderfully normal a baby shower sounded. "We can hold the shower at my place, since it's the most central. It will be insane finding a date when we can all get together, but if we start now, we should manage to set up something before the baby actually arrives. Have Emmy fax me your schedule. I'll talk to Rachel. Do you have the time to call Laurel and Kate?"

"I'd love to. In fact, how about if I check the schedules for the old gang and Kate's mom? The date is the worst aspect of party planning, and I can make phone calls from New Mexico as easily as from Maryland."

"Phone away, and many thanks for volunteering." They chatted for a few more minutes before hanging up, leaving Val cheered. When drowning in a swamp of daily details and crises, it was good to remember that friends had babies and life went on.

If she wanted babies of her own—and Lyssie was making her feel that motherhood was something she could handle—why the heck wasn't she proposing to Rob, who would be happy to participate in the project?

Before she could start brooding again, Kendra said over the intercom, "Al Coleman is on line two. He wants to interview you about Daniel. Ready to do your bit?"

"He doesn't waste time, does he? I'll take it now." Val pushed the button for line two. Like Scarlett O'Hara, she would think about Rob and marriage tomorrow.

"NOW THAT I'VE HAD THE OFFICIAL TOUR," ROB said, "may I wander around some more on my own?"

The agent smiled cheerfully. "Feel free. Since the owners moved out six months ago, there isn't anything I need to guard. Take your time—I'll catch up on my calls."

He crossed the front hall, awash in light from the leaded glass windows, and climbed the sweeping staircase. Though he liked the agent, she would probably think he was seriously weird if she saw him caressing the magnificent hand-carved woodwork.

He sat on the window seat at the top of the stairs, his absent gaze on the neglected back garden. Though he'd liked the way the house looked from the curb, he hadn't expected to fall in love with it. The better part of a century old, the structure had the exquisite details new homes couldn't touch. The spaces flowed well, creating a sense of relaxation from the moment he'd entered.

While not enormously larger than Val's home, this property stood on a spacious lot that included a surprising amount of space in the back. A relatively new three-car garage faced onto the alley and a cozy one-bedroom guest house was tucked among so many trees and shrubs that it was like being in the country.

The bathrooms and kitchen needed remodeling and the heating and air-conditioning systems were on their last legs, which was probably why the place had been on the market so long. He didn't mind. Projects would keep him busy, and he was going to need to stay busy for a long time to come.

He rose and ambled back to the master bedroom, in the left rear corner of the structure. It was a sizable room, but it would benefit by cutting into the adjacent room and turning that space into walk-in closets and a really decadent bathroom. He had a brief mental image of Val, laughing amidst masses of bath bubbles. . . .

Pivoting, he left the room.

It was too damned easy to imagine her in this house. Before their relationship crashed and burned, he'd entertained fantasies of them shopping for furnishings together. He had never done that and thought it would be fun. Val would be in charge of design, and he'd handle execution. Pick out paints and fabrics, test a few mattresses. . . .

Again he forced himself to stop thinking like that. The first lesson in family life he'd ever learned was that people didn't change simply because those who loved them wanted it. Val had serious problems with marriage, or him, or both. Despite what she'd said, he suspected that he was the problem. God knew he was no prize.

But even without Val he could be happy in this house, he thought. Or at least content. He had fled to Baltimore for refuge and gradually become attached to the place. He found that he liked knowing a broad range of people, and he found satisfaction in the work he was doing here. It was time he stopped living like a gypsy.

As he headed downstairs to tell the agent he wanted to make an offer, he wondered if the current owners would accept a contract clause allowing him to live in the guest house until settlement. It was a pleasant little place complete with kitchenette and bath, and he wouldn't risk running into Val every time he arrived or left.

As he descended the broad stairs, one hand on the silky walnut of the railing, his cell phone rang. Not Val's number. He sighed at the evidence of wishful thinking. "Hello, Rob here."

"Hi, this is Al Coleman of the *Sun*. I'd like to talk to you about the Daniel Monroe case."

He whistled soundlessly and sat down in the middle of the staircase. So Kendra's plan was off to a good start, and his privacy was about to be blown. He hoped to God that ripping open old wounds would help save Daniel's life.

From this angle, he could see that the agent was still busy on her own phone. Drawing up an offer could wait for a few minutes. "No problem, Mr. Coleman. What do you want to know?"

CHAPTER 27

❊❊❊

YAWNING, KENDRA WENT OUTSIDE FOR THE NEWS-
paper while her breakfast coffee brewed. Back in her
kitchen, she almost splashed coffee all over the counter
when she spotted the blaring headline, GUILT DISPUTED AS
EXECUTION DATE APPROACHES.

Good God, after only three days? Heart hammering, she
sat down and began skimming the story. Or rather, stories.
Al and his interns had done a great job of pulling together
the history of the case and the new evidence. All the major
players who were still alive were quoted. The coverage
benefited by the fact that it wasn't competing with any major national news stories. Heaven be thanked for the late
summer doldrums.

The main story jumped inside to a double-page spread
filled with related stories. The question of guilt or innocence provided tons of human interest, and Al Coleman
was wringing out every morsel.

Cal Murphy and Val were quoted, as was the retired
lawyer who had prosecuted the case. The latter unfortunately still thought that Daniel was guilty and should have
been executed long since. The state's attorney agreed, up-

holding her predecessor despite the new evidence that had surfaced. Kendra grimaced. Pit bull attack skills were an asset to a prosecutor, and the current state's attorney was a classic example.

Officer Malloy's widow also rated some ink. She said that having seen the videotape of Joe Cady, she believed that Daniel Monroe might well be innocent, and she didn't want to see him executed if there was reasonable doubt. *Bless you, Anne Malloy Peterson.*

Jason and Kendra got two columns of their own. She'd lent Al Coleman two photographs. One showed Daniel playing with Jason, an archetypal doting young father. The other was of Jason in uniform, looking grave and handsome, a young man dedicated to serving his country. Coleman had called Jason in Colorado and got some good sound bites, including her son saying, "This has changed the way I think about capital punishment. I used to think that murderers deserved what they got—but what if they aren't really murderers?"

There was a sidebar on Rob, too. Kendra sucked in her breath when she read his real name and history. He must have told Coleman about his past for it to be in the paper in this first barrage of news. Coleman summarized the Avenging Angel story to explain why Baltimore's Graffiti Guy had been drawn to investigate an old murder case. A file photo of a bearded Rob painting out graffiti was included, along with a quote from him that said, "There was no question of my brother's guilt. There is an enormous question about Daniel Monroe's."

She sent Rob a blessing for being willing to let his past be revealed. He had even been present at his brother's execution. How had he been able to bear it?

She was trying not to imagine what it would be like to watch Daniel die when her doorbell rang. Grateful for an interruption, she opened the front door.

On her doorstep stood a perky young woman with a television transmission truck from a local station parked on the street. "Ms. Brooks? I'm Sandy Hairston, and we'd like to interview you about the Daniel Monroe case."

Kendra tried to remember if she had ever been that young and perky. Probably not, but underneath her perkiness the girl was a competent reporter. "I know who you are, Ms. Hairston, and I'd be happy to talk to you. Can I have five minutes to get myself looking respectable?"

"Can you make it three?" the girl said without losing her smile. "Charm City News wants to be the first to get you on the air."

"Understood. One swipe of lipstick, and I'll be right out." Kendra dashed to the bathroom to check her appearance. Not bad. The cornrows were a bit funky, but she otherwise looked earnest and intelligent, not the kind of loony woman who specialized in falling in love with prisoners. She put on the lipstick, then headed outside again.

Time to find out how much power the press really had.

WHEN VAL OPENED THE NEWSPAPER IN HER KITCHen, she whooped so loudly that both cats temporarily bolted from their food dishes. The *Sun* had done the story proud. Daniel's guilt or innocence would be the talk of the Maryland legal establishment today. This morning she would deliver her petition for review by the Court of Appeals. She hoped the judges who would rule on her petition would feel enlightened rather than coerced by the publicity.

Feeling more optimistic than she had since the night when Rob had split, she decided to drive over to Springlake Way when she left her house. It wasn't her usual route, but she was curious which house had interested him.

Several blocks of the street had a grassy median with trees and a chain of pretty little ponds, but only one of the handsome residences in that section was for sale. She pulled over in front of the house to study it, not surprised to find that Rob had good taste. She had admired this house herself in the past.

For a brief, painful moment she imagined living there with Rob. It was a good size for raising children. . . .

Before she could become maudlin, she saw that an Under Contract banner had been slapped across the sign. So much for fantasies of her and Rob in this particular house. Real estate was the least of their problems at this point.

She tested the idea of marriage, like pushing her tongue against a sore tooth. Was it maybe a little less alarming than it had been the other night?

A little. Maybe. Much as she missed him, the thought of marriage still made her feel suffocated. With a sigh, she pulled away from the curb and turned on her radio, just in time to catch a news story about Daniel's possible innocence.

At least something was going right.

WHEN VAL RETURNED FROM FILING HER APPEAL PA-pers, she remarked to Kendra, "One advantage of working downtown was how much closer the courthouse was."

Kendra glanced up from her computer. "Want me to list all the disadvantages to being downtown?"

"No need—I remember them all vividly." Val gestured at the newspaper on Kendra's desk. "Great coverage. Al Coleman must have worked nonstop."

"No time to waste on this story." Kendra rolled her chair back from the desk, suppressing a yawn. "He really lit a brushfire. I've been interviewed by two different TV stations and calls have been coming in all morning. Not all of them from local journalists, either. Some of the calls were for me and some for you. There's a pile of messages on your desk. Two of them are from downtown lawyers who would like to do some pro bono work with you. You're going to end up with an empire, girl."

Glad she had finished her petitions so she had time to talk to reporters today, Val headed back to her office. As

Kendra had implied, most of the messages were from journalists, but a couple were normal business.

For starters, she returned a call from the lawyer of Mia Kolski's ex-husband. "Hi, Barney, it's Val Covington. Is your client ready to deal?"

"Steve is ready to deal," the lawyer said wryly. "He decided to reevaluate his legal strategy when faced with possible criminal fraud charges. As a human being I'll admit this is good, but dammit, Val, you just closed down my youngest kid's college fund. I made a ton of money off of Steve."

She laughed. "If he has a litigious nature, no doubt you'll be seeing him again. I don't care what he does as long as he stops harassing Mia. So what are the details?"

After a brisk round of negotiating, she said good-bye to the lawyer and called Mia, whose squeal of glee could be heard in Delaware. "Val, you are a saint, a godsend. What can I ever do to repay you for getting that albatross off my neck?"

Val thought about it. "How about if you provide live music for say, three parties of mine in the future? I'll look terribly classy without spending a cent."

"You've got it. Don't you have an open house coming up for the new office this Friday? I can get together a trio or quartet by then, no problem."

"So soon? It's a deal." After settling the details, Val called the next message on the list, her long-time client Bill Costain. "Hi, Bill, it's Val. What can I do for you?"

"I won't be able to come to the open house this Friday."

"That's too bad. I was hoping to show off my new place. Why not come by for a private tour another day and after I'll take you to lunch?" she suggested. "After all, you're my biggest client."

"Val . . ."

Hearing a strained note in his voice, she said, "Is something wrong?"

"Val . . . my wife was a Malloy." Costain drew a deep breath. "Jim Malloy was her favorite cousin. She's usually pretty easygoing, but when she read the paper this morning and saw that you're trying to get Daniel Monroe off death row, she went ballistic. She . . . she demanded that I fire you."

Val gasped, caught completely off-guard. A dozen retorts occurred to her, starting with the basic legal belief that everyone was entitled to a good defense and ending with the fact that even Jim Malloy's widow was willing to say Daniel might be innocent. But Sally Costain's reaction wasn't about logic, and Bill didn't need for her to make this worse.

After drawing a deep breath, she said, "Baltimore is such a small town—I had no idea that Sally was a Malloy. Of course this is a painful topic for her. I'll really miss working with you, but mediation begins at home."

He sighed with relief. "Thanks for being so understanding, Val. Maybe later, when this has all settled down, I'll give you a call."

Or maybe not. After hanging up, Val closed her eyes and rubbed her temples. The high she'd gotten from resolving Mia's case certainly hadn't lasted long. From the moment she decided to go out on her own, she had been counting on making good, steady money from Bill's company. That revenue would not be easily replaced. Though she was far from destitute, she didn't have a lot of ready cash since most of her net worth was tied up in her house and retirement accounts.

She pulled out her calculator and roughed up some figures. The first chunk of money from Rainey's movie had gone to set up the office, buy furniture and equipment, subscribe to legal databases, and the other costs of establishing a business, including setting aside six months of running costs for the office. She had to pay Kendra's salary, taxes, medical coverage for both of them, insurance, utilities, rent, and upkeep.

There would probably be another good-sized payment from the movie in a year or so. She would also earn some money from the cases she was continuing with Crouse,

Resnick. Nonetheless, without steady work from Bill Costain, she would soon have to go out and hustle for bread-and-butter clients.

She grimaced. It had been a nice fantasy to think hustling wouldn't be necessary. For a tough lawyer, she could be awfully naïve. Callie's influence, no doubt.

Well, she would do what was needed—even in this short time, she had developed a taste for self-employment. For now, though . . .

She checked her schedule. There was nothing critical this afternoon. A couple more calls needed to be returned, and then she could play hooky for a few hours. She needed a break after working nonstop for too long.

Hoping Lyssie was in, she called her little sister. When Lyssie answered, Val said, "Hi, hon, it's me. I know we don't have anything planned till the weekend, but since you're going back to school next week, and I have a desperate desire to get away for a bit, would you like to go on an expedition? If your grandmother agrees, of course."

"What kind of expedition?" Lyssie asked cautiously.

Val thought fast. "How about if I drive us up to Harpers Ferry? You like history and there's plenty of it there. We can have lunch, look at the historic sites, poke around the shops a bit."

"Oh, yes! I'd really like that."

"Do you think your grandmother would like to go? I think she would enjoy Harpers Ferry. My treat for us all."

"I'll ask her, but she isn't feeling well. Just a second." Lyssie put the phone down and scampered off. A couple of minutes passed before she returned. "She says I can go, and to bring her back a surprise."

"I'm sure that can be arranged." Val glanced at the clock. "I need to return a couple of calls, then go home and change. How about if I pick you up in about an hour?"

"I'll be ready."

Lyssie would be, too; she was admirably punctual. Val returned to her message pile and sorted out the most important. This big sister business had all kinds of dividends she hadn't expected in the beginning. It was nice to have a playmate.

Rob had been a great playmate—but Val refused to go there. Life was complicated enough already.

BUYING A HOUSE COULD BE DONE WITH REMARK-able speed, Rob learned. Even though the sellers had moved to the West Coast, the wonders of fax and electronic fund transfers solidified the deal quickly. Inspection and financing contingencies still needed to be satisfied, but that should be routine. Plus, the sellers agreed to let Rob use the guest cottage until settlement.

So he was a homeowner. Almost, anyhow. When he stopped by the real estate agency to pick up the key to the guest house, he said, "I think I'm supposed to start feeling buyer's remorse about now, but so far, not a trace."

The agent laughed. "Remorse isn't required. It's a fine house in a beautiful neighborhood, and you got it for a good price. You'll be happy there, I'm sure."

So was he, though not as happy alone as he would have been with Val. He had managed to avoid seeing her for several days, and that would be even easier after he relocated to the guest cottage. He wondered if he would be able to move out of the church apartment without her noticing. Probably not.

Malcolm waited in the air-conditioned pickup truck, his expression less lugubrious than usual. He was a good truck dog. "Malcolm, my lad, would you like to drive to Home-land to see your new house? Yes? Good, I was heading that way myself."

His phone rang within seconds of his turning the power on. A call from the Manhattan area code, he noticed. "'Lo, Rob here."

"Hi, Rob, it's Phyllis Greene from *Newsweek*. Remember me?"

He suppressed his sigh. Phyllis had done a story on him during Jeff's trial. She had been fair and thorough, but nothing about that period made for pleasant memories. "How could I forget you? A saintly smile and the persistence of a terrier."

She laughed. "You seem to have done your best to forget everything until this capital punishment case you got yourself involved with. I'm thinking of doing a follow-up story on you. I like the beard, by the way."

This time he did sigh. "I really wish you wouldn't do a story. There is nothing here with national implications. It's a Maryland issue."

"But this is great stuff—grieving and guilt-stricken entrepreneurial brother of environmental terrorist reinvents himself as community and capital punishment activist. It might even help your cause."

"Nothing you write would come out soon enough to affect whether or not Daniel Monroe will be executed next week."

"Maybe not, but it might help the broader cause of opposition to capital punishment. One I privately agree with, speaking off-the-record."

He rubbed the short hair on Malcolm's neck, finding the contact soothing. The dog moaned softly and rested his chin on Rob's knee. "I'm no crusader. I only got involved with this case by chance."

"I think you're becoming a crusader in spite of yourself," she said seriously. "Will you talk to me? It's easier than if I have to work around you."

He hadn't thought of himself as an activist, but the label seemed to be coming after him. First Julia Hamilton, now this. Since Phyllis was determined to do the story with or without his cooperation, he capitulated. "Okay, what do you want to know?"

If he was being given a platform, maybe he had an obligation to speak.

CHAPTER 28

❈❈❈

"I NEVER KNEW MARYLAND WAS SO PRETTY," LYSSIE said as Val steered her car along the winding highway that followed the Potomac River for a couple of miles below Harpers Ferry. The girl's nose had been glued to the window for the whole trip.

"You've never been out this way?"

"I've never been out of Maryland until today. Both Virginia and West Virginia within a few minutes!" She pushed the bridge of her glasses up with a sigh. "I've hardly ever been out of Baltimore City."

"No wonder you have a yen to travel." Val kept her voice light to disguise the pang of hearing how limited Lyssie's life had been. Amazing that the girl had such an active, inquiring mind. Or maybe her curiosity was a result of having lived within narrow limits. "I've been thinking. Maybe next spring, I can take a long weekend and drive down to North Carolina with you and your grandmother. You can visit your Lumbee relatives, and I'll go see a friend in Charlotte."

"Really?" Lyssie's head swung around, her eyes wide

behind her glasses. "Please . . . please don't say that unless you mean it."

She had the ability to break Val's heart with a single sentence. Keeping one eye on the winding road, Val laid a hand over Lyssie's. "I won't ever say anything like that unless I mean it. And if I forget something important, call me on it! You're my sister—you have the right."

Lyssie didn't speak, but she did squeeze Val's hand. Each time they had an outing, progress was made. Val liked the deepening of their relationship. For whatever reason, it was easier to accept the commitment of relationships with females.

Turning right onto one of the roads that led up the hill into Harpers Ferry, Val said, "There's a big old hotel at the top of this hill that does a lunch buffet. The food isn't gourmet, but the view from the hotel is world class. I thought we could eat first, then poke around down in the town."

Lyssie nodded enthusiastically. She seemed able to eat six times a day without adding any padding to her bony little body.

The rambling Hilltop House was just where Val remembered. She parked on the lot under a tree. "Come on, let's see if the view is as great as I remember."

It was. Lyssie gasped as they went to the flagstone landing at the end of the ridge, a few dozen yards beyond the hotel's wide verandah. No one else was around, and from their vantage point they could look down at the confluence of two great rivers.

"That's the Potomac and on this side is the Shenandoah. A railroad line runs along the river below—see the railroad bridge over the Potomac?" Val pointed out the landmarks. "I think that ruined bridge down there was destroyed in the Civil War."

"Awesome." Lyssie pointed downward. "Are those eagles below us?"

"Could be. Some kind of raptor for sure. Watching them

glide along the winds makes me want to fly." Val privately suspected that the birds were turkey vultures, but they soared as well as any eagles.

"To fly . . ." Lyssie said dreamily. She stepped off the flagged area onto the trimmed grass. To the left a cast iron fence guarded the edge, but here the hill dropped away with clifflike suddenness only a foot beyond Lyssie. The grass was damp from the previous night's rain, and Lyssie skidded as she moved forward.

A horrific vision of the girl plunging over the edge to her death kicked Val's reflexes into overdrive. "No!"

She grabbed Lyssie's shoulder and yanked her back to safety. Lyssie shrieked and folded into a ball on the grass, her arms raised to protect her head.

"Dear God," Val whispered. Kneeling, she put an arm around Lyssie and drew the small, resisting body close. "I'm not going to hit you, I was just scared that you might fall. Foolish of me, but I'm responsible for you, and I'm new to being a big sister."

Lyssie didn't respond. She kept her head down and her body tucked as she breathed in short, panicky gasps.

"Who hit you, Lyssie?" Val said softly. "One of your parents? Your grandmother?"

That brought Lyssie's head up. 'Not Gramma, my parents. Mama only hit me when I deserved it, but Daddy . . . wh . . . when he was high. . . ." Her voice broke.

"Oh, honey." Val couldn't stop herself from drawing the girl into a full hug. This time there was no resistance. Lyssie's quiet weeping tore holes in her heart. "Do you want to talk about your parents, Lyssie? You can tell me anything, and sometimes the bad stuff gets a little easier when it's shared with a friend. Or a sister."

Lyssie rubbed at her eyes, so Val pulled out tissues and handed them over.

After wiping her glasses and blowing her nose, Lyssie said, "Daddy wasn't around much, but I loved when he visited. He wasn't always mean—sometimes he was the best and most exciting fun in the world. If I knew he was coming, I would stay by the window and watch for him all day. Sometimes he took me out to see the Orioles, or to the Inner Harbor or Mondawmin Mall. Even the Aquarium once."

"And other times he was angry and scary?"

Lyssie nodded. Val cast a longing glance at the park bench a dozen feet away, but since they had the viewing area to themselves, and Lyssie seemed comfortable crouched on the grass, better not risk stopping the flow of words. "I felt the same way about my father. Since I almost never saw him, it was really exciting when I did. I would do anything to make him happy with me." Or even just acknowledge her existence.

"Did you feel bad because you wanted so much to see your father when your mother did all the work?"

Startled by the perceptive question, Val said, "I sure did. I loved them both, but my mother was the one who was always there. She made sure that I was fed and dressed and went to school. Seeing her wasn't special. My father—he was like a king who came to visit sometimes, and when he did, I felt like a princess."

Lyssie nodded again. "I loved to see him, but when he visited, he and Mama fought all the time. If . . . if he hadn't come to see me, they would both still be alive."

Sickened, Val recognized that it was probably inevitable that Lyssie would feel as if the death of her parents was somehow her fault. "Honey, when a man gets crazy and violent on drugs like your father, he's like a gun waiting to go off. It was only a matter of time till the trigger was pulled. What happened wasn't your fault. Men kill their wives and themselves so often that it has a name—murder-suicide."

"My father didn't kill himself," Lyssie said in a flat voice. "A policeman shot him. After he killed Mama, someone called the police, and they broke into the apartment because they'd been told there was a child in danger.

"When they broke in, Daddy grabbed me and held his gun to my head. He was screaming and threatening to kill me if the police didn't let him go. One of the policemen started talking to him, and when he lowered the gun a little, they . . . they shot him." She made a choking sound. "His blood was . . . all over me."

No wonder Lyssie hadn't told the whole story originally. Heart aching, Val rocked the girl in her arms. "No one should experience something like that at any age, Lyssie, especially not at the age of six. What an amazing girl you are."

Lyssie pulled her head back and blinked through glasses that were steamed again. "You think?"

Val nodded. "You survived, and you're developing into a really bright, thoughtful person. A European philosopher once said that which doesn't kill us makes us stronger. You're proof."

"Nietzsche." Lyssie frowned as she tried to see herself as a heroine instead of a victim. "Do you think surviving the . . . the murders will make me a better writer?"

"Guaranteed. You're already the most amazing girl I've ever met," Val said with complete sincerity. "Talking with you now is making me think differently about my father and how we got along. Changing how people think is part of what writers do."

Lyssie sighed and rested her head against Val's shoulder. "I'd rather have my parents alive even if they didn't get along."

Val brushed the springy dark hair with the texture so like hers. "We don't get to choose."

They sat quietly, cooled by the stiff breeze that blew along the river valleys. Val hadn't been kidding when she said that Lyssie's words had changed her thinking. She had grown up accepting that her family wasn't like others, but she hadn't really thought about how much her father's rare visits, and her even rarer visits to him, had shaped her childhood. She had been like a cat waiting by the refrigerator and hoping for cream. Though Callie had been a conscientious, down-to-earth mother, she always had her creative and romantic interests. Val had never really felt that she came first.

This had a lot to do with Rob, but she would ponder that later. Now was Lyssie's time to come first. "Shall we go inside the hotel and have some lunch? All the desserts you can eat, after you've had something healthy."

"I'm hungry." Lyssie scrambled to her feet. Though her nose and eyes were red, the tears had dried.

"Me, too." Val rose rather less lithely than her little sister. "Then we'll go down into the village. There are lots of neat little shops where we can get something for your grandmother, and the National Park Service has a terrific bookstore with practically all history books."

"Can we start there?"

Val laughed. "Start and end there, if you like." She linked her arm through Lyssie's, and they turned to the hotel.

"I'm glad I told you what happened," Lyssie said softly. "I can't talk to Gramma because she gets so upset."

"You can tell me anything, Lyssie. I know that when I'm upset, it always helps to talk to a friend."

"Helps, maybe." Lyssie smiled wistfully. "But it's never really going to go away, is it?"

"No, honey. We can get through the bad stuff, but we never really get over it. In the meantime, though"—Val smiled—"there's ice cream."

THE NEXT DAY SHA'WAN AND A COUPLE OF KIDS from the Fresh Air center would help Rob move, but this evening he was getting a head start by taking some of the more fragile items to the guest house. Not that he had a lot of breakables, but he suspected his work crew would have more energy and enthusiasm than finesse.

It hadn't taken long to pack. Though traveling lightly through life was supposed to be good, he was tired of it. He looked forward to accumulating more possessions. A new sound system, for example. He missed listening to music. Maybe a bed for Malcolm? No, the dog preferred Rob's bed. Maybe he'd like a giant leather chew bone.

Rob carried the box holding his garish ceramic canisters down the outside steps, a wary eye on Val's office. Her car was in the lot, but she was working so late these nights that he didn't expect her to leave while he was shifting his stuff.

He was heading to the steps for another load when Val came out the back door. It was the first time they had seen each other since she had bolted from his proposal.

They both stopped dead. There was complete silence, except for the *whoosh* of traffic on nearby Harford Road and a distant barking dog. Val was only a dozen feet away, and in the dim light of the parking lot she looked like a really exhausted Orphan Annie. Even her curls drooped tiredly. He wanted to put his arms around her and tell her everything would be all right. He wanted to take her to bed and give her a massage. . . .

She broke the silence before he made himself crazy. "Moving out so soon?"

"Yes. Remember that house I mentioned on Springlake Way? I decided to take a look, and I really liked it. I have it under contract now. Since the owners have moved out, they gave me permission to live in the guest house until settlement." He was babbling, trying to extend the conversation.

"You move fast. It looks like a really nice place." She checked that the door had locked behind her, then came down the steps to ground level. "If you need help with the decorating, I can probably give you some useful names. A good designer can winnow the choices down to manageable size and pull everything together."

"Thanks, I'll keep that in mind, but I'll need to do some remodeling first. The kitchen and baths are very Fifties. Too old to be acceptable, not old enough to be interesting."

"My place was like that when I bought it. I spent a fortune on remodeling." She shifted her briefcase from one hand to the other. "Any luck with the investigating? I assume you would have called if you found something dramatic."

"No smoking guns or deathbed confessions." He grimaced. "I've been wasting time talking to reporters. Being who I am raises the news value, but I would have been happy to let the dead past bury the dead."

"I'm so sorry." She took an involuntary step forward as if she was going to touch him with the spontaneous warmth he loved. Halting, she added, "This will pass soon, if not as soon as you'd like."

"I'm getting encouragement to become an anti–death penalty activist. Go around making speeches, waving protest signs. Whatever." He ran a hand through his hair restlessly. "Do you think I could do any good?"

"I know you could do good. Capital punishment is still very popular in this country, and it's going to take a lot of serious thought and talking to shift the balance." She frowned. "The question isn't whether you can do good, but whether you can bear doing that kind of work."

"What do you think would be the worst part of it?" He was surprised how much he wanted her opinion.

"Every time you speak, you're putting your personal history out there for people to throw tomatoes at. Some will respect what you did and call you a hero, which you are. Others will say that Jeffrey deserved to die and good riddance to bad rubbish. And some will despise you for betraying your brother. Not a lot of fun."

"It's getting a little easier with practice." When he had first told his story to Val, it had been almost impossible to speak. Now he was able to speak of his brother calmly, though that didn't mean the pain wasn't still there. "In the interviews I push the angle of wrongful conviction and the risk of executing the innocent. If Boeing had the same failure rate as the justice system, no one would ever set foot on an airplane."

"Hard to argue with that, and new cases of wrongful conviction turn up all the time." Her expression became thoughtful. "It would be interesting to do a study on the subject. Maybe I can get some law students to do the research. Since the story broke in the *Sun*, I've had a dozen calls from lawyers and students who would like to do some pro bono work with me. Daniel's case has really touched some chords."

If nothing else, maybe these volunteers would save a future Daniel. Mind made up, he said, "Tomorrow I'll call Julia Hamilton, the judge's wife. She asked if I'd speak to a group of prisoners' families. The idea spooked me when she first called, but I guess I'm ready now. If that goes well, we'll see."

"By the time you give that talk, maybe you'll have some good news to include."

Sensitive to the nuances of her voice, he said, "You don't sound very optimistic."

She sighed. "The Court of Appeals has promised a ruling for September eighth, the day before the execution is scheduled. It doesn't give us much time if they refuse to grant a stay, and the chances of them granting the petition are not great. Cal Murphy figures our odds of success are less than fifty-fifty."

He swore. "How can they overlook the evidence? Where is the justice?"

"They're liable to think this case was decided long since, and we're just playing games to delay the inevitable." Her voice broke and she covered her eyes with one hand. "I don't know how I'll be able to face Jason and Kendra if we fail. To do a countdown on a man's life . . . it's *obscene*."

"Val . . ." Aching, he stepped forward and suddenly they were in each other's arms, united in grief. Deep down, he had a powerful belief that if he failed Daniel, he would be forever damned. If he couldn't save an innocent man, why was he even bothering to breathe? What had he ever done that was worthwhile?

Val's face turned up, a pale oval in the dim light. He kissed her with a blind, clawing need for oblivion. She responded in kind, her nails digging into his back. He was tempted to pull her down in the grass, but he managed to say, "Let's go upstairs."

She came wordlessly as they climbed the stairs, arms around each other's waists. Inside the apartment, he turned on the light in the small foyer so they wouldn't stumble over packed boxes on their way to the bedroom. Malcolm thumped his tail in greeting, but wisely kept out of their way.

Their separation had raised passion to unbearable levels, and when they reached the bed, they fell on each other like tigers, as if they were the ones on the verge of execution. For a few moments, at least, he found the exalted oblivion he sought in her familiar, beloved body.

All too soon they returned to earth, panting in each other's arms. When he could breathe again, he stroked the curls back from her damp forehead. "I'm sorry. I didn't intend for this to happen."

"I'm not sorry." Her lips curved wistfully. "But nothing has changed, has it?"

"Not really, except that I'm reminded how addictive you are." He cupped her lovely full breast, delighting in the intimacy of the moment. "Every time I'm with you, it gets harder to imagine life without you."

She placed his hand on her heart so he could feel its pounding under his palm. "You're still determined on marriage or nothing?"

He hesitated, knowing that all he had to do was say the word, and they would be together again. God, to be able to make love with her, talk with her, bounce ideas off her. . . . The temptation was almost overpowering.

Almost. "I'm afraid so. I need to build something lasting, Valentine. I built a business once and discovered that wasn't enough. Like they say, no one ever wished on his deathbed that he'd spent more time at the office. I want to love and be loved, if that's possible. Have a normal, healthy family that isn't made up of alcoholics, abusers, and sociopaths. Have kids that I can raise better than I was raised."

Tenderly he kissed the taut flesh over her beating heart. "If I stay with you, I'll end up forgoing the dream for a reality that will be wonderful, but . . . not enough. And because it's not enough, someday it would end and then I'd have nothing. I've had way too much nothing in my life."

She sighed. "You think marriage is a guarantee that anything will last? No one is that naïve."

"Of course there are no guarantees." He paused as he tried to define why he felt this so strongly. "But surely if two people are willing to make a commitment to stay together till death does them part, it's a big step in the right direction. Maybe exchanging vows gives more reason to work through the hard times." He smiled wryly. "I'm probably kidding myself, but it's not as if I have a lot of positive personal experience to draw on. I figure taking a traditionalist approach gives better odds than most."

"You may be right. I take commitments as seriously as you do, which is why the thought of marriage makes me skittish as a three-month-old kitten." She covered his hand with hers. "Don't rush out and fall in love with someone else, Rob. I'm working on my hang-ups."

"Since I've never fallen in love with anyone else, it's not likely to happen again anytime soon." Maybe never. It was impossible to imagine another woman who would suit his body and soul as well as Val did. "Does this mean you might change your mind?"

"It's too soon to know if I can give you what you want and deserve." She hesitated. "I need to figure out why the thought of marriage sends me straight up the wall. If there was any logic here, as soon as you proposed I should have shrieked 'Yes!' and grabbed you before you could get away."

"Love and marriage don't always have a lot to do with logic."

"Don't I know it!" She stretched, the faint light from the foyer silvering her lush curves. "I've spent half my life developing a keen, logical, legal mind. I need to chuck that and get back to primal emotion. There's bound to be some in here somewhere."

"The fact that you're looking at your reactions to marriage is the best news I've heard in a long, long time." He kissed her again, opening his mouth over hers as he slid his hand between her thighs. "Stay the night."

Mistake. She ended the kiss and swung her legs over the side of the bed. "I'd better not. I need to work on primal emotion, not primal lust, which is awesome but damned distracting."

He skimmed his hand down the silky skin of her bare back, feeling the delicate strength of her spine under his palm. "You're right, unfortunately."

"It's one of my most irritating qualities." She turned on the bedside light and began collecting her scattered garments. He started to get up, but she said, "Stay where you are. I can get out to my car safely without your escort. In the unlikely event anything happens, my car key includes a panic button just in case."

He was tired enough to let himself be persuaded. She finished dressing and kissed him goodnight, then turned to leave. In the door, she turned back to look at him. "Rob . . ."

"Yes?" He rolled to his side so he could admire her figure silhouetted against the light. It was women like her who made curves popular.

Malcolm waddled into the doorway and nuzzled her calf. She bent to scratch his neck. "Never mind. Sleep well."

Then she was gone. He wondered what she had been on the verge of saying, then smiled a little. As a lawyer, she had probably just wanted to get the last word.

Consigning the boxes in his pickup to the tender mercies of the night, he rolled over and buried his face in the pillow that still bore traces of Val's scent. The bed shook as Malcolm leaped onto it—short legs but a lot of mass—so he draped his arm over the dog's barrel torso. Tonight he would sleep well.

CHAPTER 29

STANDING ON A DESK BESIDE CALLIE'S COVERED wall hanging, Val raised her hand and called for attention. Litigators developed powerful voices. "Good evening! Thanks to all of you for coming to help inaugurate my new offices. Enjoy the crab balls and smoked salmon, serene in the knowledge that they're all deductible."

As people laughed, she surveyed the crowd in the former church sanctuary. Though events had made her wish she had scheduled the open house for later in the year, now that the party had started she was having a fine time.

She had picked a Friday afternoon from 5 till 8 P.M. to catch the TGIF crowd. The turnout was impressive, aided by the publicity about Daniel's case. In the interests of safe driving, she wasn't serving anything stronger than wine and beer, but the munchies were first class. She tried not to think of how much this was all costing her.

After a few more comments, including thanks to her former colleagues at Crouse, Resnick, she said, "Now it's time for the grand unveiling. Behind this curtain is a really splendid artwork created by my mother, Callie Covington, one of the finest fabric artists in America. Callie, where are you?" She spotted her mother with Loren, both of them carefully ensconced within reach of the smoked salmon and miniature spanakopita.

Raising her glass of chardonnay, she continued, "I'd like to make a toast to my mother, who not only gave me artwork and red hair, but the rabble-rouser streak that I hope to indulge in my new firm. Thanks for everything, Callie." She was pleased to see her mother actually blush.

As others raised their glasses, Val pulled the cord that released the covering on the wall hanging. There were gasps as people saw the dramatic colors and images Callie had used in her visual meditation on the law. If she didn't get more work out of this, Val would eat the hanging herself, sans ketchup.

She had intended a thank you toast to her father as well, but he wasn't here yet, so she finished with, "Here's to justice and plenty of billable hours!"

Amidst more laughter, she descended from the desk with the helping hand of Donald Crouse. "Quite a party, Val," he said warmly. "You're off to a grand start. Taking on this death penalty case has also given you plenty of good publicity."

"That's not why I'm doing it."

"I know, but that doesn't mean it won't help your new practice." Seeing a friend across the room he moved on, giving Val a chance to catch her breath. Playing hostess was hard work. The guest list included many former colleagues and people she had worked with, as well as a good dash of personal friends. Kate Corsi, who had sent her to Rob, was here with her husband and admiring the church restoration, while their mutual friend Laurel had come down from New York and was now taking pictures of the party.

The nuts and bolts of the open house were being handled by Kendra, who had chosen the caterers and menu and was now quietly directing events. She was spectacular in a fuchsia suit that made her look like the star of a television lawyer show. Even the beads braided into her hair harmonized with the suit. Val made a mental note to ask Laurel to e-mail the best pictures of Kendra so Daniel could see them.

Only four more days till the execution date.

Kendra appeared at her side. "I just got a phone call from your father. He sent his apologies. Something came up, and he can't make it down this evening."

"Why am I not surprised?" Val managed a brittle laugh. "Thanks, Kendra."

As she moved away, she told herself it was ridiculous to feel such disappointment when she had known all along this might happen. Sure, Brad was a busy man, but most of the people in this room were equally busy. Laurel had traveled down from New York even though she was a busy art director in the middle of a major advertising campaign.

The plain truth was that an illegitimate daughter simply wasn't that high on Brad Westerfield's priority list. If she needed a bone marrow transplant and her father could provide a match, she didn't doubt that he would find the time to donate the marrow, but launching a new business wasn't as important, even if Val was his only lawyer daughter.

Though it was a good party, she found herself most aware of the people who were missing. Her father. Bill Costain. Rob. He had been invited, but declined on the grounds that it would be stressful for both of them. Plus, she suspected, he really didn't want to be in a crowd of lawyers who knew who Robert Smith Gabriel was. He was right not to come, but she would have given all the crab balls and salmon to see him here. Their unplanned tryst the night before had only made her want him more. With an internal sigh, she returned to hostessing.

Rachel arrived as the party started to wind down. "Sorry I'm late, Val. A minor crisis just before I was ready to leave the hospital."

"Not a problem. Stick around after everyone else leaves, and we can plan Kate's shower over the leftovers." Val waved Rachel over to Kate Corsi and her husband

Donovan, who were chatting with Laurel. The only member of the Circle of Friends missing was Rainey, and she would have flown in from New Mexico if she and her husband weren't acting in a play in Santa Fe this weekend. Whereas Val's own father . . .

Val mentally slapped herself. Callie had always been firm that self-pity was one of the ugliest of emotions. Brad might not be the most devoted of fathers, but he had kept in touch with her and paid child support regularly, which is more than many men would have done, and he certainly hadn't orphaned her with a crazed murder-suicide.

The thought put matters into perspective. Val moved to the door so she could say good-bye to people as they left. Laurel approached and gave her a hug. "Thanks for inviting me, Val. I like being able to envision your office when we chat." She cast her artist's eye around the church. "This is a great place. Callie's hanging is amazing."

"Any chance of getting together before you go back to New York?"

"Sorry, no, I'm taking the train back tonight."

"It was so good to see you here." Val returned the hug, thinking how well New York suited her old friend. Laurel had been a thin, dark, rather angular girl whose wit and talent were hidden behind shyness. Since then, she had learned how to transform her slim frame and aquiline features into a striking stylishness that turned heads anywhere. "We don't see enough of each other. E-mail and phone calls aren't the same."

Laurel grinned. "You know where the train station is."

"Okay, when both our current projects are done, I'll be up for a weekend. Think about what show we should see." After asking Laurel for the Kendra pictures, Val became busy with other good-byes. The last guest, except for Rachel, was gone by 8:30.

As Val collapsed in a chair, Kendra said, "Why don't you take Rachel back to your house? I can supervise the cleaning and lock up."

Tempted, Val scanned the clutter and the caterers who were busily dealing with it. "You don't mind? You must be as tired as I am."

"Not hardly. I didn't have to play hostess all night like you did. Looking effortlessly successful is hard work." With a cheerful smile, Kendra sent Val and Rachel on their way with a large bag of leftovers.

As soon as Val got home, she kicked off her high heels and headed to the bedroom to change. By the time Rachel rang the bell two minutes later, she was in a long knit skirt and cotton tunic. "I'm glad that's over. Want any of this food?"

"Please. I never did get around to lunch today." Rachel took a small plate and began choosing some of the healthier tidbits. "When we finish laying plans for Kate's shower, have you got time to kick something around with me? I'm considering whether to accept a job offer here in Baltimore."

"There's always time to discuss the pros and cons of a job change." Val popped Rachel's food in the microwave, then poured two glasses of chardonnay. "As to Kate's shower—shall we make our guests play corny party games that make people roll their eyes, but they enjoy them anyhow?"

Rachel laughed, and they settled down to serious party planning. They were about to start discussing Rachel's job offer when Val's cell phone rang from where she had set it on the kitchen counter. She groaned. "Do I have to answer that?"

"No." Rachel chose a miniature éclair from the dessert selection. "But how many people have your cell phone number?"

"Not many." Maybe it was Rob and he wanted to get together tonight, or at least ask her how the open house had gone. That was worth crossing the room for. She removed Damocles from her lap and picked up the call. "Hello?"

"V . . . Val . . . ?" The caller was sobbing uncontrollably. "It's me."

"Lyssie?" Val's fatigue vanished. "What's wrong?"

"Gramma. She . . . she. . . ."

"Take it easy, honey. Breathe slowly, and tell me what's happening."

Lyssie gulped. "Gramma fell in the kitchen and I can't get her to wake up. Her breathing is horrible and loud."

"Your grandmother has collapsed and is breathing strangely." Val repeated the words so Rachel could hear. "We need to call nine-one-one." She glanced at Rachel, who nodded. "Can you do that, or should I?"

"I already did." Lyssie sounded steadier.

"Then they'll be there any minute. They'll take her to Sinai since that's the hospital nearest you. I'm not sure they'll let you ride in the ambulance. If they're concerned about leaving you in the house alone, tell them that your big sister is on the way. I'll leave as soon as you and I hang up, and we'll go to the hospital."

"Okay." A brief pause, then Lyssie said, "The ambulance is stopping outside."

Rachel said, "I'll go directly to the Sinai ER so I'll know what's going on when you and Lyssie arrive."

Val nodded gratefully. "God bless nine-one-one. I'll see you in about fifteen minutes, Lyssie. If the EMTs take you in the ambulance, call and let me know so I can meet you there. I'll have the cell phone with me in the car."

"Okay," Lyssie said again.

"G'bye, honey. Hang on—I'll be with you soon." Val ended the call. "You're okay with going to the hospital, Rachel?"

"I didn't have anything planned for tomorrow except sleeping late." Rachel set the last of her meal aside and stood. "Besides, hospitals to me are like water to a fish."

"Thanks. For what it's worth, I've thought Louise looked unwell and might be a candidate for diabetes."

Rachel frowned. "If she's an undiagnosed diabetic, that could mean heart damage. From what Lyssie said, she might be in congestive heart failure. A good thing Lyssie was right there and thinking clearly. See you at Sinai."

As Rachel left, Val grabbed a tote bag and tossed in a couple of paperback books that might suit her and Lyssie, a water bottle, and some high energy health bars in case someone needed a boost later in the night. Then she took off, flirting with a speeding ticket as she zoomed across Northern Parkway and sent urgent prayers toward Louise.

As soon as she parked, Lyssie bolted out the front door. They met mid-sidewalk when the girl hurled herself into Val's arms, weeping. Val hugged her, saying, "Don't worry, honey, I'm here and everything will be all right." The words of comfort were pure instinct.

"It was awful, Val," Lyssie gasped. "I didn't know what to do. She . . . she looked like she was dying."

"You knew exactly what to do, honey. You called nine-one-one so she's getting the treatment she needs. You may have saved her life. Now let's go inside and get you a sweater. Hospitals can be chilly."

Lyssie took her glasses off and wiped them with the hem of her T-shirt as they returned to the row house. "Thanks . . . thanks for coming, Val."

"I promised I'd be here if you needed me, Lyssie." As they entered the house, Val asked, "Anything hot on the stove? Any food to go in the fridge? Has the cat been fed? Also, do you know anything about your grandmother's insurance?"

"Gramma's been to Sinai before so she should be in the computer. I'll check that everything else is safe." As Lyssie went to work, Val realized that this is what mothers did— keep track of the details. Anticipate what might happen and try to prepare. Take care of everyone and everything. She could do this. In fact, it seemed to come naturally.

When Lyssie was done, Val added the girl's sweater to the tote and they drove the short distance to the hospital. When they entered the ER, Rachel met them just inside the door. After Val made the introductions, Lyssie gravely offered her hand. "Is my grandmother going to die?"

Not blinking at the girl's bluntness, Rachel shook hands. "I don't know because I'm not her doctor, but calling nine-one-one got her to the hospital quickly, which is a big plus. She arrived in respiratory failure, which means breathing problems. The preliminary diagnosis is a pulmonary embolism with maybe some complications."

"I want to see her."

"This way." Rachel led them through swinging doors into the working area. The evening seemed to be quiet, though Val guessed there might be a Friday night rush later.

Louise Armstrong was in a curtained area connected to an intimidating array of tubes and monitors. A small, dark-haired physician standing beside the bed glanced up. Her ID badge had flipped so the name couldn't be read, but Kumar was embroidered above her pocket. "Is this the family, Dr. Hamilton?" she asked in a soft Asian accent.

After Rachel made the introductions, Lyssie asked again, "Is my grandmother going to die, Dr. Kumar?" Despite her size and the wild curls pulled into a girlish scrunchy, her small face showed adult seriousness.

"I'm waiting for the test results," Dr. Kumar said. "We'll know more then."

"I told the EMTs about her diabetes. Is that why she collapsed?"

"That might be part of it—the blood tests will tell us more." The doctor frowned. "I pulled up Mrs. Armstrong's records. Apparently she hasn't been taking her medications. Since she has high blood pressure as well as diabetes, that's dangerous. Do you know anything about that?"

Lyssie looked ready to hiss. "Medicaid will only pay for her medicines some of the time. Gramma is on disability, so we're too rich for full coverage." The irony in her voice could have curdled cream.

Val tried to imagine what it was like for a woman in poor health to raise an orphaned grandchild on disability. Appalled, she said, "Maryland Medicaid leaves people in need without their medicine half the time?"

Lyssie nodded. "She has to wait until her medical bills get high enough before they start helping. Every six months she has to go through the same thing, so about half the time she can't afford her pills."

Val wished she had known. Maybe if she had been filling Louise's prescriptions, she wouldn't be fighting for life in the hospital.

"You've been very helpful, Lyssie." Dr. Kumar glanced at Val. "A hospital waiting room isn't much fun. Maybe your sister can take you home?"

A nurse entered the curtained area, which was getting crowded. Val said, "Time for us to get out of the way, I think."

Not ready to be dismissed, Lyssie approached the bed on the side opposite the doctor. "Gramma?" Tears were bright in her eyes as she took the wrinkled hand between her own. "Gramma, it's me, Lyssie."

Louise made an agitated movement. Even if she wanted to speak, she couldn't with an oxygen tube down her throat. Val stepped closer. "It's Val, Louise. I'm here, too. I'll look out for Lyssie, so there's no need to worry."

"She . . . she squeezed my hand." Lyssie's voice broke. "I love you, Gramma."

As Val, Lyssie, and Rachel moved away, Dr. Kumar said, "I'll come out and talk with you when the test results are back."

As they returned to the waiting room, Val watched Lyssie with concern. Now that she had seen her grandmother and asked her questions, she looked ready to drop in her tracks. Illness in a family member was hard for anyone; how much worse for Lyssie, who had seen both her parents die violently?

Hoping Lyssie wouldn't insist on staying, Val said, "How about if I call my mother, Lyssie? She can pick you up here and take you to her house for the night." When Lyssie looked doubtful, Val said, "Since we're sisters, she's your mother, too, though she'll want you to call her Callie. She hates being called Mom. I'll stay here until your grandmother is stabilized, and they're sure what's going on."

Lyssie exhaled, exhaustion in every line of her small body. "If I go, will you call me if . . . if Gramma dies?"

"If that happens, of course," Val said, knowing that false reassurances wouldn't work with Lyssie. "But more likely they'll say she's doing fine, at which point I'll go home and get some sleep, too."

"If you think your mother won't mind . . ." Lyssie said.

"She won't." Callie might be a freethinking artist, but she knew how to deal with little girls after years of teaching school. And, unlike Val's father, Callie always came through in a pinch.

She did this time, too. Half an hour after Val's call, Callie breezed into the waiting room like a caftan-clad Valkyrie and carried off a drooping Lyssie with promises of an ice cream sundae for a bedtime snack. Val had come by her cravings honestly.

When Callie and Lyssie were gone, Val said, "I'm glad you came, Rachel, but you needn't stay. You've already gone above and beyond the call of friendship."

"I'll stick around a while longer." Rachel smiled mischievously. "It's a perfect time to talk to you about my career goals. No interruptions."

"Let's find us a couple of comfortable chairs then," Val said wryly. "It will be nice to talk about something I understand."

CHAPTER 30

✦✦✦

THE CAREER DISCUSSION LASTED THROUGH TWO
cups of bad vending machine hot chocolate and covered
Rachel's career goals and frustrations. It was nearing midnight when Rachel said, "You're right, Val. I like the idea
of working in Baltimore, but this job isn't the one. Thanks
for helping me figure out what the right job would look
like."

Val covered a yawn. "Glad to help. Clarifying issues is
one of my specialties."

"Figuring out what people aren't saying is one of mine.
What's wrong, Val? Your death penalty case and Louise's
illness are good reasons for stress, but I get the feeling
that something else is bothering you. Have things gone
south with that fellow you were dating? Rob, I think his
name was."

Val smiled ruefully. "Got it in one. I swear they must
teach mind reading in med school. Do you really want to
hear this?"

Rachel smiled, her brown eyes warm with concern. "I
really do."

Shifting her gaze to the middle distance, Val began to

describe Rob and their relationship. How they had met, how well they seemed to fit together, what an extraordinary man he was. Rachel's brows went up when she learned that his brother was Jeffrey Gabriel, the Avenging Angel, but she didn't interrupt.

Val ground to a halt when it came time to speak of her break with Rob. "It was going really well, until everything fell apart."

"He sounds like a keeper, Val. Or did things fall apart because he's one of your guys who doesn't want to settle down?"

"On the contrary. He asked me to marry him last week." She swallowed. "And instead of accepting, I freaked. It was the closest I've ever had to a panic attack, and I don't know why."

"Is it Rob, or the thought of marriage?" Rachel asked shrewdly.

Val blinked. "I'm not even going to ask how you figured that out. The problem is marriage itself, I think. In the past when I dated someone long enough for marriage to become a theoretical possibility, I'd start feeling it was all wrong and back away because the guy just didn't seem right. This time the guy is right and it still feels wrong, so it has belatedly occurred to me that I'm allergic to marriage, which is odd since I always thought I was embarrassingly eager to march down the aisle."

"You want the full Dr. Rachel opinionated treatment, pop psychology and all?"

Val smiled, thinking how when they were kids, Rachel was always the one who helped the old gang sort out affairs of the heart. "Nothing less will do."

"I think a good part of your problem is your father, or rather your absence of a father. Granted, he didn't entirely vanish from your life. It might have been better if he had. Instead, you were raised able to see him only in a very limited way."

Val thought of her conversation with Lyssie. "To make it worse, I was crazy about him. I love Callie, but we're not much alike apart from our rabble-rouser tendencies. I felt I was a lot more like Brad—smart-mouthed and analytical and not very imaginative, but at least those were traits I shared with him. It hurt that I hardly ever saw him. When I was in grade school, I wrote him two or three times a week."

"Did he ever write back?" Rachel asked quietly.

"He'd dictate a letter maybe once a month. Mostly he'd say things like keep working hard and do well in school, and then he would tell me about my half sisters. I could have hated them, except that they're basically nice girls." Even to a friend as close as Rachel, she had never spoken of the letters. The pain of that had been too sharp.

"The father who wasn't there. Callie was no help—when you were little her boyfriends were like a revolving door. Something deep down inside you interpreted all that to mean you don't deserve a full-time man. Or maybe having a man who isn't around regularly is what makes you comfortable because it's what you're used to."

Val smiled a little. "That made me think of the airline pilot I dated. Great for about two days every two weeks, then out the door. I was crazy about him. I must have gotten involved with a solid citizen like Rob by mistake."

"Well, you did think he was a carpenter. Maybe your unconscious figured that meant enough of a class difference so that you wouldn't have had to take him seriously."

"Ouch. There might be some truth to that. Luckily, Rob defies classification." Val made a face. "Why do smart women do such foolish things?"

"It could be worse. Some women who are only comfortable in limited relationships specialize in married men. They have brief periods of romance and hot sex with none of the mundane details of everyday life. They spend their holidays crying alone, and sometimes when the man actually leaves his wife, the woman ends the affair because having a full-fledged relationship goes way outside her comfort zone. At least you've avoided that."

"Adultery doesn't appeal to me." Val had never told Rachel about her one, long ago, stupid fling with a married man, and she wasn't about to mention it now. "Your theory really resonates with me. Heck, Callie was a role model for keeping relationships with men in a nice little box. But I don't want to live like that. Can you prescribe any pills that will cure me of marriage skittishness?"

"I wish." Rachel's smile was fleeting. "Naming the beast always helps. I think you need to believe that you're worthy of a loving, day-to-day, forever relationship, but that's easier said than done."

"Should I look for a therapist?"

"That's one approach. If you decide to try that, I can give you some names. Or maybe you should start a journal where you explore all your emotional kinks privately. Or you could do both. But I would start by talking to Rob. Show that you're serious about changing. From what you say, he's a listening sort of man, and if he really loves you he'll be patient, and maybe he'll have some useful insights."

All good ideas. Val rested her head against the wall behind her, wondering why hospital waiting room chairs were so blasted uncomfortable. Did they think people would stick around a place like this for fun?

Seeing Dr. Kumar approach, Val got to her feet. "Thanks, Rachel," she said quietly. "As you said, naming the beast helps. Maybe now I can tame it." Raising her voice a little, she asked, "How is Mrs. Armstrong doing?"

"She's resting comfortably," Dr. Kumar said. "The embolism damaged her lungs, and she'll need to stay in the hospital for several days, maybe longer, but we're giving her drugs to dissolve the clot. Her blood pressure was sky high and so was her blood sugar, but they're also being treated. Later she'll need some cardiac tests to see how much damage the diabetes has done, but so far, so good." The doctor looked down at her clipboard. "You're Lyssie's sister but not Mrs. Armstrong's granddaughter?"

"Lyssie and I are in the Big Sister/Little Sister program so there's no blood relationship," Val explained. "I don't believe there's any other close family in town."

Dr. Kumar nodded, accepting that. "Mrs. Armstrong simply must take her medications regularly. The next time, she might not be so fortunate."

"I'll see to that in the future," Val promised. "I'm a lawyer, so I know how to work the system." And if she had to pay for the meds herself, she would.

Rachel asked a medical question, and the doctors exchanged some technical talk about things like deep vein thrombosis and Greenfield filters and the relative advantages of cheap aspirin over expensive Coumadin for blood thinning. When Rachel was satisfied, Dr. Kumar turned to Val again. "Mrs. Armstrong really wants to speak to you. It's very important to her."

"What about the oxygen tube?"

"She has a tablet and a pen and much determination. I don't think she'll rest until you've seen her."

"I'll be happy to go in. Rachel, do you want to come in or head for home?"

"Home for me. We'll talk tomorrow." Rachel touched Val's arm, then left.

Val followed Dr. Kumar to Louise. "A bed is being prepared in the ICU and she'll be moved up there soon," the doctor said before moving on to another case.

Val pushed aside the curtain to Louise's area. The older woman looked gray and drained, which made sense when she had been flirting with the Pearly Gates, but her tired eyes were much more aware than earlier.

"Lyssie's fine, Louise," Val said. "My mother came and took her home. Between us, we'll make sure she's taken care of until you're out of the hospital. Is that what you wanted to know?"

Louise's eyes closed and the tension in her face eased. In the still room, the soft sounds of the ventilator that breathed for her were unnaturally loud. Thank God Lyssie had been in the house when her grandmother collapsed.

Opening her eyes again, Louise fumbled for the lined tablet lying beside her. Val lifted the tablet and held it in a position where Louise could write more easily with her felt-tipped pen. "Adopt Lyssie when I die?" she printed in large, sprawling letters that filled most of the page.

The message jolted Val like an electric shock. "You're not going to die. Dr. Kumar thinks you'll be able to go home in a few weeks."

The dark eyes looked impatient. "Diabetes hurts heart," she wrote. "Won't make old bones." Next page. "Could drop dead anytime. Want Lyssie safe. Take her?"

Val drew an unsteady breath. From Louise's expression, she must have hoped and prayed that a deep relationship would form between Val and her granddaughter, but she surely hadn't expected the situation to turn critical so soon.

Val was being asked for a commitment greater than marriage. There could be no divorce if she adopted Lyssie. But when she thought of Lyssie's intelligence and vulnerability and courage, she knew she had no choice. Saving the world was beyond her ability, but if necessary, she could save this one precious child.

Feeling a deep sense of rightness slightly tinged with panic, she said, "Of course I'll adopt Lyssie. I've always wanted a child, and she went straight to my heart as soon as I met her. You'll have to specify me as her guardian. I'll get papers drawn up, but first we need to ask Lyssie what she wants. She might have other opinions."

Louise reached for the tablet again. "Won't. Loves you."

Val found her eyes tearing. This must be akin to what new parents felt when contemplating their baby: a mixture of awe and fear and determination to do right by their child. "This sure is easier than nine months of pregnancy and stretch marks. On the down side, the terrible teens aren't that far away."

Louise's dark skin crinkled with silent laughter. Val took the older woman's wrinkled hand. "I think you're going to live to see Lyssie grow up. You're not that old, and I promised Dr. Kumar that from now on you'll have all your medications, plus Lyssie and I will both nag you to take care of yourself."

This time, it was Louise's eyes that filled with tears. Val leaned forward to kiss her cheek. "Thank you, Louise," she whispered. "I've never received a greater compliment than this. Even if the need to adopt Lyssie never arises, I promise I'll be there for her as long as I live. Think of me as a godmother."

Louise feebly squeezed her hand, then fell into exhausted slumber. She must have been maintaining consciousness by pure will. Now, finally, she could rest.

Val left the hospital feeling equal parts exhilarated and bemused. Even if she never became Lyssie's guardian, a seismic shift had occurred in her life and in how she saw herself. If she could take on a child, maybe she could do the same with a husband?

She drove back across Northern Parkway on autopilot, glad there was little traffic at this hour. Though her car had plenty of gas, she was running on empty herself. The last couple of months had been drainingly, exhaustingly full.

Was she in a better place than she had been? Yes, she was glad to have her own business and to have found Lyssie and Rob, even if so much caring was painful.

As she turned down Charles Street and prepared to turn into her Homeland neighborhood, she glanced at the Stony Run Meeting on the opposite side of the street. She had driven past it literally thousands of times since she had stopped attending Meeting in her adolescence. And every single time she thought about going inside again.

Tonight was far too late, but maybe, someday, she would work up the nerve. . . .

VAL OPENED CALLIE'S DOOR WITH HER KEY. "HI, IT'S me," she called. "Here to take a certain young lady to visit her grandmother."

Lyssie appeared, looking refreshed. Val had called first thing in the morning to confirm that her grandmother was doing well, and the news had lifted a huge load off those thin shoulders. "We had waffles for breakfast," she announced. "With fresh sliced peaches and real whipped cream. Can I take some to Gramma?"

"I don't think so—she'll probably be on the ventilator for at least a few days." She put her arm around Lyssie's shoulders and headed to the sunny kitchen at the back of the house where Callie was sitting lazily with a cup of designer coffee.

"Hi, Callie." Val poured herself a cup of the coffee, then sat down with a fork and began sampling leftover peaches and cream. "Thanks so much for taking my little sister. Now that I've imposed on you once, can I ask you to keep her for the next few days, until . . . the Monroe case is decided?"

"Not a problem." Callie waved a hand dismissively. "Lyssie is easy to have around. She has a first-rate imagination."

Val recognized that her mother was ready to turn Lyssie into another surrogate daughter who had the talent her real daughter had lacked. Well, Laurel had benefited by the arrangement, and no doubt Lyssie would, too. "She's a born storyteller as well as having artistic ability. Maybe she'll end up a writer and illustrator of books."

Callie's eyes narrowed. "I've been thinking. The school year is just starting, and I think Lyssie should transfer to the Hanover School. That's where I teach, Lyssie. It's a good place for children who have talents that might not get enough encouragement in public schools. What do you think, Val?"

Val recognized that speaking glance. She was being asked not only her opinion, but whether she would foot the bill. The Hanover School was not cheap. Though Callie might be able to wrangle a partial scholarship, more would be required, and neither Callie nor Louise could afford it. Well, Val could manage it with some belt-tightening, and it seemed that it was the sort of thing a new godmother should do. "I think that's a great idea. I went to Friends

School myself because it was a better fit for my abilities, but Hanover is super for creative types like you."

Lyssie perched on the edge of a chair, looking uncertain. "I might be too weird for a private school."

"Not this one," Callie said confidently. "I think you'll make friends there easily. It will be like finding your own tribe."

Val had told Callie about Lyssie's Lumbee blood, and referring to a tribe was the perfect way to convince the girl. "Then I'd like to go there, if Gramma agrees."

"I'm sure she will. She wants the best for you." Thinking this was a perfect cue, Val caught Lyssie's gaze. "Your grandmother is doing well, and I think she'll make a good recovery, but last night she asked if I would adopt you if . . . if something happened to her. I said yes, as long as it was okay with you."

Lyssie's eyes widened, looking enormous behind her thick lenses. "Did Gramma talk you into that even though you didn't want to?"

Val shook her head. "I agreed as soon as she asked because I thought it was a wonderful idea." She glanced at Callie, sending a silent message of her own. Making Lyssie part of the Covington family meant that if Val got hit by a truck, her mother would inherit the responsibility for Lyssie. After a brief hesitation while Callie absorbed that, she gave a faint nod, accepting the possibility.

"You'd really do that?" Lyssie asked in a whisper.

"I will indeed, and with pleasure, though I'd rather your grandmother lives long enough to see her great-grandchildren." Val rose and hugged Lyssie. "I had no idea how effective the Big Sister/Little Sister program would be, honey. We're family now."

Lyssie wrapped her arms around Val, her hug as unreserved as her tears. Val patted her on the back, feeling six kinds of wonderful. Any doubts she'd had about her fitness for becoming a mother were gone for good. Parenting would have its difficulties, but it would be worth it.

CHAPTER 31

KENDRA APPEARED IN THE DOOR OF VAL'S OFFICE, her eyes wide and black. "Petition denied," she said starkly as she offered a handful of faxed papers.

Even though Val had been expecting this, the finality of denial was paralyzing. "So it's over. We've failed."

Kendra nodded. Her beautiful caramel skin was tinged with gray.

Val took the fax and skimmed through. The opinion was exactly what she expected. "In spite of everything, I never believed that an injustice of this magnitude could really happen." By concentrating, she was able to stand without wavering. "I'll go downtown to tell Daniel. Do you want to come?"

Kendra shook her head. "I've promised myself not to cry in front of him, and I . . . I wouldn't be able to do that right now."

Val picked up her handbag and headed from the office. At the door she paused to rest a hand on Kendra's arm. "I'm so sorry. Except for Daniel himself, you're the one injured most by our failure."

"Maybe. Luke might disagree." Kendra's gaze came

into focus. "For you it's not as much a personal loss, but maybe something even worse—you're losing your belief in the law, and in yourself."

Val caught her breath, startled. "You may be right. At the moment that's too heavy a thought for me to handle. Will you call Luke and Jason to let them know?"

After Kendra nodded, Val left the church, taking extra special care in buckling her seat belt. She was feeling the kind of numbness that required mundane details to keep her anchored to the real world.

In eighteen hours Daniel Monroe would be executed. The drugs would flow into his veins and stop his heart and lungs. All that life and strength would depart, leaving only the shell of what had been a special man. But weren't all men and women special?

An avalanche of emotion cascaded over her, leaving her feeling bruised and bludgeoned. Instinctively she drove from the lot and turned the car north rather than south. She needed to see Rob, who should be in his guest house. Rather than phone, she wanted to tell him the news in person. Even more, she desperately needed for him to hold her. It wouldn't hurt to spare Daniel the bitter truth for a little longer.

As she drove, Kendra's words buzzed around her head. Though she liked winning as much as the next lawyer, failing to save Daniel undermined not her professional ego, but the articles of faith by which she lived. No amount of intellectual understanding that it would be hard to save her client had prepared her for the emotional devastation of knowing that she was part of a system that was about to commit murder.

Would she be able to continue as a lawyer after this? She exhaled roughly, knowing it was too soon to decide any big questions. She was like an accident victim whose severed limb was still bleeding—still in shock, unable to comprehend the magnitude of her injury.

As she turned south on Charles Street, her gaze went automatically to the Stony Run Meeting, the plain old building barely visible on the other side of the Cathedral of Mary Our Queen. She had been tempted so often to stop by. If only . . .

Abruptly the turmoil of her spirit overcame her doubts, and she turned into the Quaker parking lot. Ordinarily it would have been necessary to ring for admittance to enter the meeting house at an off-hour, but as Val approached an elderly woman with a serene face exited. Seeing Val, she politely held the door open. Val nodded but didn't speak, not wanting to disturb the other woman's peace.

The meeting house was just as Val remembered. She turned slowly, absorbing the atmosphere. Decorated not with stained glass or statues or carved wood but God's own light, the room was a well of silence and peace. Val settled onto the nearest bench, closing her eyes as she remembered the traditional Quaker injunction: *"Turn in thy mind to the Light, and wait upon God."*

As a child, she had done that instinctively, quieting her mind to make room for the inner light. She had lost that ability at adolescence, and her inability to recapture quiet had led to her abandoning the meeting. She hadn't known real peace since. Awash in hormones, the discovery of boys, and a desire for success and the security of money, she had known that she didn't belong at the meeting house. Today she needed to seek at least an echo of faith to sustain her through a dark night of the soul.

Since stilling her mind would be impossible, she formed a mental image of Daniel, then tried to surround him with light. When she couldn't manage that, she focused on igniting a single spark of inner light in her heart. She was on the verge of giving up when she found a faint, pure glow of illumination deep within.

Expanding the light, she was able to encompass her image of Daniel. Once she felt him beside her, she knew that he would be safe in the light despite the fierce injustice of his imminent death.

As she became more centered, she reached for Louise and Lyssie. They had both had such hard lives. Louise already lived in light, and it was simple to bring her close. Lyssie was more difficult, all jangled edges and wariness, but in time Val felt her little sister's presence as well.

Her spirit, so long deprived, slowly flowered, bringing the peace that surpassed understanding. One by one, she sent light to Rob, to Jason and Kendra and Luke, to her friends and family, to the Friends she had known years before in this meeting house.

She wasn't sure how long she prayed, but when she opened her eyes tears were running down her face. Healing tears that softened her own jangled edges and wariness.

Her mind a kaleidoscope, she rose to leave. Why had she stayed away from the Meeting for so long? Clearness was an important concept among Quakers, and she was experiencing a moment of true clarity. She had been living life with a spiritual void at the center of her soul. No amount of success or material possessions or busyness could fell that elemental emptiness. No wonder she had done so badly with relationships. She had lacked faith in herself and in the power of love.

She was still an imperfect, deeply unworthy Quaker. But she would no longer be an absent one.

IN THE BACK OF ROB'S MIND A CLOCK TICKED away the hours of Daniel Monroe's life. Rob had experienced the same surreal horror when his brother's execution was approaching. Though Rob disagreed with the rough justice of an eye for an eye, at least he could understand it, and Jeff had committed terrible crimes. The death of an innocent man was infinitely more harrowing.

Needing a break from the case notes he was scrutinizing, he walked from the guest house and sat on the top step of the little porch. Malcolm joined him, so he draped an arm over the dog, receiving a moan of comfort in return.

He had spent the last long days digging ever deeper into the life of Omar Benson, hoping to find a definitive piece of evidence to clear Daniel. Nothing, nothing, nothing. His gaze wandered over the unruly garden that would soon be his. Tomorrow these flowers would still be blooming, and a man who had become a friend would be dead.

He saw a movement from the corner of his eyes, and turned to see Val rounding the corner of the house. She was dressed in crisp professional mode and her expression was calm, but one look into her eyes and he knew what had happened.

Though her face showed the marks of tears, her voice was steady when she said, "I wanted to tell you the bad news in person."

"The petitions failed." He stood and moved toward her, Malcolm at his heels.

"The Supreme Court refused to grant cert. Only to be expected when the chief justice once said that actual innocence is not a constitutional argument. The state Court of Appeals has already agreed that it's essential for cases to achieve finality. After seventeen years of appeals and post-conviction proceedings, the testimony of unreliable witnesses isn't enough to make a difference." Her voice broke. "I knew it was a long shot, but even so . . ."

He wrapped his arms around her shaking body, his emotions as bleak as hers. "We tried our damnedest, Val. It's the most anyone can do."

" 'Nice try' isn't good enough! In a capital case, only winning counts." The tears she had been trying to control began spilling from her. She wiped at them angrily. "Dammit, I thought I was done with crying."

He handed her his handkerchief, which was wrinkled but clean. "This situation deserves tears. It deserves sackcloth-and ashes and wailing to the heavens."

"I keep wondering if the Court of Appeals was affected negatively by all the publicity. Maybe they didn't want to seem influenced by media opinions."

"There's no way to know, and no point in speculating." He held her tight, glad he could do this if nothing else. Even if Val wouldn't marry him, they would always have the battlefield bond of having fought to save a man's life. If only they had succeeded.

He steered her to the guest house steps and sat down, tucking her under his arm. When she had mastered her tears, she said, "I've been thinking about my relationship issues and found some clarity, but maybe today isn't the right time to talk about it."

"Give it a try," he suggested. "We could both use a distraction."

"I suppose you're right, but if I don't make any sense, hit your mental delete key." She sat up and made a futile push at her hair. "My omniscient friend Rachel suggested that my allergy to marriage might stem from having my father be such a small part of my life. I got used to the men in my life being limited. Sort of like growing up with an alcoholic, then meeting an attractive drunk and thinking 'This feels so right! It must be destiny!' If that makes sense."

"It makes a lot of sense." He thought of his own mother, who mostly wasn't available. Mentally and often physically, she was somewhere else. That had to be an aspect of his own relationship issues. Speaking as much to himself as to Val, he continued, "Recurring patterns are hard to recognize, and even harder to change."

"The funny thing is that I can handle committed, long-term relationships with females. My closest friends date back to elementary school. My mother and I are pretty different, but we like and trust and understand each other. Friday, when Lyssie's grandmother collapsed and was hospitalized, I agreed to become Lyssie's guardian if Louise dies before Lyssie is of age."

"That's major, and good." He drew her closer, thinking this surprising announcement boded well for his prospects. "If ever a little girl deserved to be taken care of, it's Lyssie. How is her grandmother doing?"

"It looks like she'll pull through this time, but it's too soon to judge her long-term prospects. Whatever happens, Lyssie is now part of my family. I felt a pang or two of claustrophobia when Louise first asked me, but no real doubt that it was the right thing to do. It's only with men that my judgment collapses and I panic."

"You couldn't trust your father to be there for you, and that set the pattern of your relationships with men ever since. Not to mention that falling in love makes us terribly vulnerable." As he was where Val was concerned. "Safer never to fall all the way."

"Maybe that explains why one of the best relationships I've ever had with a man is with Kate Corsi's brother, who's gay," she said thoughtfully. "He was the big brother to all of us, and I would trust him with anything."

"Because he wasn't a threat, and even as a kid you sensed that." Rob frowned, trying to find words for an elusive concept. "If sex and love intertwined are dangerous, maybe your natural sensuality—in other words, sex—could only be expressed freely if you controlled the love end of the equation by avoiding it."

Her eyes narrowed with thought. "That's an interesting way to look at it. Makes me sound almost rational. Does that mean that if I fall in love, I'll have to give up sex?"

"I certainly hope not!"

She smiled at his vehemence. "The scary thing about you, Rob, is that you're offering unconditional love, and I just don't know how to get a handle on something with no edges or limit. My over-educated mind can say cooly that I have self-esteem issues, but somewhere deep inside a funny looking redheaded kid is shrieking 'Wrong!' and 'You don't deserve a great guy like this!' "

"Careful—if you're too flattering, I'm going to start suffering self-esteem issues myself," he warned, but hope sparked inside him. "We both have things we need to sort out, Val. The first and most critical step is to recognize that so we can get to work."

She lifted her gaze to his, her eyes transparently honest. "On the way over here I stopped at the Stony Run Meeting on the other side of Charles Street, and I think I have some new insights. It's still an open question if I can change in the ways I need to, but I really intend to try. Just . . . can you be patient?"

"I can be very patient when the rewards are so great." He smoothed back her hair as he studied her eyes. "You're going to need some patience with me as well. I know I'm in love with you, but that doesn't mean I know how to build a happy, lasting marriage. I've never seen one close up."

"Thinking about your childhood puts my problems in perspective," she said ruefully. "When you drew your line in the sand, you said I couldn't cross it until I was willing to seriously consider a long-term relationship. I'm serious now. Does that mean we can be a couple again?"

"It sure does." He kissed her, feeling levels of openness that were new. This is what he had wanted and been unable to find when they first came together. "I love you, Val. It may be a long journey to where you'll be comfortable with marriage, but at least we're finally on the same path."

She settled against him trustingly. "My friend Rachel said I should talk to you because you sounded like the listening sort. Rachel is always right."

He laughed. "I'm glad she is, because I'm not."

"Neither am I. That's why I hold onto my smart friends."

He stroked her arm. "I'm feeling this odd mixture of emotions. On the one hand, I would like to take you inside and make mad, passionate love as a symbol of reconciliation. And yet . . . it feels as if it would be wrong to be so happy and self-indulgent when Daniel is facing death."

"I feel the same. We can wait. We have time. Daniel doesn't." She sighed. "It's time for me to go down to the SuperMax and tell him the bad news. He won't blame me, but that won't make me feel any better."

"Let me do it. I had already decided to visit him if this turned out to be his . . . his last day. There's no point in you torturing yourself when I'll be talking to him anyhow."

She hesitated. "You're tempting me, but it seems a dereliction of duty."

"You're going to be there in the morning to . . . to bear

witness, aren't you?" When she nodded, tears glinting in her eyes again, he continued, "You can say your good-byes then. I'll be there, too. Will Kendra? Daniel asked me once to keep her away."

"She'll be there." Val closed her eyes in anguish.

"No one could have fought harder to save Daniel's life than Kendra has."

Val's full lips thinned into a narrow line. "She and I agree that Yoda was right—there is no try, only do or not do. And we couldn't do it."

"Yoda is a cute little lawn ornament even if he never did master the use of subjects in sentences, but in this he was wrong. Trying matters. Fighting the good fight matters, or what's the point of living?"

"Cal Murphy said much the same."

"Maybe it's a guy thing." He kissed her. "Go home or back to your office while I visit Daniel. I guess I'll see you at the penitentiary at what, seven A.M.?"

"That sounds right. I'll check with the prison people and let you know if another time is better." She patted Malcolm, then rose wearily to her feet. "Maybe we can drive down together, but for the rest of today and all night, I'm going to be hunting through my files for a miracle."

"Same here." Unfortunately, he didn't believe in miracles. "Maybe we should work together at your office tonight."

She regarded him for a moment, then nodded. "I doubt it will help Daniel, but for sure I'll feel better with you nearby."

And so would he. Maybe a fellow traveler would make a night without end a little easier to bear.

DANIEL WAS ABLE TO READ ROB'S EXPRESSION AS easily as Rob had read Val's. He sat heavily in the chair on his side of the barrier and picked up the handset. "The courts played Pontius Pilate and washed their hands of me, right?"

"I'm afraid so." Rob relayed Val's brief summary of the courts' reasoning.

When he was done, Daniel sighed. "I said from the beginnin' that I didn't expect this to work. But you know, it's impossible not to have at least a little hope. I'm ready to die. I've been expectin' it for a long time. But I'd rather live."

The quiet words were a dagger in Rob's heart. "I'm so damned sorry that we've made this worse for you. Maybe the road to hell really is paved with good intentions."

"You didn't make things worse, Rob. It means a lot to me that two smart folks like you and Miss Val have worked so hard for a black man you didn't even know. And because of your investigation and Kendra's publicity, plenty of people have found out that I'm no murderer."

"None of them on the Court of Appeals," Rob said bitterly.

"Yeah, but even my family had doubts sometimes, I think. Not anymore. Best of all, because of your efforts I got a chance to see my baby all grown up." Daniel gave his rare smile. "Isn't Jason somethin'? Did you see that he called me his father in the paper? He's not ashamed of me, and that's more than I ever dreamed of. So thanks, Rob, and thank that pretty little redhead of yours."

On the verge of breaking down, Rob said, "You can thank her yourself. She'll be here with me in the morning."

"What about Kendra?"

"Val said she's coming. Maybe you can ask the warden to keep her out, but as Val once told me, our womenfolk are adults and capable of making their own decisions."

"God never made a finer woman than Kendra, and she's been with me every step of the way. I guess I don't have the right to keep her from the last one."

Glad about Daniel's decision, Rob said, "Lethal injection is a calm, painless death. Nothing ugly. Not like the gas chamber or the electric chair."

"A more peaceful death than most people get." Daniel

shrugged. "Funny, I believed in the death penalty. I figured only really horrible criminals were executed."

If only that were true. "Are they treating you all right?"

"Oh, yeah. Not many executions here, and everyone is goin' out of his way to be nice. Real weird. For my last meal, I asked 'em to get food from my brother's restaurant. Luke will deliver it himself." He smiled faintly. "I always wanted to taste Angel's cookin'. I not only get that, but Luke will serve it to me in my cell. For the first time in seventeen years, I'll be able to touch someone I love. A pretty good last meal."

Rob could barely speak past the lump in his throat. "You're handling this way better than I am."

"We all die. Not many of us have as much time to prepare as I have." For a moment, a crack appeared in Daniel's composure. "I don't deserve this, but life isn't fair. I'm dyin' a better man than I was when I was arrested, and that's God's mercy."

Rob had been wrong earlier, he realized. Miracles happened, and Daniel was one of them.

CHAPTER 32

When Rob joined Val in the church confer-
ence room to spend the night sifting through case files and
notes, he acknowledged bleakly that their vigil was merely
symbolic, but it was essential to do something more than
watch the clock. Every hour or so he would stand and
stretch, then give Val a hug. Physical contact helped keep
the demons at bay.

It was almost 11 P.M. when Rob's phone rang. He
frowned as he dug it out of his tote bag. "Who would be
calling at this hour?"

"It's either the governor with a stay of execution, or a
wrong number from someone trying to reach a pizza
place," Val said with bone-dry humor.

"Hello, Rob here."

"Mr. Smith? This is Virginia Benson-Hall, Omar Benson's mother. You left your card and said to call if I came
up with something useful?"

Despite himself, he felt a flicker of hope. "I'm glad you
kept the card. What did you think of?"

"It's not much and surely too late," she said uncertainly.
"But I've been reading about that poor Daniel Monroe and

racking my brain, trying to remember Omar's friends since you had asked about them. I just thought of something Omar said once, not long before he was arrested and sent to prison."

Which was not that long after Malloy's murder. "What did you remember?"

"Omar said that Darrell Long had done him a real big favor, so he needed to do something in return. I remembered the name because Darrell's family is in my church. His mother threw him out when he started stealing from her for drug money."

Rob suppressed his sigh. Darrell Long, the perjuring witness. Nothing new about that. "He lied to protect your son from being arrested for shooting James Malloy. That was a pretty big favor that Omar owed him."

"It surely was. According to the newspaper, that Darrell was the one who persuaded the other fellow to lie. That's a lot to do even for a good friend. And poor Mr. Monroe is paying for it. Is he really going to be executed in the morning?"

"I'm afraid so. The courts have refused to intervene."

"I wish I'd thought of something more useful. I'll pray for his soul."

"That's all any of us can do, Mrs. Benson-Hall. I appreciate the time you've taken to think back over what must have been difficult times."

"It was the least I could do, since my Omar is responsible for Monroe's execution. Good night, Mr. Smith."

He said good night and hung up, but something was niggling in the back of his mind. Val started to speak, and he shushed her with a hand gesture. Something Omar Benson's mother had said? Something he had heard earlier, jumbled together with the details of a hundred interviews?

Darrell Long had done him a real big favor. Maybe more than lying to protect Omar. What had Sha'wan suggested about the weapon? If it had been him, he would give it to a homey to keep. Someone he trusted.

Half my attic is filled with boxes of stuff belonging to Joe and Darrell from the days when they were best bud-

dies . . . Worthless stuff, or they wouldn't have left it. One of these days I need to sort through and toss, but it's easier to put it off.

He spun around to face Val. "This is a crazy long shot, but Omar Benson's mother just mentioned that Omar felt he really owed Darrell Long. Joe Cady's sister has an attic full of possessions from Joe and Darrell, boxes that have never been opened. Do you suppose there might be something there? Something that Omar gave to Darrell, like maybe the murder weapon?"

"It's possible." Val glanced at her watch. "It's awfully late."

Late to call Lucy Morrison, and very, very late to save Daniel. "It's worth a try."

Rob dug into his files for the phone number of Joe Cady's sister. When she answered, her voice was sleepy, as if she had been awakened by the telephone ring.

Knowing how alarming late calls could be, Rob said, "I'm really sorry to disturb you so late, Mrs. Morrison. This is Rob Smith Gabriel." It was the first time since he left California that he had introduced himself by his full name. "And I have an enormous favor to ask you."

VAL WHISTLED SOFTLY AS SHE ASCENDED THE STEEP stairway into the Morrison's stifling attic. "Look at all this. No wonder Mrs. Morrison hasn't wanted to sort through it."

Rob took her hand to help her to solid footing. "I'm glad there are two of us to go through this. It will take hours."

"No kidding." Val classified this search as grasping at straws, but it wasn't any more useless than sifting through their files for the thousandth time, and it gave them the chance to go down fighting. "Let's see, she said the boxes from Joe and Darrell are in the area over the garage." Using a flashlight Rob had provided, she picked her way to the far end, doing her best to avoid the bodies of long dead bugs. She wondered what her attic looked like and resolved never to find out.

A low door led into the area above the garage. "It's not much more than a crawl space, and the light is really feeble. A good thing you came prepared."

Rob had brought two construction lights with long cords. After plugging them in, he found nails for hanging at the peak of the low roof so the boxes were well illuminated. "There's just enough room to start searching here, then transfer the searched boxes to the side."

Val heaved one of the top boxes to the floor, then sat cross-legged beside it. Her slacks would never be the same. Inside were LP records and audiotapes and a sweatshirt that hadn't been washed before it was packed away. She poked through the contents gingerly, hoping not to find a loose hypodermic needle. "It must have been backbreaking work to bring all this stuff up here."

"A good place to hide something you didn't want found, though." Rob started on a box of his own. In return for the Morrisons' permission to search, Rob had offered to use his truck to haul off anything they wanted to get rid of. Val guessed the elderly couple would have agreed to help anyhow, but it was nice of Rob to offer.

Looking for a miracle, she reached for another box.

AFTER TWO HOURS OF SEARCHING, THEY WERE almost through the pile of boxes and the trash bags containing household goods like stained sheets and blankets. No wonder Darrell and Joe had never bothered to retrieve this stuff.

Rob's eyes were stinging so badly from the dust and fatigue that when he opened the next to the last box, his first reaction was that he must be hallucinating. He wiped his eyes with his wrist and looked again, his heart starting to accelerate.

In the middle of a pile of moth-eaten athletic gear was a brown paper bag, the wrapped shape looking very much like a handgun. He had brought a pair of plastic gloves just in case, so he pulled them on before lifting the bag and peering inside. "Eureka," he breathed. "Val, take a look."

She was beside him in an instant, eyes widening as she saw the sleek, deadly semiautomatic pistol. "Is this the kind of gun that killed Malloy?"

He carefully ripped the bag open to get a clearer look, not touching the gun and minimizing contact with the paper. "Yep. Walther PPK 765. That's the caliber that killed Malloy. This particular weapon is the one James Bond carried in most of the movies. It all fits. Omar wouldn't have wanted to get rid of an expensive gun with fantasy value, so he gave it to his buddy Darrell to keep for a while. Then Omar got sent to prison and never retrieved it."

"A James Bond gun." She stared down at it. "That's almost pathetic."

"Omar's fantasies might have been pathetic, but I'd bet my back teeth that we're looking at the long-lost murder weapon."

Val bent so close he almost warned her not to touch the pistol before she looked up, eyes blazing. "There are little rusty-looking spots on it. Reddish-brown spots."

"Good God, do you think that's blood?"

"Yep." She sat back on her heels, brows knit in thought. "Darrell Long was no fool. Sure, he was willing to hold the weapon for his buddy, but keeping it in crime scene condition might have seemed a prudent precaution. Suppose he was picked up for some other crime and wanted to trade information to the prosecutors in return for his freedom. A weapon that killed a cop would give him plenty of leverage."

His brows rose as he recognized the possibilities. "You have a sneaky mind."

"Thank you. It's one of my lawyerly stocks-in-trade." She gave a swift smile that lit up the attic. "It's even possible there might be fingerprints. I've read of forty-year-old prints being taken off objects that had a smooth surface and were protected from handling and the elements."

He whistled softly. "I wonder if Darrell deliberately chose a brown paper bag like the crime scene techs do?"

"Could be. Or maybe we just got lucky."

His gaze returned to the pistol. "Now that we've found it, what do we do with it?"

"We go to the governor. Sure, there's an election coming up, and he doesn't want to look soft on crime, but now that we've found the probable weapon, the media would tear him to shreds if he allowed an execution to go ahead without this being tested."

He straightened, swearing when he banged his head on the roof. "Makes sense, but how do we get his attention? Somehow I don't think we can just phone the governor's mansion in Annapolis."

"No, we phone someone who *can* call the governor's mansion." Her eyes gleamed. "Rachel's father, Judge Hamilton. He's politically well-connected and had a large hand in getting this governor elected. He'll know how to get through."

JULIA HAMILTON ANSWERED THE PHONE, SOUND-ing more asleep than awake. "Julia, it's me, Val Covington," Val said quickly. "Is the judge there? This is literally a matter of life and death."

"Val, what on earth . . . ?" Julia came more awake. "The Daniel Monroe case?"

"Exactly."

"Hang on a moment."

Muted voices could be heard, then Charles Hamilton's familiar baritone came on the line, husky with sleep. "This had better be good, Valentine."

"It is." She drew a deep breath. "We found the smoking gun."

DAMN VAL AND ROB. THEY HAD SAID THEY WOULD be here, and they weren't. Kendra needed to damn someone or something. Maybe it would relieve some of the anger and anguish that were consuming her as she moved restlessly around the viewing room that was separated from the execution chamber by a large window.

When she arrived at the penitentiary, she had to push through pro- and anti-capital punishment protesters, reporters and TV trucks, not to mention the merely curious. With all the publicity in the last week, there was a good turnout.

Becoming a witness to the execution wasn't easy. Reporters drew lots to attend, and family members of the victim could come. In this case, only one did, a tight-faced woman who was Malloy's sister. Val was allowed as Daniel's lawyer, and she'd managed to persuade the warden to admit Kendra and Rob as well. Except that Val and Rob weren't here. Probably screwed all night and overslept. Even as she thought the words, Kendra didn't believe that, but she wanted to lash out at someone, and Val made a convenient target.

The half dozen reporters chatted easily among themselves, but the five civilians like Kendra were silent, sipping coffee and not meeting each other's gazes.

Where the *hell* were Val and Rob?

Quarter to eight. Not long now. Her gaze went to the gurney in the execution chamber, and she wondered if it was large enough for Daniel. It would be undignified for his feet to be hanging off the end.

She supposed it didn't matter, but her mind kept fastening on small details. Next to the gurney was some kind of cardiac monitor. Daniel would have already been checked by a doctor to see if he was healthy enough to die.

There was a collective inhalation from the witnesses, and she turned to see Daniel escorted into the chamber. Show time. Kendra went to the window and stared inside, trembling in every cell of her body. Maybe Daniel was right, and she shouldn't be here.

He looked dignified and remote, a man who was already halfway to a place where no one else could follow. She pressed a hand to her heart, agonizingly aware of their shared history. Joy and grief and injustice had bound them together forever.

Though he couldn't have heard her, he looked toward the window. Their gazes met, and gravely he inclined his head in farewell. Then he lay down on the gurney. After restraints were snapped in place, a technician started setting up the IV lines.

Tears obliterating her vision, Kendra retreated to the back of the viewing room, stumbling into someone in the process. Maybe it was time for her to go, because she didn't know if she could bear this. She half fell into a chair and buried her face in her hands. *Sing for me, Kendra.*

How often had Daniel asked that? She could almost hear the words in her mind. Was he sending that thought to her? Shaking, she tried to think of a spiritual that suited the occasion.

"Swing Low, Sweet Chariot." Of course. She'd heard that the song was a secret way of talking about the Underground Railroad which carried slaves to freedom, but it was also a song about death. So softly that no one could hear, she intoned the words of her last song to Daniel. *"Swing low, sweet chariot, / Comin' for to carry me home . . ."*

She had reached the verse that said, *"I looked over Jordan, and what did I see? / Comin' for to carry me home, / A band of angels comin' after me . . ."* when a sudden chatter of excited voices pulled her from her dazed thoughts.

She looked up, disoriented, and saw that the reporters were pressed against the window of the execution chamber. Wanting to see, she stood on her chair to look over their heads and saw that the chamber was filling up with people. Daniel lay on the gurney. Was he dead already? No, two guards were unfastening the restraints. When they were done, Daniel sat up, his expression stunned.

What was going on? She clasped her hands together and pressed them to her mouth, wanting to scream from tension.

The viewing room door opened and a forceful man in a

dark suit entered. "Good morning, I'm Warden Brown. We've just received a phone call from the office of the governor granting a temporary stay of execution."

"Why?" several reporters asked in unison.

"New evidence." The warden hesitated, debating whether to say more. "The likely murder weapon has been found, and the governor feels that in the interests of justice, the execution of Daniel Monroe should be delayed until tests can be run."

As a babble of voices rose with the reporters asking more questions, Kendra dropped back into the chair, weeping prayers of thanks to God.

Daniel was alive, and all of a sudden she had a pretty good idea of what Val and Rob had been up to.

CHAPTER 33

❋

BY THE TIME THEY RETURNED TO THE CHURCH TO meet Kendra, it was early afternoon and Val was dead on her feet. She had even asked Rob to drive her car because she was too tired to be safe. She had enough pride left to walk inside rather than let him carry her, but it was a near thing. Covering a yawn, she said, "How long will the ballistic and DNA tests take?"

"Several weeks, at least. Then the court will have to process the information, assuming the tests clear Daniel." He slung an arm around her shoulders and steered them toward the back door of the church. "I keep telling myself that the gun might have nothing to do with the Malloy murder, but I don't believe that. The pieces of the puzzle fit too well for this to be a red herring."

"Agreed." She yawned again. "I'm glad you were there to deal with all the cops and prosecutors. I would have collapsed under the strain."

"They weren't happy to have their thinking reoriented, especially the deputy state's attorney." He reached past her to open the door. "I thought Daniel was doomed when the governor turned out to be in Europe. Judge Hamilton is amazing."

"I told you he was well-connected, not to mention tenacious. If he hadn't been able to find the governor, I think he would have gone down to the penitentiary and stopped the execution himself. Wouldn't that have made a great story?"

"It's headline news even without the extra drama." Kendra swung through the door at the far end of the hall. "Val, you look like something the cat dragged through the fence."

Val didn't bother to check her appearance since she knew Kendra was right. Her clothes were smudged and wrinkled and her hair was living its own life, wild and free. "You, unfortunately, look terrific."

"I had time to go home and freshen up after I left the Pen. Oh, Val . . ." Kendra's levity vanished into a heartfelt hug. "When I first asked you to look into Daniel's case, it was a shot in the dark. I never thought that a decorative little corporate shyster like you could make a difference."

Val laughed, thinking they'd never had such easy banter at the old office. They had gone far beyond being coworkers. Now they were truly friends. "If that's your real opinion of me, I'm not sure I want to know it."

"My real opinion is that you're a goddess."

"Rob gets the credit for his investigative work. I just shuffled papers."

"Okay, if you're not a goddess, he must be a god." Kendra turned to Rob and put her hands on his shoulders. She was close to his height, so when she kissed him with slow deliberation he reacted as if she had just injected caffeine into his veins.

When she ended the kiss, he gasped, "That was certainly an unexpected bonus, but better not do it again. I'm trying to convince Val that I'm worth keeping."

"'Bout time you two stopped smoldering at each other and made it legal," Kendra said with a grin. "I've been thinking that you two are starting to look like you belong together. Are congratulations in order?"

"Not yet, but I'll keep you posted."

He put an arm around each of the women and they ambled forward into the high-ceilinged reception area. Directly ahead of them hung Callie's tapestry of justice, the colors glowing in the afternoon sun. "I don't know about divinity, but have you two incredibly lovely ladies—"

"Magnificent women," Val said firmly as she plopped onto the sofa and pulled Rob down beside her.

"Kick-ass warrior sisters," Kendra suggested as she sat on his other side.

"Whatever." He kissed Val on the tip of her nose. "It was a team job. All of us were essential, and we got a lot of help along the way. Have you considered doing more wrongful conviction cases? There's no shortage of worthy subjects, I suspect."

"It's work worth doing." And worthy of an aspiring Quaker. During the course of Daniel's case, Val had worked herself to exhaustion and the emotional toll had been enormous. Yet what had she ever done that was more satisfying or worthwhile? "I don't know if I'd want to do wrongful conviction exclusively—it's intense, and it doesn't earn the money needed to run the office. But yes, I would like to do more. I assume you'd do the investigating?"

He nodded. "I'll need to get a license if I'm going to do this seriously. We can also draft some of the volunteers who have been calling in order to take on more cases. Get some journalism students as well as lawyers and law students. As for the money—well, maybe you could get annual grants from the Brothers Foundation to help cover your overheads."

Rob's own foundation? "That would be . . . very appropriate," Val said softly. "Kendra, how are you at grant writing?"

"She doesn't have to be too good," Rob said with a grin. "I . . . know someone at the foundation."

"As a matter of fact I've done some grant writing for my church and a couple of local community groups, and I'm darned good at it," Kendra said. "Though maybe the money situation will take care of itself, Val. Bill Costain called half an hour ago. I suspect that he wants to bring his work back here."

"That would be nice. I always liked working with Bill." She cocked her head to one side. "I've got an idea, too. Kendra, have you ever considered getting a law degree? The University of Baltimore has a part-time program."

"Girl, I've been taking courses part-time for years, and I haven't even finished my bachelor's! It would take ten years before I was qualified for the bar. I'd be fifty."

But Kendra wasn't saying that she disliked the idea, Val was interested to note. "How old will you be in ten years if you don't go to law school?"

Kendra opened her mouth to reply, then closed it again. "Good point. Maybe I'll kick the idea around." Her eyes narrowed. "You are one mean little redhead."

Val chuckled. "I try."

Rob said, "When and if we get Daniel out of prison, I have an idea for him, too. Kendra, do you think he might like to work at the Fresh Air Center? Do some counseling, shoot some hoops, act as a kind of surrogate father. The place could use a mature man like him who's learned wisdom the hard way."

Kendra stared at him in awe. "That's brilliant. He doesn't have a lot of regular job skills, but he would be wonderful at mentoring fatherless kids. Suggest this the next time you visit. I think he'd love it."

Maybe helping other young boys would help make up for all the years he had missed with Jason, too. Val leaned tiredly against Rob's side. "Now that we've settled the future, can I go home and go to bed?"

"Good idea." Rob stood and lifted her against him so that she had to cling monkey style. "Any other loose ends can wait."

With a sigh, she let her head drop on his shoulder as he

carried her out to the car. She had a loose end to take up with him, but like he said, it could wait.

Though not for long.

IT WAS EARLY EVENING WHEN VAL AWOKE IN ROB'S arms. They had come to his guest house because Malcolm needed to be fed and walked. Cats were much lower maintenance. By the time Rob had walked the dog, Val was dead to the world.

The slanting sunshine found blond streaks in his hair and sculpted his strong features. He looked good enough to eat. She filed the idea for later and gently touched the day and a half of stubble that shadowed his jaw. Sexy.

His eyes opened, regarding her with such warmth that she had trouble remembering that the light color had once seemed icy cold. "Feel better?" he asked.

"Much." She rolled on her side, eliciting a small snort of protest from Malcolm down by her feet. "We'll need a king-size bed to accommodate us and all the critters."

"Are we at the stage of buying beds together," he asked with interest, "or was that a rhetorical comment?"

"Not rhetorical." She trailed her fingers through the soft hair on his bare chest. "I hope you don't entirely give up remodeling work. The results are so splendid."

"Glad you think so, but let's go back to the subject of beds. That had promise."

Promises . . . Her mouth dry, she said, "I'm still working on this marriage idea. Though I think my panic factor is down by at least a third, there's still quite a way to go. But there is one thing I've figured out."

He raised his brows encouragingly.

"I love you." The words were amazingly hard to get out. Love meant vulnerability, commitment, for better and for worse—all those scary things that she hadn't been able to accept, but was no longer sure she could live without. "It wasn't until meeting you that I even realized I didn't know what love is. Friendship, lust, broken hearts—I was pretty adept at those, but love, no. I still don't understand all the nuances, but there can't be a better teacher in the world than you."

"Love goes both ways, my Valentine," he said softly. "You are the light of my life, quite literally. You bring me joy I've never known, and didn't think I'd ever know." He wrapped his arms around her and rolled her on top of him. It wasn't just his chest that was bare, she discovered.

"You really want to get this conversation back to beds, I see," she laughed before bending into a kiss. Was she imagining the lightness she sensed in him? No, this was real. Their success at saving Daniel had freed him at the same time. Though grief and regret for his brother would always be part of him, he was no longer imprisoned by those emotions. They had both come a long, long way since meeting each other.

There were more journeys ahead. Thinking of the previous day, she said, "Were you raised in any particular religion?"

He shook his head. "As a kid I'd sometimes go to Sunday school at whatever church was closest because I wanted to know the things the other kids knew. It helped me blend in, but wasn't exactly a comprehensive religious education."

"As you know, I was raised Quaker." She crossed her arms on his chest and used them to cushion her chin. "I fell away from the meeting when I discovered boys and developed the urge to be a killer lawyer, but the values are still a part of me. More so than I had realized for many years. Visiting the meeting house yesterday . . . filled some missing holes in me."

He caught her gaze. "Is that why now you can say that you love me?"

She blinked. "Maybe so. I felt better for being there, and I'm going to start attending First Day meetings again. Would you be interested in coming with me?"

"I like what I've heard about Quakers. They seem like people of principle," he mused. "What do they believe?"

"There isn't a lot of specific doctrine. Everyone is encouraged to pray for guidance and follow their inner light. Friends are a community, not a hierarchy."

"I think I'd like that. Shall we attend a meeting this Sunday?"

"We call it First Day and yes, I'd love to take you. You'll fit right in." Her eyes drifted out of focus. "It takes enormous spiritual rigor and faith to become a good Quaker. I suspect that I'll be trying for the rest of my life and still not make the grade."

He grinned. "Yoda to the contrary, I think that trying counts for a lot."

"I hope so, because I'm never going to be the perfect woman." She wriggled her hips against his, loving the way his eyes darkened with desire. "But I'm beginning to think I can be good enough."

EPILOGUE

❦

THE DAY BEFORE THANKSGIVING WAS COOL AND crystal clear, so beautiful that Kendra thought even the grim exterior of the penitentiary looked good. It had taken only a few days to identify the fingerprints of Omar Benson and Darrell Long on the Walther PPK. The DNA tests that conclusively identified the specks of blood as James Malloy's had taken much longer, over two months. Once that was proved, the courts had ordered Daniel's release in less than a week.

Finally the hour had come. The inner circle of people waiting included Kendra and Jason, Val and Rob, Lyssie and Rob's friend Sha'wan, Luke and Angel Wilson. Resplendent in his uniform, Jason murmured, "I'm more tense now than when I was waiting to find out if I'd been accepted by the academy."

She tucked her hand in his elbow, grateful the Air Force had allowed him to come home for his father's release. "So am I, Jay. Hard to believe this day has finally come."

Also present were well-wishers and a crowd of reporters and cameras. Al Coleman was anticipating an exclusive interview with Daniel later, but for now he and his colleagues stayed back a respectful distance.

The door of the penitentiary opened and Daniel stepped out, tall and powerful, a free man for the first time in over seventeen years. A cheer went up from the onlookers, stopping him in his tracks. He looked—stunned. Exhilarated. Maybe even afraid. She could only imagine the complex feelings that must be surging through him.

Lyssie broke the tension by skipping up the steps to present him with a bouquet of autumn blossoms. "Welcome to the world, Mr. Monroe." Her voice was very clear. She and Val had worked this out in advance. "Lots of people are glad to see you."

Daniel's expression softened, and he went down on one knee to accept the bouquet. "You're Lyssie. I've heard a lot about you. Thank you for the flowers." His fingertips skimmed over the petals of the gold and bronze chrysanthemums. "In the old days, I never noticed how beautiful flowers are."

Beaming but suddenly shy, Lyssie scooted back to Val and Rob.

His expression more sure, Daniel rose and walked down the steps to Kendra and Jason, straight into their arms. "Oh, baby, baby, baby," he said hoarsely.

She wasn't sure if he meant her or Jason. Both of them, probably. His powerful body was both familiar and unexpected. They had been lovers once and would be again, she knew in her bones.

To her shock, she began to cry, burying her face in Daniel's shoulder as great wrenching sobs tore through her. "I'm sorry, honey," she gasped. "I . . . I wouldn't let myself cry in front of you when you were in prison, but now . . ."

"It's okay, girl," he said with a grin. "If I weren't such a big mean dude, I'd be cryin' myself."

As she and Jason laughed, Luke and Angel came forward, then Val and Rob. After greeting his brother and sister-in-law, Daniel gave Val a hug that swept her off her feet. "Just a bit of a thing," he said fondly.

He turned back to Kendra and said in a voice so low that even Jason couldn't hear, "The first time I met your mama I said I'd marry you, but I never got the chance. I'm not fit for marryin' now any more than a bulldog just off his chain. I've got a lot of learnin' and livin' to do. But a year from now—well, by then I should be ready to ask you a question. Think about it between now and then."

She smiled through the tears that insisted on stinging her eyes. "Yes, Daniel, I'll think about it." She'd think, she'd weigh the pluses and minuses, maybe even make a neat list of pros and cons. She would think about whether they still looked as if they belonged together.

And then she'd say yes.

VAL WATCHED MISTY-EYED AS DANIEL AND HIS family moved forward into the crowd of reporters. Lyssie's gaze had the sharp observation of a potential writer. Val could almost see the mental notes her little sister was making. With the improvement in health Louise was showing now that she had better care, Val was unlikely to become Lyssie's guardian, but they were sisters forever.

"It's been six months since I decided to open my own office so I could practice more do-gooder law," Val said quietly to Rob. "So much has changed."

He put his arm around her shoulders. "Pretty much all for the better, too."

For sure. Rob had taken to the Meeting like an eagle to the air. His hard-earned clarity and integrity made him a natural Quaker. She would spend her life working to be a better Friend, but that was another battle worth fighting. "I've been thinking. Now that the weather's getting colder, surely you and Malcolm would be more comfortable living at my place until you finish the main remodeling work at your house."

"If that's an invitation, we accept," he said promptly. "But didn't you say that people who lived together first were more likely to get divorced if they later got married? Maybe we need to do something so we don't become victims of a statistic."

"I've thought of that." With a grin, she stuck out her palm. "Hand over the keys to the Corniche, and let's start looking at dates."

AUTHOR'S NOTE

Capital punishment arouses strong opinions on both sides, but just about no one is in favor of executing innocent people. While any thinking person has to assume that sometimes the justice system makes mistakes, the advent of DNA testing has proven how alarmingly often those mistakes occur.

Ever since then public awareness of the problem has been stimulated by stories such as those coming out of Illinois. With the help of energetic journalism students from Northwestern University, more men were released from death row as innocent than were being executed. The stories were so outrageous and horrifying that eventually the governor of Illinois declared a moratorium on executions.

While my characters and plot are fictional, most of the details are derived from real cases. A major inspiration for this book was the case of Michael Austin, imprisoned for murder in my hometown of Baltimore. Austin was convicted by the flip-flop testimony of a lying eyewitness, and a business card that turned out to be totally irrelevant. Not only had several other eyewitnesses described a killer of very different appearance, but Austin had been at work at the time of the murder and had a time card to prove it. It took twenty-seven years for the truth to set him free.

With the intervention of Centurion Ministries, a New Jersey organization dedicated to helping wrongly convicted prisoners, Michael Austin was released after spending half his life in prison. Anyone interested in learning more about wrongful conviction can find more information on the Internet. One good site is www.justicedenied.com, which has a bibliography of books and articles on the subject.

MARY JO PUTNEY graduated from Syracuse University with degrees in eighteenth-century literature and industrial design. A *New York Times* bestselling author, she has won numerous awards for her writing, including two Romance Writers of America RITA Awards, four consecutive Golden Leaf Awards for Best Historical Romance, and the *Romantic Times* Career Achievement Award for Historical Romance. She was the keynote speaker at the 2000 National Romance Writers of America Conference. Ms. Putney lives in Baltimore, Maryland.